A Novel

DARK
TRADES

KEN HARRIS

Copyright © 2017 by Ken Harris

ISBN: 978-1-943258-40-6
Library of Congress Control Number: 2017937958

Edited by: Amy Ashby

Published by WARREN Publishing, Inc.
Charlotte, NC
www.warrenpublishing.net
Printed in the United States

To my grandfathers, Oscar McWashington and Waymon Harris who, despite overwhelming oppression, obtained land, lived in dignity, raised large families and navigated the swirling waters of discrimination and racism to the benefit of their descendants.

To my wonderful wife, Felecia, and our extraordinary children, Christian and Sydney, the blessing you are allows my creativity to rise. You are the focus of all that I do and I love you dearly.

To my parents, Sterling and Lois Harris, you poured a lot into me — my perspective, my work ethic, compassion, complexity — thank you for always being there. Parents make the child!

To N. Alexzander Smith, Kenya Redd, Star Spencer, Leonard Graham, Fred Braziel, Greg Bailey, Amy Ashby, Mindy Kuhn and Tahnya Williams – You are the best. Your involvement concerning Dark Trades made this dream a reality.

Dark Trades is dedicated to the 2 million or more slaves who lost their lives in the middle passage and to the 10 million or more who made it to South America, the Caribbean and Brazil. To those hundreds of thousands of ancestors who made it to North American, we can only imagine what strength it took to make it through that dreadful journey and then to persevere through slavery. Our lives are a testament to your commitment to survival. If not for that commitment…there would be no us.

CHAPTER 1
THE CROPS

I stood at the window and watched the sun go down. This was the very best moment of the day. It had been a long, difficult afternoon and my work never seemed to end. Finally, it was my chance to unwind.

I turned toward the kitchen sink, looked down, and there it was; a large, succulent piece of Salisbury steak, thawed and ready for action. All during the work hours, I'd wondered if I had any onion to spice things up. I opened the refrigerator to check and, to my delight, I was in luck. There was one onion left in the bottom tray. I pulled it out and sliced it up slowly and methodically. I then folded the onion into the Salisbury steak and made three misshapen patties. I tossed a chunk of butter into my only skillet and watched it skip around as it melted to a golden brown. I then carefully laid each patty in, side by side. Oh, the smell was so wonderful I thought I might faint. I stood there, reveling in this moment of pure joy.

I knew I better enjoy this. Thomas wouldn't be along for another month and so I wouldn't have access to any Salisbury steak before the end of March. I turned the burner up and crossed my fingers that it wouldn't go bad on me. My one-bedroom apartment was so neglected, I had only one working burner left. But there was no one to complain to. The Admins cared only about livability; they had no concern for our comfort. A maintenance request was responded to only if it was a matter of life and death. So, the lights flickered off and on, sometimes ten or eleven times in a night. The power grid was worked to the max. After all, there were five thousand people living in this complex. To keep things regulated, all lights had to be off by 12:15 AM. The Admins knew we had to have time to unwind, but there was no way to avoid massive power use within such a dense, consolidated project. So we obeyed and conserved the best we could.

As the patties began to sizzle, their intoxicating aroma filled the air. I flipped on the TV. It was a damned shame that we had only twelve channels to watch, six of them managed by State TV. The other six were a combination of closely monitored game shows and movies. Each film they showed featured characters who were submissive and cooperative, a not-so-subtle reminder that we better stay in line. But, at least it was some form of entertainment. Tonight, I opted for the game show. Some guy was attempting to answer a series of questions. If he answered them all correctly, he got a two-week vacation away from the Crops. The dream.

We dubbed the large complexes that we lived in "the Crops," because they were basically massive incubators. The crop? Human beings. Each of the large apartment buildings in the Crops housed hundreds of one-bedroom apartments. Each unit held just one person — no sharing allowed. That said, all of the apartment buildings were co-ed. The Admins decided long ago that it was healthy for us to mingle with the opposite gender. This dynamic was a positive in the event that a person was designated a late "breeder."

Take me, for instance. Here I was, a thirty-five-year-old man, strong and in good health, who hadn't been selected to breed. I was no virgin, though. Some six or seven years ago, I was selected to participate in the sex education program. The program allowed for some individuals who lived in the Crops to spend a two-month period learning the "ins and outs" of sexual anatomy. For me, the program was eye-opening, to say the least. There were at least forty people in my class. Of course, I was already excited to be out of work for two weeks. I was more excited to be in a classroom of mixed-gender people talking about sex all day. Who wouldn't be?

Then came the kicker.

After the two-week orientation, we were each placed — with a partner — in a fancy apartment to experience the sexual process for a full two days. I had a lot of anxiety until I saw who my intended sexual partner would be. She was a beautiful girl, about my age, who was more than willing to teach me the nuances of sexual interaction. To say that the two-day training process was glorious was an understatement. Although our interaction was somewhat clinical, she focused on teaching me every position achievable and made sure I could accomplish each and every sexual goal should I ultimately be selected as a breeder.

When the two-week training period was over, we each underwent a debriefing period concerning the breeding process. While the experience was somewhat pleasurable, it was also dehumanizing. Were we people or commodities? We, as slaves, had an obligation to procreate, to leave behind a new generation to serve our white superiors. But hey, at least I'd had sex.

I flipped the Salisbury steak over one more time and turned toward the TV. Tragically, the game show contestant failed to answer the final question correctly. Instead of a two-week hiatus from the Crops, he was awarded a new microwave oven. I chuckled, knowing that there were many people in the Crops who'd choose a microwave over the two-week hiatus.

It was done. The Salisbury steak was finished and I slid all three patties onto my plate. I sat down and relished the best meal I would eat for a month. Salisbury steak was a delicacy that didn't come often. We were allowed to go to the supply center once per week and there was no flexibility concerning the supplies we could pick up. We'd present our lanyard for scanning, and then we'd receive a bag of groceries based on our predetermined need. Salisbury steak was never on my supply list. However, I had Thomas.

Thomas was what we called a Provider. He knew how to get things not normally available as part of our weekly regimen. Simple things — nothing too special. Thomas could provide items that made life a little bit more tolerable and, sometimes, more exciting. Thomas could get you an extra set of razors or a fancy birthday cake. He could even get you CDs that matched your taste. And most importantly, and for the right price, he could get you a nice Salisbury steak.

Special treats like these cost major coin, so extras came only about once or twice a month. I was more than happy to give Thomas extra for Salisbury steak. He would leave it right outside my door on the second Thursday of every month. And on the second Friday of every month, I'd give him two coins. Coins were the only measure of currency in the Crops, the only measure of currency a slave was allowed to hold.

The Admins believed that compensation for work was a key form of incentive. I received ten coins a week for the work I did at the cleaners. It was difficult and strenuous work. I must admit, those coins did make me work harder. There were many jobs that paid less, so, I treasured the opportunity to make that many coins at my job. If a person saved up enough coins, he or she could buy a hiatus. It took a number of years to save up for time away from work, but it was worth it. So, I worked hard every single day and saved my coins as best I could. You could even save up enough coins to improve your living quarters, but it didn't happen often. There was an old saying: "Once in the Crops, always in the Crops."

My feast complete, I looked out over the Crops. In the distant horizon, I imagined our one-time capital city, Washington, DC. The area across the bay always seemed aglow and it looked magical from where we lived. Here in Baltimore, we were more industrial — lots of factories and service-oriented businesses. And we were crowded;

there were "fields" of Crops in Baltimore. I would have loved to, just once, venture over into DC simply to see what it was like. I bet the Crops weren't pushed up against one another there like they were here in Baltimore. I bet there was space to hang out and cook out and even picnic, with lots of room to run around or relax. I bet they even had lakes, fishing, and boating. But, that was just a dream. The Crops were my present and future reality. And I had learned to make the best of it.

CHAPTER 2
MEAGAN

I guess you could say she was multiracial. She had light caramel skin and grayish eyes. She was so graceful and beautiful. I saw her every day. She lived right next door. Some nights, I would turn the television down and simply listen to her move. I could hear her washing the dishes or watching television. I often wondered what she was thinking about as she did those things, and I would muse about what her day had been like. I wondered where she worked. We weren't allowed to interact, and, as frustrating as it may have been, I didn't dare to break the rules. Communication amongst individual slaves was prohibited unless in public places. And there certainly was no unmonitored interaction between male and female slaves, even in the Crops. That's just the way it was.

The Admins had affixed a tracer to each one of us slaves. The small anklets fed the Admins twenty-four-hour knowledge of our every step. It was such a small, slim device, that it was almost forgettable. Yet, occasionally, I'd catch a glimpse of it as I dressed myself or bathed; a constant reminder that I was just another blip on someone's monitor. Its light pulsed like a tiny heart that never skipped a beat. I guarded my every movement, unable to risk my "freedom" in an effort to find out where she worked.

It was a challenge to watch such a tantalizing creature pass me by each and every day. Sometimes I would time my comings and goings based on the sounds I heard coming from next door. I'd hear her pace quicken and would open my door just in time to see hers open, too. I'd pretend that my door was jammed or that I'd dropped my keys, just so we could walk past each other on the way to work. Sometimes, I'd walk behind her as we left the elevator, hoping to get a sense of her direction, but careful to remain subtle. She stepped briskly and gracefully in her slender high heels. Perhaps she worked in hospitality; she was always dressed professionally. I'd fantasize about who she was and where she went, but all I had to go on were the clean and tidy dresses she wore to work each day.

And her name: Meagan.

In truth, I wish I had never heard her name, its every letter a temptation in a world of forced anonymity. But it was loudly imposed upon me during many nights. *Meagan!* Her fate was inescapable. She was an exotic-looking woman forced to live as a slave in the Crops. And, she was mixed. It was widely assumed that a mixed slave was the result of interactions between slave owner and slave. While her days were burdened with what was surely a difficult work environment, her nights were blemished with something entirely more sinister.

About once a week, Meagan's owner would come to visit. I'd only seen him through my door's peephole, but I always knew when he was coming. I cringed every time I heard those loud, plodding steps in the hall. He didn't even have the decency to knock softly. He would pound on the door loudly and yell her name, "Meagan!"

The first few times, I'd turn my television down and listen, just out of sexual curiosity. But as the years wore on, I'd turn the television up, unable to bear the sounds from her apartment. He'd stay for an hour or so and then I'd hear the door open, and those big feet would trudge down the hallway toward the elevator. I could hear Meagan turn her television off and then all would go quiet.

The next morning, as always, I'd time my exit for when she left for work. Her door would open, and she'd tiptoe past me with her head down. We were all required as slaves to walk with our heads down.

Any unsolicited eye contact with the masters was not tolerated. But, on those mornings after her master visited, Meagan's chin would graze her chest.

This had been going on for about four years now, and the Meagan I'd first seen was slowly disappearing. Her life force was draining. I feared it would dry up completely.

As much as I wanted to march out into that hallway and confront her master, man to man, there was simply no way. So, each and every night her master came to the Crops, I sat and listened in agony.

As a man — a slave — I was helpless.

CHAPTER 3
SLAVERY

Someone should have long ago coined the phrase, "Arrogance can destroy a generation."

Such was the case with William T. Sherman. General Sherman commanded the Union forces during the latter parts of the Civil War. In fact, General Sherman had a tremendous opportunity to end not only the civil war, but slavery as well.

At a point in time when General Ulysses S. Grant was given control over the Union forces in the east, General Sherman was given command over the massive Union forces in the south. Sherman commanded the sixty thousand strong army of Cumberland, the twenty-five thousand strong army of Tennessee, and the thirteen thousand strong army of Ohio during the latter part of the civil war campaign. In an aggressive effort to end the war, Sherman decided to march his troops southeast.

His strategy was to move into Savannah and Atlanta and decimate the very heart of Confederate forces. In this process, Sherman engaged in a one on one, ego-filled conflict with confederate General John Bell Hood. As Sherman's troops headed east, Hood circled his forces and placed a strangle hold on Sherman's supply lines to the north. Sherman's once brilliant strategy of relying on the land's resources proved inadequate. The end result was that Sherman's supply-starved troops were eventually defeated just outside Atlanta.

As a result, the Union's core forces were decimated and the Confederate forces were able to move into the northeast, advancing against the troops commanded by Ulysses S. Grant. Ultimately, Hood's Confederate forces were then able to advance against the very heart of the Union in Washington, DC. President Abraham Lincoln was expelled from the country, and John Bell Hood became president of the United States.

Slavery became deeply entrenched in the progression of American history. Despite outcries from many of our foreign allies, slavery only grew in strength over the years. Slaves quickly became the United States' most abundant resource; an entire system of programming was developed to grow the slave population and exploit black Americans for generations to come.

Over the years, there were several episodes of non-violent resistance related to the slave trade. In the nineteen sixties, there were a number of non-violent protests that arose in the southern states aimed at shaming the United States into abolishing slavery. Those non-violent protests failed miserably as the majority of slave owners moved forward with a violent, yet efficient response.

The government publicly executed many who were involved and the government amplified their harsh and violent response to anyone opposed to slavery by showcasing the deaths in newspapers across the country. The perpetuation of slavery became a tremendous economic foundation, allowing the United States to become a global industrial powerhouse.

It was first thought that the best course of action would be to keep all black slaves in ignorance. But the white slave owners soon realized that a calculated program of education for the American black slave would be the best course of action to grow the desired industrial base. Older laws that prohibited slaves from reading gave way to a program of calculated education. Slaves were not only allowed to read, but slave owners were encouraged to identify certain talents within their slaves so that, at an early age, they could be directed into a discipline that allowed them to reach their underlying potential and best serve the community.

However, it soon became apparent that individual slave owners were more focused on the individual benefits of slave ownership than growing the underlying talents of their slaves for the benefit of the commonwealth. As a result, in 1975, the legislature enacted the Slave Licensing Act (SLA).

This act mandated that each and every slave in the United Sates was now the property of the federal government. The act represented the most substantial eminent domain taking of property in United States history. The justification of the legislation was that a universal program related to the growth of the slave trade and industry was necessary to promote the well-being of the United States.

As a result of the SLA of 1975, all slaves were owned by the United States and then licensed back to the individual slave owners. If a slave owner failed to abide by the requisite education requirements set by the federal government, their privilege to maintain slave ownership was revoked. Shortly after the SLA came the Breeding Program. This program was established to allow the federal government to designate which slaves were appropriate for procreation. Slaves selected as "breeders" were placed in a program for up to two years. Owners were compensated for the length of time that their slaves were held for breeding.

Breeders were identified and selected by the federal government and were given absolutely no choice in the matter. Regardless of the slave's current position in life, their selection as a breeder was the compelling concern. As a result, a slave could be snatched from his or her daily environment and placed in the program without any prior notice. Upon program completion, slaves were re-acclimated back to their Crops to continue their daily routines.

Over the years, the government expanded academic, cultural, and social outlets to prevent complacency or unproductive behavior.

During the eighties, a massive computer program was developed, whereby each slave was issued a computer and mandated to engage in a two-month training program related to computer usage.

The initiative was thought by the federal government to be a critical component in its workforce upgrade program. As a result, all slaves had computers in their apartments in the Crops. We were told that our computers were monitored twenty-four hours a day. I found it hard to believe that the computers could be monitored every second of every minute; however, that didn't really matter because the computers were limited in terms of the actual content that an individual could access. For example, there was no ability to interface with other slaves or our masters. The computer did allow a limited interface with the Admins whereby we could send a maintenance request, but the requests were typically ignored if they didn't involve a very serious matter.

The computers provided us access to all sorts of educational information. Historical data, although somewhat slanted, was available to us all. My computer was the only thing that expanded my world beyond the Crops, and I couldn't get enough. So I was always probing, researching, and consuming information. I was enamored with the history of our country and how our government worked. Our president was Richard Hood. I had read that he was the descendant of a prior president. I enjoyed reading about how a president managed our country and our relationships with other countries. The United States was very powerful. And we had very favorable relationships with many countries around the world. In particular, I loved to study how the world's economics worked. The United States was a growing energy power. Strangely, I took pride in our country starting to produce so much natural gas and oil. *Man, I* thought, *somebody is making some real money out there!*

I dreamed of going to other places like Germany, China, or Saudi Arabia. I knew it would never happen, but even a slave could dream. I knew full well that my fate was to live and die right here in the Crops.

The Admins felt that this ability to obtain information was critical for the slaves. It was an outlet that allowed us to fulfill our innately human curiosity. The Admins had chosen education over provocation, feeling that anxiety and hostility could be defused by this distraction. Their premise was sound. I found myself engaging in hours upon hours on the computer in order to understand the history of our country, our growth as an energy power and the activities of other nations around the world. Were it not for the computers, I surely would have been a mess, searching for any opportunity to vent about the frustrations of being a slave in the Crops. Despite the fact that there was no interface with other slaves, the computer did help me feel connected to the rest of the world. It reminded me that I mattered.

My computer also provided information that could be damaging to the Admins and their system. On a number of occasions, I was able to access news reports from other countries that were critical of the United States' reliance on slavery as its industrial engine. I saw reports from France and China suggesting that the United States was engaging in international hypocrisy by criticizing the actions of other countries that were also still relying on an archaic and inhumane system of oppression.

It was a promising dialogue. I often wondered whether these other countries would utilize more than words to combat the moral issues related to slavery in the United States. But the sobering truth was that the US was an overwhelming international power. There had been three world conflicts since the Civil War and each ended fairly rapidly when the United States became involved. There was simply no way that the other world powers could keep up with our pace concerning the production of weapons. Love it or hate it, slave labor was just too efficient. The US simply dominated when it came to weapons of warfare and there were slaves who'd had their whole lives dedicated to working in large plants. This dynamic provided the technological and industrial foundation for the advancement of our military.

However, slaves provided more than just support from an engineering and technological standpoint. They were also part of our active military. I had no idea how big the force was, but I saw military slaves walking our city's streets every day. They were trained from youth to serve, and it was said that they enjoyed many perks.

Slave soldiers received more coins than the average slave worker and were treated with a sort of dignity that was not allowed in the general slave population. At one point in my youth, I thought that the military might be a great option for me, but it was not something you elected to participate in. And, upon deeper reflection, I realized that there was a great likelihood that the slave soldier had a life that was not valued substantially by his "free" military peers. I'd heard that slaves were often placed on the front lines of any military exercise. I'm sure that their mortality rate was extremely high concerning any conflict. While they did enjoy elevated status when not engaged in conflict, the truth was that it was a dead end job.

I used to wonder how many slaves there were. I researched and learned that there were far more slaves in the United States than I had imagined. The breeding program was wildly successful. I heard that there were Crops all up and down the East Coast, each one filled with thousands upon thousands of slaves who were regulated by the government. The slave population must have been massive but I couldn't find an accurate head count. There was no evidence of any group activities amongst slaves other than those that were explicitly allowed by the government. But, as you walked around the city you could sense the overwhelming population disparity.

On an average day when I left for work, I would see thousands of black slaves yet I would encounter only hundreds of slave owners and whites. There simply weren't enough whites to police the slave population. So there were slaves who were trained as a lower tier police force. Those slaves did not hold guns, but were instead issued tasers.

In the Crops, there were many black "police officers," and we called them Monitors. Monitors were readily apparent at the entrance of every apartment complex. They, like slave soldiers, were paid an increased wage and experienced elevated status. There were Monitors in the courtyards and on the streets every single day. Their job was to observe any unusual activity and report it immediately to the Admins.

I watched the Monitors and studied their habits. They did not appear to be any happier or more conflicted than the rest of us; they simply completed their tasks day in and day out. But the truth is they were pretty much useless. Crime was virtually non-existent in the Crops. Each slave tried to stay as far under the radar as they could, for becoming too obvious meant risking being sanctioned or punished.

When conflict did arise amongst slaves, those involved would simply disappear. We called these kinds of transgressors "transfers." Once a slave was transferred, they were never seen or heard from again. The government refused to let any bad seeds exist in the Crops lest they become the beginning of something much larger and more difficult to manage. My guess was that "transfers" were actually executed rather than transferred, but, I had no evidence to support my suspicions.

Transfers weren't the only slaves who went missing. Oddly enough, there were no slaves over the age of sixty-five to be found anywhere in the Crops. I never saw them at home, on the streets, or at work. We were told that older slaves were transferred into a different type of Crop, a Crop that was organized to provide for aged slaves and their specific personal and medical needs. But if there were separate Crops for older slaves, wouldn't they still be present in our daily service areas? Why were they never in line to receive food or medication? Why didn't we see them when it was time to pick up new software or equipment?

I had long suspected that the grim reality was that once a slave reached a certain age, the Admins eliminated them. Our society was based on productivity, not compassion. A slave's usefulness was directly related to age. We were a commodity, and cost-benefits analyses were constantly conducted relative to each slave. This was something I believe all slaves knew and never discussed. I can't imagine what it was like to live life as a slave after you turned sixty-four, knowing that there was some type of transition ahead and just counting down the days. There were times when I saw elderly slaves being escorted to the vans to be transported to their new Crop. The fear was apparent in their eyes, but there was never any resistance. It was useless to resist.

At least, that's what we had been taught.

Chapter 4
The Beginning

I could say that something in me changed on April 15, 2018, but that would not be accurate. Instead, the change happened gradually, beginning much earlier, but April 15, 2018 was a true turning point in my life.

I woke up that morning and put on my all whites. I had to wear white tennis shoes as well. My master at the cleaners said the appearance of all white gave customers the confidence to believe that we did an excellent job cleaning their clothes. Clean appearance, clean clothes. I walked out the front door of my apartment — no Meagan today.

Downstairs, I stepped out of the elevator. Careful to keep my head down, I strolled past the two Monitors and into the sunshine. It was a beautiful day, about sixty degrees and not a single cloud. There were some days when the weather was so beautiful that I almost felt free. I inhaled a long draw of the cool breeze and stepped onto the government shuttle that would deliver me to the front door of the cleaners. I was always fifteen minutes early, no exceptions, and my supervisor appreciated the dedication.

I normally worked from eight in the morning until six in the evening with a thirty-minute lunch break. There were about twenty-five other slaves who worked at the cleaners. To make the time pass, I would lose myself in the mundane task assigned. Each shirt and each pair of pants were important, and there were days when I pressed hundreds of garments. Sometimes the days went very fast because I got lost in the repetitive nature of my work. The very best moment was when I would look up and see that we had only about twenty minutes left in the workday. I would always step up the pace toward the end of the day to get my garment count up. *Finish with a bang,* I always thought. So I put on a show those last few minutes, and would leave with a customary salute to my supervisor before getting back on the shuttle and quietly enjoying the twenty-five-minute ride back to the Crops.

On this particular evening, I walked past several Admins and onto the elevator with my head down. I lived on the fourteenth floor and sometimes, I wondered if the elevator would even make it that high. It rattled all the way up. There were twenty-eight stories in my building, the elevators were always somewhat crowded at this hour, and, I was always waiting for the day when I'd get stuck halfway up.

Safe on the fourteenth floor, I stepped off the elevator and into my apartment and turned on the TV. For some reason, I was in no mood for my usual game show. I switched the channel to one of my favorite Westerns, happy to relax for a while.

To me, this was just one day in a million. The evening wore on. I ate dinner and began to doze off in front of the television. I didn't even feel like doing research on the computer. I was tired and just wanted to recline and relax.

That's when I heard it.

The elevator bell. It was already after eleven o'clock and I knew it could be only one person: Meagan's master. Though his steps were heavy and somehow different tonight. They were inconsistent, staggered, and of all things, he was singing. His stumbling got louder and louder until he stopped outside my door.

He knocked on my door and yelled loudly, "Meagan!" I looked through the peephole and could see directly into his face. He was an older white man about fifty-eight or fifty-nine years old. He stared blankly into the peephole for a moment, then looked up and realized that he was at the wrong door. His face was flushed and sweaty with intoxication. He slid toward the next door — Meagan's — and began to bang loudly on it, yelling her name.

Within seconds, I could hear her unhook the locks and open the door. He continued singing. The door closed but I could still hear them through the walls. I put my ear to the wall and listened. Her master's stammering was incoherent at times. But then he began to yell, and I could hear him say something about how one of the other masters at the hotel had inquired about Meagan. I was right! She did work at a hotel! He began yelling that he would never sell her — it would never happen. "You're mine now!" he shouted, "Your ass will be mine forever." Meagan said not a single word in response. "They think my money is short," he continued. "They think I've lost it, but I'm still the same man I was ten years ago. A few bad deals and they think you're worthless!" He laughed, sounding almost deranged.

Then it happened.

I heard a loud smack that hung in the air. Its echo reverberated through the wall and I felt as if I myself had been struck. The room spun.

It had become a federal offense to damage slaves under the Federal Slave Possession Act of 1987. As of 1987, the government advanced the premise that all slaves were property of the state; therefore, any damage to a slave was damage to government property. In my opinion, this was just an effort by the government to avoid the costs associated with resolving conflicts caused by violence against slaves. The law allowed the United States government to keep slaves in as pristine a condition as possible and save itself some money. As a result, there were very few instances where slave owners physically assaulted slaves. The slave "owners" or masters held only a license to the slaves. Damage to the slaves was considered to be both a civil and criminal offense that could, in certain instances, be punishable by incarceration.

Despite the laws against it, this bastard had just hit Meagan. I took a deep breath and calculated. Was I to do the unthinkable and go next door to assist her? It could be the end of my life. I would be transferred and likely executed. In reality, all I could do was listen. He hit her again, and I could hear her fall against the furniture. For the first time, I heard her voice as she muttered quietly, "No," and he slapped her again. I heard her body hit the wall as he yelled, "You're mine! You're mine, aren't you?"

Then there was an indistinguishable struggle and rustling of bodies and limbs, followed by his heavy panting and moaning. The gravity of the situation took hold, I slid to the floor, and listened to Meagan, freshly bruised and battered, being raped by her master.

All I could do was listen to her sobs.

When it was finished, he breathlessly mumbled, "That'll teach you," then coughed a couple of times. I could hear the rustle as he put his clothes back on. I heard her apartment door open, then close. Meagan didn't utter a word. He was still singing as he sauntered through the hallway, obviously still drunk. His hand slid across my door and the knot in my gut tightened. Within seconds, he was in the elevator and gone.

There was no way I could let this go. I'd sat idly by as he raped Meagan time and time again, an act that while malicious, was still sadly permissible by law. But this time a line had been crossed; I feared she was in more danger than ever before.

There were limits to what I could do. Any action on my part would be to stick my head above ground, and the axes were always swinging. However, there was one step I could take without consequence. I could report to the Admins that I'd witnessed an assault. And that is exactly what I did.

I ran over to the computer and filed a report stating that it sounded like two slaves were fighting in the apartment next door to mine. I didn't dare report a master. I took a deep breath and hit send. At this point it was 12:08 AM, our lights would be shut off at any minute, so I hurried to bed.

I lay there for some time hoping and praying that I hadn't overstepped my boundaries or elevated myself into a position of harm. I prayed that I had also done enough to put Meagan's master in a position of peril. Hopefully, the Admins would get the report.

The next morning, as Meagan and I each left our apartments, she had bruises on the side of her face. I knew she needed medical attention. Her appearance, plus the probability of her seeking medical treatment and the report that I made to the Admins, would surely create some scrutiny. I hoped this would bring that bastard to justice. He'd damaged a slave. This was a crime against the government, and justice must be served.

June 29, 2018 is the second date I'll never forget.

It had been over two months since the assault and I'd grown more comfortable and proud of my actions. I'd done something. I'd finally taken a step to intervene. It was a significant step for me. It made me feel alive, like I could affect the world — a stark departure from the way I'd lived my entire life prior. I'd seen Meagan multiple times since the incident, and on two occasions she darted her eyes at me and smiled. Could it be that somehow she knew? I began to experience something that I can only describe as self-esteem, a feeling that I had somehow been empowered to do the right thing. It felt good.

Then disaster struck.

On the evening of June 29, at 11:15 PM, I once again heard the elevator bell chime. I figured it was one of the Monitors until I heard those familiar, plodding steps. The beat of those heavy shoes trudging slowly down the hallway.

Only, this time he didn't sound drunk.

His steps were almost methodical as he approached Meagan's door, and his knock was much quieter than usual, almost gentle. I heard some shuffling inside the room, and then the door opened and closed quickly. Ten minutes later I heard his moaning and groaning.

It lasted almost thirty minutes. I sat there on the floor with my back toward the wall listening to the all-too familiar sounds. When he finished, I heard him collect his things and head for the door.

He mumbled a pitiful, "I'm sorry," then quickly made his exit. I didn't hear Meagan crying that night, but I'm sure that's what she was doing. I must have sat there for two hours with my back against the wall — long after the lights went out for the night — and it was in that moment I decided I could no longer live like this. Here I was: a helpless slave with no ability to impact my own future let alone Meagan's. My actions were wasted and my life counted for nothing. If nothing changed, I would live and die in the Crops. I would leave no legacy. I would influence no other human beings. I was a mere pebble on the beach, walked on and then washed out to sea, never having affected the overall landscape. It was a thought I couldn't bear. In that moment of desperation, I decided I had to take some action. I needed a plan, and it had to be perfect. I didn't sleep at all that night.

Around six o'clock the next morning, I took a shower, attempting to wash away the desperation of the previous night. As I put on my all whites, I looked down at my pristine, white shoes and realized I'd spent my whole life looking down. What had I missed?

I'd read on the computer that prize horses could never be successful thoroughbreds until they were broken. They had to be reduced to their lowest point. They had to be robbed of their very thoughts, their very basic methods of doing things. This breaking down and abandonment of all previous habits bore a thoroughbred. This was my breaking point.

When I'd heard those familiar steps the night before, I realized that the system, with all its lauded power and security, would never protect Meagan or me. The law would never choose a slave over a master. Protection was an illusion.

Meagan had been beaten, raped, and degraded, and there was not a single measure of recourse. While my own individual experiences were limited, I'm sure that, in perpetuity, the transgressions of slave owners (or license holders) were overlooked in favor of continuity. In all likelihood, only the most serious physical transgressions against slaves were prosecuted. I felt stupid for thinking there could ever be justice for a lowly slave.

Dressed and ready, I had fifteen minutes left before I had to leave for the shuttle. I looked out my window. The courtyard of the Crops was already getting busy. I sat at my kitchen table, pulled out a note pad and pen and stared. Something welled up inside me and I wrote three words, "Commit to Resist."

Those three words would define the rest of my life.

I reached into one of the drawers in the kitchen and pulled out a magic marker. Then, in bold black letters I scrolled across the top of my pristine white shoe, "COMMIT." It was an empowering step, but I also knew this step was dangerous. The mere action of doing something different, something beyond the norm, could lead to my death. Yet, oddly enough, I felt alive. For the first time in my life, I felt like I had some control of my destiny. I didn't care whether that destiny was life or death. I just wanted to have some impact, some significance. I sat at the kitchen table, leaned over and stared at my feet. Commit. Commit.

My plan was simple: to break the mold. But I knew of only one person who operated outside of the system, and that person was Thomas, my provider. Once a month, he would bring that delicious Salisbury steak by my apartment. Obviously, he knew how to get things. Thomas was a slave as well, but he knew how to reach beyond the system's normal protocols and he had operated outside of the system for many years. Though seemingly lax in his routine, his was a controlled sort of chaos. Thomas was designated to allow us slaves some level of unusual comforts as a part of the overall process of controlling us. His offerings provided the illusion of freedom in an otherwise mundane world. I didn't know where Thomas lived or who controlled him, but I felt as if he might hold the key to the world beyond the Crops.

About twice a week, I would intersect with Thomas as he went about his routes in the Crops. The intersection would take place during the morning hours when I walked across the courtyard to the shuttle. Once a month, I would stop to place my order for Salisbury steak and hand him the coins. He would kind of laugh, take the coins, put them in his pocket, and move on.

You could tell that Thomas took pleasure in his job. He brought a rare joy to an otherwise joyless environment. It seemed like he took pride in the ability to interrupt our mundane existence. But truthfully, I had no idea where his loyalties lay. Still, I was determined to commit no matter the consequences. The risk was worth it.

Commit. If anybody noticed, I could always suggest that I wrote the word on my shoe as a sign of my dedication and loyalty to the system. With that thought, intentions were set. I walked out my front door and into an uncertain future. I headed toward the elevator, my pulse quickening with each sure-footed step. This day all my senses seemed heightened. Each step seemed somewhat heavy.

The elevator smelled damp and pungent, a reminder of the staleness I was prepared to leave behind. It wasn't crowded that morning; only four people rode down with me. When I exited the elevator and walked out into the courtyard, I noticed that the sun wasn't shining. It was a somewhat overcast and gloomy day. Yet the courtyard was active with no indications that this day was any different from any other in the Crops. I was the only difference.

I was careful to walk at my normal pace. Head down, I glanced toward my right and I could see Thomas entering the courtyard area. He walked slowly toward me, face down, expressionless. I timed my steps perfectly so that we would intersect right in the middle of the courtyard. There was no way for him to get around me. He had to walk right through me to finish his course of progress.

Once we intersected, I'm sure he thought I'd ask for my usual Salisbury steak. But, I just stood there and said nothing. I reached into my pocket as if to grab some coins, but instead, I just stood there. I darted my eyes toward his, and for one split second our eyes met, his expression one of puzzlement. Then, for a full minute we stood there both looking downward. I shuffled my feet, hoping and praying that he'd see the word scrawled across my right toes. *Commit*, dammit, *commit*.

But nothing else happened. He moved around me and continued on his way. I continued on to the shuttle. I had no idea whether or not he saw the word on my shoe. But I knew I'd see him again over the next few weeks and I was determined to keep trying. My resistance had begun. I had no idea of knowing where this course would lead me, yet I knew I could not turn back.

Two days later, I woke early and wrote the word "to" on the toe of my right shoe. Again, Thomas and I intersected at the middle of the busy courtyard. There were so many people in the courtyard each morning that I was sure our actions would remain inconspicuous. There was simply no way for anyone looking to think that anything was up other than Thomas and me bumping into each other, or perhaps conducting a trade related to comfort food. Again, our interaction resulted in no meaningful communication. I had no idea whether or not he noticed the second word on my toe. But desperation led me to stay the course.

Early the following week, on a day when I knew I would intersect with Thomas, I got up early and wrote the word "Resist" on the top of my shoe.

I'd hesitated; this was in fact the most dangerous word. "Resist" could not be misinterpreted. If either the Monitors or the Admins saw that word on my shoe, I would surely be arrested, detained, and "transferred" to my death.

When I finished the word, I took a deep breath. I knew that this was it. Somehow, I didn't feel empowered this time.

As I entered the hallway, I felt an uneasy sense of fear. However, the momentum of my actions had been set. There was no turning back. Not this day. Not even a week ago. I had to do this.

I walked off the elevator and scanned the courtyard for Thomas. But today, he wasn't there. I walked nervously to the shuttle, staring at my feet and at my possible demise. I rode to work knowing that I could be arrested at any moment.

Two more days passed and to my astonishment, nothing had happened. No arrest, no unusual activity in the Crops, nothing. This time I saw Thomas slowly approaching from my right again. I paced myself and we intersected. I had written the word "resist" a little bit larger than the two previous words. There was no way he could miss it. We stood there for what seemed an eternity. Standing at an angle in the midst of this busy courtyard, both looking down, we said nothing.

Then suddenly, in a flash instant, Thomas reached out his left hand and grabbed my right arm, his eyes shifting for a second to meet mine. He then moved around me and continued on his way as if nothing had happened. But he'd touched my arm. He'd made actual physical contact with me — an action that was strictly forbidden. An action I'd never before experienced. An action I had no real way of understanding or interpreting. I could only hope that I'd somehow gotten through to him. And I could only pray that the Admins and Monitors had not spotted us. I slowly walked away and proceeded to work as usual.

The rest of the day seemed just like any other.

Chapter 5
Exposed

It was a dumb move.

I knew absolutely nothing about Thomas. I didn't know where he came from. I didn't even know what his true job description was. I had taken a huge risk in attempting to communicate with him and feared it was a road to nowhere. Even if he did respond in a favorable way, I had no plan beyond that first contact. It was a move fated to end in my destruction. All I could do now was wait for things to self-destruct.

Over the next two weeks, I saw Thomas at least four or five times. Each time I passed him in the courtyard, he kept his head down and walked right past me. He said absolutely nothing, and his expression never changed. As the weeks continued to pass, my bravado transitioned into palpable fear. The pressure was too much. I knew some type of repercussion was inevitable. I would get a knock on my apartment door and the Monitors and Admins would be standing there, armed with a needle to make my execution quick and painless. I would be whisked away from my apartment to be replaced by a new slave. My body would be taken to some isolated area where it would be unceremoniously disposed of like trash… . With no real way of knowing what happened to transfers, I could only imagine the fate that lay before me.

On the other hand, it could be that Thomas failed to understand my communication. Or, perhaps he understood the communication, but did not have any ability — or will — to help. I was just another slave trying to find a way out, and Thomas obviously was going to be no help. If he simply chose not to respond to my message, then there would be no problem.

I spent my days living whilst thinking of dying. In reality, I didn't know which was best. At this point, I felt like dying was almost a suitable alternative to living the rest of my life in the Crops. I began to lose track of the days. Thomas's Salisbury steaks didn't taste as good. I had no interest in watching television. Even more disturbing, I had a diminishing sensitivity to what happened to Meagan — after all, she was just another helpless slave like me.

In effect, my life was slipping away and I didn't even care.

Almost a month after my interaction with Thomas, I received notice on my computer that my master would be making a visit to my apartment. It had been almost three years since I'd seen my master. He was a distinguished looking gentleman in his forties. During his last visit, it appeared he wasn't a malicious person. His only interest seemed to be that his investment in me was progressing. I don't know when he purchased my license; I only knew that he was interested in getting a good solid return on his investment. His major concerns were that I was healthy and active and had a long work lifespan ahead of me. He received the majority of the wages from my work at the cleaners and I'm sure he would be satisfied with my productivity. I did a great job and I'm sure my supervisor at the cleaners had made positive reports. I was hopeful that the visit would be brief. We really had nothing to say to each other, and I knew that my master had no real concern for my welfare other than to make sure I was still an able-bodied and productive slave. And wasn't I?

I straightened up the apartment the night before my master's visit. I wanted to make sure that everything was in order so his visit would take as little time as possible. The knock on the door came about eight o'clock on a Thursday night. I opened the door and attempted a smile.

"Come in please," I said, my voice hoarse from so seldom being used.

My master had two ladies with him. One of the women had a medical bag with her, a nurse of some kind. The three of them squeezed in together on my one, small couch. I pulled up my kitchen chair and took a seat across from them.

"Harrison, how are you doing?" my master asked, his brows furrowed as he attempted some semblance of concern.

"This is my girlfriend, Janice," he continued before I could answer. "We just wanted to come by to check and see how you are doing. Obviously, we hope that you continue to do well. We want to let you know that we are here to support you concerning your continued work activities."

I muttered a quiet, "Thank you," hoping my response would be the end of the conversation.

But my master continued, "You know this visit is all about us getting a good feel for your health, right? We really want to make sure you're in great physical condition. And, we want to make sure you receive any medical attention you might need. This is nurse Anderson. She's going to conduct a quick examination and we'll be out of here."

Examination? This bastard must be crazy.

Then he added, "So, Harrison, I need you to disrobe."

In my mind I was thinking this guy must have lost his mind. Here we were sitting in my living room and he wanted me to get naked in front of everyone, so a nurse could prod at me.

He said it again with a firmer tone, "Harrison, I need for you to go ahead and disrobe."

His countenance changed and he was now very serious. Where was all that concern he had a few minutes ago? I stood up and hesitated. I looked my master dead in the eye just to make sure this was what he wanted.

He held both hands out and said, "Let's just get this done." Then he crossed his arms and legs and sat back in the chair, his eyes fixed on me with a focus that I will never forget. I took off my shirt, then pulled my pants down. There I was standing in my living room with just underwear and socks on.

Nurse Anderson said, "I'm going to need you to take down your underwear."

Instinctively, my mind left my body. I pulled my shorts down and off. Now I was completely naked except for my socks. The nurse asked me to turn and face the window. I stared out over the Crops, hoping nobody could see in.

She then asked me to bend over. The nurse then proceeded to perform a full anal prostate examination in front of my master and his girlfriend, who watched as if I were some show on late night TV. It was absolutely sickening. After the anal examination, the nurse took several blood samples. I was not allowed to get dressed until she had completed taking the blood samples. She threw the gloves and the needles into my trash can, put the samples in her medical bag, snapped it shut, and without a single word, let herself out of the apartment.

My master turned to me and said, "Thanks again. Remember, if you need anything please feel free to contact me."

My hands shaking, I slowly dressed myself while avoiding his eye contact. My body was covered, but my dignity was diminished. I escorted my master and his girlfriend to the doorway. He stepped out into the hall, looked down the hallway to the right and then to the left toward the elevators, checking that we were alone. Then he turned back toward me and with a wink, he said, "Keep up the good work."

He and his girlfriend then walked away without so much as a glance backward. I slowly closed the door but I could hear the bell ring as the elevator reached our floor. I heard the door to the elevator close and sighed deeply. I glanced out my window into the courtyard and watched until I saw them exit my building.

I muttered to myself, *I bet your girlfriend wishes she could come back and get some of this after seeing what she saw.*

It was all the revenge I could muster out of the situation. I sat down in the chair and turned the TV on. Maybe a nice game show would be on? I released a mischievous smile and then, to my surprise, a laugh.

Some Salisbury steak would taste real good right about now.

CHAPTER 6
THE ABYSS

I woke up each morning with a solemn demeanor. I'd begun to lose motivation concerning my work. It was no longer a point of pride for me to be meticulous or dedicated. I was never late for work, but I began taking the second or third shuttle in rather than the first. Sometimes I would even get to work within five minutes of my start time. I knew that my pace was down at work, and I didn't complete as many garments each day. This act of defiance affected the number of coins I received. Somehow, it didn't really matter to me.

The grim reality was I didn't know what I was saving the coins for anyway — to take a vacation to nowhere? To obtain a temporary and meaningless break from this monotonous existence? My life no longer made sense. I had read on the computer about an illness called depression. Depression was a heavy weight that you carried each day regardless of the circumstances. A dark, muggy feeling that you couldn't escape. Escape? My whole life was depression.

My apartment began to feel like the prison it was. I no longer worried about Meagan day to day at all. I became consumed with following my routine and just getting through the day. I started to think about death a lot more often. Maybe death would lead to a better existence. Somehow I felt that death raised the spectrum of possibilities. After all, life offered no possibilities, no deviations, and no future.

Just to the back of the Crops were a series of benches. From the benches you could sit and look over a three-mile, open field. A tall fence separated the benches from the field, but you could look out over it and see all the way to the bay. The field used to be an industrial complex and it housed several buildings that hadn't been used for years. Each of the structures was an old vacated apartment or office building. Some were probably used at some point in time to house slaves. They were tall buildings, some about eighteen stories high. I wondered why officials had never torn the buildings down.

The fences prevented any slave from entering that area and walking out to the bay. I liked to sit on the benches and look past the fences and the dilapidated buildings. I could see a shadowy skyline in the distance. It was my dream city: Washington, DC.

While Washington, DC was considered the industrial gateway to the North, I heard the slaves in Richmond also lived very, very well. Richmond was the capital of the United States and some slaves there even had positions as administrative aides to the president. Of course, none of this information was on the computer, but I did have a chance to talk to other slaves during our yearly socials. The socials were a unique opportunity for slaves to get together and eat, dance, and sing. Socials happened once every year and the location wasn't determined until a few days prior to the event. There were multiple socials held at the same time. Normally a thousand or so slaves would attend a single social. You were selected to attend the socials at random in order to avoid the possibility of any organized slave activity.

I enjoyed the socials. It was an opportunity to exhale for a minute and meet other people. The one unfortunate part about the socials was that once you made a connection with another person, it was likely that you would never see them again. Nonetheless it was good to get together, laugh, and interact, even on that limited basis. I had never seen Meagan or Thomas at the socials, but I had seen many other people whom I saw on a regular basis out on the courtyard. I even attended socials in the past that included some of my coworkers. I think the socials were seen by the Admins as a way for us to blow off steam. It was their way of ensuring that we didn't build up enough frustration to organize or rebel.

DC probably would have been a better place for me. I sensed that it had more activity and more opportunity to make coin. However, now that my motivation was gone, all I wanted to do was sit on that bench and look over the field into the Chesapeake Bay. I fantasized about what used to take place in those old apartments. I realized that many slaves had probably come and gone there. Slaves had probably been born and died in those buildings. Now the buildings were worn and useless with no tenants. There were no other mementos to suggest the lives they'd housed, no other remnants to suggest the many memories that had been created there.

I wondered if the slaves who'd lived in those old apartments had dreams and ambitions similar to mine. Dreams and ambitions that were dashed long before mine. I wondered how many had been transferred at a young age — or been executed. I also wondered how many of those slaves had reached the age of sixty-four, knowing that within the next year they'd receive the ultimate "transfer."

My ten minutes of relaxation was up. It was getting late and I needed to get inside. I walked through the somewhat quiet courtyard and into my building. When I reached my apartment, there it was, on the floor in front of my door… this month's Salisbury steak.

I managed a smile. It wasn't a great night, but it was tolerable. Every part of my life felt like an abyss. My environment had no escape. My job had no end game. I would never live in another apartment. I sat in my chair and stared out into the water. Here was a huge channel that could take a person into a great ocean and to many corners of the world. But dream as I may, I could never access that channel. I continued to stare and welcomed the time when I was overcome by sleep.

CHAPTER 7
WINTER BREED

Fall soon became winter in the Crops. I hated the winter months in Baltimore. It was freezing cold, icy, and muddy, and I dreaded leaving my apartment complex each day. Walking outside and across the courtyard to a shuttle stop was a challenge for everyone. The courtyard was poorly maintained and there were icy spots everywhere. Even though the shuttles were crowded when we headed to work, there never seemed to be enough heat. I always felt better when I arrived at work and was able to take off my jacket and warm up. The cleaners was always much warmer than my apartment.

Winter in my apartment was just tolerable. Each unit came with a heater, but mine was barely adequate to keep the temperature up. Each winter, there were a couple of occasions when the power went out in the Crops. On one occasion, the power was out for almost twenty-four hours.

My heater went out because it was electricity driven. My lights, my refrigerator, and my television also went down. But I noticed that when I turned on the one remaining burner on my stove, it came on. Gas power! Fortunately, the electricity and natural gas ran on different systems, so, one could be down while the other one was still up and running. I ran that one burner all night and it provided me just enough heat to not freeze. I wondered whether others had discovered the same thing.

One night when the power went down, I looked out the window and into the entire area of the Crops. All of the apartment buildings were dark. I could only imagine what the other slaves were thinking. This power outage gave us all something in common. If only we could unite over something more substantial. For now, the darkness was all that we had in common.

As winter progressed, I prepared myself for a dull and monotonous season. One day, as I geared up for the end-of-the-workday hustle, my supervisor approached me and asked me to come to his office. It was a terrifying moment for me. Going to the office could only mean bad things and I prepared myself for the worst. I had taken a chance on communicating with Thomas earlier. Could this be my moment of truth?

My supervisor sat down and pulled out an envelope. I stared at the envelope as he unfolded its contents.

He smiled slightly and said, "Well, son, you have been selected as a breeder."

My jaw dropped.

I had to ask him to repeat himself.

"You said a breeder?"

"Yes. You've been selected as a breeder. You're not surprised, are you?"

I explained that I was somewhat surprised because, at thirty-five, I was getting up in age. He noted that I'd been a consistent worker for over a decade, never once being late. He also told me that he had considered me for many years to be his smartest employee.

"For those reasons and a whole lot more, I recommended that you be selected as a breeder. The world needs more just like you."

He managed a half smile, handed me the envelope and said with a wink, "Enjoy."

I grabbed the envelope, stood up, and shook my head in disbelief. When you were selected as a breeder, they didn't give you much time to prepare. I knew I'd have just two days to get ready and I was immediately relieved of my duty.

At the end of my work shift, I took the shuttle back to the Crops. As soon as I got home, I opened my computer and looked at my messages. In my inbox was a message detailing my admission into the Breeding Program. I would need to take a shuttle to the bus station to be transported to a breeding area. Then I'd remain at the breeding facility for no less than two weeks. It was hard to believe, but it was truly a welcomed diversion. No one ever complained about being a breeder. Anything different from the heavy depression I'd been experiencing was a welcomed change.

Two days later, around midday, I headed for the shuttle. The shuttle took me to a busing annex that was about five miles from my apartment. I pulled out my bus pass and schedule, and showed them to the attendant who directed me to a large bus. There were about forty other men on the bus. Any expectation of comfort or dignity was quickly dispelled, as the Monitors walked through and placed us all in secured handcuffs.

The bus pulled out of the terminal and for the first time in decades, I was able to see the rest of Baltimore. The first thing that struck me was that there were so many different Crops in Baltimore. We passed complex after complex filled with slaves. For the first time, I saw the many stores and businesses that filled the rest of the city. Baltimore was an active city with a substantial white population. It was fascinating. As we moved toward the outskirts of the city, I noticed more and more whites and fewer blacks.

Living in the Crops gave you the impression that there were blacks everywhere. This, apparently, was not the case. We began to exit the dense city area and enter the more remote areas of Baltimore. Once we got about five miles out of center city, I began to see miles upon miles of fences bordering the highway. Much of the fencing had barbed wiring along the top of it. On the other side of the fences were large residential areas. Many of the neighborhoods contained large houses and I could see white children playing in the backyards.

It took us about two hours to get to the breeding facility. It was a large facility with about twelve rows of housing. Each row appeared to have a least ten to twelve different units, and in between each unit was a small black unit that contained the nursing and scientific staff. As we walked off the bus, each of us was given a card with a letter and a number on it. I was given a card that said *D1*. We were then led to one of the black units where each of us was given an examination and blood test.

After my blood test, I underwent a physical examination. Thankfully, there was no prostate exam this time! In fact, I had no problem at all with the female nurse who performed my exam. It felt like a massage to me, so unaccustomed was I to physical touch. I was then escorted into a dark room where I was given an x-ray and then placed on a large scanner. The scanner moved over me from head to toe. One of the nurses told me it was an MRI machine. It took about twenty minutes for the nurses to read the results.

I was then asked to step into an adjacent room where there were about fifteen other male slaves. We all stood around in this small room in surgical gowns just looking at each other and wondering what was going to happen next. Another female nurse came in and escorted us into a large bathroom area that had about thirty shower stalls. We were each given a hand towel, a larger towel, and a bar of soap and instructed to bathe. I have to admit that the soap they gave us was the best smelling soap I'd ever experienced. My initial apprehension gave way to submission. I graciously lathered up, savoring the luxurious aroma.

We finished our showers and dried off. By the time we left the shower area, the nurses had laid sweat suits on the benches for each of us. I put on my sweat suit, took a seat, and waited for the next step. I was getting excited. At this point, all of it seemed good. A nurse came back with a clipboard and read off each of our names. As each of our names was announced, we'd be led to our designated housing unit.

When my name was called, I was promptly escorted to the yard in front of unit D1. The sun had set an hour or so before, and just a few flickering lamps lit the way. The nurse walked me to the door and then put her hand out to suggest I enter. I obliged and she slowly closed the door behind me. The unit was somewhat small. Four walls and not much else. But it was very homey and comfortable. It had a large bed with lush pillows and a thick, colorful blanket. On one of the walls was a large flat screen television, and there was a kitchenette area with a working stove and refrigerator. There was also a lounging area with a table and two chairs. There was even a small refrigerator beside the bed. For me, this was the lap of luxury.

I walked over to the refrigerator and opened the door. It was full of fruits, drinks, sliced meats, and other delicious items. I moved things around and saw that there was also a carton of milk. I opened the milk to smell it and to my delight, it smelled wonderfully unlike the somewhat sour milk I was used to.

I opened several cabinet shelves and found they had one of my favorite cereals. So I sat down and fixed a bowl of cereal, while wondering what in the world was going to happen next. My stomach full, the long day began to take its toll, so I decided to lay down for the night. I lay across the big, soft bed and turned on the television. But I soon turned away and simply stared at the ceiling. It had a lovely wooden ceiling fan, and I watched it rotate over and over again, utterly transfixed by something so simple. The room was warm and cozy. I had a full stomach, no worries, and no one to bother me. This was the kind of night I loved.

Then, there was a knock at the door. Damn, I knew it was too good to be true. I stood up and walked toward the door, anticipating a nurse, Monitor, or Admin.

But when I opened the door, I was shocked. There stood a jet-black-haired, brown-skinned, statuesque, supremely beautiful woman. I simply stood there in front of her with my mouth open.

Finally, she said with a laugh, "Can I come in?" I nodded and she entered. She smiled and said, "What were you doing, sleeping?"

She walked straight to the bed and sat down. My heart began to pound. She crossed her legs and then, in a sharp and articulate way, began to pepper me with personal questions.

I sat at the kitchenette and looked over at her, careful not to stare too intensely. It felt like this was some hazy dream. I managed to get a few words out.

"Well, I'm from the Crops in Baltimore and my name is Harrison."

"Well, Harrison, you must be a great guy to end up being a breeder, huh?" she said with a smile that made me skip a breath.

I replied, "Nothing great on my end, just another slave." What was there to say? I added a few details about my job and growing up and living in the Crops.

Her name was Denise. She was twenty-five years old and of course, a slave. She didn't know who her parents were. She had lived in the breeding complex for the last two years. She'd already had one child through the breeding program, and this was her second pregnancy assignment.

Denise was certainly pleasant to talk to and seemed very outgoing. She was not reluctant at all to share her experience as a breeder and mentioned that she had also lived in the Crops in Baltimore at one time. She believed that she was selected for breeding because of her looks. I didn't say so, but I agreed. After working for a number of years as a cashier at a retail store, Denise was reassigned as a breeder. At the time, she was only twenty-one. Initially, the reassignment was extremely disturbing to her. She envisioned poor living conditions and repeated abuse by men. Fortunately, it didn't turn out that way for her at all.

The breeder women were treated very well. Denise had been assigned to luxurious new living quarters, and even had a maid service. Each female breeder was also assigned a dietician who made sure that breeders received the very best of foods. They received advanced educational training and some breeder women even went on to obtain college degrees. Breeders were exposed to cultural and arts programs and lived lives that I could only dream of. Once a breeder woman became pregnant, she was reassigned to another unit where she would receive the very best prenatal care.

However, in the midst of relative luxury, there was also tragedy. After a breeder bore a child, she had only about six months with the baby. At six months, the baby was taken away to be raised in a controlled environment. If the pregnancy was successful in producing a vibrant baby boy or girl, the breeder woman was then encouraged to engage in a vigorous exercise and diet program. Once the recuperation from the pregnancy was complete, the breeder female was then returned to the breeding program to mate with a new breeder companion and the cycle continued.

Denise paused here, smiled, and said, "In this case, that would be you."

She moved over to the refrigerator and turned to me and said, "You about ready to get this show started? You seem a bit nervous."

She was right — I was nervous. She was so beautiful that I found it difficult to look directly at her. I stared at the top of the kitchenette table and listened to her fumble around in the refrigerator. Finally, she pulled out a bottle and said, "Okay, okay, maybe this will help."

The bottle had a greenish clear tint and a very long neck unlike anything I'd seen before. Denise reached into one of the drawers in the kitchenette and pulled out an apparatus that she placed on top of the bottle. Then she proceeded to screw the top of the bottle upward. Once the top was out of the bottle, she then went into the kitchen and took out two glasses and poured some of the liquid into each glass.

It was a dark purple liquid with a strong, pungent odor. Denise asked coyly, "Have you ever tried this?"

I angled my chair toward her hesitantly and said, "What is it?"

She said, "It's called wine. It's delicious."

As she handed me the glass, our fingers touched. Soft hands. To me the "wine" tasted like juice that had spoiled. It had a somewhat bitter taste and as I drank a little bit more, I decided I would rather just have juice. We sat and talked for another twenty minutes or so and I began to open up. I talked more about myself. I told her about my experiences in the Crops and how I was ultimately selected to be a breeder. The more I sipped on the liquid, the more I liked it. Not only did the liquid start to taste good, it started to make me feel good, too. The feeling was hard to describe; it was a little bit of light-headedness combined with a heightened sense of happiness. Wine. I could get used to it.

I was almost a full glass in when Denise said, "Hey, that's about enough for you. Come on, let's lay down. You won't need any more of that." She tugged on my sweat pants and I slid them off slowly, then my sweatshirt. I pulled the covers to my chest and watched as she removed her clothing. She was perfect. Long, flowing black hair and a stunningly beautiful body.

We were here for one thing only: breeding. And happy was I that that was the case. It was one of the most pleasurable nights that I had ever or would ever experience, and I took full advantage of it. Slowly, the evening turned into the dawn and I fell into a deep, blissful sleep.

I had to remember to thank my supervisor when I returned to work — he was the man!

During the days at the breeding compound, the men would get together in a large recreational room. There were computers, a cafeteria, and a gymnasium area. There was also a lounge where you could watch television. I stayed up on the news, worked out, and even played a little basketball. I knew about basketball from the recreational programs that I had participated in as a kid. Organized sports were just another one of the diversions that the Admins had come up with to keep us distracted. As a young man, I was encouraged to play both soccer and basketball.

Around five o'clock each evening, we were escorted back to our units to await our breeding partners. We were treated so well that, at times, I almost forgot I was a slave. My depression lifted completely. I began to get comfortable with the routine of being a breeder.

My blissful spirit began to dwindle, however, toward the middle of the second week as I began to feel anxious about the end. I knew that at some point, my breeding session would end and I would be taken away from Denise. More than likely, I would never see her again. That's how it was with slavery. Transitions were devastating and heartless, and there was no consideration for emotional attachment. The more I concentrated on this disturbing fact, the less I was able to enjoy the breeding experience.

Toward the end of the second week of breeding, Denise knocked on the door as she did each evening. She walked in with a smile on her face and said, "I have something for you."

She handed me a small folded up piece of paper. I unfolded it and laid it flat on the kitchenette table. It was a wonderfully drawn illustration of Denise. The detail was fantastic.

I looked at her, my eyes wide, and said, "Did you draw this?"

She said with a grateful smile, "Of course. I wanted you to have a picture of the mother of your child. This way you can always remember."

I folded the picture back up and put it into my jacket pocket. Denise took my hands in hers and looked me straight in the eyes. "You know, this may be the last night we end up being together. I wanted you to know that I've had a wonderful time with you. Even though we'll never get to truly know each other, I can tell you're a wonderful person. Our child will have the potential to do great things." Her words were sweet and gentle, though I wondered what potential — if any — lay ahead for our child.

"You know you're pregnant already?" I asked. I hadn't been around pregnant women before and wasn't sure of the exact timeline for these things.

She squeezed my hand and replied with a sigh, "No, I say these things just in case. These are things that must be said depending on what the future holds."

Over the next few hours, we talked about how frustrating it was to be a slave. How we could never achieve our true ambitions. How we could never experience family life. How we could never grow to know other people or build relationships. Then, we made love one last time. This time, it was only for us.

By the time I awoke in the morning, Denise was gone. The shades in the unit were open and my sweat suit was lying on the chair in the kitchenette. I got up, got dressed, and opened the door. I looked to my left and noticed that the bus that had brought us to the breeding compound was parked in the circular driveway of the complex.

A Monitor walked by the unit, turned to me, and said, "It's time to get your things."

I pulled together my belongings and then walked toward the front of the complex. The other male breeders were already gathered. The Monitors told us to line up; we were handcuffed and led to the bus. The drive back to Baltimore seemed shorter than the drive to the breeding complex. I felt relaxed as I stared out the bus window, watching fences pass on the side of the highway. I wondered what it was like to live on the other side of those fences. I wondered what it was like to be a white man with a family and a good job. What was it like to have potential and a real future? It was midday on a Saturday when the bus pulled back into the courtyard at my Crops.

I was un-cuffed and told to walk toward the front of the bus. I stepped down onto the courtyard and my gaze instinctively fell to my feet. There was no welcoming committee, no celebration, no nothing. I rode the elevator to the fourteenth floor and trudged back to my apartment. Inside, I opened my refrigerator door and, to my surprise, it was full. Perhaps this was the Admins' way of helping me adjust to normal life after being a breeder. Of course, I didn't have any choice. Tomorrow would be like it never happened. Then, come Monday morning, I would be right back at the cleaners.

CHAPTER 8
THE SOCIAL

Being a breeder had rejuvenated me. I no longer felt the overwhelming depression day by day. I don't know why, but I had a heightened sense of optimism. I was still a slave but somehow, being a slave didn't seem so oppressive after being a breeder. My pace picked up at work. I again started going in at least fifteen minutes early. I had spoken to my supervisor about my performance. He indicated that if I continued to have excellent performance, within the next couple of years, he would again recommend me to be a breeder. That said, I knew that the likelihood of my being selected again was slim. By the time he recommended me again, I would be approaching forty. That was right on the verge of being too old to breed. Nonetheless, it was something to strive for. I used the possibility of it as motivation.

I started enjoying television more and more. The game shows were not of any great interest anymore, but the educational shows were good. Coupled with my studies on the Internet, the shows served as a real source of knowledge. Sure, the information was screened, but there was more than enough substance to occupy an evening. I became less and less concerned about Meagan. She was still very beautiful to me, but my mind often wandered to Denise. I wondered if she'd gotten pregnant during our sessions. I wondered if I was soon to be a father. Of course, I would never know the end result. Just the thought of it, however, filled my days with much needed spice.

Not knowing the true answer allowed me to fantasize about the possibilities. Was it a girl or a boy? Was she beautiful or was he handsome? These thoughts were more than enough to erase the mundane nature of my day-to-day tasks. Even the cold, cloudy days didn't diminish my renewed enthusiasm for life. I began to think of new ways to make my life even more interesting, and there was one way. I was eager to explore this new opportunity, but it would take some nerve.

As the winter months dragged on, I began to consider the possibility of another scheme. It would involve some risk, but the rewards could be life-changing. It was an overcast morning in January and the temperature was in the low forties. I put on my all whites and my jacket and sat at my kitchen table. After a moment, I stood up, went over to the kitchen drawer, and pulled out my black marker. On the side of the thick pen were the words "magic marker." Magic indeed.

This marker had created many possibilities for me, and I was going to exercise its full power today. I sat back down, leaned over, and carefully wrote across my left toes the word "Wine." I then headed for the elevator.

I'd given myself extra time this morning because I was going to have to make a quick stop. I hoped that Thomas would be out today, and to my delight, I looked to my right and could see him entering the courtyard.

I timed my steps perfectly and we intersected about fifty feet from where the shuttle normally pulled up. We met at an angle, both of us, as always, with our heads down. We stopped for minute right in front of each other with only our silence separating us. Thomas then reached out with his left arm and grabbed my right arm. He shook it briefly, and then walked on without a word. As I continued to the shuttle stop, I took in the crisp morning air. Involuntarily, I started smiling. Maybe, just maybe, he'd gotten my message.

Two days later, I saw Thomas again as he crossed the courtyard. This time, however, I noticed how he adjusted his pace once he spotted me. I adjusted mine as well and we met in the same spot before. He paused and for a moment glanced up at me and then back down toward his shoe. My gaze instinctively followed his. On the top of his left shoe was written in dark magic marker, "Four coins." I was amazed; my plan had worked.

Once I got Thomas his coins, it took about two weeks for my request to be granted. I started to fear that he'd let me down. Then, one evening after work as I walked down the hallway toward my apartment, I noticed some items at the foot of my door. There was a fairly tall bag and another package. I hurriedly took both items into my apartment, knowing full well that if anybody saw my wine, I'd be a goner. I was getting away with murder.

Once inside, I had a little difficulty opening the bottle of wine. There was a spongy type of stopper in the top and I didn't know how to get it out. I took a nail from my cabinet and slowly pushed the stopper down into the bottle. I then poured myself a cup and sat down to eat. The wine wasn't as delicious as juice, but had a distinct taste. And drinking it helped me to visualize a few very special times with Denise. I savored the Salisbury steak and wine combination. This was luxury.

I drank about two glasses, mindful of Denise's warning about two cups being enough. By the end of the meal, I was starting to get that nice smooth relaxed feeling that I had enjoyed at the breeding complex. I fell asleep right there in the chair in front of the television. I was the most relaxed I'd been since the breeding. I saved the rest of the bottle. This was a feeling I wanted to relive once every couple of weeks, and I knew I was going to have to make some serious additional coin to satisfy this habit.

Many of the slaves in the Crops went to church each Sunday. The church was about three blocks away from my apartment complex and it was a relaxing walk. I think many of the slaves looked at church as a welcomed diversion. It served as a benchmark for each week and a lot of slaves seemed to enjoy the fact that they had a quiet walk from the complex over to the church facility; it was almost freeing in a sense. I was not as enthusiastic about the habit of going to church each weekend. At least some of the sermons were kind of interesting.

The pastors were always white and the associate ministers were black Monitors. The Monitors were never allowed to give sermons and it was clear that the sermons were designed to give us a controlled educational experience. There was always one underlying theme. A typical theme amplified the superiority of white masters over their slaves. We did learn about Jesus, the disciples, Noah, and many others, but the pastors always talked about the importance of obedience and the overwhelming benefits of having a system. They talked about the virtues of being a slave and providing maximum effort to benefit the overall enterprise. Somehow, I doubted Jesus would agree.

There were additional activities that took place at the church, including Bible study and self-help programs. The programs were aimed at vocational enhancement. For example, there were workshops concerning activities like wood work and automotive. All of the activities were very closely monitored, as independent communication was limited amongst slaves.

When the two-hour church service was over, we would all walk back to our individual apartments. The walk was kind of awkward because we had just received a lot of information, but we were not allowed to communicate with each other. Instead, the whole lot of us would walk back to the Crops in silence.

There was one thing I used to like about the walk home, however. Every now and then I would see Meagan and I'd try to get close to her and make her notice me. Over time, however, my enthusiasm waned. It seemed useless; I'd never be able to have any real interaction with Meagan. My fixation on her was becoming tiresome. And as time wore on, I was less interested in trying to intersect with her after church or in the courtyard. I didn't even try to make eye contact in the hallway. In truth, church allowed us to have a connection from a religious standpoint, but it also emphasized our distinct limitations related to interaction.

While we were limited concerning individual interactions during and after church, the socials were another matter. I loved the socials. It was the one time a year that we as slaves could get together and interact and talk and dance. As the winter began to fade away, I began to look forward to the social. It was always thrown during early spring, though we were never given any precise notice as to when it would take place.

Meanwhile, my relationship with my supervisor continued to improve. He constantly complimented me on my job performance, so this made for a comfortable work environment. I was picking up more and more coin as time went by. I had saved enough that I could take a short hiatus from work if I wanted to, but doing so would exhaust almost all my extra coin. So I decided not to pursue it.

Instead, about once a month I would use my extra coin to purchase wine from Thomas. Those bottles of wine added a wonderful new element to my life. I now had the ability to unwind during a few evenings each month, which was great because I knew the socials were coming. I planned to drink a glass or two of wine just before the social so that when I got there, I would truly be in the spirit.

The notice was put up during the first week of March and on the Friday before the social, Thomas brought me a nice new bottle of wine. It was a type of wine that I had never tasted before — "Riesling." It was a clear wine with a sweet taste. I enjoyed it even more than some of the bittersweet wines he'd brought by earlier.

On the Saturday evening of the social, I took a long shower. I pulled out a pair of my best work pants and my nicest shirt. There were four socials in our area on the same evening and the start times for the socials were staggered so that there wouldn't be a large number of slaves on the move at the same time. My social was the last one to start. All evening I'd watched as other slaves traveled across the courtyard dressed in their best work clothes. The atmosphere felt much lighter and happier than usual as everyone prepared for an evening of dancing and laughter.

When the time came for me to head out, I pulled on my shirt, careful to smooth the wrinkles the best I could. I entered the hallway, and to my delight, Meagan was just leaving her apartment, too. That could mean only one thing — we'd finally been assigned to go to the same social. I turned toward the elevator and walked ahead of her without saying a word. The two of us entered the elevator together in silence, with about five other slaves. It was a ten-minute walk to the social that was housed in a large, heated warehouse.

By the time we turned the last corner to the warehouse, a long line had formed. None of the slaves were speaking to each other as that was only allowed within the confines of the social. There were Monitors and Admins outside at the warehouse, along with several armed guards, but I tried to put them out of mind. All I wanted to do was get inside, hear the music, eat some food, and communicate for a change.

After these many months of not paying Meagan any attention, I became intrigued by the possibility of communicating with her. This may be my one chance and it was a dream come true. I stood in line and stared straight ahead, focusing on what I might say to her. This was an opportunity I could not mess up, and there was no way I was going to do anything to bring attention to myself before I got through that doorway. I couldn't risk spoiling my only chance by alerting a Monitor or Admin with conspicuous behavior. So I kept my head down. I didn't even look back behind me to see if she was there. Of course she was there — it was fate. This was my one opportunity to speak to her.

Finally, I was at the front door. The Monitors scanned my lanyard and let me enter. This was a large warehouse and there must have been about two thousand slaves in attendance. We were Social Number Four according to the signs around the warehouse. There was no rhyme or reason for this designation from what I could tell; we were just a random mix of black slaves thrown together at an event for the purpose of defusing any pent up anxiety or hostility.

But tonight was far more than that for me. The music was perfect, a mixture of jazz and rhythm and blues. It had a strong beat that made me want to dance and let go. I'd had a couple of glasses of wine before I left and I was feeling good. The food was good as well. There were several large pigs that had been roasted for the event. Bread, vegetables, and fruit filled long tables on the sides of the hall, along with several savory-looking meats that I didn't quite recognize. It was spectacular. And to top it all off, I finally had my chance with Meagan.

Despite the lavish food and music, socials always felt a bit awkward. Some people were tentative to eat. Others just sat and ate, but didn't talk to anyone. It was a good mixture of men and women, but we were all so unaccustomed to social interaction that many didn't know where to start. I got in line and grabbed my plate. My goal was to taste everything that was there.

My plate full, I stood in a corner and enjoyed my food as I scanned the room for Meagan. It didn't take long for me to spot her. She was on the other side of the warehouse standing alone with a plate in hand. I'd have to find the perfect moment to approach her.

About an hour into the social, many of the slaves had begun to warm up and to talk and mingle. Some of the slaves were laughing and joking with each other, and many of the guys took the rare opportunity to chat with women. Even though we knew there'd be minimal interaction beyond the social, a precious opportunity to talk to a female slave in a social environment was too good an opportunity to pass on. At least for one night, we could pretend that it was about more than this limited interaction. This fantasy would energize our lives for the next couple of months. With that thought, I gathered my courage and walked across the room toward Meagan. I slowed my pace as I approached, careful to not seem overly eager. Just then, another male slave walked up beside her and started talking to her.

She was clearly one of the most attractive women in the room, but to me she was more than just beautiful. She was mysterious and alluring and at this moment represented a rare opportunity for interaction. I didn't care at all that she was talking to another male slave, because the fact remained I had lived beside this woman for many, many years. I knew more about her than anyone else in the room. In a way, I felt like she knew me, too. Confidently, I walked right up beside her while the other male slave was talking.

She turned her head and looked at me. Our eyes met. She seemed stunned, though she said nothing. She just stared. The other male slave got the point and walked off. The wine as my courage, I made the first move.

"Well, I guess it is what it is. All these years and I've never had a chance to talk to you, though I've always wondered what you were like. Since we only have a few hours here, I'd like to get to know you, if you'd like that," I exhaled, happy to finally get those honest words off my chest, even if they weren't as smooth or romantic as I'd always pictured.

She turned and looked in the other direction. She smelled like flowers and I inhaled deeply.

"Well, what good would that do?" she said apprehensively and her eyes lowered. My heart ached knowing that she spoke the truth, but still I had to try. I looked around to see if there were any Monitors or Admins nearby. I knew the cameras were on us, but I didn't care.

I grabbed her hand and said firmly, "You never know what turn life may take. It's about right now. I'm damn sure not going to waste this opportunity to get to know you. Even if it's just for a couple of hours."

She looked up at me for a moment, her beautiful brown eyes catching the light of the room, then lowered her head again and smiled. "Ok, well here's what I know. We're slaves. I'm thirty years old now and I don't know who my parents are." She lowered her voice. "I've got a master who comes and violates me once every couple of weeks. I work at a hotel as a hostess. It's a good job and I've saved up some coin. Above all that, I'm a slave. I have no rights and no future. My name's Meagan. Now, what about you?"

Her sarcasm flowed like honey over me and I couldn't help but smile. It was a sad life, but it was all we knew. There was no need to hide the details of a grim existence that we all shared.

The music grew louder as the night wore on and I eased myself into a comfortable exchange with Meagan. We broadened our conversation to cover all sorts of things. What would life be like if we weren't slaves? How would it be if we were able to date and get married? What would it be like to have a family? We talked about the difficulty of being oppressed day in and day out. How hard it was to keep a positive spirit.

Then, we danced.

Oh, how we danced! I didn't really know any dance moves, none of us did, but I swayed back and forth to the music. They played a lot of up-tempo songs and the atmosphere grew more and more festive as the night wore on. Even the Monitors seemed to be having fun. I saw a few of the black Monitors mingle with some of the other slaves. Toward the latter part of the evening, even the Admins seemed to relax a little bit. It was a rare opportunity where we almost felt like equals.

They played a slow song and I was able to hold Meagan's hands and dance. I gently put a hand on her hip and we swayed back and forth to the music. I stared into her eyes the way I'd always wanted to and she smiled, this time more confidently than before. The dance seemed to last a long time as I tried to hold on to every second. For a second, I almost forgot where I was and thought of leaning over and kissing Meagan. But I corrected myself — that would be too overt and would surely alert the Admins. So instead we just continued to dance and talk, enjoying the profound fact that, for a moment, we felt like normal people.

All too soon, the DJ announced that there would be only one more song. Meagan and I danced the song out, and then very quickly our demeanors became solemn. It was the ending of a wonderful evening and more than likely, there would no continuation of a friendship, a relationship, that had just begun to blossom. This was it. It was time to move on with our lives.

As soon as the song ended, the Monitors and the Admins descended upon the crowd, pulling and shoving us in a random manner so that any coupling was impossible. I was quickly torn away from Meagan. I didn't even have a chance to say goodbye.

We lined up and walked out of the warehouse in an orderly manner. The streets were lined with Monitors, quickly dispelling my hopes of walking back with Meagan. Each slave began the slow, shameful stroll back to his or her respective living quarters. It was a long, dark walk with no talking at all and the transition was soul-crushing.

When I got back to the courtyard, I paused for a moment and took a deep breath of the cool night air, hoping it would taste of the freedom of just a few minutes ago. The elevator was packed tight with about twelve other slaves, but Meagan was nowhere to be seen. I walked to my door and scanned the hall, but she was not there. I opened the door and closed it behind me then sat in my chair and looked out into the courtyard. There were still a ton of slaves walking back from the social. I couldn't pick her out of the crowd.

Finally, about five minutes later I heard her door open and close. I wanted to go over to the wall and sit and listen but it simply wasn't enough. It hurt too much. The best thing I could do was lie in bed and fall off to sleep. I almost wished that the social had never happened. It was just too tough now that I knew that Meagan and I had a connection. It felt as if we were fated to be together, but there was no way for that to ever happen.

Unless I came up with a plan.

Then, suddenly, I had it. I had stepped out of bondage when I wrote that first word on the top of my shoe. I had risked everything in an effort to change my circumstances. And I was more than willing to do it again. There was no way I was going to sit here and not interact with my soul mate. She was just a wall away. I knew what I had to do. I would put my plan in action tomorrow. It might cost me everything, but somehow, I wasn't afraid anymore. I felt alive. I drifted off to sleep with the scent of Meagan's rose-scented perfume on my skin. Tomorrow would be a big day — a new beginning.

CHAPTER 9
GATEWAY

Sunday was the beginning.

I took a pencil from one of my drawers and drew the outline. I'd create a small passage from the bottom corner of my apartment into Meagan's. It would take only a day or two to carve through the drywall, but I'd have to make sure I didn't do too much damage so the passageway could be obscured. As for obscuring the passageway, that would be easy – I'd make the cut behind my couch and slide it out of the way anytime I wanted to enter or exit.

I'd work on carving through the frame and then I'd cut through the drywall on her side. My most critical concern was that I would make too much noise. In addition, my master might come for an unexpected visit and see my work. Any visit by my master, a Monitor, or the Admins could create a very dangerous situation for me while I executed my plan.

I was also obviously concerned that Meagan might not be excited about me barging in. But it was a risk I was willing to take. Based on her reaction at the social, I hoped that she'd be happy to see me, although I wasn't sure. Still, it was better to risk it all and get caught than live another day of my life without Meagan.

I saw Meagan on Monday morning as I headed out to work. She looked at me and smiled. It was the warmest smile I'd ever experienced and suddenly my plan didn't feel as crazy.

That night, I thought about just knocking on the wall to share my plans with Meagan. But my master's unexpected visit had left me guarded. The better course of action would be to keep my head down and work on building the gateway between our apartments as discretely as I could. I needed to do it quietly and without arousing any suspicions, so I decided to limit my interactions with Meagan in the meantime. There were cameras in the hallways and cameras in the elevators. So the best course of action was just to lay low and not interact lest anybody begin to suspect my feelings for her.

That Monday was a normal day. I went to work, did my job the best I could, then boarded the shuttle home. I noticed that the two large television screens in the corner of the courtyard were on. Normally, the screens were on only for one of two reasons during the evening hours. First, if there were any special notices that the Admins had to get out to slaves, they would have the screens on in order to efficiently communicate to the masses. The second reason, however, was more concerning, and for some reason I had a bad feeling about them this time. The glow from the screens was foreboding and slaves moved about more skittishly than usual. The entire scene was unnerving.

About an hour and a half later, just as I was settling down for dinner, the horns blew out a loud, extended alarm. It was the sound that we all hated to hear. Horns meant we were all required to meet outside for an announcement, and within minutes, thousands and thousands of slaves flooded the courtyard and focused on those ominous screens. Beneath the screens sat an eight-foot tall tree stump with a crudely-formed wooden seat nailed to it, about three feet up. Almost like a throne, but its purpose was much more ominous.

All of us stared at the stump and the still blank screens, knowing that nothing good was about to come. A long twenty minutes later, fifteen or so Monitors escorted a shirtless slave through the yard and to the stump. There were at least twenty Admins with weapons standing in and around the courtyard. Several Admins held shotguns, while others carried pistols and assault rifles. In silence, the slave was directed toward the seat, his back toward the crowd and his arms and legs wrapped around the stump where they were then bound on the other side. It was a terrible sight to see, and I couldn't decide if it was better or worse that we couldn't see his face.

One of the Admins walked up behind the slave holding a shiny black briefcase. Methodically, he opened the briefcase and pulled out a whip, then stepped back and gestured toward the screen. The screen then showed us the charges against the slave: "Disobeying a Master" and "Assault on a Master." The screen went to black and the word "Guilty" faded in. His punishment was thirty-two lashes, the maximum for such a crime. I'd seen eight to ten lashes cause irreparable damage — *thirty-two*, I thought, *could kill a man.*

The Admin slowly backed away from the slave and then, rather unceremoniously, began the beating. The first strike was so blunt and forceful that it caused us all to grimace. I was scared to look away because I knew that might draw attention to me. So I stared right at the slave. I had long ago learned to look without really seeing anything. I removed myself from the moment the best I could, but each strike seemed to last an eternity.

Surprisingly, the slave didn't utter a sound. With each strike he arched his head back but he didn't utter a single word. The beating took maybe thirty minutes, though it felt like eternity. The Monitors untied the slave and he sunk, limp and unconscious, onto the ground. Three nurses in pressed, white uniforms came and laid him face down on a gurney, and with the help of four Monitors, took him to a medical vehicle. The horn let out one short blast, and we all promptly returned to our apartments.

On the crowded elevator, no one moved, no one breathed. Fear hung in the air like a stale odor. Back at my apartment, I stared out into the courtyard that had already emptied, as if nothing had happened. Somehow the work on the gateway to Meagan didn't seem as important now. I would wait until tomorrow to begin in earnest.

For the next couple of days, I found myself falling into my old state of depression. The Admins always seemed to be able to strike a balance between punishment and incentive; however, this latest beating seemed over the top. It placed a dark cloud over the entire Crops. Everyone seemed to be down. Once again we were slapped with the stark reality that we were less than human and our lives were not our own.

Late in the week I was crossing the courtyard on my way to the shuttle when I noticed Thomas approaching and heading my way. I altered my course slightly so that we'd intersect. When we got close, head down, I immediately noticed he had writing on his shoes. And there it was on his right shoe, the words "He died."

I stood there in the cool March air, frozen in place for a minute. Thomas stood there as well and we said nothing to each other. Then, hesitantly, he squeezed my arm and continued on without a word. I entered the shuttle that morning with a clear understanding of what those words meant: the slave that had received the beating a couple of days earlier had died. My head spun. Thomas had inside information and had chosen me to confide in. Our strange interactions were the closest thing I had to a friendship, and yet my heart sank. I was certain that there were many times that slaves were killed by their masters or by the system. If you were age sixty-four you'd better prepare, because at age sixty-five you'd disappear. If you were traded to a new master, you could be taken away and executed. Now it seemed that even public executions were not out of bounds. It was a sobering situation and for the next few weeks I couldn't find any inspiration, not even inspiration born of my desire to cross that wall and be with Meagan. I set my plans aside for now.

CHAPTER 10
DOWN AND OUT

I was really starting to go down fast. The weight of my circumstance was starting to bear down. I found no happiness in my days and I knew I needed a boost. So one day I approached Thomas in the courtyard and handed him four coins and whispered quietly, "wine." I couldn't wait until he delivered it to me. I didn't even need the Salisbury steak at this point. I just needed the boost and the euphoria that the wine provided. Maybe it would somehow catapult me out of this dark reality that I had no way of escaping.

The following Monday, just two weeks after the beating, as I returned from my workday, I noticed two Monitors standing just to the side of my door. I felt my shoulders tense with anger, figuring they were sent by Meagan's master to confront her. But as I approached, I noticed that one of the Monitors had a bottle of wine in his hand. They both turned to me and laughed.

"Man, you get the good stuff, don't you?"

I opened my mouth to speak but no words would come out for fear of saying the wrong thing. I then noticed that the top of the bottle of wine was open. Careful to keep his back toward the hall cameras, the Monitor then pulled the bottle to his mouth and took a generous swig before handing the bottle to the other Monitor who took a swig, as well.

The first Monitor, a short and stocky black slave, looked me in the eyes and whispered, "You know this stuff isn't legal, right? We could have you punished for this."

The other Monitor, a bit taller and with a deep, stern voice, added, "But if you keep it coming, we can pretend this never happened. Understand?" Simultaneously baffled and fearing for my life, I nodded.

The two Monitors then brushed past me, with the wine carefully stashed in its original bag, the shorter one muttering, "Thanks for the drink, bud."

I breathed a sigh of relief just as the taller Monitor turned back and with a quizzical look said, "Hey — you don't know anything about secret messages from someone called, 'Phoenix,' do you?"

My anger combined with the notion of secret messages sent a chill through my body. Did they think I was this 'Phoenix' character? I shook my head emphatically, scared for what might happen next.

The short, stalky Monitor laughed in a way that suggested he'd been sipping my wine well before I showed up. He sneered, "Nah, man. This idiot is too stupid for that." Then they walked away, laughing and slapping each other on the backs. Sometimes it was hard to believe that the Monitors were slaves, too.

Once they'd disappeared into the elevator, I opened the door to my apartment. My mind was conflicted over them stealing my wine, the promise I'd been forced to make about supplying them with more, and this 'Phoenix' who may be associated with me somehow. I threw myself down hard on the couch with my mind racing. The only other person I knew who fit the Phoenix description was Thomas. I slid the couch over a little bit and looked at the outline of the passage that I had carved to Meagan's apartment the night I'd made my plans. Then I slid the couch back to its original position, and sat there for a moment before falling into an uneasy sleep. At this point, life really wasn't worth living.

The Monitors taking my wine was a real wake up call. I was always aware of the possibility of being harassed by the Admins, but

I had never experienced harassment or oppression by the Monitors. It was the most personal form of oppression. This was slave on slave humiliation, and I'd quickly learned that the Admins weren't my only enemies.

This served as yet another reminder that I was at the bottom of the totem pole. It was a devastating thought and it was a struggle each morning to find the energy to get up and get to work on time. My garment count at work fell substantially and I knew I was in deep trouble. I needed to correct myself before my supervisor noticed, but it seemed fruitless.

When I got home each evening, instead of engaging in the delights of cooking or watching television, most of the time I just sat and stared out the window. I couldn't even find enough energy to start work on the gateway to Meagan's apartment. I was stuck, and I began to worry that I would never find my way out of this dark world. I didn't even have the wine to rely on.

I resolved to focus on the small things. Taking pleasure in doing my work at a considerable pace; taking pleasure in any positive comments my supervisor said; taking pleasure in the sunset each day; taking pleasure in the fact that I had wonderful memories over the last couple of months, including the fact that I had been a breeder and had a chance to interact with Meagan. I even began to fantasize about a future with Meagan. What would happen if I did, in fact, complete the gateway? What if there were no more barriers? These thoughts were my inspiration, and I began to rely on those possibilities to get me through the day.

I was just coming out of the abyss when I received another devastating blow. It was a late afternoon right after work. In the elevator this afternoon were about seven other slaves, but no Meagan. When the elevator stopped on my floor, I stepped out and, to my horror, noticed two Admins and three Monitors standing by my door.

Instinctively, I began to head back to the elevator, but as I began to turn, a third Admin appeared out of nowhere and grabbed me roughly by the arm. He pushed me forward and I anxiously ambled down the hallway, making no effort to resist, as I knew it was strictly forbidden. My mind began to race. Were they here to ask me about Meagan? Had they discovered the drawings and outline I'd made for the gateway? They had access to my apartment after all. How could I have been so stupid? I was going to be transferred and executed, I just knew it. I braced myself for the conversation ahead.

Silently, the men escorted me to my room and sat me down. To my surprise the couch had not been moved, which made my mind race in anticipation. They had to be here for another reason. What was it? I had really done nothing else wrong. Maybe it was my interaction with Thomas. Could he be an informant? Maybe they thought I was this Phoenix guy. Maybe it was the writing on the tops of my shoes. It had all come back to destroy me.

One of the Admins, a shorter, muscular white man with a crew cut, slowly sauntered over to me with his hands behind his back. "You think you're smarter than the rest of us, don't you, young man?"

I laughed inside at that title: Young man? I was certainly not that. I responded, "No, sir."

"Well, you've had some interesting activity on your computer over the last couple of weeks, haven't you?" I searched to recall whether I'd had any strange or unusual behavior on my computer, but I couldn't think of anything.

The Admin continued, "You know we monitor each computer twenty-four hours a day, don't you? And in the event that we discover any unusual or threatening activity, we reserve not only the right to take a computer away, but to imprison the individual at fault."

I avoided direct eye contact, lest I unintentionally provoke him. His voice became louder as he continued, "Due to suspected illicit online behavior, we will be taking your computer with us today. Consider this fair warning. We will also be keeping an eye on you over the next couple of months. Any unusual activity whatsoever could result in your being transferred."

My breath escaped me. Transfer. Death. This was it and I had no idea what I'd done wrong. I finally mustered up the strength to say a few words, "But sir, with all due respect, I have not engaged in any unusual activity on the computer."

The Admin raised his brows and with a silence that made my palms tingle, motioned for two of the Monitors to bring my laptop over to the kitchen table. He then gestured for me to take a seat in front of it.

He continued, sternly, "In the past two weeks, you have conducted over one hundred separate searches using the words 'rebellion,' 'insurrection,' and 'revolution.' Such usage is a direct threat to the state and any rebellion, whatsoever, will not be tolerated. Son, let me remind you that even the thought of such actions will result in severe punishment. You need to watch what you think and you need to watch what you do." Even my thoughts weren't free. My head spun. I hadn't searched for those words — had they confused me for somebody else?

With a single, jerking motion, he yanked the computer cord out of the wall, causing the lights in the room to dim. He wrapped the cord around his arm, slammed the computer shut, and gestured for the others to leave. As he followed behind them, he turned back and added, "Remember, any action against the State and you're done."

He slammed the door behind him and I sat there at the kitchenette table wondering what in the world had just happened. I hadn't conducted any illicit searches on the Internet, and I certainly had not looked up the words, "rebellion" or "revolt" or whatever those guys thought I was looking at. Could they have the wrong guy? My life was no longer my own.

Just as I'd begun to process my thoughts, the lights in my apartment flashed on and off. What next? Were they going to turn my lights off? I stared out the window, trying to clear my mind, and slowly and fitfully, fell into sleep.

The next morning as I exited my apartment, Meagan was leaving, as well. I glanced her way, but this time there was no smile. She simply looked down and walked past, completely ignoring me. I wondered if she'd also had a visit by the Admins. Could she be avoiding contact with me? I certainly didn't want to draw any attention to either of us, so I let it go.

When I got to work, I noticed that things felt different. None of my co-workers would look at or speak to me, and even my supervisor was quiet. He had nothing at all to say to me other than to keep up my pace. And to think, we'd just established such a positive relationship. Despite everything, I put in a hard day at work remembering that any misstep on my part could lead to dire circumstances.

I continued to ponder why the Admins would accuse me of searching for those words, because the truth was plain and simple, I hadn't done it. I don't know if this was some targeted way to get at me or if they had actually found out about my shoe writing. There was a target on my back and I felt it was all because of Thomas. He had to be Phoenix. They had begun the process of eliminating me.

The next day at work was my worst ever. I couldn't think straight and fell way behind. My garment count was down and my supervisor was becoming more and more distant. I began to worry that I might lose my job and be placed in another less desirable position. I needed to wake up and put in more effort toward my workday.

I rode the shuttle home and watched the world outside my window. Normally I didn't take notice of much on the way home as it was always the same; slaves going back and forth to their workplaces. But today I took a particular interest in the many white people going about their daily activities: shopping, going to work. I watched several white children walking and playing on the sidewalks with their parents. They seemed so carefree with not a worry in the world. Not only did they have their parents to take care of them, they also had slaves. I, as a slave, was subservient to mere children. It was a depressing thought.

When the shuttle dropped us off, I had a strong desire to just get back to my apartment, eat, and go to sleep. As I walked toward the building, I noticed my apartment light was on. This was concerning to me as I had a precise routine and was always very cognizant about preserving energy; I always turned my lights off. When I got off of the elevator I instinctively looked behind me to see if there were any Admins around, but didn't see any. I walked to my apartment, opened the door and there they were, the same two Monitors who'd taken my wine.

"Come in," said the shorter man.

I slowly walked inside and hadn't even finished closing the door when he blurted out, "I'm sorry to inform you, but you have just been transferred." His face was solemn and apologetic and his words hit me like a blow to the gut.

Transferred.

The word was practically synonymous with execution. I thought about running, but I knew there was no way to escape. I wanted to shout, but I couldn't get a single sound out. The taller Monitor told me to turn around and I did. He handcuffed me behind my back and without another word, they escorted me out.

I had somewhat of an out of body experience. I felt and thought nothing — my body was an empty shell. They escorted me to the elevator and we began the ride down in silence. It felt like an hour passed before the doors opened again. I wondered how it would feel to be executed. How would they do it? How long would the pain last? Could I give up, and turn off before I died so I wouldn't have to experience the agony?

When we exited the building and got out to the courtyard, there were only a few people milling around. It was after dusk and just a few lamps shone across our path. A couple of slaves walked past us, heads down. I'm sure they wanted to look up and see what was going on, but that was strictly forbidden.

The two black Monitors walked me across the courtyard — slaves escorting a slave. I assumed they would turn me over to the

Admins and then I would be taken for my ending. I noticed an Admin approaching in the darkness. He was in full uniform, here on official business. When he got close to us the two Monitors stopped. Their arms were interlocked with mine; I was trapped.

"What's the deal here?" the Admin asked, as casually as if he were asking for the time.

"This is a transfer," said the shorter Monitor.

The Admin asked for my slave identification number. The Monitor quickly provided it, and the Admin pulled out his handheld computer. He ran the number and nodded, "I see he had a violation related to computer issues."

The shorter Monitor replied, "Yes and he had a second violation last night." Last night? I hadn't done a thing last night. I didn't even have my computer. What was happening to me?

The Admin furrowed his brow and said, "I don't see it here."

The Monitor shrugged, "We were notified this morning that he has been scheduled for a transfer."

The Admin took a step back, studied me from head to toe, shook his head, and told them to carry on before continuing on his way.

The Monitors lead me away without hesitation and began to move toward the left side of the courtyard. However, instead of walking to the street where I was sure a car would be waiting to take me to my final destination, we instead walked parallel to my apartment building. We continued to walk toward the edge of my apartment building and then made the turn toward the back of the building where the benches and field were.

My heart raced and I felt as if I may throw up. Were they going to kill me right here? Was I going to be left to await a whipping? I was terrified of what might happen next.

The Monitors led me toward the fenced in area. Their grip tightened as we approached the fence and I assumed this was it. Now they'd lower me to my knees and shoot me in the head. We got closer and closer to the fence and I began to resist every step.

Finally, we got to the fence and I turned to one of the Monitors and said, "I guess this is it, huh?" I knew speaking without being spoken to was forbidden, but what did I have to lose?

I glanced over my shoulder at my building one last time — there was nobody around. There was the bench where I'd sat many times and looked out over the field past the two dilapidated buildings and over into Chesapeake Bay. It felt like a serene place to die. I'd rather it happen here than anywhere else. The moments before my death, I could focus on the Chesapeake Bay area and wonder what was next. Just as I began to kneel out of instinct, they shoved me forward.

The taller Monitor pulled back a part of the fence. It was cut open. Then, to my amazement, the other Monitor unlocked and removed my handcuffs, and took off my ankle monitor. He then pointed to his shoes. On the top of his right shoe there was drawn an arrow that pointed in the direction of the fence and toward the two dilapidated buildings.

He pulled me toward him and our eyes met as he slowly nodded with an assurance that made my stomach somersault. He pushed me through with one word, "Go!"

I turned back scared and desperate, my hands gripping the fence as if it could protect me. "Go?" I cried.

"Go!" he repeated, this time more urgently, and pointed at the top of his shoe.

They both flashed a quick smile and the taller one said, "Thank you, Phoenix, for giving us hope!"

Phoenix! My mind reeled with a thousand questions about how and why these men knew a thing about me, what they knew, and how far the news had traveled. Before I could utter a single word, they both turned around and hurried away. I stood by myself in the dark, hands clinging to the fence, facing the Crops and not knowing what to do next. I had just escaped death. My pulse raced and my eyes welled with tears, so happy was I to be alive.

After a moment, I turned toward the two dilapidated buildings behind me. The arrow on the top of the Monitor's shoe had pointed toward them, so I headed in that direction. It was a long, difficult walk. The vegetation in this field had grown to about three quarters of my height, though thankfully, I figured, it would help to obscure me from any prying eyes. I pushed back some of the taller stems and grass and waded my way through, squinting into the dark and heading directly toward the buildings — about a mile or so ahead. I was thankful for the light of the moon and the late March air — it was cool but not cold. It took me almost twenty minutes to get to there and I was lost in terms of my expectations. Why lay ahead? Was this my end or my new beginning?

Why had the Monitors taken me away from my apartment? Who were they? Were they in fact instructed to execute me and had they disobeyed orders? Why had they directed me to head toward these two buildings? Was this all a trap? Was I still headed toward my execution? And was I their Phoenix? I felt sick with worry.

Given no other choice, I continued my journey forward, until I reached the front door of one of the old buildings. Upon closer inspection, it looked like an old slave apartment, one that had not been used in many years. Hesitantly, I entered into a lobby area and instinctively scanned the room but I saw no one. Just as quietly, I exited and walked over to the second building. As I entered, I looked down and noticed an arrow painted on the ground. *A clue from the Monitors? Or someone else?* I followed the arrow to the elevators that sat across them. I chuckled nervously; this building was so old and in such ill repair, I was certain the elevators wouldn't be operable. I pressed the button anyway, praying that the elevator wouldn't fall and crush me to death.

To my surprise the elevator arrived, the bell rang, and the door opened. Inside, I stared at the buttons. Despite the few dozen stories that were above me, there were only three buttons, P1, P2, and P3 — and they all led downwards. It felt like one of those game shows where the host makes you choose from three doors for your prize. Only each of these options seemed more ominous. I pressed P1. The elevator lurched roughly downward; however, P1 was nothing but the dark, charred remains of a huge, empty room. I pressed P2. The elevator continued down to P2, the door opened, and my mouth fell open in alarm.

There were three people standing there, two black males and one black female. One of the male slaves, a tall, striking man with dark brown skin said, "Well, I'm glad you made it, Phoenix." He reached out his hand and grabbed mine and gestured for me to enter the long, bare hallway. His handshake was firm and assuring.

All I could do was stare at them dumbfounded. After a moment, I managed, "My name is Harrison, not Phoenix."

They all laughed and the man shaking my hand said, "Please, let us take you on a tour of your new life here and we'll explain everything to you."

Chapter 11
Alive!

I followed the three slaves down a long, wide hallway. Black uniformed individuals scattered each side and there were slaves everywhere. They milled past us with importance, dressed in work attire and clearly eager to complete one task or another. Some had papers in their hands and there was a healthy mix of both male and female slaves. Occasionally some would look at me in awe and say, "Welcome Phoenix," "Thank you, sir," and other greetings that confused me even further. I'd never been called "sir" in my life. Was I dreaming?

I could not believe what I was seeing. When we got toward the end of the hallway, we took a sharp right and walked into a large, open area. It was like a huge warehouse facility, though quite rough around the edges. Some of the walls were dirt and rock; the vast room had clearly been carved into the ground with haste. At least a hundred slaves sat at folding tables, busily typing away on computers. There were other slaves who fussed over stacks of boxes and seemed to be sorting out some type of inventory issue. Equipment was piled up in one area and food and bottled water and other supplies, lay to another side. This warehouse was larger than the ones where we'd had our socials. I could not believe that such a large facility existed here underground, completely hidden from the Crops and the world above. We walked to the far end of the warehouse, and I noticed that there were three large tunnels leading from the facility. How vast was this space and how long had it been here?

At last, the young man who had shook my hand spoke, "Well, let me get introductions out of the way. My name is Barry and these two are my assistants, Christian and Nora." Christian was a young man of maybe eighteen with a baby face and a wide grin, and Nora was an attractive, slender woman with a bobbed haircut and tall, stiletto heels that clicked on the concrete floor as we walked about.

The two assistants gave a quick nod and left us, heading in the opposite direction.

"I know you have many questions right now but let me first thank you for your mantra, "Commit to Resist." It's positively refueled our revolution. Thanks to your words, Apex, our leader, has given you the code name, Phoenix. You raised our hope out of the ashes." How could my one small action have had this type of impact? There was only one way: *Thomas*. If I ever saw him again, I'd be sure to thank him for paying me mind and saving my life.

We exited the warehouse through a large door to the left and walked through a set of rooms containing desks, chairs, and other office equipment. My mind was barely keeping up with Barry and his summation on how all of this came to be.

"Apex began work on this facility about fifteen years ago. He was one of the slaves originally housed in these apartments. He has always been a computer genius and was able to use his computer to obtain all types of information, including insider information about the government's plans to build a tunnel under the Chesapeake Bay from Baltimore to Richmond.

"The government had begun work on the tunnel years before, but found that it was simply too expensive to complete. During the Reagan Administration, folks were more focused on the Cold War and threats from the Soviet Union, so the whole process was aborted. Apex, however, was able to connect the dots and formulate a plan that he had in the works ever since he was a young man of twenty-one. His discovery of the abandoned tunnel was just a happy addition to his plans."

A few more slaves passed by and one stopped Barry, asking him to sign off on a document. We continued on through a maze of rooms and Barry barely paused for a breath. I remained quiet, listening to his mythical and epic history of Apex and this astonishing facility.

"Apex knew that with some extremely hard work, these old, unused, and incomplete tunnel could be extended to connect to the bottom of this very building. He developed an ingenious platform to communicate with other slaves online without being detected by the Admins.

"Over time, Apex hand-selected three other slaves who he felt he could trust to help him with his vision. I was one of those original three, and you'll meet the other two later. Then, through a lot of planning and meticulous computer hacking, he was able to remove our names and slave ID numbers from the grid and we all moved down here. The facility you see before you today has slowly expanded over many years, with plans to expand further in the future.

"Apex has recruited slaves for many years but he has always been careful to make sure there was a certain set of indicators that a slave was ready to be removed from slave society. All of the black men and women you see before you are *former* slaves — yourself, included." *Former slave?* At first the words didn't even make sense, so unaccustomed was I to the idea of it. But there it was: in an instant, my shackles were gone. I was a free man. I wanted to weep, but instead I continued forward, eager to learn more about the new life that lay ahead of me.

Barry continued his conversation after turning a corner into a control room of sorts. "We have a network of Monitors that work for us as well," he said, gesturing toward a very impressive area of computers being manned by different male and female *former* slaves.

"All men and women in our facility communicate via an internet platform that Apex himself designed to piggyback off the Admins' protocols. Apex pays for the entire operation by hacking into the various financial systems around the country. By taking just a little bit here, and a little bit there, we've been able to collect enough money to keep operations running smoothly without being detected. We even have a few Admins here and there on the payroll."

"Apex is such a genius that he has been able to dispel any comments about missing slaves or about the possibility of there being an operation like ours whenever there has been any kind of suspicion amongst government officials. Many so called 'transferred' slaves end up here, and our Admin and Monitor allies have been instrumental in seeing to it, oftentimes creating false allegations against slaves so that they may be 'removed' without suspicion."

It was all coming together — that inappropriate computer behavior I'd been accused of had been my ticket here. And those Admins who'd taken my computer away… did they work for Apex?

He continued, "So far, we have remained undetected. We have an underground, self-sustaining system of tunnels that house not only our food and provisions, but also our entire way of life."

My mind tried to keep pace with Barry, "While it's not entirely comfortable, it is certainly better than living on the surface as a slave. Our strength relies on the vision that Apex has for not only us, but every one of our brothers and sisters still being oppressed above."

The more Barry talked, the more I wanted to meet this Apex character. He sounded like a Greek god. Barry's admiration was evident, and I couldn't imagine why Apex thought I could help with something this major. I felt unworthy.

Then, Barry's tone shifted from praise to clear foreboding, "Apex knows that at some point and time we will be detected. And at such a time, the government and Admins will decide to take action against us. But Apex has always preached that he doesn't feel as if the State has enough heart or resources to stand against a rebellious slave population as immense as ours. It would simply be too costly for the State in terms of resources. The white masters have always been complacent and reluctant to become engaged in any substantial confrontations; especially ones that would involve the possible loss of lives. They understand the complexity of using a large population of black Monitors and soldier slaves to attack an organization like ours. The majority of our nation's armies is black; can you imagine an army of black slaves attacking their own? I, for one, cannot. Imagine the riots it would cause. Apex has always said that even if the government did detect us, they would focus on containment rather than destruction, and I think he's right. There's even a chance that the Admins already know about us, but at this point they are just reluctant to act due to fear. In the meantime, we are preparing for an offensive that would be stunning and effective. One that could potentially end the slave trade for good. Apex has it all in his plan and the time is coming."

The end of the slave trade? Peaceful negotiations with our white leaders? I thought back to the severe beating I had witnessed just weeks before. I had serious doubts that our government would even so much as hesitate to take us all down — and without remorse. On this point, Barry, Apex and I vehemently disagreed. I kept this to myself for now, however, as I needed to learn more about Apex's wild plans to end slavery altogether. From my recollection, slave rebellions in the past were dealt with harshly and quickly. Barry's words sounded too good to be true.

We turned down one of the many tunnels and walked toward a door on the right. Down this tunnel, there were many doors that gave the impression of some type of living quarters. Barry opened a door about halfway down and we walked into a modestly-sized, but cozy apartment. There was a refrigerator, a television, and a large, comfortable-looking bed.

Barry smiled, "I know it's not much and it's not luxurious, but here, you're not a slave. This apartment is all yours — so make yourself at home, Phoenix. Someone will be back later to bring you clothing and additional food. We have a large cafeteria where everybody eats three meals a day. Someone will be by later with further instructions. It was an honor to meet you, sir. The work that you've done has already changed lives."

He paused, smiled, and held out his hand for me to shake. Barry was a young man of about thirty years of age, but he had a class and dignity about him that I'd never seen in any other slave. Then again, I'd never had a chance to interact, face to face, with other male slaves on this level. I shook his hand and said "Thank you," and with that he was gone. The door closed behind him and I stood still in the middle of the room, uncertain as to what to do next.

A million questions rattled inside my head and I didn't know where to begin. But it had been one hell of a day — how late was it anyway? — and now all I wanted to do was dive into my new bed and pray that I didn't wake back in my old apartment, waiting to be executed.

It was one of the longest, deepest, and most satisfying sleeps I had ever experienced. For the first time in my life, I could sleep without fear of imminent harm or danger. I was a free man. I must have slept for twelve hours. I woke, halfway thinking that all that had transpired was a dream and as I lay still for a moment and realized that it wasn't, I wanted to shout.

I opened my eyes and looked around me. I was in a new room — my room. It was small, but it was beautiful in my eyes. I looked around and noticed that it had a table, a television, a computer, a small refrigerator, a bed, and a sink. It was all that I needed. Most importantly, I wasn't at the Crops. I wasn't stuck in an environment where at any moment one of the Monitors or Admins would burst into my room. I had complete privacy, and it began to dawn on me that I could probably even invite others to my room if I wished. It was beyond my imagination.

I stood up, stretched, and then there was a knock at the door. I halfway expected someone to bust in, but when they didn't, I walked over and opened the door, slowly. Standing at the door was Christian, Barry's young assistant from last night. He smiled and said, "About time you woke up, brother! Barry sent me to get you; you got a lot to do today. We need to get your briefing started immediately. Someone will come to escort you to the showers. Get dressed, and then we'll bring you over for breakfast. After that, we need to start." I glanced to the left of my door and found a stack of simple clothes, a toothbrush and toothpaste, and a bag of groceries — milk, fruit, cereal and the like. I thanked Christian, collected my things, and returned inside.

I'd just sat down on the bed for a minute when there was another knock. I opened the door and there was Barry, smiling.

"Alright, Harrison are you ready to go?" *Harrison.* I was so unused to hearing my own name — it was like we were already friends.

"I thought your assistant said you were sending someone to collect me?"

Stepping into the room Barry laughed, "I couldn't just let my assistant escort our Phoenix around on his first day!"

He had a towel rolled up in his arm and some more clothing that he gently tossed onto the bed.

"Grab that stuff and let's go get you showered up."

I grabbed the clothes and towel and walked out with him. As I exited out into the hallway, I noticed there was already a lot of activity. Men and women walked back and forth; all of them walking with urgency, yet none were panicky. They walked with their heads held high and greeted each other as they passed — it reminded me of watching white people interact on the streets on my way to the breeding facility. Everyone seemed relaxed and comfortable, and they all wore clothes much nicer than what we wore in the Crops as slaves. I looked at the clothes Barry had just given me and they appeared to be of some soft, lightweight cloth.

I walked behind him down the hallway. Every once in a while, someone would take an extended look at me and smile. I guess they knew I was the new person here, the famous "Phoenix," a name I wasn't fully ready to claim just yet. We walked down the tunnel and made a left into an open area. We walked into an open area where there were old lockers pushed into the walls. There must have been hundreds of lockers and a bench extended all the way down the length of the room. Barry walked me over to locker number "687."

"This is yours, man. Make sure you remember your number and here's your key."

I asked Barry, "How do y'all get all this stuff?"

Barry responded nonchalantly, "Apex got all of this for us. He was the first. He and his guys started it all. He knows how to get any and everything with his tunnel network. He's an absolute genius. Everything that you see here is a result of his hard work. It will all make more sense soon."

Barry walked me around the corner past a long row of sinks into a shower area. "The water comes from over the tunnels," he explained. "It rolls in here and we funnel it into the showerheads, sinks, toilets, and the like. Apex has been talking about a water recycling center, but for now, because of the bay, we have a natural unlimited source of water. We divert gas from the pipelines into the tunnels as well, so we have an unlimited source of heat. So you will find that we have ample hot water. It's very refreshing." I had grown used to cold showers, as there was never enough hot water to go around in the Crops. This was paradise.

I took a long, relaxing shower, trying still to wrap my mind around this new situation. Each of the showers had a small partition that extended from the tunnel walls and out in front of the stall, so you had a little bit of privacy for bathing and dressing. I finished my shower, put on my new, impossibly comfortable clothes, and walked out to the front of the shower area. Barry was there waiting.

"Now, let's go get you something to eat."

We walked down yet another hallway and into the mess hall area. It was a big, well-furnished room, though the equipment was clearly used and old. There were people behind the serving areas. I expected the worst of foods. I figured there was no way they could get good supplies down here.

Barry escorted me up to the counter and asked, "What would you like, Harrison? It's pushing eleven o'clock, but they're still serving breakfast." Eleven o'clock? I really had slept a long time.

I said, "Do they have any eggs?" Barry laughed and said, "Of course. Give him the works," he told one of the male workers.

"Sure thing, Barry," he replied. Everyone knew who Barry was down here.

The server grabbed a plate and piled it high with scrambled eggs, grits, bacon, and the freshest-looking fruit I'd ever seen and handed it to me. It was a spread that beat the heck out of the cold cereal I was used to. I walked down the end of the line to a big barrel full of juices of every kind. I grabbed an orange juice and went to go sit down with Barry. He sat directly in front of me with his own plate. There were about seventy or eighty former slaves sitting at the tables, eating and chatting.

Before eating I leaned in and whispered to Barry, "Man, there are a lot of slaves here."

He raised an eyebrow; "Hey, look, man. We don't call each other slaves here. We are all free, and that includes you. We are black, or as Apex says, we're 'African American,' but that title hasn't stuck quiet yet since none of us has ever been to Africa," he chuckled at the last part and I smiled.

"I'm a free man!" I repeated, and let out a laugh. It felt incredible. Then, without another word I dove into the food before me. Having missed dinner the night before, I was very hungry and the food was absolutely fantastic. The eggs were fluffy and cooked perfectly. I gobbled it all up, drank the juice, and reclined back against my chair. "Wow, for a tunnel, this is a pretty good situation, huh?"

Barry laughed. "Hurry up man. You need to finish up. We're going be late for your briefing."

As we exited the cafeteria, we entered a large lobby area where there were three pairs of double doors by a set of elevators. Barry walked me through the center door and what was on the other side shocked me. There was a gigantic hallway with private offices to either side.

As we continued down the hall, I commented, "I'm going to need a map or a trail of breadcrumbs to get back to my room. This place is huge!"

Nodding in agreement, Barry said, "Trust me, I've gotten lost on several occasions. Just remember that the cafeteria is in the middle of everything. If you go left from there, that's where the living quarters, showers, and loading dock are located. If you go right, like we're doing now, you'll be headed to the offices. By the way, you'll have your very own office once we clear it up for you." My jaw dropped for perhaps the fifteenth time since arriving at the facility. My own office! What would I use it for?

Before I could respond, Barry opened a door to the right that led to a plush and ornately decorated conference room. There were men and a young woman with anxious eyes and hard expressions waiting for us. They stood to greet me. The attention was overwhelming and I automatically went into my eyes down mode. Barry nudged me to look up, whispering, "It's, okay, man. They don't bite!" and everyone smiled at me kindly.

Barry directed me to take a seat near the end of the table and then everyone else sat down. For a couple of moments, we just sat there and stared at each other. At this point, I was really wondering what the hell was going on. Here I was in a gigantic basement with three slaves — correction — people, wearing fancy clothes and sitting in a fancy conference room. Last night I expected to be executed; this morning I was attending a meeting about revolution.

The door opened and another black man walked in. His skin was a little lighter than the rest of us and he had thick, curly hair. He sat down at the head of the table to my left.

"Harrison, the Phoenix!" he said excitedly. "Allow me to introduce myself. My name is Chris." He gestured to the young lady who was a darker-skinned beauty. "This is Lynn, you've already met Barry, and this is Ray."

Ray was an interesting-looking guy. He was older than the other folks in the room, and he seemed like he might have been in his late fifties or early sixties. I wasn't used to seeing many older people around, and he had a distinguished look about him as if he'd done a lot of living. Ray smiled and nodded his head at me. *This has to be Apex*, I thought.

Chris continued, "It is an absolute pleasure to meet you, sir. You are an innovator. 'Commit to Resist.' Brilliant. Your motto is something we have lived by for over the last six or seven months. It's a model for the ages."

Ray chimed in, "And man you can't forget the shoe writing! Who would have thought that such a useful and powerful way of communicating could come from such simplicity? We are all very grateful."

This stunned me. My small act of rebellion had this type of importance?

Lynn reached over the table and grabbed my hand and said, "It is certainly an honor for me too, sir. We look forward to working with you." I almost jumped — a female grabbing my hand, of her own free will, without consequences.

"I... thank you," I muttered, uncertain of what else to say.

Chris then became very stern. "The process and transition may feel somewhat difficult. It's always hard when you leave the regulated world of being a slave and then transition into life in the tunnels. But I can guarantee you will enjoy your life here a whole lot more than you did in the Crops. What an absolute waste of human talent. One day it will change. One day soon."

Aside from my conversations with Denise back in the breeding program, I had never heard black people talk like this. I was a little reluctant to respond, but I mustered up the courage.

"Where am I? Am I still in line to be executed by the Admins?" I chuckled nervously, only half joking.

Chris laughed and said, "Nah, man. You're not going to be executed, not even close. This is the beginning of your new life. There's a whole bunch of work to do and you've come at a very crucial time. We are now at the point where opportunity meets action, and you have been a big part of our efforts so far."

I replied to him, "Well, what have I done? I'm just a lowly slave... I mean, black man," I corrected myself, unused to the new title. "I didn't really do anything."

Chris responded, "You've done more than you could imagine. Your actions have been an inspiration. It took a lot of courage to do what you did. We orchestrated..." before he could finish, the door to the conference room burst open.

It was a very muscular black man who stood a commanding 6'3" and looked like he was in his early fifties. He was a stunning-looking guy. He had a thin, grayish beard and his eyes looked right through you. He was escorted by three other men.

He walked in and said, "Ah, Harrison. Good to see you."

He walked to the head of the conference room table and stood expectantly. Chris looked up at him, got up, and walked to another seat. The gentleman sat down in the head seat, crossed his arms, and looked directly at me.

"My name is Apex; it's good to have you join us."

His voice was bold and powerful; it was obvious he was a leader.

I shook his hand firmly, and without missing a beat said, "Thank you, but I'm really confused right now. Don't get me wrong, I'm thankful for being rescued, but I have so many questions."

Apex replied, "You're here because we made it happen, Harrison. We have been watching you for some time; monitoring your activities. We knew that you were special the moment you came up with a new way for slaves to communicate. You may have guessed this already, but Thomas works for us and has for many years, playing a dual role.

He works for the State and they have no idea that he has connections with our movement. He told us about the writings on your shoes. It was an absolute stroke of genius; something that the Admins would never expect. They tell us to always keep our heads down. You turned that weakness into a strength.

"It was not only that, but the words you communicated, 'Commit to resist.' Those words have become our motto. For that, I am grateful. We knew that you were working your way into a bad situation. Your interactions with Meagan created a scenario where you were now conspicuous and we assumed that after the social you might do something stupid like try to interact with her. We had to get you out of the Crops before it was too late."

My heart began to race at how closely Apex and everyone else had monitored my actions from then to now.

"It seemed inevitable that the State would have you transferred if you continued with such rebellious activity, so we made moves to make it happen earlier. We gained access to your computer and entered the keywords so that the Admins would take your equipment. We knew that that would make you uncomfortable. We knew that the execution in the courtyard had already made you uncomfortable. We also arranged for the Monitors to drink your wine. Don't know if you noticed that the Monitors who escorted you out of your apartment last night were the same ones that drank your wine."

"Yeah, they drank a very good bottle," I said with a chuckle, which made everyone else laugh.

Apex continued on, "We were the ones who shut off your power. We had to make you as uncomfortable as possible. We had to weaken you and depress you so that there would be very little resistance when we decided to make your 'transfer' a reality. We wanted it to come as no surprise. Thank goodness it worked. You're the type of person who could benefit us here. That's why we brought you in."

I put my head down on the table, feeling as if I might faint. It was all so overwhelming. They had carefully orchestrated me out of the

Crops. It was as if I were dreaming and I couldn't wait to hear what was going to happen next.

Apex said, "Look up."

I immediately obeyed the command without thinking about it.

"This is the beginning of a new life for you, but you have responsibilities, understand? Responsibilities to yourself, and responsibilities to all the others like us. We are in the process of a movement, a rebellion and the time is coming for us to act. We have the resources to move our entire race into a position of freedom, but we need your help. I need to know that you are committed... committed to resist. We've given you your freedom. Are you willing to do the work necessary to help others obtain theirs?"

I didn't know how to respond to such a loaded question, so I just remained silent, foolishly assuming that it was rhetorical.

He repeated himself, "Harrison, are you willing to help?"

I looked him directly in the eyes, and thinking of Meagan and the future that could be ours, said with conviction, "Yes."

Apex got up and walked toward the door with his escorts, then turned back toward me and said with more levity, "Well then, let's begin!" With that, he walked out and everyone else quickly followed suit.

This man certainly has a flair for the dramatic, I thought, as I followed the others in Apex's wake.

We all headed down the hall to another conference room that had four monitors on the wall. I found my seat at a large table with about a dozen other people. The attendees included Barry, Ray, Chris, Lynn and of course, Apex at the head of the table, along with several other people who seemed to study me with great detail.

"Harrison, this is the council. We manage this great complex and I thought it would be important to give you a feel for how we got here."

Barry walked over to a computer and booted up a slide show that displayed on one of the monitors.

Apex stood at the front of the room and began his presentation, "The population of the United States is now approximately three hundred and fifty million. African Americans represent about ten percent of that population."

I noticed everyone's faces when Apex said 'African Americans.' A few rolled their eyes.

The screen switched to a map of the United States.

Apex continued, "But the black populations are very heavily concentrated in a few cities, primarily Baltimore, DC, New York, and Chicago. We also occupy several other heavy industrial areas across the US. The slave population has been used for many years as a foundation of manufacturing growth here in the United States, both in the northeast, and in the Silicon Valley areas of the west. This heavy concentration of slaves has several benefits to the white majority."

Barry advanced to the next slide, in which a pie chart listed several resources and other information that I didn't understand just yet.

"First, it allows whites to manage the slave population effectively with limited expenditure of resources. They house us in large complexes, allowing them to focus their organizations and administrative infrastructure in smaller areas, rather than the slave population being spread out over the United States. It has allowed the white majority to coordinate their slave commodity, and to be very efficient in generating products via the slave population.

"The Crops allow for the systematic cultivation and monitoring of the black slave. Masters keep their slaves in one area so they can monitor activities through cameras and computer usage.

"The State is able to easily impose a mental stronghold on the slave population through the use of the outdoor monitors, television programs, and State-administered computers. They have been very successful in utilizing the slave's workplace as another method of control and monitoring. As you know, a slave's actions and demeanors are scrutinized on a consistent basis within the workplace."

Apex walked back from his spot in front of the monitor and leaned with his hands firmly planted on the table. He glanced upwards as he gathered his thoughts.

"However this system comes with one significant flaw. Congregating slaves in large industrial areas also gives them strength in numbers. In fact, if there were a stimulus — an ignition point — they could take very significant action against the State."

This speech began to make me nervous. Sure there was a large group of slaves in the Crops, but even if something were to ignite them, it would be more likely to scatter them out of fear, than to unite them.

"Our mantra, thanks to you, Harrison, is 'Commit to Resist.' You gave voice to a plan that has been in effect for over a year now. We've been working diligently to gather all the weapons and hardware that we can, so that we can ultimately begin our resistance. Our goal is to begin within just a few months' time. Between now and then, we will mobilize by delivering weapons, resources, and information to a number of densely slave populated areas in large cities here in the northeast. Our primary focus will be on DC, Baltimore, and New York, with plans to expand down the line."

I listened intently while Apex matched his speech in time with images on the screen, and I tried to absorb it all to comprehend the full scope of his vision. The more he spoke, the more I envisioned a terrible outcome. Arming slaves with guns wouldn't be so cookie-cutter perfect. I imagined pure mayhem — not the clean, organized resistance that Apex spoke of.

Apex continued, "We're aware that this initiative will take some sacrifice. Our operatives will deliver large weapons caches to the very heart of slave populations. These actions will take place right in the middle of the day when slaves are most active.

"Once our slave brothers and sisters are confronted with fellow African Americans who are committed to resist and armed with weapons, we expect they will take up arms as well. We will seize the very heart of the financial district in Washington, DC. This is critical as DC is the financial capital of the world.

"The downtown area houses some of the largest skyscrapers in the world and is our largest manufacturing base. We plan to seize many of those buildings by mobilizing the Crops. The overwhelming number of blacks with weapons in hand will force them to surrender. Same will happen in Baltimore and New York." His confidence was astounding, and I couldn't help but shake my head in disbelief. "We now have the capacity to deliver weapons in an effective manner throughout each of these cities; our tunnel network is vast and expanding each day. All we need is for our black brothers and sisters to take up arms with us and each one of those cities will be ours by the nightfall!"

Apex paused for a moment, clasping his hands behind his head. His arms were enormous; the guy was ripped.

I had many objections and concerns, but was too afraid to question his plan. Everyone around him looked upon him with zeal. And besides, who was I but a former slave, still learning to breathe free air?

He said quietly, "It has taken us years to build the appropriate armory, and it has taken us even more time to develop a sophisticated way to deliver these arms to the slave population. This is revolt on a grand scale. It *will* work. And the world will be forever changed. All we need is for each of our brothers and sisters to *commit to resist.*"

He let his eyes land on me after saying my shoe mantra. I was beginning to wish I'd never written those words. This plan had too many assumptions. How could I tell this man, this leader of such a grand movement, that his plan was bound to fail? I had to come up with something to aid in his vision, but didn't know exactly what it was just yet.

I slowly nodded my head in agreement and he continued, "Every week for the next two weeks, we will continue to gather our weapons, and we must continue to grow our arms count to ensure we have enough for a successful operation. We must not become single-minded in feelings, for there will be a great number of losses on the day of the initiative." My mind fell to Meagan and I had to shake the thought of her being harmed from my mind. "Those delivering the arms slaves are at greater risk, as they are the first ones that Admins will try to stop. But, it's an absolute fact that Admins and employees of the State are simply too few in numbers in these heavily populated areas to resist us once slaves take up arms. White America has become suburban in nature. They have become sedentary. They have never been less prepared."

Apex paced around the room while he spoke, patting each of us on the shoulder. It seemed that everyone had heard this same speech before, and they all gave him their full and undivided attention.

"State employees no longer desire to live in the city side by side with slaves. Nor do they desire to live near industrial or manufacturing facilities where many slaves reside. They prefer instead to live lives of luxury with fancy homes and fancier meals. In doing so they have become fat with themselves; fat with the fact that America is an overwhelming international powerhouse; fat with the fact their slave population provides them a never-ending source of ingenuity, energy, and power."

Apex's baritone voice was inflected with steel undertones, "I don't think white America has the heart to fight the slave. They are too used to putting blacks on the front line to fight wars overseas, they are too used to letting black Monitors punish their slaves. They are too used to having their every need met by the slave population. Without us, they crumble."

The room grew silent; his speech inspired and chilled me to the bone at the same time.

Turning sharply around, Apex looked around the conference table and threw his hands up in disgust, "They don't want to get their hands dirty! And once the revolution begins, you will see them come quickly to the table to try to negotiate a resolution. Let me repeat myself: They do not have the heart to fight us. That's why they provide so many concessions in the Crops. That's why there are computers in the Crops, and socials, and church services. They have, for many years now, practiced accommodation over provocation."

Apex then turned his attention to me.

"You are now a part of this council, Harrison. Your contributions preceded your presence. You not only provided us a slogan, but you also provided us a method of communication. Much of the information that we disseminate to Monitors is delivered on the tips of our toes, so I thank you for your contribution." I smiled and nodded, still amazed that my simple act had been carried so far.

Apex pointed back at the screen, "Each of those industrial areas will be ours on the day of reckoning. We must continue to push. Thank you."

Then, without another word, Apex left us with the same burst of energy with which he'd entered, followed by two of his administrative assistants.

The next two weeks were a wonderful blur for me. It took quite a while for me to get used to my newfound freedom. I was able to get up later in the morning, wash up, and walk around the complex in freedom. I was even somewhat of a celebrity here in the complex. It seemed as if everyone had heard of my simple act of defiance, which had become the motto for the revolution that I was now part of. I began to feel a renewed sense of value.

Commit to Resist. Those three simple words were printed on walls and banners throughout the complex.

It was also hard to get used to communicating however and whenever I wanted. These folks actually laughed and joked with each other. They could say whatever they wanted. They engaged in long, intellectual conversations — the type I'd had only with Denise and Meagan. Our computers were unlimited and unrestricted. I could now read without censorship about the government, news items, and world affairs – and all from the comfort of my own office. My world had been completely opened and it was spectacular.

I began to communicate more with Ray as well. He seemed more level-headed and less intimidating than some of my other new acquaintances. Even though he was older, he had a youthful vigor about him and always seemed to listen first. He would digest what you said and then comment on it expertly. On a number of evenings, Ray would come over to my room and ask me about how things were in the Crops. He wanted to know about living conditions and our mental and emotional state. He knew that the slaves were mistreated, but he wanted to know how much of an impact it had on our way of thinking and our emotional well-being. This was critical knowledge for our resistance.

Ray also gave me some insights on the complex. There were about four hundred and fifty blacks in the complex, split about half and half between males and females. Dating was not only allowed, but encouraged, and we had every intention of growing our population. The blacks in the complex, or African Americans as Apex would say, were strictly prohibited from going into the upper world without explicit permission from him. Apex deemed it too dangerous for just anybody to roam above ground, however, he knew that some interaction was necessary in order for the community to achieve its ultimate goal.

A few days after my orientation, Ray showed me the armory. It was absolutely astounding; one gigantic room full of weapons of every kind. I stood in awe and finally asked him, "Ray, how were you guys able to accumulate such an impressive arsenal?"

Ray explained, "When Apex started growing the complex, he targeted Monitors who worked on military bases and had access to equipment and weapons. His practice of targeting such Monitors grew over the years; and eventually he had ample access to weapons."

Running my hands over a box labeled "GRENADES," I listen in fascination to Ray recount how the Monitors would steal weapons, one by one, from military bases and deliver them to the complex. Apex would cover their tracks via his ability to hack into the military and government computers. He now had dozens of trained hackers working for him.

"Apex is pure genius," Ray said to me as we entered my room after our armory visit.

"He may be a genius concerning weapons, but I have some real concerns about his plans for the Crops," I told Ray, taking a seat on my bed.

"What do you mean, 'concerns?'" Ray asked with a raised eyebrow.

"Well, the one variable he has failed to include in his analysis of the resistance is the slaves' mentality. I know because I have experienced it, and I'm still trying to adjust to thinking like a free man. Can you imagine slaves up there all of a sudden being told they are free and 'here's a gun' to fight for their freedom? I can't. It's not going to be a rallying cry for most of the slaves, because of their conditioning. Because of their fear. Apex has been away from it for so long that he's not factoring slave mentality into his analysis," I responded.

"What do you mean?" Ray said, sitting down on the bed beside me. I paused to gather my thoughts, still learning how to express myself clearly.

"Well, a slave has lost everything, right? His identity, his desire, and his goals. In many ways, a slave has lost his sense of self and any sense of courage or dignity. For a slave, being passive is not just a way of life, it's a way of survival. Over the years, even the strongest, most determined of slaves gets to the point where his depression is overwhelming and his sense of helplessness is overbearing.

"These weaknesses cause you to be paralyzed and fearful. Even under circumstances that stimulate that bravery — a social or a breeding situation, let alone an unexpected revolt — a slave will hesitate to act. I know the power of that uncertainty."

I thought of Meagan and her master raping her and how all I could do was listen.

I had Ray's attention, so I continued, "I know what it's like to hesitate when your gut instinct screams for courage, and it's that hesitation that will be fatal to Apex's plan. When the weapons are delivered, it is very doubtful that many slaves will have the courage to take action against their Admins or owners. And, think of all the Monitors who still don't know about us — they're on *their* side. Would they take action against their own peers?" Ray wrung his hands together and looked ahead, thoughtfully.

"Most slaves will hesitate or even resign themselves back into the Crops for fear. As a slave, you are trained not to do anything that makes you conspicuous. Very few slaves would react under those urgent circumstances to take up action against the State."

Ray's silence became heavy and uncomfortably awkward. Instinctively, I lowered my head, fearful that I had spoken out of line.

At last he spoke, shaking his head, "I hope you're wrong, my friend, because I'm not living in a tunnel for the rest of my life. This is about our collective future and Apex has spent years developing this plan. Right now, it's all we have. It's all we believe in." Ray rubbed his forehead, trying to hide the disappointment in his eyes. Then, without a word, he walked out of the room.

CHAPTER 12
WRONG TURN

After my confession to Barry, I felt that I'd said too much and decided to remain quiet and lay low. I really didn't know what they expected me to contribute. I knew the plan needed to change to ensure that Apex's vision would go off without a hitch. He told us that the revolution would begin on Christmas Eve. It was early August — we had a lot of work to do.

The next month or so was wonderful for me. I was easier to please, of course, than blacks who had been free for longer. Even the simplest opportunity was a luxury for me. Waking up in the morning was an absolute delight. I was able to leisurely head to the cafeteria and grab a bite to eat, take a shower, watch television, and enjoy the infinite information that was available online.

I had an acute interest in the history of slavery. I learned that we could thank the Portuguese for the wicked and inhumane practice of enslaving Africans. The institution was initiated with the Portuguese gold trade in Africa. It then grew through Africa's Guinea and the practice gained momentum when the Europeans arrived on the West African coast. In the Crops, we had always been told that slavery was a part of our nature, that Africans had enslaved each other; and that the submissive role of servitude was a part of our inherent make-up.

The true reality was that the slavery amongst Africans was vastly different from that inflicted upon our race by the Europeans and ultimately by the plantation system. Slavery amongst Africans was more in the way of serfdom. So-called slaves in African society had the right to marry and own property, including other slaves. Slavery did not pass from generation to generation amongst a slave's family. Also, it was a common practice that slaves in Africa would one day earn their freedom, and it did not carry the implicit and horrible assertion that whites were superior to blacks.

This revelation shook me to the core. I had always thought that being a slave was my natural course; that I was not biologically equipped to be a true equivalent to our white masters. The very distrust in my own abilities and intellect caused me to initially underestimate my ability to contribute to the mission of the blacks in the tunnels. But still, they told me my "invention" of a way of communication and my slogan "commit to resist" were valuable. As my self-confidence grew, I began to look at Apex's genius in another way. He was not just a former slave formulating a path to resistance. He was a true innovator; someone akin to an Einstein. Someone who was creating a new unchartered path, and the foundation for his plan was generated through his profound intelligence.

I was also liberated in terms of how I used the Internet. In the Crops, we had filtered access. Any information that was critical of the United States was blocked. I especially could not access information critical of the institution of slavery. However, the access in the tunnels was unlimited. I was able to read articles about slavery and it was clear that other countries were extremely critical. I read about how countries like Russia, China, Iran, and even our allies in Germany and Great Britain felt the United States was engaged in hypocrisy by asserting a moral high ground concerning world affairs while still practicing slavery. This had led to a huge trade imbalance in favor of the US. Cheap, almost free, labor provided a huge advantage for our nation's companies. And, now, many countries were attempting to renegotiate or eliminate existing trade agreements because of the imbalance. I loved being able to read how slavery was viewed around the world and the impact it had on our international relationships.

Despite my expanding knowledge and education, I also began to take pleasure in the trivial. I loved the fact that I could now communicate with other blacks without having to censor my comments or thoughts. I sought ways to engage my peers, even in the most mundane of conversations. I greatly enjoyed my many conversations with both Ray and Barry. Most of the conversations were about the Crops or our plans to mobilize the slaves, though we also talked about history and what we thought our families might have been like.

I also finally had an opportunity to talk to women openly and freely. What an absolute pleasure this was! There were so many beautiful women here in the tunnels. However, beauty wasn't my only criterion for a potential partner. I wanted someone to talk to, someone who could teach me, and someone who could help me make the transition to this new, strange way of living.

One day in the middle of fall, I met a lady named Tyra in the cafeteria. I'd seen her around before, but hadn't had the courage to speak to her. But the weeks that passed had made me bolder, so I took a chance.

Tyra was dark-skinned, attractive, and extremely articulate. She appeared to be in her early thirties, and, as far as I could tell, she had no husband, no boyfriend, and no children. She worked as an engineer, and had been taken out of the Crops ten years prior after being identified by Apex as a potential talent. I noticed Tyra sitting by herself one day and decided to join her.

The first thing I noticed about her were her eyes. They were a beautiful caramel color and stunning. They seemed to pierce through me and even before she spoke, I could tell she was very intelligent.

From the very first day, our conversations were deep and meaningful, and she was fascinated by my recent life as a slave. She wanted to know about the effects of oppression on my feelings as a man and as a person. Somehow, we seemed to hit it off naturally. After a couple of weeks of eating breakfast and lunch together in the cafeteria we began spending time together in the evenings. It was somewhat of an odd feeling, having this much freedom with a woman. Even during my time as a breeder, my interactions with Denise had been controlled.

I began to wonder how I could have had such a profound caring for Meagan without any real ability to communicate with her. My discussions with Tyra became a foundation of my daily life. After my traumatic experiences as a slave in the Crops, I became comfortable with life in the tunnels and began to feel like I could live this way forever. I didn't long for anything else. It was a selfish but comforting thought and I began to lose sight of any real drive to participate in Apex's plans for revolution.

My desire to help others began to slip away and my entire focus turned to my new comfortable life in the tunnels: getting up each morning and going about my routine tasks, then interacting with Tyra. I'd spent my whole life working, but I'd never known enjoyment like this. As Tyra and I became closer and closer, I became more aware of issues like hygiene. I began shaving every day. It was almost laughable. I'd really had no strong awareness of my physical appearance when I was in the Crops; life back then was all about getting to the next day.

I was brushing my teeth one morning when there was a knock on my door. My mouth still full of toothpaste, I opened the door and to my surprise, there was Apex with two of his assistants. He looked at me with those cutting eyes of his and said, "May I come in?"

It was more of a command than a request, and I was so shocked I rushed over to the basin, spit, and stammered, "Certainly."

Apex walked in and looked around the room. "Comfortable surroundings, huh?"

I nodded to him and said, "It's obviously much better than what I had in the Crops."

Without hesitation, Apex took a seat on my bed and directed his assistants to wait by the door. I took a seat at my table.

Apex spoke, "You know, comfort can be very intoxicating, can't it? You start to make a life here in the tunnels, and it can lull you into a false sense of security. It's easy to assume that this life is all there is and that this is all you could ever desire, but pleasure is not what life's all about my friend. You have responsibilities, Harrison. You are here for a much bigger purpose than to find peace and a relationship."

His remark felt like a slap to me, and my mind raced back to the conversation I'd had with the Admin who took my computer away. I quietly asked, "What do you mean?"

"Well, it seems like you're getting real close with Ms. Tyra and you've made no attempts to make any contributions to our efforts here in the tunnel, despite the fact that you have considerable skills that would advance our cause. I chose you for a reason."

Before I could respond, he waved his massive hand and plowed on, "I think the question now becomes, do you plan to aid our many brothers and sisters who are still bitterly enslaved in the Crops? Or are you going to continue wasting time?"

His words cut into me.

I took a deep breath and responded, "I have every intention of meeting my obligation to the other slaves. If one were to listen to you, I have already contributed."

Apex eyes softened at my remarks, and I continued saying, "But I must admit that I have serious concerns about your plans for the revolution."

Apex nodded his head, "So I've heard, but you must understand that any action is better than inaction. I believe the plan is sound, because the human spirit will overcome any reservations. When the time comes, I am confident that our brothers and sisters will choose the possibility of freedom over the cold certainty of enslavement. We come from a strong people. It is in our nature to be free, not enslaved. It is that very innate and instinctive reality that will lead every slave that is touched by this opportunity to take immediate action. I believe... ."

Before he could continue, I cut him off, "Well, what if you're wrong, Apex?" He turned and furrowed his brows at my directness, but I felt compelled to continue. "What if years of oppression, being beaten down both physically and mentally, years of insecurity, and years of diminished self-esteem are so powerful and so ingrained that the slaves cannot and do not react? What do you do then? What do you do if those weapons lay on the ground and no one picks them up? Or, God forbid, they fall into the wrong hands? It will be a wasted opportunity and a disaster in the efforts to free our people. Don't you think it would be better to wait and develop a more realistic plan?"

Apex stood up and hovered over me. His presence was overbearing.

"A realistic plan compared to what? Compared to living like this?" He stretched his arms out wide for emphasis. I wasn't sure how to reply. How could I help if I wasn't being heard?

Folding in his arms across his chest, Apex continued, "This is what's real. We live here each day in a *tunnel,* and without action we have no hope for anything better. Down here we are not truly free. We are slaves to our environment, slaves who are just as captive as in the Crops."

Nodding my head in agreement, I replied, "Apex, you're right! I want to help you succeed in this plan. However, my concerns are real. You've been out of the Crops for so long, you really don't understand the mentality of the slave right now. For this to work, we have to think of something to add to your plan!"

The eagerness in my voice fell on deaf ears and a stone face.

He added coldly, "We can't walk out of this tunnel and be free, own property, marry, or even love. I will not resign myself to a future in which our people live in caves for the rest of their lives. The time to act is coming soon. You, Harrison, are a great asset and I hope you will begin to see your responsibility to others. This isn't just about you finding a girlfriend and relaxing each day. That's a selfish way to look at the world and it isn't why I saved you." Then, in his always abrupt manner, Apex walked out, followed by his two assistants, and left the door wide open.

The next few weeks were a blur. There were constant meetings amongst the council about the upcoming attack. I spent most of my time sitting in those briefings day dreaming about the alternative plan that I had begun to develop. Apex became more and more anxious as time moved on. He asked very few questions in the briefings. The meetings were all about him barking out directions, and it was hard for anyone to get a word in edgewise.

We learned that roughly a hundred and fifty of our men would be deployed during Apex's initiative. They would be divided up and sent into various Crops, driving vehicles loaded with weaponry through various tunnels that led to the surface. It was expected that the Admins or Monitors would attempt to intervene or stop some of these vehicles. Confrontation was inevitable and it was clear that not all who were deployed would return home. Another key risk factor was that, for the first time, our position in the tunnel would be potentially exposed or compromised. It was beyond dangerous, but Apex maintained an all or nothing approach.

It had taken me no time to realize that Apex's behaviors were obsessive – even manic. He saw this as his once in a lifetime opportunity to give slaves a chance at freedom. It would be impossible to convince him that his plan was not the only — or even the best — solution. In his mind, it was this or nothing at all.

One day in late November, Barry and I once again visited the armory, this time to check on recent deliveries. I had to acknowledge that it was very impressive. There were so many types of weapons, hand guns, machine guns, grenades, missile-launchers, you name it. It was certainly enough to inflict a great deal of damage, but all this weaponry would have very little effect if the State mobilized their military in response to our attack.

I shook my head and said to Barry, "Man, this is a lot of fire power."

He smiled and chuckled. "Yeah, Apex, has done a great job here. Who would have thought it possible to gather this many weapons underground — and all by former slaves!" He chuckled again. Apex had done a phenomenal job building something out of nothing.

"You have to give him a great deal of respect for that," I acknowledged, then paused to gather my thoughts. "There is certainly no doubt that this man is great beyond measure, but I also think he's narrow-minded. That kind of lack of perspective may rob us of our sole opportunity to attain freedom for our brothers and sisters across the country."

Barry's eyes widened. I had his attention and it was encouraging.

"We need to further analyze where slaves are located across the country. I've been doing some research, Barry, and it appears that there are Crop locations in just about every major urban center, including out West. In fact, some of the largest Crop densities are in urban areas in California."

Barry nodded and replied, "Of course, affluent cities like Detroit, Chicago, LA, and Houston; these are all cities that have significant commercial or industrial bases. Slaves drive industry out there just as they do here. The State benefits from slavery across the US and it's just tragic. Whether white society needs a computer chip from California, a car from Detroit, or natural gas from Maryland, it's all processed and built on the backs of slaves. It's surprising that the United States has been able to survive the international criticism for this long. It's hard to carry yourself as the moral leader of the free world if freedom is not pervasive in your own country."

"So true, Barry," I nodded in agreement. "I think we need to go bigger. Apex wanted to focus on the Northeast — but is that going to be enough?"

"You may be right," said Barry. "I knew we picked you for a reason." It was reassuring to speak to someone who listened.

I picked up one of the machine guns and stared at it. It was cool to the touch and sent chills running through my body. "I need to learn how to use one of these, don't I?" I asked apprehensively.

Barry laughed, "Perhaps. But first, let's brush up on those computer skills."

We left the armory and headed to the computer lab where Barry continued my lessons in our complex's internal systems. My new job was as Correspondence Captain, a title that Apex bestowed on me and two others. We were to relay orders and progress updates to everyone in key positions.

After a few minutes, Ray came in and asked if he'd missed anything important. Then he began filling us in on new plans that had just come down from Apex.

The men who would be going into battle had already been selected by Apex. There was a total of one hundred and fifty-six who would be transporting weapons.

Both Ray and Barry had become convinced that there needed to be an ancillary plan to supplement Apex's efforts. I knew that they had struggled with this. But, my argument about the potential reluctance of slaves was compelling.

I asked Ray if there was a list available and he said he would provide it to me as soon as he could safely get a copy without raising suspicion from Apex. If we were to make any progress, we'd have to do so without Apex's knowledge — at least for now.

I had spent years studying the energy infrastructure of our country while in the Crops. It was one of my passions. So my plan was centered around power plants. With Barry's help, we'd gather information about the power plants in each of Apex's three targeted cities — Baltimore, DC, and New York. We would get one chance at this and one chance only. One week prior to the attack, we'd begin sending test emails to slaves who had been identified as employees at the power plant.

The test emails would contain a subject line with my slogan, "Commit to Resist." The goal would be to get as many slave workers as possible to stay home on the day of our revolt — an organized strike of sorts. The greatly diminished workforce would cause power plants to shut down. The test emails would help prepare them for something bigger.

Barry had explained previously that the power plants could not be manipulated from outside hacking. The on and off switches were operated by workers within the plant and we had to have someone on the inside obtain the codes related to the internal operations of the plant.

I'd crunched the numbers and now clarified to both Barry and Ray that we needed at least five or six insiders at each power plant to obtain all codes and permissions for overriding the computers. Once those codes were obtained, Barry could manipulate the operations of the plant from the outside. However, to engineer a complete shutdown of the power plants, he'd need to continue working with insiders who could send him information in real time. This dynamic presented a great deal of risk. Whoever we sent in would need experience. They'd have to be brave and remain cool under pressure. Whoever went in faced the possibility of never coming back out. I wrung my hands as I spoke to Barry and Ray, "The only way we'll be able to convince our high-tech workers to enter the plants is if they believe this was part of Apex's plan all along. It's not just risky for them — it's risky for us, as well."

Over the next few days, Barry identified a hand full of operatives who would serve the purpose. These were men who had substantial work experience related to computer operations within the tunnels. They were also tough guys who'd lived in the tunnels for quite some time. Ray confirmed that these were men we could trust, but they were also used to taking Apex's directives as law. We began the process of altering what they believed were Apex's orders so we could begin our manipulation.

The plan was coming together quite nicely. On the day prior to the revolt Barry would send out a final email to all power plant slaves with a coded directive to stay home. Despite our thorough planning, we expected that many of the slaves would still go to work. However, we also suspected that some would not and those missing workers could be the advantage we needed. Either way, the emails would prepare slaves for the possibility of change.

On the day of the revolt, we'd send operatives into the power plants with weapons to pave the way for our techs to reach the operations rooms of the power plants. Surprisingly, the natural gas facilities were not seen as facilities deserving of very substantial security. They weren't like older nuclear power facilities that had required a ton of security and were nearly impossible to access. The natural gas power plants were actually quite accessible. You could drive up to the facility, park in the parking lot, and stroll into the lobby area without any real obstacles to entry.

It was our hope that attacks closer to the Crops would be a significant diversion. The Admins' focus would be on managing those crises. Who would suspect an incident at the natural gas facility? Our guys, armed with machine guns, would be able to enter the lobby area and quickly move toward the operation room in each plant. The total operation at each facility would take less than twenty-five minutes. Each team would remain in contact with us. As soon as they arrived at the operations room, workers would be cleared or subdued so that codes and other necessary information could be communicated back to Barry and a small team of computer technicians at our facility. Barry and his team would then seize control of their systems, recoding the operational protocols and setting up firewalls to prevent further access from the State. At that point, the plants would be shut down and the power would be in our hands.

A month or so before the attack, the stress level inside the tunnel had grown significantly. You could see the pressure on Apex's face. In each briefing session he became more and more intense. His face was gaunt and you could tell he was losing weight. The planning and structuring was beginning to take a toll on him — on all of us, really — as we began to face the reality that our lives were about to change for good. I began to seriously fear the outcome if the State decided to take action directly against the tunnels based on information that they gleaned from one of the operatives involved in the attack. These were indeed dangerous times.

I decided to spend some of my remaining time with Tyra. I missed spending so much time with her and I wanted to know her thoughts about whether Apex's plan really had merit. I continued to be very careful about what I communicated because I didn't want her — or anyone else — to know about the ancillary plan that we were working on.

One evening I knocked on Tyra's door and she answered. It was getting late and I halfway expected her to be asleep. But I couldn't stop thinking about her and decided to take the chance anyway. She had on a white robe and her face was calm, relaxed. She invited me in and after a few minutes, I asked her what she thought about Apex's plan.

Her response, as usual, was very direct. "Apex is a genius. All that you see within these tunnels was built and initiated by him. These are all remarkable accomplishments, Harrison. Look at all the technology around you. Look at the infrastructure. These are things that don't just happen by chance. Apex put it all together and it became one massive operation that allows us the chance to one day be free. He gave me my freedom. He gave you your freedom. Because of that, and so much more, I will stand by Apex and whatever decision he makes concerning our future." Those stunning eyes of hers studied me, searching for objection.

I took a deep breath. I had to be honest with her. "Well, what if he's wrong about the attack and the revolution? What if these are our last days of freedom? What if the revolution fails and the State decides to move against the tunnels? This would be a tragic loss of opportunity — don't you think?"

"If Apex is to succeed — if we are all to succeed — then we need to believe that we will succeed. If I were you, I'd keep that doubt to yourself," she paused. Still studying me. "But you're right. For the revolt to succeed, we must have a million things go correctly. But none of this initiative will be successful unless our morale is high and we are determined to see the entire initiative through." We were sitting on Tyra's bed. As she spoke with such authority, she'd never seemed more beautiful to me.

I put my arm around her assuredly. "I am truly committed to Apex, Tyra. Although I believe his plan has flaws, I also know that I owe my freedom to him. He has earned all of our respect — we should support him regardless of what we think."

She nodded and smiled hesitantly. "Exactly. And one key thing to remember is that Apex has always been about others. He doesn't have a selfish bone in his body. He has always worked to make sure that our community, our slave brothers and sisters, have an opportunity to one day taste freedom."

I took Tyra's hand in mine. Her fingers were long and graceful. It felt wonderful to be able to act without over thinking. To act how I wanted to. I looked her in the eyes.

I lowered my voice. "I think the anxiety is getting to us all. The stakes are as high as they'll ever get. I guess it's now or never."

I leaned over and kissed her. We both knew that time was short and with that, I simply lost all reservation. I knew she was special from the first time we spoke. I hadn't felt this way, of course, since my time with Denise in the breeding program. However, this was much more.

This wasn't a pre-scheduled night with some stranger. Nobody was forcing us. Tyra and I had become great friends — maybe something else. There was potential here, and for once, I felt like my emotional state was in my own hands. It even occurred to me that Tyra could someday become my wife. For the first time in my life, I made love to a woman I truly cared about. It was a night I'd remember forever.

I fell into a wonderful, dreamless sleep, and the next thing I knew Tyra was tapping me on my shoulder telling me it was time to get up. "You must have been tired. It's already late," she said, leaning down to kiss my forehead.

I looked at her computer for the time. It was already ten. I had started the habit of getting up around eight and meeting with Barry and Ray concerning our plan. I'm sure that they had already been by my room.

I sat up in the bed and looked over at Tyra. She sat at her table, brushing her long hair. It was odd that she didn't seem anxious at all; despite all that was about to come.

She glanced over her shoulder at me, "So, are you going to help Apex complete the plan?"

I paused for a moment, thinking of my own plan and wondering how to answer her. I nodded and replied, "There's no way in the world that I'll let Apex down. If this is our only chance, then it will take everyone's support — including mine." She smiled. That was what she'd wanted to hear. "You know, Tyra, this is our life. If we don't make this happen, then we could be stuck as slaves forever. I can't let that happen."

She smiled and continued brushing her hair. "You better get going."

With that, I got up and quickly dressed. Then I crossed to Tyra and gave her a soft kiss on the cheek before heading out. As I closed the door behind me I looked out around the tunnel. Under normal circumstances I would have been a little bit apprehensive about leaving her room during the morning hours for fear of causing any gossip. But today there was so much activity, I wasn't noticed at all. The plan was in full implementation and everyone was focused on his or her tasks. I rushed back to my room. I needed to shower and get dressed for the council meeting at eleven thirty.

This council meeting was somewhat different. The tone was much more animated than usual, and Apex was very aggressive in his tone. It was all about the details. Apex quizzed Barry repeatedly about the various protocols related to the attacks and asked him to repeat the sequence of events leading to the deployment. Barry read off the sequence effortlessly and flawlessly. It was all going smoothly.

Then Apex began to break down what would occur during each step. The ammunition trucks would leave the tunnels at precise intervals headed toward various Crops in Baltimore, Washington, and New York. The trucks headed to New York would leave first, their journey being the longest.

Apex spoke sternly but passionately, "This plan doesn't get off the ground at all unless we are able to take control of a large number of Crops; it will and it must happen. I *know* it will happen. We have too much resolve, too much spirit, and too much strength for our people to miss out on an opportunity at freedom. You'll see, it's in our nature to be warriors. When those weapons are dropped, we will take up arms and we will control the Crops. With this foundation, we will forge our freedom nationally."

As we left the meeting, I motioned for Ray and Barry to follow me to my room. As I closed the door behind us, I shook my head solemnly.

"Do you think we're doing the right thing?" I asked, trepidation dripping from my tongue.

Barry was quick with his response, his tone direct and honest, "You know, Harrison, I have analyzed Apex's initiative over and over again. If what you say about the slaves' mentality is true, this plan has absolutely no opportunity for success." I shook my head again. That's what I was afraid to hear. Barry continued, "But we all know at this point that Apex is obsessed with moving forward. There's no turning back. I must say that your plan for a continued initiative after the initial thrust gives meat to the plan. With our efforts here, we can add what might be the final straw to the initiative. I truly believe it's in our best interest to quietly move forward. We cannot allow this initiative to fail."

I thought for a second, then replied, "Do you think we have enough infrastructure available to pull this off relative to the power plants?"

Barry nodded, "We'll have more than enough firepower to make it happen if the power stations aren't guarded. At this point, we've done our research concerning the power plants and I feel confident that any security there will be minimal." He paused, worry cast across his face. "Another critical issue is that we must have enough man power to take control of the power plants and to send data to me and my men in the control room. We have about sixty men available — I hope that will be enough."

"I hope these guys are brave," I sighed. In truth, I didn't know if they'd come out alive once the plants were taken. The State would move in with a military presence and there would simply be no way out. The thought was a sobering one, yet it was something that must be done for the well-being of us all.

When I saw Apex again a few days later he was no longer clean-shaven. He was starting to grow stubble on his angular face. Nonetheless, he was still as assertive as ever. Each day he'd go over the plans step by step, in meticulous detail. Like a dictator, Apex would not relent, and he would not change his plans. In a way, I would have been more comfortable doing nothing at all. We needed more time at the very least.

I felt somewhat cheated. Now that I finally had my freedom — and a future with Tyra — we were immediately facing a situation that could set us all back to where we started. Apex had decided that it was time to move forward, and there was no way of talking him out of it.

During our meetings I had begun sitting on the far end of the room, putting as much distance between myself and Apex as I could, and I began to tune him out. Instead, I focused my attention on my own plan.

We needed more power, more influence, and an ability to affect whites not only in the urban areas but also in the suburbs. Ray, Barry, and I had worked diligently to come up with a plan that would utilize the aggression of the first strike and divert some of the man power to specific areas related to the power infrastructure in New York, Baltimore and most importantly, Washington, DC. Although our plan wasn't fool proof, it was one that could work.

During one meeting, I pulled out a pencil and started making additional notes concerning my plan. Apex must have noticed that I wasn't paying attention and in front of the entire council, he blurted out, "Harrison! You're not paying attention. What's up? You're not interested? This is the type of attitude that would cause our plans to fail. We need all hands on deck. And if you're not in, you're out."

I looked up, stunned that he had directed so much energy toward me. But he was right, I *had* been an insignificant participant in the council meetings. And now he was making a point of it at my expense.

Always quick to intervene, Ray stammered, "Apex, no worries. You know he's new here. I'm sure it's difficult for him to integrate at this point in our process."

I turned my head toward Apex and stared him directly in the eyes. The room was so quiet you could hear every breath. Apex moved from behind the podium and took several pointed steps toward me.

"You have something to say, Harrison? You sit there in the back of the room in meetings and say nothing. We all know you're an intelligent guy, but you've done nothing at all to contribute. I'm starting to regret that we ever extracted you. Get your head together, man. This is it! This is history! It's time to act! We've given you an opportunity at freedom and you've done *nothing* to contribute back. Get off your black ass and start doing something! What are your thoughts? What do you have to contribute?"

I took it all in, knowing full well that I should hold my tongue. But my instincts got the better of me and it all came out.

"What if the plan doesn't work?" I said, practically shouting. "What do we do then? Is that it? Do we just wait around like sitting ducks and let the State come and take us into custody? We'll have nothing left. What if your plan doesn't work?"

The veins had begun to bulge on the side of his head, *"What if the plan doesn't work?"* he repeated, his tone heavily mocking mine. "We've got just a few weeks and now you're talking this shit? My plan is all that there is! We will *make* it work regardless of your late-ass opinions!"

Ray stood up and threw his hands in the air, exclaiming, "Calm down, man! He's only been here a short time. He doesn't know the full complexity of the plan and why it's destined to be successful."

Apex pushed Ray out of the way, and crossed the rest of the way to me, shouting, "You know something, Harrison? You think you're pretty hot — Mr. 'Phoenix' — but to me you are a one-trick pony. A guy who had some great ideas but when we were all counting on him, was totally unprepared and unwilling to assist the revolution." He wiped sweat from his forehead and set his jaw in a way that I'd only seen the white Admins do before they doled out lashings. "I hate that I brought you here. When you were in the Crops you seemed like a guy who was ready to do something about his situation, his circumstances. You get here and all you want to do is sleep and eat. You need to wake up man. This is it! Either there's a tomorrow, or there's not. Either you're a revolutionary, or you're not. One thing I know you're not is a leader. What a waste of talent."

He spat that last sentence at me, his white teeth fixed in a grimace, and I just sat there not saying a word. There was nothing I could say. Apex had equity here. He had all the power. He was the alpha dog, and the omega. So I sat there quietly and bided my time. Ray ushered Apex back to the podium and the details of the plan were advanced once again.

The rest of the meeting continued without a hitch, everyone seeming to brush off Apex's outburst as if it were completely normal. We must have gone over the plan about two or three times. But despite his aggression and his monotonous lectures, I knew that deep down Apex was a great man who had done so much for so many. The fact that we'd even have an opportunity to remove the shackles of slavery for others was a testament to his abilities and his dedication. I decided I'd visit Apex's room later to apologize for my comments.

In the big picture, it wasn't and it couldn't be about me versus him. It was about us fighting slavery together. I couldn't let him know what I was doing at this point; Apex had no idea that there was an alternate plan in progress. But I could certainly let him know that I'd support him and all that he'd worked to accomplish. Maybe my comments could ease his stress.

Apex's room was located down a long hallway, just past the armory. Apex had two attendants with him during most hours of the day. They stood by to make sure Apex's orders were disseminated amongst those in the tunnels, and to protect him in the event there was some type of uprising or instability in the tunnels.

As I approached Apex's door I noticed there were no attendants present. I was glad because I wanted to catch him without being announced. The door was already cracked open. As I was about to knock, I heard Apex speaking to a woman. I knew that voice anywhere — Tyra. My heart skipped a beat. What was she doing in Apex's room?

I could tell that the discussion was not entirely positive. Apex was talking in his usual aggressive manner, but his demeanor was somewhat tempered. I could only hear parts of the conversation, but it was mainly coming from Tyra.

She raised her voice, practically shouting, "You don't talk to me that way and you shouldn't talk to him that way! You are the leader here for goodness' sake, so start acting like it!" Tyra's tone startled me. I'd never heard anyone talk to Apex like that. I knocked and then quickly let myself in. Apex and Tyra sat on the edge of his bed, his arm draped around her waist. At my entrance, they both turned to see who'd interrupted them.

Apex rolled his eyes and muttered sarcastically, "Ah, the resident genius. Come on in."

I stepped just inside the doorway and pushed the door closed behind me. Tyra looked at me, her eyes wide. She reached for the shawl that lay next to her on the bed, wrapped it around herself, and hunched her shoulders forward as if she'd caught a chill. I raised my eyebrows at her and she silently raised a finger to her lips as if suggesting I should stay quiet. Then lowered her eyes to the floor. My heart sank.

I turned to Apex, "I wanted to apologize for today. I certainly meant no disrespect. You're doing all that you can to advance the overall cause. Not only for everyone in the tunnels — myself included, but for every slave across the United States. I just wanted to tell you that I respect all that you've done and all that you're doing. You have my full support."

Apex didn't move a bit. He looked at me and stated, "I appreciate the fact that I have your support. I only wish that you'd do more. These are critical times for our entire race, but since you've been here, you've only stood still. You haven't embraced the urgency. And for that reason, I am truly disappointed."

I looked to Apex, then to Tyra, her eyes still avoiding me, and said, "Sorry to disappoint you. I will try to do better."

I left without another word and headed toward my room, my steps heavier than ever. The friction between Apex and Tyra told me all I needed to know about them. They weren't just acquaintances, and they weren't just soldiers in the same battle. They were a couple.

I'd always wondered why Tyra — such a beautiful, intelligent woman — would be sitting alone in the cafeteria each day. While I considered myself to be a desirable guy, I also wondered why she was so fast to take a liking to me. She had been in the tunnels for some time. Certainly at this point she would have developed other relationships, right? But now it all became clear. She was Apex's girl, and she must've also been a plant. It was very fortunate that I didn't tell her about my alternate plan. I assumed Apex had no knowledge of the depth of our relationship. She'd been sent to monitor me; to make sure I wasn't a threat to the tunnels or to Apex, and yet it had become so much more. I made a note to myself to never talk to her again.

Deep down I knew that Apex's motivation was to protect the others in the tunnel. After all, he hardly knew me at all, and he'd done what was necessary to make sure I wasn't a threat.

Over the next couple of days, I purposely avoided Tyra and focused on the task at hand: implementing my plan with Ray and Barry. As we worked together, I became more and more aware of the technical expertise that Barry had. Barry was a uniquely intelligent young man. He'd gained Apex's trust not only through his demeanor, but also through his capabilities. Barry, I'd learned, managed the day-to-day technical operations of the tunnel. While Apex had laid foundations for the systems, Barry was the guy who managed not only the staff, but also the physical systems day-to-day. His staff programmed and ran the hundreds of computers throughout the tunnels. He had complete control of the operations room, and more importantly, he had Apex's complete trust. Whenever there was a technical issue or problem, Apex turned to Barry. Barry himself was a unique talent in terms of hacking. While Apex had been able to hack into the State's mainframe, Barry had quadrupled that access over the past few years. He was the technical expert behind the slave extraction process and had orchestrated my extraction personally. He was *the* expert when it came to hijacking outside systems.

I also liked Barry's demeanor. He was a reserved guy. He never wanted any accolades over his accomplishments and he was always very goal-oriented. Oddly, as far as I could tell, Barry hadn't developed any close relationships in the tunnels. Instead, he was all about the activity, the progression. The one exception was his apparent friendship with Ray. Their relationship seemed to be based on their shared reservations about Apex's leadership.

Ray seemed to be the ultimate father figure in the tunnels and I felt like my initial confidence in him had been well placed. Ray's gift seemed to be that he analyzed each situation based solely on merit. Personalities did not play a role in his decision-making. I believe he saw me as the same kind of face-value person, which made us very compatible. Ray understood that my motives were based solely on trying to forge success out of a plan that was fated to fail.

With our intentions aligned, the three of us set to work.

On December 22, two nights before the revolt, Ray, Barry and I met in my room to review our plans one last time. Apex would hold his last council meeting in the morning, and I'd do my best to stay attentive and show my support.

Barry sat at the table and Ray sat on my bed with his hands clasped. The tension was so thick you could almost taste it in the air. "Barry," I said with exasperation, "I'm still worried we don't have enough personnel for this thing."

Barry shook his head and replied, "Well, I feel comfortable with what we will develop. A technical team is intact — I have at least eight. They will be notified of our plans on a need-to-know basis as the plan unfolds, and they've all been briefed on Apex's mission. I have padded his protocols with additional details that will assist us. In the moment, our men will do what's necessary to make sure we pull this off."

Ray chimed in, "Do you expect any internal resistance?"

"Well you can never be sure," Barry responded, "however, the energy and confusion in the moment should be enough to mask any insecurity about whether or not they are receiving the appropriate directions. Of course, I will have technical and operational control during our initiative. So at this point, I don't anticipate any problems. Apex seems to be weakening physically and I know that the stress is getting to him. I'm certain he'll stay in the command room during the entire process, monitoring the results of the attack. He will rely on me completely for all operational issues."

Ray and I listened intently as Barry reviewed the overall plan once again. Somehow his explanation gave it complete validity. The pieces seemed to fit. Still, I feared the likelihood that the plan would fail miserably. As I'd reiterated over and over again, the slaves were in no way ready to initiate any type of resistance against the State. While some slaves might be willing to take up arms, I envisioned that armed resistance from the State would only lead to their martyrdom. I fully expected a harsh response; there would be bloodshed.

I took a long sip of whiskey from the bottle Ray had brought. It was a strong tasting drink, but I'd grown to like it. I asked, "Barry, do our men know that some, if not all, won't make it back here once this is over?"

Barry sat upright and wrung his hands, "Yes, they all know the risks. And, they all understand how important it is to not disclose our location here no matter what."

Ray placed his hands together and said, "Only God knows the course of our actions. I pray that he guides us all to a safe and triumphant victory."

"Amen," I added.

Our plan was now complete. We all agreed to get some rest. It would be a very trying next couple of days and tonight would probably be the last night that we'd get sound sleep for a while. I shook each of their hands while they left my room. I was exhausted mentally and physically and once I lay across my bed face down, I was asleep within minutes, exhausted from the possibilities.

Morning came too soon and I woke up with my alarm screaming for me to get ready. On my way to the council meeting, I saw Tyra standing outside of the control room. She stood there staring at the computers, watching as others focused on their individual tasks. All of the workers appeared to be running analytics. The foot traffic throughout the tunnels this morning was substantial. Most of the activity surrounded the control rooms and the armory as weapons were prepared for transport to the various attack locations. I walked up behind Tyra and tapped her on the shoulder. She jumped, surprised, and her lips pursed nervously when she saw it was me.

"Well, well, well. Fancy seeing you here," she said ruefully. I managed a chuckle. We hadn't spoken since the night I found her and Apex together.

"Yep. How are things with Apex?" I asked with a smirk. She frowned. We both started to speak but as usual, Tyra took control of the conversation.

"Look, I apologize for how things worked out. But there are some things you need to know. First, Apex and I are very, very close. For Apex, you were an issue from the beginning. There was a ton of debate amongst the council about whether or not to extract you, but we all recognized your talents. 'Commit to Resist' had become an important part of our culture and we understood that you had a strong desire to get out of the Crops and contribute to a resistance.

"Apex was your biggest advocate, yet even he had reservations about taking someone out of the Crops so close to the planned revolution. We felt it was unfair to bring someone out, just to throw them right in the middle of this initiative. Apex told me that the council meetings got heated when he decided to move on your extraction. Others in the council wanted to the focus only on the initiative and not bring new people in."

I nodded. I could understand their thinking this way. If the roles were reversed, I knew I wouldn't want to bring in new blood so close to the revolution. Tyra continued, "Once you arrived, Apex had a responsibility to make sure you would be an asset. He also wanted to make certain that you wouldn't do anything to derail the operation. You know, you're kind of a cult hero here, Harrison. Or should I say, 'Phoenix.'" She smiled and I felt dizzy. I wish I could reverse any feelings I'd ever had for her. "Everyone knows about what you did in the Crops and Apex wanted to make sure things didn't move in the wrong direction with you being here.

"It was a tough decision to make, but we decided that I would create an interface with you. I'm sure you've figured this out by now, but I planned to be at the cafeteria each day sitting alone. Apex figured that at some point you would talk to me. You did exactly what we thought you would do. I did what I was instructed to do," she paused, gathering her thoughts, "...which was to vet out your feelings for Apex and his plans." She looked up at me, shame cast across her face.

My ego was bruised big time, "But we... ."

She didn't let me finish, "Yeah, we did. That wasn't really a part of the plan. I'd expected any interaction between the two of us would be on a 'friends only' basis. Apex has been difficult and over the last few months, his life has been all about the operation; the attack. Not much time left for a relationship. I made a mistake with that. I hope you will forgive me. And I hope that you will be discreet. Apex still doesn't know about us — and I'd like to keep it that way."

I wanted to be angry with her, but I knew it was best to let it go. I grabbed Tyra's hand, looking into her face with those beautiful, caramel eyes. She was so articulate, and her face was soft and welcoming. I squeezed her hand tight and let go. "These next few days will be tough on everybody, Tyra. I hope we're still here to continue our friendship three days from now."

Tyra smiled confidently. "I'm sure we will be. Apex will make sure of that." She planted a quick kiss on my cheek and then went on her way.

CHAPTER 13
CHRISTMAS EVE

We had been taught about Christmas in the church sessions in the Crops. I remembered the decorations in anticipation of Christmas day. Of course, slaves were not able to celebrate holidays other than the ceremony, but I remember the demeanor of the customers in the cleaners just prior to Christmas day. They'd all show up to get their best clothes cleaned. On the streets, people carried bags of gifts. I used to daydream and imagine how wonderful Christmas day would be; the great anticipation and opportunity that came with opening gifts. It was a feeling I'd never had, but the way I felt now in anticipation of our revolution must have been similar in many ways.

That anticipation was also mixed with anxiety and fear. Tonight would be a very difficult night for sleep. Tomorrow it was likely that our lives would change — in one way or another. If the attack failed and my initiative failed, it was very likely the tunnels would be attacked and destroyed by the State. If pressured, our operatives might be forced to disclose where the tunnels were located. We all worried that if unsuccessful, our activities could adversely affect the lives of many slaves across the country. It was a point not lost on Apex as he spoke to us during the last council meeting before the attack.

The atmosphere was solemn, almost somber. We were sending so many of our men into an uncertain and deadly situation.

Apex spoke slowly, but with assurance, "Well this is it. We've worked for years to get here. This is the opportunity we've all been waiting for. It took years to consolidate our technology and advance to the point that this could all be possible. It took years to siphon off the weapons contained in the armory. It took years to gather all of the computers and monitors necessary to have a pervasive ability to contact slaves across the country."

His booming baritone fell silent for a beat before he continued, "Every single African American man and woman here in the tunnels will be involved in the attack tomorrow. Many will be deployed to our attack sites to initiate in battle. The remainder will remain here in our operations room to man our computers and ensure we have continuous communication with our slave brothers and sisters in the Crops. I've asked Barry to brief you concerning the technical side of the operation."

Barry stepped to the podium and said, "This is all about precision. We must make sure that the effort starts at the exact same time in each location. We've mapped out travel times to each attack site. We've already begun loading our trucks and they will be prepped by sundown. Each designated truck will leave the tunnel at a coordinated time to reach its desired location and deploy arms at around five-thirty a.m. tomorrow."

Barry turned to another chart before continuing, "We will monitor the success of each individual location through contact with our operatives. We not only have one hundred and sixty or so soldiers prepared to act tomorrow, but we also have many Monitors and an untold number of slaves who will share in our efforts. This will be a glorious day. I encourage you all to be focused. If you have any questions tomorrow, I will be in the command room manning the computers. We are heavily dependent upon the slave population to make this happen. Let's hope that the urgency of the moment is apparent."

Again, I sat there without saying a word. I was eager to get back to my room and meet with Ray and Barry about our operation. We'd developed a script for the sixty or so men who would be diverted into our operation. They would be sent in teams of three or four into eight power plants; one in New York, five in Washington, and two in Baltimore.

I no longer wanted to talk about it, I was ready for action. I felt it in my bones that come hell or high water, this plan would not fail.

CHAPTER 14
ONE DAY

It was mere hours before the attack. The intensity in the tunnels had ramped up to an almost unbearable level. I got up, brushed my teeth, and headed to the showers. After my shower, I headed to the cafeteria to grab a quick bite to eat. The cafeteria was unusually quiet but still full of people. No one was talking much and everyone seemed to be eating a little bit faster than normal. I was quite nervous. I felt a buzz inside me as if my senses were heightened. I was excited about the possibilities that were about to unfold. Today would be the ultimate changing point. The possibilities were endless. In the next couple of hours, I could be a free man, *completely* free. Free with the ability to finally chase my dreams as a normal, fully vested member of society. On the other hand, it was also equally as likely that I would be incarcerated — or dead.

Initially, I planned not to attend the council meeting that morning. I figured Apex wouldn't miss me. I wanted to take the additional time to sharpen the details of our plan. However, I decided skipping out would be too risky. So, as usual, I took my seat at the far end of the table away from Apex. He started the meeting with one final briefing. His weight loss was so severe at this point that it made him look almost sickly. You could tell he hadn't gotten much sleep the night before. He walked back and forth between the monitors, emphasizing the various points of attack.

My mind drifted and I thought of all the equipment Apex and his men had amassed. Monitors, computers, weapons, lights, showers, boardrooms, and bedrooms — it was phenomenal. For the first time, I began to wonder if his plan could actually succeed.

Maybe I had been wrong about my projections related to slaves participating in the resistance. After all, I myself was a part of the resistance. When asked, I'd stepped out of the boundaries of slavery and was now taking a chance to fight back. Everyone in the Crops had experienced the same oppression I faced when I lived beside Meagan. Maybe that was enough to start a fire. Maybe all they needed was a match.

On the other hand, I knew that even if a substantial number of slaves took up weapons the next day, it would likely not be enough. Sure, they could start a small insurrection, but even with our ability to contact slaves across the United States, I doubted that this course of action would provide enough firepower to truly challenge the State. No, my plan was necessary. We needed to take down the power plants and hit our oppressors where it hurt. That would serve as the additional firepower necessary to change the course of history.

Following the council meeting, I visited our docking bay. At the far end of the tunnels, heading toward Chesapeake Bay, was a man-made ramp that Apex and his men had built for the transportation of equipment, machinery, and weapons. The ramp led up and out of the tunnels, onto a dirt road, and eventually out into the streets of Baltimore. This ramp had served as a gateway for all the instruments of progress that Apex had amassed.

I walked up to the very end of the ramp. At the end was a gate that was never unlocked, except for during those times when goods were being received. I looked out and up to the dirt road. It was the first time I'd seen daylight since becoming a free man. I relished this serene moment, for in a few hours, this area would be chaotic. I took in a breath of fresh air and my lungs felt heavy. Instead of a gateway of possibilities, this ramp could be a gateway to death. By the time I got back to my room, Ray and Barry were standing outside.

As we stepped inside, Barry spoke up, "Alright, big man, you ready to get this done? Do you have any reservations?"

I gestured for Barry and Ray to take a seat and I stood, my hands resting on my hips. "No reservations whatsoever. This is it. I think the plan is solid but we must be able to execute it in tandem with Apex's overall design. I'm not going to lie; I do have some concerns that some of our guys will want to verify with Apex prior to heading to the facilities."

Ray chimed in, "Well, yes, there's that possibility. But I believe Apex will be inaccessible for the majority of the day. He already has plans to be holed up in the command center. He'll be monitoring the screens and dash cams to ensure that the attacks are moving efficiently. I think we have a chance here."

Barry pulled out a map of the areas that would be involved in the attack. Apex's plan was highlighted in blue and ours was in red.

As I scanned it, I noted, "Do you guys anticipate problems from any of the other council members?"

Barry said, "I doubt they'll have any effect. Most of them aren't involved on the operational side. I will be in full control of the command room, the computers, and the flow of information. I fully believe that the three of us will be able to direct traffic in the appropriate manner and get this thing off the ground."

We talked for another hour or so until it was time for us to hit our posts. I really didn't want Barry and Ray to leave; it seemed as if the longer they stayed, the slower time moved. We all knew this discussion would be the last calm moment we'd have for the next few months. Our lives would be entirely changed in a matter of hours — for better or worse.

As we left my room, there was activity everywhere. People were running back and forth, carrying equipment and documents. I parted ways with Barry and Ray for a moment and paced nervously, deciding what to do next. I was not scheduled to enter the fray until about one o'clock. With nearly three hours to kill, I decided to take a walk and collect my thoughts. I headed toward the control room.

In the control room, at least thirty-five people sat at computers, all chattering away. In the corner stood Apex, nodding his head and nervously wiping sweat from his brow.

I walked up the tunnel and headed once more toward the armory. At this point, its doors were fully open and there were twelve or so men busily stacking and organizing weapons. They paid me no attention as they worked to prepare for the arriving vehicles. At the base of the ramp were about twenty people waiting on the trucks. The gate was open and the mid-morning sun shone down onto the ramp, providing some optimism that today would be the beginning of a bright new horizon for slaves across the country.

None of the trucks had arrived yet but they were already bringing weapons down into the dock area to be organized for load out.

I decided to walk all the way back to the council meeting room to see if anyone was there. Along the way, I glanced over into the command center and saw Barry standing over one of the computer technicians, pointing out some details on the monitor. As I walked by, he glanced up at me and gave me a thumbs up.

I opened the door to the conference room and was taken aback by its eerie emptiness. I walked toward the podium where Apex had stood so many days lecturing to us about the attacks and the future of "the African American population." The conference room was now full of flat-screened televisions in preparation for today's events. On the center monitor, three words were displayed:

"Commit to Resist."

Despite our differences, it was clear that Apex saw something in me. After all, he had devoted resources to bring me up from the Crops at such a late point in time. And he had allowed me to be privy to the council meetings when he could have just as easily relegated me to any other job within the tunnels. While I did not fully believe in Apex's plan, I certainly held a deep appreciation for what he was doing for others and what he had done for me. His heart was in it.

My plan was a supplement, not a substitute; but it was something that had to take place. Standing there seeing my words on the screen, I felt my stomach turn to knots. It was time for me to step into some big shoes, and I wasn't sure I could fill them. The only thing I knew beyond a shadow of a doubt was that I could no longer live like a slave. Either this revolt would be successful, or we'd all die trying.

I walked out into one of the open areas of the tunnels and stared at all of the activity. It made me very, very proud. *My* people were doing this. We were prepared to fight regardless of the consequences. It was what I'd dreamed of when I had been in the Crops. Here stood people with no hesitation. With no fear. Whether a success or failure, this would be an inspiring undertaking that bore proof to the fact that we were, in fact, equal to those who held us as slaves.

Around twelve-thirty, I once more headed toward the dock area. The first trucks had just arrived. They were plain white commercial vehicles, the kind used to move furniture and the like. They could transport weapons and troops without anyone becoming suspicious.

Each truck was labeled, "Vince's Movers." Apex had relationships with Monitors who had an in with a moving company that let us borrow their trucks. As the seventh or eighth truck pulled forward, the driver got out and I was shocked to see an old familiar face.

It was my good friend, Thomas. I grinned and ran after him. I had not thought about Thomas much since my move to the tunnels and it was a welcomed sight to see him. I owed my freedom to him and had never had the chance to thank him.

"My friend." I reached over and grabbed his arm as he had done to me so many times in the courtyard.

He turned to me, let out a huge smile, and embraced me. "My old friend! Man, am I happy to see you."

We continued our conversation as we headed toward the cafeteria. The other drivers had collected there to grab a quick bite to eat before the long drive that lay ahead.

"Well, this is the day," I said as we took a seat.

"This is what I've always dreamed of — an opportunity to see freedom," said Thomas with a smile as he looked up and watched the activity going on around us. "It's a great day," he continued, "And this is something you had a lot to do with, my friend. I always knew you were special. When you stepped out that first day and I saw the writing on your shoes, it inspired me."

I looked down at the table; his enthusiasm was overwhelming. "Well, I'm no Apex, but I do believe we deserve a better life. And that's what today is all about, isn't it?"

Thomas smiled again, "That's it. Today is about a chance at freedom. I've seen both sides of life. I've watched our masters go day in and day out enjoying life with the unlimited ability to pursue their dreams. They have families. They also have opportunity. They do not live in constant fear. Their thoughts and creativity are not controlled or hindered. We deserve those same basic human rights and this country has been built largely on the backs of slaves. It's high time we start to enjoy the rewards."

"You're right, Thomas." I said. It was wonderfully strange to finally be able to speak to him after all this time. "Listen, I never got to say thank you — "

Before I could finish, Thomas interrupted. "Don't mention it, man. *I* should be thanking *you.*"

We sat and talked for a few more minutes, temporarily forgetting there was a full-blown assault in effect. A man walked past us, stumbled, and dropped his tray with a loud crash. In an instant, we both snapped back to reality. Thomas finished his food and got up. We shook hands and hugged once again. We both understood that this might be the last time we saw each other. I was in awe of Thomas and his calmness despite the fact that he was about to drive into the Crops with weapons. This was no longer about him.

In a moment, Thomas faded into the activity of the day. It was nearly time for the trucks to leave.

It was fast approaching one o'clock. There was just one variable that could cause us huge problems. There were no cars to be used in Apex's plan. All the vehicles in the ramp area were to be trucks. Ray, Barry, and I decided to use cars for our operation because they were less conspicuous. A car could pull up to a power plant without arousing suspicion.

Barry would be in the ramp area at one o'clock when our first car arrived to be loaded. That first car would leave the ramp area at about one fifteen with another fifteen minutes later. They were both on their way to a power facility in New York City. Barry would direct the attention of those we selected to drive and inform them of "the change in plans." Barry had already prepped each technician for their entry into the power plant and everything concerning the methods by which they'd obtain the codes. Barry was prepared to use force concerning the change in directions should anyone begin to question the validity of his orders.

The key was to make sure Apex didn't enter the ramp area as our cars were being loaded. My job for now was to keep an eye on the common area when a car was in the loading area. I was to keep an eye out for Apex.

Meanwhile, Ray would supervise the command room and make sure there were no questions being raised concerning our activities. The first car would be arriving any moment now, so I headed toward the conference room to see if I could find Apex.

When I arrived, he was sitting at the end of the long table looking up at the screens. He glanced up at me and nodded.

I responded, "Big man, how you holding up?"

Apex responded, "Of course I'm a little nervous. This is the beginning. I'm just hoping all goes well and we lose as few lives as possible."

He had all eight screens in the conference room going at one time. They showed the various Crops areas where the attacks would take place. One screen was dedicated to the news stations and another monitored the ramp area outside the tunnels.

My heart began to race. Apex would be able to see cars coming in and out of the dock. I politely excused myself and hurried back down the hall. We were about to be shut down even before we got started. If a car entered the ramp area when Apex was looking at the screen, he would immediately want to know what was up.

My first thought was to run down to the ramp to warn Barry, but it was too late. The car would be arriving at any moment now and I had to do something quickly to prevent an uproar from Apex.

Just then I saw Tyra walking down the hall. I ran over to her and grabbed her arm.

"Tyra, I need your help. If you don't help me now, this plan is going to turn into a complete disaster." I stared into her eyes, hoping she'd sense my urgency.

Tyra pulled her arm away, "What do you mean? Everything is going fine."

"I know you don't trust me, but I need you to go to the conference room and pull Apex out for just a few minutes. Engage him in conversation — any type of conversation. I just need him out of the conference room for the next ten minutes."

Tyra stared back at me like I was speaking Greek.

I continued, my tone increasingly urgent, "Tyra, if you don't do this now, Apex's plan will completely fail."

Tyra's eyes grew large and she quickly turned away from me and stomped toward the conference room. She opened the door and I feared she'd tell Apex I was losing my mind. But then, just a moment later, Apex followed her out of the conference room. They stood outside the door, talking in an animated fashion. As she leaned in to kiss him, I turned away and began to head back toward the ramp. As I got closer and closer to the ramp, I saw something that was beautiful to my eyes. They were finishing the load out for the first set, and only one car remained on the ramp.

The technician and his assistant climbed into the passenger's side. Barry leaned his head in to give a few last minute instructions and then the car drove up the ramp and into the glorious sunlight. We were off.

I dashed back to the conference and to my relief, Tyra and Apex still stood in the hall, her hands flailing as she caused a big fuss. She briefly glanced up at me and lowered her brows before she turned back to Apex, raised her hands in exacerbation, and walked off.

Apex raised his arms, shook his head, and went back into the conference room. We'd had our first close call of the day. I was sure that there would be more to come, but our plan was underway. Lives would be changed today, for better or for worse.

It was five-thirty in the evening. About twenty-five of us were crowded in the conference room eagerly watching the screens. Three screens were connected to dash cams on trucks that were entering the Crops. The other screens were on television stations that displayed news activity. There was also a monitor that tracked the movements of all vehicles that had been deployed. Of course, those monitors were not tracking our cars.

The hallways in the tunnel were empty. Everyone else was congregated in the command center. It was an eerie feeling. We'd all been waiting for the vehicles to arrive and for our guys to get out and start handing out weapons. The screen tracking the location of all the vehicles now showed that all trucks were in place.

Apex sat at the front of the table. He had a small radio in his hands. The room was completely silent. He put the radio to his mouth, looked around the room, and with a deep breath boomed, "Go!"

At that point, the activity on the screens exploded like angry bees defending their hive. Men dashed out of trucks and dust flew as they loaded out the weapons in a series of desperate assembly lines. Men shouted and swore and then came a sound that we didn't expect this early.

Someone had fired a gun.

We heard a flurry of gunshots and then voices shouting, "Go, go, go!" Then someone yelled, "Get the guns! Faster!"

There were slaves running around in every direction on the monitors. The activity was frenzied and it was hard to keep track of what was going on. There were people running in front of the camera constantly. We could hear men and women screaming.

There was another flurry of gunshots, but we couldn't tell where the gunshots were coming from or at which location. Apex shouted for people to stop crowding the monitors. I glanced toward Apex and saw Ray standing behind him with his arms crossed. Ray's demeanor was amazingly calm. He stared at the TVs intently, but his expression was like that of poker players I'd seen on the game show channel when I lived in the Crops.

A couple of the people in the room lowered their heads. The carnage had begun. I got up out of my seat and walked out toward the command center. There were more screens there and it would be a better vantage point to see what was transpiring. Plus, I needed to know what was going on with our cars.

Barry followed me out and then ran ahead of me into the command center. He shouted to a technician, "Tell me where the gunshots are coming from! I need to know where the gunshots are coming from! Which location?" It was the only time I'd heard panic in his voice.

As I focused on two or three screens, it became apparent that gunshots were taking place at multiple locations. To my astonishment, I watched as several — dozens — of slaves took up arms. One young man raised a gun over his head shouting, "It's time! It's time!" *Yes, my man,* I thought, *it is time.*

In one location, I heard one of our operatives directing slaves to get back in their buildings. I fixated on the screen. I knew that courtyard. I was looking at my own Crops in Baltimore. Instinctively, I put my head down. Then, just as quickly, I threw my head back toward the ceiling and let out a massive sigh. My people were there. Meagan was there. I nearly wept.

As with the other locations, the activity in Baltimore was chaotic. Slaves were running back toward the building, some of them armed. A few Admins were running toward the crowd. The gunfire had greatly reduced, but we could now hear conversations between our operatives and some of the other slaves. There were slaves at each location coming to the trucks for weapons.

I was floored. So far, it was working. The screams and gunfire continued for what seemed like hours, though it was likely not even five minutes. Then came the sirens. I didn't know whether the sirens were from ambulances or police vehicles, but they grew louder and louder. Every few minutes or so, you could still hear gunfire, but for the most part the slaves had obtained weapons and gone back into their buildings. Now it was just a waiting game.

In the relative silence, I once again became aware of my immediate surroundings in the command room and turned toward Barry. One of the technicians was explaining that he'd lost both audio and visual contact with at least three of the trucks.

The screens showed that one truck was moving away from its Crops area. The truck's camera was pointed directly out its windshield. As the truck pulled away, a police car screeched to a halt in front of it, blocking the road. The truck was forced to stop. The police piled out of their vehicle, weapons drawn, and a panicked voice inside the truck muttered, "This is it." The police walked up to the vehicle and we heard the door open and then screaming, but no gunshots. A few seconds later, our two operatives were torn from their vehicle and escorted back to the police vehicle where they were roughly shoved into the back.

Another vehicle left its Crops and began to head toward the highway. A voice was heard saying, "Mission complete. Let's get back to the tunnels." As for the other vehicles, I didn't know if they'd been disabled or if the operatives had taken up weapons and entered the Crops. But at most of the locations, the police had now arrived.

Two of our operatives were contained within each complex with the now armed slaves. The stage was set for a standoff at each location.

Barry looked back at me and said, "Stage one." I slapped him on the back — this was progress.

In the command center, there must have been about ten screens monitoring local and state news stations. On one of the big networks, the NNC (National News Channel), a reporter shared a breaking news story about a violent attack going on at several Crops in the Baltimore area. She didn't mention the DC or the New York attacks, but instead noted that the attacks appeared to be at isolated Crops in Baltimore and that it appeared to be more than one location involved. She spoke with urgency and fear in her voice, stating that there were police on the scene and that some slaves appeared to have been armed.

As the report finished I couldn't help but smile. We had made an impact on the national consciousness, but it was only the beginning. As the story broke, Apex came in and walked over to Barry. His voice calm and even, he said, "Barry, let's get that email out."

Barry signaled to his technicians that it was time to go. At this point a mass email was being sent to slaves across the country that stated:

Commit to Resist. The insurgence has started. Do not go to work on Monday.

This message would impact millions of slaves. The question was how they'd react. There was no way the State could avoid slaves from getting information about what was happening in Baltimore, New York, and DC. They simply had too much access via their computer and there was no way to "cleanse" all of the information about the attacks on the Internet. I had to give Apex a great deal of respect. If, in fact, slaves became aware of the insurrection and the work boycott, the plan would still have a huge national impact no matter the outcome. I doubted that the State would take direct physical action against an entire *mass* of slaves who didn't go to work. After all, they were the State's biggest industrial and economic asset. The State certainly wouldn't move to diminish or dissolve that asset without a great deal of thought. That said, they'd certainly take corrective action that would be punitive in nature. A strike would be necessary to serve as a deterrent to future similar actions by the slaves. It would have to be a very calculated response.

The email was sent. Our standoff had begun. Now we waited for retaliation. This was the part of the plan for which there was no adequate calculating. Would this make a change or were we just sitting ducks? Would any of the operatives disclose the location of the tunnels? And would we be attacked ourselves? I also wondered if any of the operatives would make it back to the tunnels. We were only thirty minutes in, and none of us knew what was going to happen next.

We now faced impending repercussions from these United States, and at the helm of any response would be President Richard Hood.

CHAPTER 15
SLAVERY'S ADVOCATE

Richard Hood was the third president elected from the Hood Family, beginning with the Civil War. He was the descendant of John Bell Hood, the notorious general and former president of the United States. Richard had narrowly won the 2016 election, campaigning as a strong advocate of slavery. He reiterated over and over again on the campaign trail that slavery formed the fundamental foundation for the worldwide economic success of the United Sates. He was a tremendous orator and his speeches stimulated a strong southern constituency. In fact, Hood had won over 90 percent of the votes in the south and that support gave him a foundation for success in the election, even though he lost the key states of New York and California. Richard Hood was a polarizing president. He embodied the balance in the United States between human rights and economic success. He also repeatedly leveraged the fact that slaves served all industrial and military segments of the American engine. He noted that should slavery end and should slaves no longer be forced into military servitude, many white boys and girls would be placed on the front lines. That scared many voters, all of whom were white of course. It set the foundation of fear that primed Hood for a firm reelection in 2020.

Apex knew that tonight was an important night for Richard Hood. Hood had already been campaigning for months and tonight was a huge fundraiser. This first event would be held at Chickahominy Bluff. This location was selected as it was the very place that Robert E. Lee led more than twenty thousand infantry-men in advance across the Chickahominy River – one of the critical turning points in the Civil War for the South. Hood, known for his extravagant and well themed parties, was hosting some of the most prominent United States businessmen and women for a Christmas Eve dinner. The event had already been discussed at length on national news channels and would be an extravagant affair. It would be held outside with almost five hundred tables set up for the potential donors. The food would be served by slaves dressed in old Civil War style slave attire, as a festive throwback to the "old hallowed days." Slaves would play an integral part of the party by providing not only waitressing and butler services, but performing in the live band as well.

Through coverage on television and online, we'd learn that President Hood was seated at a long table along with some of his most honored guests, including the governor of Virginia, Thomas Quarles. Various other dignitaries and lead businessmen and women were also in attendance. The first lady, Barbara, was also seated at the head table. Slaves were beginning to serve tea and other drinks.

The president had apparently dressed down for the affair, trading his usual suit for a white shirt — top button undone, sleeves rolled up — with expensive slacks. This was to be a relaxed environment and the president made every effort to affect just that. He was amongst his own — elite white supporters who, in the past, had donated millions upon millions of dollars to his campaign.

The dinner was hosted at the presidential mansion. Although his family was originally from Kentucky, the president's mansion was in Richmond, a city that had been the capital of the United States since the Civil War. Hood had become accustomed to Southern life. He'd even begun to speak with a deep Southern drawl. Many of Hood's constituents believed that he had actually been born and raised in Virginia, the Carolinas or Georgia, and he played this up to grow his southern political base. Hood also had the advantage of being a taller man. At six foot three with dark hair and a chiseled, weathered face, he was an imposing figure. These attributes, combined with his folksiness, gave him the persona of being sort of a political cowboy. He could mingle with the down home folks in the South but also converse with the most astute and complex businessmen.

Despite his well-crafted image, Hood struggled mightily to overcome the growing sentiment in the United States that slavery had passed its day. Many liberals could not stomach the fact that the US was seen nationally as a human rights violator. But Hood was relentless and unashamed. He stood strongly with his constituency, proudly asserting the virtues of slavery. None of the supporters tonight would question his advocacy of slavery.

According to reports, the president and his guests had just sat down to tea as Secret Service received word of our revolt. Being a high-profile event, camera crews stood at the ready to capture the president's speech and B-footage of Hood mingling with his guests. It was just the beginning. In the weeks to follow, news stations would repeatedly air footage of a flustered and embarrassed Hood receiving word of the attacks. That footage would show a Secret Service agent whisper in Hood's ear. Hood nodded before rising up angrily. The president's guests can then be seen staring on in concern as they watch the president being escorted from the party.

An agent directed two other men to escort Mrs. Hood out of the reception and into the nearby mansion. The first lady appeared visibly shaken.

Meanwhile, the atmosphere in the tunnels was tense. I watched as Apex paced back and forth across the conference room, waiting for additional information to be broadcast. We were still waiting for direct contact from the men who had actually participated in the attacks. We had the dash cam footage, but it only provided clarity concerning the beginnings of the attacks.

One camera was pointed at a large apartment complex, but you could see very little activity, though you could hear gunshots every now and then.

Finally, a technician opened the door and said, "We've got a call."

Apex answered the call on the room's speaker phone. One of the men involved in the attacks in Baltimore was calling from inside the complex. He was breathing hard and his voice shook with panic.

"I'm in an apartment on the first floor. We distributed the weapons to a number of slaves. There was a fire fight and we retreated into the building. Several Admins are down, but we are surrounded at this point by Admins and police. I don't know if there is any way out at this point. I need back up!"

Apex replied with a calm, steady tone, "Son, I know this overwhelming, but I need you to take a deep breath and relax."

We all could hear the fear in the young man's breath. He swallowed loudly before he said, "How in the hell am I gonna get out of here, Apex? I'm surrounded! I hear gunshots every few minutes — can't tell where it's coming from. Are you guys going to send some help?"

"What's your name, son?" Apex asked in a calm, soothing tone.

"Michael, sir," he said shakily.

"Michael, help is coming real soon. You aren't alone, but we need help in locating your exact location to send help. The more information we have, the better we can help you. Which building are you in?"

I listened to Apex calmly suggest that help was on the way and knew this was a lie — a mere placation on Apex's part. There was no help for this young man. We didn't have assets for any additional resources. The young man was trapped and he was likely to be killed or captured. Apex told Michael to keep feeding us information and that we would be back in contact with him within the next thirty minutes or so.

The news was now reporting that there had been at least eight attacks. One station indicated that an attack had occurred at a facility in New York, two Crops facilities in Baltimore, and five facilities in Washington, DC. The report made the attacks seem much larger than they were and reporters suggested the possibility that there were additional attacks coming. We'd achieved the element of surprise and the country was in mass panic. Reporters and anchors expressed their confusion about how slaves could have the mental capacity to develop a plan like this or the physical capacity to carry it out. All responses were uncoordinated as the State scrambled to understand what was going on. But I knew that, sooner than later, the harsh retaliation would be coming to us. At that time, my counter plan would go into effect.

I walked out of the conference room and back over to the command center. Barry was still there managing the technical aspects of the operation. The technicians continued to monitor the attacks, relying on news stations and websites to gather additional information.

I walked over to Barry and whispered, "Any news on what is happening with our phase of the operation?"

Barry responded, "Nothing yet. It's kind of good. I'm glad we haven't hit the radar yet. That means our guys are still undetected."

At this point I really didn't know what to do next. My hope was that we would hear something about the attacks on the power plants as soon as possible. It was critical. Our guys had to reach the operation rooms. If they didn't get there, our plan was a complete failure. With all of the commotion related to the attacks in the Crops, we had an increased chance to be successful. No one would expect that we'd be bold enough to attack power plants, and they certainly wouldn't expect us to be sophisticated enough to gather codes to shut those facilities down. Our guys just had to get there.

I walked back over to the conference room, unable to stand still for all of my anxiety. The first phase of our mission complete, everyone took a moment to breathe. Apex finally took a seat in the middle of everyone. Tyra sat beside him as they discussed some issue related to the latest newscast.

As I entered, Apex stood up and said, "It's time to make contact. Someone get Barry in here so we can make our presence known to the world."

The talking quieted immediately when Barry walked in and over to one of the computers. Using the same email address that had been used to contact the slave population, he began drafting an email. His fingers flew over the keyboard as he let the State Department know exactly who we were, that we were the ones responsible for the attacks and that they needed to contact us immediately. We'd baited the hook with Apex's plan, now we waited to see if they'd take it.

Barry and Apex had selected email as the best means of contact. They feared that a call could be immediately traced to our location. It was imperative that they not know our location until an attempt at negotiation had been initiated.

We knew it would take a while to get through to the State Department. There would probably be anti-slave organizations trying to take credit for the attacks. Plus, the State Department would probably be more focused on responding to the attacks rather than communicating with the perpetrators.

After a tense fifteen minutes, Apex said in irritation, "Have they responded?"

Barry shook his head and said, "Nothing yet, Apex."

Apex let out a growl of frustration, throwing his hands in the air.

Ray calmly said, "Patience, Apex. This is expected. They are probably looking for some well-financed, large organization. Surely they're investigating liberal anti-slave groups. They aren't expecting that it's a group of slaves."

In the meantime, we had begun to gain contact with more of our operatives in the field. The word from each of the Crops was they'd distributed the weapons, moved into the facilities, and were standing down. We'd also received several reports of operatives being shot or captured by Admins. This concerned me as these young men knew the exact location of the tunnels. If the State was aggressive against them and engaged in torture, they may give up our location.

This was an issue that I knew Apex had not prepared for. Apex had taken an all or nothing approach to the attacks with the hope that they'd stimulate some type of massive response by the slaves within the next day or two. It was a response that was unlikely and I hoped he'd soon realize that the attacks were merely an isolated irritant to the State. Still, this "irritant" could very well help to stimulate widespread work boycotts on Monday.

Although Apex had proposed the attacks as an ultimate means to end slavery, I also felt that his back-up plan was to make a symbolic statement for times in the future. In this moment, watching Apex pacing back and forth in anticipation of the inevitable end of this revolt, I knew he meant for us to be victors or martyrs. His revolt was, in part, a signal for future generations to take up arms and fight.

Barry continued his efforts to contact the State Department. After an hour had passed, he indicated that he was having active communication with one low-level official at the State Department.

Apex's face lit up, "What is he saying?"

Reading the incoming email from the official, Barry replied, "He's asking questions on why he should believe that we are the true agitators of these incidents." Barry laughed and cracked his knuckles as he continued, "He's not ready for me, but I'm gonna wake him up right now."

Barry typed his response detailing how and where the attacks started. After a moment, Barry indicated to Apex that we were developing some traction in terms of communication with the State Department. Without contact and communication, the minute that we were identified as the location or the epicenter for the attacks, we would probably face a very strong and effective attack on our facility. This gave us an opportunity to mitigate negotiations. Barry, Ray, and I would also need that contact with the State Department relative to our secondary attack. Barry gave me a quick wink once contact was established.

Barry said, "Apex, they want to speak to you directly."

Apex donned a calm demeanor and, for a moment, seemed like the commanding and dynamic leader I'd first met.

Barry said nervously, "I tried my best to scramble the signal, but it's good to assume they can trace this signal back to us. Be ready for anything." That last comment was for us all. Everyone shifted closer to their various weapons located around the room.

Apex said, "Let's do this," as Barry dialed in to the State Department. An anticipating hush fell over the conference room while Apex spoke in his rich baritone voice.

Apex said stoically, "Who am I speaking with?'

The man on the other end of the line said, "My is David Jackson and I'm a Deputy Director here at the State Department. Whom am I speaking with?"

Apex advanced in a stern voice, "Hey, David. I'm the mastermind behind today's attacks and I want to speak with someone who has the power to discuss a potential resolution of this situation."

The deputy director responded harshly, raising his voice in anger, "Resolution? What resolution? People died today. This was an attack on the United States — domestic terrorism. There will be no negotiation. What I need to know is whether there are additional attacks planned and how we can ensure that nobody else gets hurt."

Apex's voice went cold, "Slaves died today as well. They died pursuing freedom. We are all human and what we want is freedom for all slaves. We need an executive order from the president of the United States that will immediately free all slaves nationwide. With that, we will cease our aggressions."

"That's not going to happen tonight, son," the deputy director replied, though his tone was increasingly assertive. "We don't concede to terrorists here in the United States. I'm assuming that you had some type of outside help. I need to know if this was a domestic issue or whether we should be concerned about outside forces attempting to perpetrate additional attacks."

Apex responded, "No, no, no…, there was no outside help here. This was purely a response by the slave population here in America. We've joined forces to fight the institution of slavery and it must end immediately. We will fight to the death if the president gives us no alternative. Hopefully we can resolve this without any further violence, but we will not relent."

This time David laughed, "Well, we have each of your facilities surrounded. Police are on the scene and there is no way that these attacks will escalate."

Apex waited for a moment to respond before saying, "We'll see. It's your move, brother."

Apex then nodded his head and Barry cut the communications.

I was impressed with how Apex handled the deputy director. He was very forceful and had successfully injected uncertainty. At this point, the State was likely certain they were dealing with the people who had perpetrated the attacks. Now we had to sit back and wait for the chain of communication to escalate. It was a good start for us and I felt very comfortable with Apex's direction.

Meanwhile the president had arrived back at Chickahominy Hill and was escorted back to the bewildered guests at his fundraising event. Hood walked up to the microphone and began to deliver a speech that was broadcast to the entire nation.

"Ladies and gentlemen our nation faced a crisis tonight. There have been slave attacks reported in Crops in New York, Washington DC, and Baltimore."

The crowd let out a collective gasp.

Holding up his hands to calm them down, Hood continued speaking in a soothing voice, "This is no reason to panic, the attacks have been subdued. The attackers are now surrounded and we will be able to put down this situation in very quick measure. The institution of slavery will continue in perpetuity here in the United States. No effort, by slaves or otherwise, will change that!"

The crowd broke out in boisterous applause and many members in the audience began to stand and cheer. Then, without further word, the president continued as if everything was normal, giving a speech about the economic strength of the United States and its growing and dominating prosperity in international affairs from a military and economic standpoint. He talked about the country's power relative to the energy trades, and he discussed the strength of the United States as an exporter of natural gas. I watched the report, utterly stunned that he'd brush off our attacks so quickly. It was clear that he was trying to save face.

"We are blessed with an invaluable resource here in the United States," Hood continued. "We have far more natural gas than we can use domestically. Due to this surplus, we have become a huge net exporter of natural gas, an economic engine that will fuel the United States for years to come."

The crowd again broke out into applause. The president finished his speech by discussing the importance of order in the United States. He noted that slaves were a commodity to be managed not people to be coddled and respected.

Hood's tone was matter of fact as he said, "Look around you. Look at the slaves here tonight. They are happy with their condition for they are well taken care of. Aren't you happy, folks?" The camera panned to several slaves who stood by one of the serving tables and they nodded their heads subserviently. "Yes, see? They're well provided for and although they don't have the same mental or physical capacity as we do, they are huge assets to our country. I respect the slave. I believe in their contributions and I believe they are happy with their status in life. Thank goodness they have someone to care for them. The State will always be there to provide for them and to advance their growth."

A thunderous applause broke across the crowd with cheers of, "Four more years!" Hood smiled and waved as he left the podium.

I was somewhat disappointed that the president seemed to minimize the attacks. His less-than-serious tone could possibly undermine the fact that we were relying in part on the chaos and confusion caused by the attacks. My concern was short lived. It was about eight o'clock in the evening when Hood once again came on the air to address the nation. We were crowded once more in the conference room with all of the flat screens tuned in to his speech.

The screen faded to black and then the president came up, this time looking very somber. It was obvious that he now had a clearer understanding of the extensive nature of the attacks.

Hood began, slowly and carefully, "At about five thirty this evening, the United States came under a vicious attack. We were subjected to violent and deadly attacks in at least five of our Crop facilities in Baltimore, New York, and Washington, DC. These attacks have left numerous innocent individuals dead and countless more injured."

Looking down for a moment, Hood then looked directly into the camera with an iron look in his eyes and said, "This unprovoked attack will not go unpunished. Early indications are that the attacks were orchestrated by a small group of abolitionists. We have never let terrorists alter the course of United States government activities and this aggression is no different. I have already authorized the use of force against those who perpetuated these attacks. Military forces have moved into each of the Crops locations where the attacks took place. Every individual involved will be captured and punished to the maximum extent under the law."

Small gasps of concern rose through the conference room before Apex demanded silence so he could hear what the president was saying.

Hood continued, "And if it is found that any slaves either participated in the attacks or brandished weapons during the attacks, they will be arrested and punished harshly. The secretary of state will be updating you as the remainder of the evening progresses. We have brought the entire force of the United States to bear on this unfortunate situation. I expect that the situation will be fully controlled by the late evening or morning. We will be working diligently over the next few hours to restore normalcy to all areas affected. Thank you."

The president left the podium and fled to a back room without answering a single question. I looked over at Apex. There was not an ounce of fear on his face and he seemed to have a great sense of accomplishment. He shook hands with some of the other members of the council. They even smiled, proud of what they'd done. Their actions had led to the president taking notice and having to address the country. Apex grinned in satisfaction that his goal was accomplished and that we had been able to affect the government at the highest levels.

Within minutes, Barry ran into the conference room. Catching his breath, he stated, "We've got the secretary of state on the line, Apex. He wants to talk to you."

Apex motioned for everyone in the conference room to be still and quiet. He put both hands on the table and looked up at one of the middle Monitors.

Apex walked back to his phone and said, "Put him through."

On the screen was now John Moore, the secretary of state of the United States. I knew that Apex wasn't allowing Mr. Moore to see his face, but we could all see Mr. Moore's face. His face was round and ruddy, and his tight collar was damp with sweat.

Mr. Moore started by introducing himself, "I am John Moore, secretary of state for the United States. We understand that you have attempted to claim responsibility for the attacks today."

Apex spoke loudly and strongly, "Yes, we are the responsible parties. We organized and executed the offenses. This is all about slavery, John. It's time for this evil institution to end, and these attacks are just the beginning."

Moore responded harshly, a smirk forming across his face, "Yes, you're right. This is the beginning. The beginning of the end for you. As soon as we can unscramble your signal and locate you, our troops will be there in minutes. There will be no negotiation. You attacked our facilities and our people. Individuals have died because of the attacks today. We will bring the full force of the military down on you."

Apex shook his head and responded, "Well you have to do what you have to do. But, I'm telling you, something started today and it will not stop. We will destroy slavery no matter how long it takes. It's time for all blacks to walk free, be able to earn a living, to marry, and grow a family. The institution of slavery, as of today, is dead."

Moore paused, not knowing how to respond to such an audacious speculation, "Slavery is dead? You have to be kidding. All of your operatives are now surrounded and trapped. You have no way to continue the offenses. Troops are arriving at each one of the attack locations. As soon as we're able to turn one of your guys, we'll know your exact location. At that point, we are going to come and get you, and your punishment will serve as a lesson to everyone who thinks in a similar way. You will serve as the deterrent."

Apex didn't have a response and his well-composed face of leadership slipped a little. In his heart, he knew that the secretary was right. There was no backup plan and the fact that the individuals that perpetrated the attacks were now surrounded in the Crops or captured meant there would be no additional offenses. There would be gunfire in the Crop facilities where the operatives were held up and there may be some armed slaves who would continue to fight, but ultimately it was a no-win situation. There was no way for those folks to get out of the Crops. All Apex had to rely on at this point was the mass email that went out suggesting that people stay in from work. Apex was dealing from a position of profound weakness and he knew it.

The secretary of state took advantage of Apex's silence and said, "When you start an offensive like you did, you have to have an end game. For you, there was no end game... was there? It was just go out and attack. The attack has failed utterly and we will clean this mess up in the next two days."

Apex gathered his courage and stated proudly, "If this is it — if this is the point we go down, I am proud of the people who took part in this operation. We made it happen and there will be more after us. It may not be today, but there will be more after us." The council members stared at Apex, their eyes wide with shock. They assumed he had more to give than just a kamikaze mad dash to death.

The secretary of state replied, "Well, there may be more like you later but it won't be today, it won't be tomorrow, and it won't be in the foreseeable future. We will put sufficient systems in place to safeguard that this never happens again."

The finality began to sink in that all of this planning was for nothing. The secretary was going to crush us all under the foot of the US military like ants at a picnic to ensure we no longer had any thoughts of attempting such a foolish undertaking.

John spoke after a brief pause, "Your only option now is to surrender. Surrender yourself and all who helped you concerning the attacks. Make all of your operatives in the Crops surrender and drop their arms. This is the best course for everybody. This will allow you and your workers to receive the least amount of punishment. There is no way out for you at this point. By conceding you would be protecting not only yourself, but your people as well."

It seemed for a minute as if Apex was considering the surrender and that infuriated me. I walked toward Apex and squeezed in beside him.

The secretary began pressing Apex for a response, "What do you want to do? This is your opportunity to cut your damages. You made a point about slavery. It's not something that is desirable long term. Maybe your actions will stimulate thought and promote some type of change. However, right now, it would be better if you surrendered. There's simply no way out at this point and no way for your plan to be successful. We will come after you."

I couldn't hold it any longer. I stepped right in front of Apex and blurted out, "What about the power plants?" It was a shot in the dark. Without confirmation, I couldn't be sure our attacks had been a success — but if they were, surely the secretary would have heard about them by now.

The secretary of state looked as if he'd seen a ghost. His face was a dead giveaway; he *did* know about the plants. Furthermore, he and the president had intentionally avoided mentioning anything about the attacks on the power plants, so now he realized there was only one way we could know about them.

John tried to regain his composure and responded to my question, "What do you mean power plants?"

Apex looked at me and scowled. I took over the conversation.

I spoke slowly but with authority, "We attacked seven different power plants today in addition to the attacks from the Crop facilities. I'm sure that you already know this though. What you may not have accounted for is that we still have the shutdown codes for at least three large power plants in the Washington, DC area. If we decide to shut those plants down, it could throw all of DC into chaos. I'm telling you, sir, we have the codes and we are fully able to shut the plants down unless you're willing to come to some sort of negotiation."

I turned toward Apex. His mouth hung open and he stared at me, stunned, without anything to say. I looked back up to the screen at the secretary of state.

"Washington, DC is the largest city by far in the United States. It's the financial capital of the world and I am telling you now that I intend to start shutting those power plants down one by one. So, you will not initiate any attacks against the individuals holed up in the Crops and you will definitely not initiate any attacks against us should you at any point determine our location. If you do, the codes to turn these power plants back on will be lost forever. Your world, as you know it, will be in the dark. Don't make me do that, sir."

There was dead silence not only from the secretary of state but the conference room as well. Moore, I'd later learn, was well aware that someone had attacked the power plants. He did not know the full extent of the damage, but now he fully understood the implications of the situation.

He bluffed, "I am completely unaware of what you are talking about, son. Let me have a moment to check with my sources and then I will get back with you."

Without another word, he disconnected the video call leaving everyone looking at me with awe.

Apex looked me dead in the eyes, "What happened here? Does this mean that you diverted men from our core attack to advance against some power plants? Does this mean that you, after being down here for only a short period, have issued orders and undermined my command?"

I stared back at him, aware that everyone in the room was listening to our conversation. "Apex, I told you. Your plan was never going to work. You have done something great here. You started a resistance that can be success, but the plan was only going to go so far. It would only get people killed and I don't know about everyone else here, but I don't want to be a martyr. I will not be a permanent and painful reminder for every slave after us who doesn't have the guts to commit to resist slavery. You needed something else, and I gave it to you."

Without a word, Apex threw a punch to the right side of my face that knocked me to the ground. The room spun and I could taste blood.

Apex yelled, his eyes glassy and red, "This is the type of thing that destroys a once in a lifetime opportunity. You diverted resources; you've weakened us all. I can't believe this has happened at the last minute! I can't believe I brought you in. I brought in some smart ass, one-trick pony, and you destroyed our plan. I hope you burn in *hell!*"

Apex then stormed out of the room. Ray ran over and helped me to my feet as I wiped the blood from the corner of my mouth. As I looked around the room, Barry grabbed my other arm in support.

I said the words that had been burning in my chest for months, "This had to be done this way. You all have followed Apex. He's a good man but the plan was not going to work and you saw the evidence of it yourself. What, we were gonna let kids like Michael get captured or die in vain? The secretary of state said it himself — he has our operatives surrounded. There's nowhere to go. What Apex created was resistance. What we have collectively created is an opportunity to end slavery."

I was now gathering my senses and I shook myself a little bit and stood taller.

"This is now about success. This will be a turning point in all of our lives. This was never about sacrifice and suicide. This was about achieving freedom for every slave in the United States."

I don't know where the words were coming from; they just seemed to flow. I was emboldened. And what I was saying was true. We had added to Apex's plan. We had given it an opportunity to succeed. We now had the government scared to death of us. We were communicating with the secretary of state. I knew that all of our conversations were being communicated to the president. We had not only made a profound impression, but we now had an opportunity to affect some type of change. I was not about to let the opportunity pass us by; it may never come again. It was time for our people to make a decision – they could continue to blindly follow Apex, or they could start following a plan that could change history.

I nodded to the group, then walked out into the hallway where Apex was still standing. Nobody followed me.

I turned to Apex and said quietly, "I'm sorry. I respect everything that you have done and all that I have done was supplement your plan."

Apex said nothing but gave me one last cold stare before slowly turning his back to me. I wanted to continue to explain myself, but decided against it. I knew what I was doing was right and I had to follow this through regardless of Apex's ego. I had to continue what I started.

I then walked to my room, opened the door, and lay across my bed. I needed at least ten minutes of silence. It had been an excruciating day and I knew that the next call from the secretary of state would be coming soon. The only question at this point was who would accept the call, Apex or me? This decision could affect the fate of millions of slaves across the United States from now to forever.

I had almost drifted off to sleep when came the inevitable knock at the door. I shook off my developing haze, walked over to the door, and opened it hesitantly. Standing there were Barry and Apex. I allowed them in, anxiously anticipating what each would say.

Apex took a seat at the table and began first, "Look, this is a very difficult and stressful situation for everyone involved. The one thing I know is if we don't work together, we won't be successful. This is the end game for us. It's not about ego; it's not about personalities. It's about whether we can do something to affect slavery."

I began to speak, but Apex promptly interrupted me, "Look, Harrison, this may be the most important day in our history. I'm not going to have today's significance reduced because of pettiness. I'm authorizing you to fully command our operation today. You will continue to command this revolution as long as it continues. You'll report directly to me, but our strategy will be yours. While I'm not happy that you diverted resources from the central plan, I can't argue that our initial plan had no true end game. So, now you and I will share the responsibility to move our overall strategy forward. Thank you, Phoenix."

I felt dizzy, so overwhelmed was I with Apex's change in perspective. Barry smiled as I walked toward Apex and extended my right hand to shake his. Apex took my hand, as a hint of a smile crept across his face for the first time since I'd met him. "It's just Harrison, man," I said with a smile.

Barry interrupted the niceties and said, "Harrison, come on. We need to get out on the floor. We are going to start receiving reports from our operatives concerning the power plants. We need to be out there ready to receive the information and process."

I shook off the last of my cobwebs and Barry and I walked over to the command center while Apex returned to the conference room. Barry stood behind a computer technician who was busy at work.

Barry shook his head and said, "At this point it's clear that we've lost at least three of the teams. There's been no communication from the teams headed up to New York and it also appears that we've lost the teams that were to strike the power plants in Baltimore. The good news is that we've secured codes for three of the power plants in Washington, DC, including the Capitol power plant near the old White House." His voice was dim, almost defeated.

I noted, "But that's three power plants in the largest and most influential financial center in the world! Pull the numbers again for how many people will be affected when we shut down those plants. How are the power plants fueled?"

Barry replied, "The Capitol power plant is a coal-fueled plant while the other two plants are natural gas fueled. The last two have a much larger service area."

It was critical for us to not only retain control of the power plants, but we'd have to shut them down. We had no choice but to exhibit our fortitude and move forward with the plan at all costs. There was no way we were going to receive a favorable reaction from the government.

"Do we still have operatives on site at each of the power plants?" I asked, gathering my thoughts.

Checking his data, he said, "We have operatives at each of the locations and they have secured the codes. They've all made contact with us."

Breathing a sigh of relief, I said, "This is good news."

I knew that the order had to be given, but I wanted to consult with Ray, Barry, and Apex before issuing the order. I decided to convene the four of us so we could decide on whether to start shutting down the plants. However, before we could get together, the secretary of state interrupted with a call.

Barry answered the call and turned on the screen to show the secretary of state's red, stern face.

"Well, you've done it now!" he exclaimed. "You've threatened millions of citizens in our country's largest city by taking control of the codes at these power plants. How many plants do you control?"

I stepped in front of the screen and replied calmly, "We control at least three facilities and unless certain demands are met, we plan to shut those facilities down." Apex walked into the room and stood behind me, resting his hand on my shoulder and giving me a nod of confidence.

John chuckled, "Demands? Son, you'll be lucky if you can get out of this without us annihilating you and your operatives. This call is to give you one last opportunity to surrender. If you fail to do so, then I will authorize the military to begin taking action against the Crops. We will regain control of every single facility regardless of the cost."

I looked up at the screen, a bead of sweat running down the side of my face, and said calmly, "Well, you're going to have to do what you have to do, John, but we are not surrendering." The Secretary tensed upon hearing a supposed slave use his first name in such a casual manner. "We are going to move forward with our plans and we look forward to seeing the chips fall where they may."

It was a very bold move and one that I was uncertain of. It was early in the crisis and we were already practicing brinksmanship. But we already had one significant wild card — the ability to cause a mass black out. If and when we did that, the effect would be devastating on the city of Washington's morale and our country's economic fate. Not to mention the world stage and the nation's confidence in our president. I knew that these variables gave us the upper hand and I was emboldened.

Moore shook his head and said, "Son, you just got a whole lot of people killed."

The screen went blank. I knew his was a move that was used to instill shock in our team. Barry motioned that John was still listening to us; sneaky bastard was trying to intimidate us into submission.

I had to say something to reaffirm some confidence, "No, John. You just put a lot of people in the dark. Merry Christmas." With that, Barry ended our call.

Giving the nod to Barry, he walked over to the technician who had the codes to cut the power to almost two million in Washington, DC. We had no choice. Time had run out and if we delayed any further, the military would act.

Barry stated quietly, "It's your order."

I paused for a moment and looked around the facility. We had a huge command center with over fifty computers and monitors, and everyone had their heads down working diligently to try to make this happen. The hopes and dreams of all African Americans lay within this room. We had had a good start with Apex's initial plan. Maybe it had been a success after all. Apex's aggressive actions had provided a gateway to my more technical plan. The president and his Administration were reeling from the attacks. It was now time for us to take the actions necessary to show our true capabilities.

I turned to our lead technician and firmly gave the order, "Shut two of the facilities down, but leave the Capitol power plant operational. For now."

The technician relayed the command to our guys in the plants. I knew this would likely be our last communication with them. After the plants shut down and the power was gone, they would be unprotected and left to their own means to return here. I feared for them and prayed to God for making them brave and dedicated to the cause. I'm sure they knew they'd be isolated and vulnerable. Still, they responded without question. This was their opportunity to make a huge difference and like me, this was probably the first time in their lives that they felt truly empowered.

I knew that the quickest way I would find out that the operation had been a success was to watch the news. This would inject a new sense of reality concerning the insurrection. Not only were we aggressive and violent; we were smart.

Barry, Apex, and I slowly walked over to the conference room. I knew the rest of the council would be there watching the TVs. I walked in and several of the council members nodded to me with knowing smiles on their faces. I gave a quick wave and then collapsed into one of the chairs, exhausted. I looked up at the clock. I couldn't believe it was now approaching eleven o'clock. The events of the past few hours were historic and unbelievable. I rested my head in my hands and waited. The truth is I didn't have to wait very long. About twenty-five minutes after I gave the order, there was breaking news.

An anchor came on frantically saying, "Ladies and gentlemen, we are getting reports that large areas of Washington, DC have completely lost power. We are unable to confirm the exact locations of the power outages, but we can say that the outages appear to be massive. At this point we don't know the source of these power outages, however some have speculated that this may be related to the slave attacks earlier this evening. We will keep you informed as the evening progresses."

A powerful eruption of cheers came from the council and other rooms throughout the tunnels. It was an amazing feeling. We had taken down much of the power infrastructure in one of the world's largest cities. The president, his cabinet, and the entire free population of the United States had underestimated us. Now they were paying for it. It wasn't about those people who were living without power. It was about the mental uncertainty that we had added to the equation. People would now be scared. They wouldn't know how to act or where to turn. For the first time, they'd realize that the government couldn't protect them. This was no longer about race. Each man or woman, black or white, fears the dark.

As soon as the report ended I stood up in the conference room in front of the council and Apex gestured for me to speak. "Tonight is the beginning of the future. Many people died today in our pursuit of freedom. We had to do some things today that are not characteristic of us. However, those actions were necessary. But we have one other necessary action that we must undertake. We must prepare to move. We will not be able to stay here in the tunnels. The military and the Admins have surely taken some of our operatives as prisoners. No matter how much our men try not to betray us, if they are tortured, they will ultimately disclose our location." Several council members nodded their heads in agreement. I continued, "Let's please take a moment of silence to honor those who lost their lives for our future. Their sacrifices will not be in vain. They will be honored with our victory." Although we have leverage with the power plants, that still does not insulate us from the wrath of the government. So, I suggest that we be prepared to move by tomorrow evening. We'll only be able to stay them off for so long. One advantage that we have is their uncertainty, but we have to be out of here by tomorrow evening."

Tyra stepped forward and stated, "Are you kidding me, Harrison? Leave all of our equipment, supplies, and weapons? No way. It's not going to happen."

"Tyra, I certainly understand your reluctance, but this is not a question about whether we stay here and try to survive, the question is whether we stay here and die. We don't have an option at this point. We must move."

Apex, with his arms crossed on his chest, asked, "Well, Harrison, where do you expect us to go? We are not able to just move our operation to some beautiful facility in downtown Baltimore or downtown Washington, DC."

With adrenaline pumping through my veins, I spat the words out, "Oh yes, we are. That's exactly what we are going to do. We are going to move our operations into the heart of DC, and we are going to make our move tomorrow night. That's an order."

I sent everyone to their rooms for a few hours of sleep. It would be a big day tomorrow and we were all fatigued from today's events. We knew we were taking a calculated risk letting down our guard for a quick four or five hours, so I quickly assigned teams to guard the gates in shifts. I made sure to shake Apex's hand before I left the conference room.

Barry walked me to my room and we discussed initial plans for the morning. Our destination was set and he'd send word immediately to our allies throughout Baltimore to supply cars and trucks that would be ready to begin loading first thing in the morning. Then we'd take it from there. I patted him on the back and then finally entered my room close to 1 am.

I wished I'd had some of that wine they gave us when I was a breeder. Before I could doze off to get some much needed sleep, there was a knock at the door.

I opened it and there was Tyra. I knew either she or Apex would be by to question my actions.

"Can I come in?" she asked, meekly.

I reluctantly allowed her to come in, "Look, Tyra, I'm tired. We have a long and dangerous day ahead of us tomorrow. What do you need?"

Tyra said, "I'm sorry for the outburst during the meeting. I know how difficult it was and you have my full confidence moving forward. Your decisions hold the key to our future. Apex says you have what it takes to finish this job; to take us to a better place. More importantly, he believes in you. And... I believe in you, too. You did great today."

This woke me up out of my stupor and I looked at her dumbfounded.

Laughing a bit, she said, "But he also wants to be valued for laying the foundation for us to have a chance. I know that you understand all that he has accomplished and what he has built here... it's tough to just get up and leave. This is the only security that we've ever known. It's the only place we can live with some degree of freedom and dignity. Now you're asking us to leave it all. I totally understand that we don't have a choice. I just wanted to let you know that we both believe in you."

I looked up at Tyra. I'd never seen her look so vulnerable and scared. I wanted to reassure her the best way that I could. I walked over to her and embraced her.

"Tyra, I can't thank you two enough for your trust. These are delicate times, but we're going to make it through this. We have a good plan. All we need to do is believe and execute. See you in the morning."

She gently kissed me on my cheek and smiled while I opened the door and she walked away, the bounce returning to her step. I closed the door behind her, and took a long sigh before lying down. Tomorrow would be here quick enough and I didn't know if I'd awake a free man or a slave.

CHAPTER 16
THE MOVE

It seemed like I had been asleep for only an hour before the knock at the door came. I jumped up, rubbed my eyes, walked over and opened the door. It was Barry.

"Harrison, it's time for us to roll and get this thing going."

Rubbing my eyes, I asked, "Man, it feels like it must be seven AM... . What time is it actually?"

Barry gave me a punch on the arm and said, "Man, it's nine thirty. We let you sleep in. We knew how exhausting yesterday was, but now we have to get moving. I already have the cars and trucks on the way here, but we have to be careful."

I threw on some clothes and then quickly followed Barry into the hall as he brought me up to date with the ongoing plans.

"You know the one thing that could cause us a big problem is a curfew," he said. "If a curfew is put in place as part of the state's response, we will have problems moving around at night without being noticed. We have to move our timetable up. The president is indecisive. We need to use that indecisiveness to our advantage."

Picking up a large cup of coffee, I looked at Barry with pride. He had done a tremendous job with coordinating our move. He had intimate knowledge of all of our equipment and he knew exactly what needed to be moved to keep us operational. Most of the equipment that would be left behind would be destroyed lest the State get hold of any inside information. We also needed to move weapons and this could not be seen by the public as a coordinated move. We could not travel as a convoy, which could make us vulnerable. If there was no curfew, we had the technology to move in a practical manner without being stopped. Barry had provided credentials to all of the drivers and everyone on our team.

I was nervous and afraid that my insecurities about my plan would make me falter. I wasn't fully prepared. Although I knew our plan was solid, I also knew many of our key operatives would not be going with us. We had planned for only some of our people to make the trip to DC. Some brave souls would stay behind in the tunnels — decoys, as it were. Others would be relocated to various Crops. Barry's team had already hacked into the computers to make their integration possible. Only our core group of about thirty would make it into DC. At this point only Barry, Ray, Apex, and I knew our final destination. All I could do was hope and pray that there would be no curfew.

The day progressed in a very efficient manner. Equipment, food, and weapons were gathered toward the dock area. We continued to monitor the news stations. It seemed that things were becoming quite chaotic with the power outage. Millions of people would be eating their Christmas dinners in the dark. News outlets reported that the State was working vigorously to get the power plants back up and running, but we knew they wouldn't be getting access anytime soon. We still had those facilities on lockdown.

It was Christmas morning, so there was still a fair amount of activity on the highways and in the cities as people traveled to see their loved ones. We had to be up and running before the evening in case the president enacted a mandatory curfew. For that reason, I told Barry we needed to move in the late afternoon versus the night. We needed to be ready to head into the DC area at around five o'clock.

Late December meant it would already be getting dark; we'd have some cover.

The cars and trucks were ready and waiting at the dock, and the workers pressed to get everything ready for immediate loading. The critical pieces of equipment included the computers and monitors. Those would be loaded onto trucks and moved independently of our other vehicles.

We briefly paused as another news outlet reported that the president was making attempts to get the power grid up without the use of the power plants. In addition, supplies were being gathered to provide any needs in the DC area resulting from the power outages. Generators were being provided for essential facilities like hospitals, senior citizen homes, and daycare facilities.

It was about three o'clock in the afternoon when a call came in from the secretary of state. As usual, we all gathered in the conference room and watched him on the screens. We still didn't dare to let him see our faces.

The secretary of state started without any pleasantries, "Well, you've messed it all up. You have got the power down in DC and tonight we are going to be in a desperate situation. In the dark, crime rises and people lose their minds. People may even die because a lack of power — it's the middle of winter for crying out loud. You're going to have that blood on your hands, son!"

I responded without hesitation, "How much blood do you have on your hands, sir? What about the millions upon millions of slaves who have had their hopes and dreams dashed by your imprisonment? What about all those slaves who have died or been killed by their slave masters or by the Admins? Just a few months ago, I watched a slave get beaten to death. Whose hands have his blood on them, sir?"

As if he had not heard me at all, Moore continued, "I have a proposal. This proposal comes directly from the president. Release the codes to us immediately, so we can get the power back on. As a result, I will provide you and all of the folks with you complete amnesty. You will be relocated to Richmond and placed in a safe facility where we will allow you all to live comfortably without any punishment from the state."

"That's punishment enough," I said with a laugh. "Comfortable or not, we'll still be slaves and we'll still be away from our loved ones and friends, won't we? We live one heck of a life, sir, treated as less than human. Not allowed to live up to our ambitions or talents. Respectfully, I decline your offer."

Moore frowned. "I knew you'd fail to accept the offer. That's a big mistake. It was your only hope. We're getting close to finding out where you guys are. When we do, we'll rain down on you like you've never seen."

I walked closer to the monitor and looked into the screen, wishing for a second that he could see my face.

"Good luck," I said, and walked out of the room leaving the secretary of the state flabbergasted.

It took about another hour and a half to load the cars and the trucks. Barry and Ray were pushing everyone to get their belongings together and move toward the docking area, for time was short. There was no telling when the president's men would find our exact location. If they did attack before we got out of here, we'd be goners. Barry gave the signal, and the trucks carrying our supplies started moving one by one. It was still daylight and there was still a lot of activity out on the roadways and in the city. People were moving around trying to prepare for an evening in the darkness. The weather was cool, not cold, so there was no real threat that anyone would suffer from any weather-related catastrophe.

We finally got into the car that Barry had arranged for us. I was in the car with Barry, Ray, and a driver. Apex, Tyra, and Apex's assistants followed in the car behind us. This was an odd journey and I knew that the people traveling with us would be shocked by where we were heading. As the car climbed up and out of the tunnel, I squinted into the sun. It was beautiful.

I wasn't surprised to see that there was a substantial amount of traffic on the highway — it was a holiday after all. There was also an increased police presence. We were sure to be stopped along the way, especially riding in a car full of blacks. Fortunately, there were plenty of slaves moving about to carry out the tasks of their wealthy masters who had stayed in to make the most of the holiday — and also, likely out of fear. Though many whites feared that this was the beginning of a slave revolt, they still required their slaves to be out and about handling their daily tasks. I counted this as another sign of disrespect. Slaves couldn't even celebrate a holiday like Christmas in dignity.

As we drove along the highway toward DC, I noticed the beginnings of a military buildup. Thankfully the military was more focused on the Crops areas than the highway. Where we were headed would be one of the most unprotected areas in Washington, DC. The entire time Barry was on his laptop, piggybacking off the Wi-Fi from various places to leave his trail scrambled. I looked in the backseat at him and laughed to myself. In that small laptop, he controlled the two largest power plants in the Washington, DC area and the former Capitol power plant. It was funny to think that the fate of all slaves across the United States was controlled within that small machine.

Our group was coming in from different directions and everyone was instructed to call in or signal if they were stopped by the feds or by the Admins. The plan was working to perfection. We were slated to arrive at our destination after dark. I expected we'd have the most difficulty once we got onto the Baltimore-Washington Parkway, and I felt like we would be stopped once we got into the middle of DC.

My fears began to ease, however, once we got to Main Avenue. There was no police presence on Main, no presence on East Street, and no presence on Executive Avenue. This was a part of Washington, DC that was considered a relic of the past. There was no interest in protecting this area. In fact, my impression was that the powers that be likely wanted this area destroyed to solidify Richmond as a national powerhouse for good. This area would become the epicenter of all of our efforts from this point forward. I checked with Barry to make sure our generators were on the way.

"Yes, Harrison, they are being delivered now," he said, not looking up from his computer.

We'd worked with one of our Monitor contacts to obtain generators. Those generators had been loaded onto a tractor-trailer truck with other supplies and were on their way to our location. The driver's cover, in case he was pulled over, was that the generators were being taken to a hospital in DC.

We had made it to our location and I knew it would shock everyone once they saw the place.

Our driver gasped in awe, "Oh shit, it's the White House!" I couldn't help but laugh. It was a sight to behold.

The former White House was now a museum that was infrequently visited and poorly maintained. There was still a large fence around it, which appeared to be poorly maintained as well. There had not been a president housed here since Lincoln and it had been all but forgotten. The sign at the front said that admission cost was ten dollars. We knew that with everything going on, the facility would be closed. From previous reconnaissance, we knew there would be one or two security guards out front. Unfortunately, we would have to subdue those security guards, but fortunately, we had enough manpower to do so. The critical question would be whether we could subdue those individuals without them signaling any type of outside assistance. After we gained entrance into the facility, we'd be golden. Once again we'd exploit the administration's failure to provide adequate security to strategic representative facilities.

We had to move rapidly. Our other cars were arriving as well, and I anticipated that the trucks would also be arriving soon. We needed to find access as quickly as possible. The main gate had already been locked for the evening, so we drove around to the side of the gate and began the breech. There was a lock on the gate, but we were prepared with lock cutters and it easily fell away. We opened the gate and drove into the driveway with five more cars from our convoy.

My heart was racing and I knew that at any moment the guards would be approaching. Right on cue they came down a walkway from the back of the White House. There were two of them and surprisingly, one of the guards was an elderly white man. The other was a middle-aged slave. They both had on the guard uniform and they were both unarmed.

The elderly gentleman asked, "Hey, what's going on here?"

I walked toward him and said, "Don't be afraid, sir, but we are getting ready to occupy this building."

He asked quizzically, "Is there some type of problem here?"

I noted, "No problem, but I need you to stay calm so that everything works out without anybody being harmed. I'm afraid due to this circumstance, neither one of you can leave this facility. "

The old man chuckled and removed his hat as he scratched his head, "Well, this is the night shift, son. We didn't anticipate going home until the morning anyway."

Barry, Ray, Apex, and I escorted the two guards back inside the building while the other members of the team began to unpack the cars.

We opted to use our code names in case somehow these guards got bold and tried to run for help.

I said, "My name is Phoenix and I need to know where your back entrance is. We have more coming in. Tell me, do you have a place where we can hide our vehicles?"

The old man replied, "My name is Charles and this is Lewis," the slave tipped his hat and kept his eyes to the ground, subserviently. His face bore a look of bewilderment, for he was likely unused to being addressed by another black man. "To answer your question: yes, we do and I can show you."

We walked through a door into the first floor of the White House and I immediately noticed how beautiful the rear lobby area was. "I'm going to need you to help me understand the layout of this building. Is that okay?"

The old guard nodded his head. He seemed calm.

The slave seemed confused.

Outside, our trucks were beginning to arrive with all of the remaining equipment. We had arrived at the perfect time. We could begin the process of unloading the vehicles and organizing our equipment in a manner that was undetected. I was very pleased at how things were progressing. There was some critical business that needed to be taken care of immediately.

I walked around the inside of the White House and took in the beautiful paintings. There were ropes and half walls set up to protect some of the antique furniture downstairs. It was overwhelming to be in the old presidential residence. It housed the finest of everything from many years ago. This was where our head of state had resided and here we were, making ourselves comfortable. It was overwhelming.

My curiosity and nostalgia tempted me to stay and linger here and take it all in. However, I knew I needed to work my way back to Barry, Ray, and Apex. We had one critical moment ahead and the fact that we were now in the White House only solidified my resolve. We had achieved the unbelievable and there was no reason to stop now. It was time to take the next step, and a bold next step it would be.

CHAPTER 17
THE PRESIDENT'S MEN

Updates on the NNC showed the president scrambling to take adequate action against us. It was clear that Hood was in a panic concerning our bold actions and activity over the last few days. He had been forced to respond to an attack in the Crops. The Crops had become an institution in America. They represented, from the president's perspective, all that was good, positive, and progressive about the institution of slavery. But now that institution had been attacked in the most violent way and it was up to him to formulate the appropriate response. For Hood, this posed a difficult challenge. A heavy-handed response could result in the loss of many lives, including the lives of valuable slaves. But on the other hand, a failure to respond with appropriate force would make Hood appear weak and unstable — something he simply could not tolerate.

It was announced that the president would pull together his cabinet for a special, executive meeting at the presidential mansion in Richmond. President Hood was a man of great conviction in terms of his belief in the superiority of white Americans. He had a strong southern-based belief that slaves were fortunate to be in the United States and fortunate to have their stations in life. Hood believed that the institution of slavery resolved the plight of the slave. In his words, it gave them "direction and opportunity," and Hood certainly didn't entertain any thoughts that slaves had substantial intellectual capabilities. He knew they could use computers and that they had achieved certain benchmarks in terms of the industrialization of America, but he attributed those accomplishments to the systematic education of slaves.

'They are merely following habit," he was often quoted saying.

Any achievements beyond those trained processes were an anomaly according to Hood. Slaves were limited in terms of their potential, and whites were naturally superior.

The vice president, Frederick Benz, was somewhat older than the president, and he held the same deeply southern convictions. Benz, however, had grown more and more concerned about the capability of the slave population. He often worried to other members of the cabinet — and the media — that, because the slaves were constantly traded in the facilities up North, they had ample opportunities to congregate and develop a plan to challenge their enslavers.

Benz had often advocated a plan that would disperse the Crops and the slave populations into the general population. But President Hood would have no part of that, saying that doing so would be a waste of resources and funding could be used better elsewhere. Benz had also opposed the substantial use of slaves in critical industrial trades and in security-related positions. Benz adamantly vocalized his reluctance to Hood about allowing a substantial slave population in the military. Benz knew the more slaves who had access to machinery and weapons, the more likely it was that there would be an armed rebellion at some point in time.

Defense Secretary Collins Wright had also been advised of the seriousness of this situation. The media indicated that it was Wright who had immediately issued orders for the military to advance on the Crops and begin the process of taking down any resistance. Those forces were moving into place and the cabinet felt as if the crisis could be cleaned up within the week.

The evening following his cabinet meeting, Hood threw a brief press conference, during which he stated, "Ladies and gentlemen, this is a crisis of an unprecedented nature. These slaves have initiated what they hoped would be the beginning of an armed, massive revolution."

Wiping sweat from his pepper gray mustache, Hood continued, "The resistance was started by a small group of highly-trained slaves who have developed some substantial technological capabilities. We are working diligently to target their location and we have been in direct contact with the perpetrators of the attack. We are in the process of exposing them. Rest assured, we will see that justice is served."

Hood paused for applause, the recognition as usual, going straight to his head. "In the meantime, we are dealing with an energy crisis in the Washington, DC area. Two major power plants were disrupted during the rebellion, leaving millions throughout the DC area without power."

Just then, a young, lanky, male reporter in the front row yelled out, "Mr. President, will you be issuing a curfew in the DC area as a result of the attacks?"

"No, sir!" Hood barked. "I do not feel that a curfew is necessary as all threats have been contained. We will re-evaluate this decision in the days to come should the outages persist. But please note that we are doing all that we can to restore power to DC residents." Hood smiled nervously, clearly agitated by the unexpected question.

"But aren't you concerned that the outages could continue? This was, after all, a highly-coordinated and sophisticated insurrection," the reporter said, reading from his legal pad. "Aren't you concerned that... ."

"Nonsense," said Hood firmly and with agitation. "Where did you hear that? It's ridiculous to think that slaves would be intelligent enough to coordinate... I mean... ." A collective gasp was heard from the crowd and Hood paused for a moment to gather his thoughts. "This is an isolated incident and we have it under control."

These last words boomed across the conference room with an air of finality. "Once again, we will keep everyone updated as events continue to unfold. Thank you."

As the president stepped down from his podium, the busy hive of reporters burst into a flurry of "Mr. President!" and "One more

question, sir!" Hood could be heard shouting roughly, "No questions!
No questions, please!" as he exited the room.

Meanwhile, on the other side of the political equation, Bradley Crest,
a Democratic senator from Massachusetts had risen to power. Crest
was as close to being an abolitionist as he could be without damaging
his political career. He had always been outspoken about the difficulty
of maintaining our slave state in a worldwide economy. Crest had also
repeatedly noted that African Americans would be more valuable to
the United States if they were free to realize their ambitions and goals,
versus the forced servitude that existed under slavery.

Crest had commissioned repeated studies concerning the cost
of housing and maintaining slaves as a commodity. He had also
commissioned studies that indicated that an individual's productivity
was stunted and diminished in a situation where they were not properly
incentivized by freedom. In each interview related to the slavery issue,
Crest repeatedly hammered home the results of those studies.

Many Americans were affected by his opposition to slavery.
Because of consistent pressure exerted by Crest and many other white
abolitionists, slavery was now seen by many in the United States
as an institution that diminished America's potential. Even still, it
was unpopular in many circles to voice such opinions. Many white
Americans who internally disfavored the institution of slavery failed
to voice those opinions publicly because of the economic benefits
that they experienced personally.

Crest was a tall, distinguished gentleman with a chiseled, clean
shaven, dimpled face. He was a combination of an old western figure
and a suave businessman. Many in more liberal circles viewed him as a
potential presidential candidate, but he had not declared his candidacy
for the upcoming election. Nonetheless, he was well respected not just
by Democrats, but by many Republicans as well, despite his views on
slavery. The American people always seemed to take a keen interest in
what Crest said — whether on the issue of slavery or otherwise.

On NNC, just minutes after Hood had concluded his press conference, a young, blond, female reporter came on the air and announced that Speaker of the House Bradley Crest was giving a live speech.

Crest stepped up to the podium at the State House in Richmond. He cleared his throat and looked into the camera, his eyes expressing sincere concern. He began, "The past few days have been difficult. First, let me note my heartfelt condolences related to the loss of a number of Americans during the assaults. We will continue our prayers for the families of those lost during this course of this inevitable rebellion."

Crest took a moment to pause before continuing and then said, "We will do all that we can as a government to ensure that there is no additional loss of life. We have some substantial concerns as to whether this event is over. It is our understanding that the same individuals who perpetrated and organized the attacks in the Crops may have also organized and orchestrated the takeover of two power plants in the Washington, DC area. This is apparently a very intelligent and sophisticated group of slaves.

"With that said, we must be diligent in our response and efforts to contain this situation. I am calling on the president to utilize all resources available to bring this situation to a peaceful conclusion, and I emphasize 'peaceful'. It is my strong feeling that taking military action against these highly organized instigators would be unwise. I will continue my efforts to update the American public as best I can. However, I would note that the president is in the best position to provide comprehensive updates relative to the current position. I would also note, and with concern, that there is currently no curfew in place for the Washington, DC area. I have substantial concerns for the safety of DC residents and I strongly urge those residents to stay home this evening, should power not be restored."

Crest then left the podium without making any additional comments. He had done what he always did — and that was to subtly and respectfully contradict the president's antiquated beliefs without directly calling him out. Crest had made a point of describing the attackers as intelligent and sophisticated. He urged the president not to use military force, for it would be heavy handed to attack intelligent and sophisticated people like these. In just a few words, he had humanized the black community and equalized the playing field in a way that was guaranteed to make Hood's blood boil.

In the meantime, Ray, Barry, Apex, and I, along with a select group of council members and individuals from the tunnels, watched both speeches from the White House, the glow of a computer monitor lighting my desk and my black skin as I sat at my new post in the Oval Office. This had been Lincoln's desk and belonged to countless other presidents before him. These walls had been built by slaves, and now they were ours once again.

I listened intently to their every word. Every word of hatred and ignorance spoken by the president was fuel for our cause. His words had given me further confidence in our plan — if we could instill uncertainty in President Hood, then perhaps we could sway the American public, as well. And with Crest on our side, I was more confident than ever that we could succeed.

CHAPTER 18
OUR VOICE

As soon as Crest's press conference was over, I turned to Barry and said, "Get me to NNC immediately."

Barry began the process of sending repeated emails to NNC. The emails stated that they were from the head contact for the leaders of the insurgency. It took about ten minutes for a NNC executive to get back in touch.

The executive, a young woman named Lydia, got right to the point, writing, "I need you to verify that you are who you say you are."

Barry typed a prompt response, "We are responsible for the Crops attacks and arming our brothers and sisters with weapons to fight the infamy of slavery. We are also responsible for shutting down power to DC and are ready to do more if not taken seriously."

"What is it that you really want from all of this? What do you expect?" was her reply.

Barry's response was simple: "To be heard." With that, Barry gave her a username for making an online phone call. This was a much safer option than a telephone that could more easily be traced.

Within seconds, a call came through and we could hear the scratching of pencil on paper before at last Lydia spoke, "Is there something you want to communicate to the American people?"

Glancing at me, Barry said, "Yes, one of our leaders would like to provide a comment. Before I let you speak to him, will you let this response be aired to the world?"

Taking a pause before speaking she said, "We reserve the right to edit for content and inappropriate language. Other than that, I see no issue getting this to the public later today — pending further network approval."

Barry nodded his head in a positive affirmation and gestured for me to go ahead. Everything that we worked for had come to this moment. My nerves began to get the better of me until I felt Apex's hands on my shoulders.

Apex whispered, "You got this, Phoenix. I couldn't bring this movement to this conclusion. You saw the holes in my plan and forged ahead to make this happen. I'm glad I choose you to do this. Now do me proud."

All I could do was smile at his kind words. Apex was the first person who had made me feel like what and who I was really mattered. I mouthed a "thank you" to him, and cleared my throat to say, "My name is Phoenix and I'm one of the leaders of the insurgency that has taken place over the last few days. These have been difficult moments for us all. However, for years African Americans have yearned to no avail for an opportunity to be heard. The truth is that freedom is not a luxury or a commodity; it is a right. It's time that America allowed all of its citizens to experience that right."

The executive interrupted, *"African Americans?* Why would you choose this label to describe slaves?"

Without hesitation I said, "Because, Lydia, our ancestry is from Africa before the slave trade began. We are their forgotten brothers and sisters. By adopting this name, we honor our new history and their legacy."

I could hear her writing as I continued speaking, "Our goal is freedom for all African Americans. This would not only benefit our community, but all of America related to its growth and progress both domestically and internationally. These are issues to be discussed later but for now, I have an offer for the American public, and in particular, an offer for our American president. Mr. President, we are willing to disclose our location with a commitment from you and from the military to allow us immunity from any intrusion or arrest over the next two months while we initiate a dialogue and negotiate a resolution to the slavery issue. In return for these concessions, we will agree to immediately restore power to those areas in Washington, DC that have been affected by the shutdown of power plants. We have the codes, we control the on and off switches, and we can restore power immediately. But that is up to you."

The executive's tone was increasingly excited as she replied, "What if your demands aren't met? Then what will be your course of action?"

"We must have an absolute commitment from the president that our activities will not be disrupted over the next two months and that there will be no arrests or prosecution of our operatives. In return, we will issue no additional attacks."

I could hear the eagerness in her voice, "I'm going to green light this immediately, and I'll be back after the president responds."

With that, she quickly disconnected. I could almost hear everyone's heartbeats as they stared at me, waiting for some sort of affirmation.

Smiling, I said, "They're about to broadcast our statement to the world."

Everyone shouted and began clapping. I caught Tyra's eyes as they welled with tears while she and Apex embraced. It was almost too much to believe. Just a year ago I was a slave stuck in the Crops with no hope or opportunity to affect my future. Now, unbelievably, I found myself in the White House, in Washington, DC communicating with NNC as a driving force to make a positive change for every African American from today until the end of time. Apex had planted the initial seed of change, and it was growing into a plan with real impact. No matter what came next, I knew beyond a shadow of a doubt that we would be victorious.

It felt like an eternity waiting to see whether NNC would actually air the story. But less than ten minutes after we had made the communications, there was a breaking news report on NNC. A reporter came on and noted that the network had been in communication with the alleged perpetrators of the attacks in the Crops and on the power plant facilities in Washington, DC.

And then he read my statement. It was amazing to hear my words being spoken over live television. A few minutes later, four analysts called in to discuss what was next. One noted that the statement put a lot of pressure on the president. The analysts began to argue over the ramifications of ending the slave trade, each individual presenting pros and cons. The four of them represented a microcosm of the American public, the two sides in stark disagreement.

After thirty or so minutes of heated debate, the reporter once again appeared and said, "It is the president's widely known belief that slaves are not intelligent. But no matter which side of the slavery debate you support, it is clear that these reports challenge that assumption."

The camera cut away to a quickly darkening sky and the reporter added, "With evening fast approaching and many DC residents still in the dark, it would behoove the president to open negotiations with these African Americans, as they have proven they are no mere slaves."

The network then segued back to the analysts and Apex placed them on mute in the midst of everyone cheering.

I felt very comfortable about my statement. The pressure was on for the president to provide us some security from interference over the next two months. The grace period would give us an opportunity to advance some dialogue about slavery and provide time for our cause to take root.

It was perfect that we had left a few operatives back in the tunnels in Baltimore. This would be the very facility that I would "give up" in response to any inquiries from the president. The people that we left in the tunnels were well aware that, at some point, the authorities would be coming to the facility. They had volunteered to stay behind and continue operations, understanding that they would likely be the first ones apprehended. Their courage gave us the opportunity to cause an additional distraction and confusion concerning any effort to take us down.

I knew that it would be only a few minutes before we heard from the secretary of state. Now that our word was out there for the American public, the pressure was on the administration to make contact with us immediately and to respond to our demands. True to form, the secretary of state called within five minutes of the broadcast. Apex and I gathered everyone around the computer before I picked up.

The secretary of state's red, sweaty face appeared on the screen as he addressed us in his usual irreverent tone, "Well, I assume it was you all that made the statement to NNC. It's a pretty desperate statement, son. You know that the American government does not negotiate with terrorists."

I chuckled, "Come on, John. You know we're not terrorists. We are former slaves yearning for freedom. We want our citizenship and rights, and it's overdue that America live up to its founding principles."

"Well, there's no way we are going to give you immunity for two months," he replied. "So, let's just start with you putting the power back on and then maybe we'll consider some dialogue."

I let steel coat my tone as I responded, "If you don't provide us with your assurance of immunity in the next thirty minutes, we will push back any restoration of power to the DC area for two days," I smiled knowing that the generators we'd brought with us from the tunnels would keep the power on at the White House for the time being. "It's in your hands now. We made a good faith offer to restore power, John. The American public is expecting it. We've asked for no more than a delay in any ultimate determination about our fate. This will give you an opportunity to investigate and determine next steps while we present our case and continue discussions. That's a very small price to pay when you're talking about power in the largest city in the US."

I knew in my heart that the president didn't have a choice. The dialogue was already out to the American public and he could not appear indifferent to the fates of so many people in the Washington, DC area.

"I will get back to you in a minute, son," John replied, and he disconnected the video call.

The room had once again fallen silent, the tension thick in the air. There wasn't much for us to discuss as we waited for the secretary's response.

Within five minutes, he called back. His shirt collar and upper lip damp with sweat, John spoke, an air of defeat in his voice, "Son, we will agree to your terms. "

"Thanks, John. We'll need a public statement to that affect."

The secretary of state responded, "I've already scheduled the president to provide his response as a public white flag, stating that we have agreed to your terms. Now when are you going to restore power?

"The very moment the president makes his statement, we will restore the power. Also, if you recant your position and attempt any further action, we will have no choice to turn off the power not only in DC, but in Baltimore and New York, as well.

"You have my word," John said solemnly and disconnected the call once more.

Thirty minutes later, the NNC announced that they had just received communication indicating that the president would be responding to the statement issued by the insurgents. Moments later, Hood appeared on the screen looking red-nosed and crestfallen. It was publicly known that the president was a fan of aged scotch, and given his appearance, I wondered if he'd just had some.

The president cleared his throat and said, "After much negotiation from the slaves... the uh, African Americans... involved in this insurgency, we have agreed to their terms and granted them immunity for the next two months. Let us build a bridge to peace in this new era that fate has thrust upon our strong and beautiful country."

I was stunned. The thundering screams from our council members made it hard for me to think. I had to hush everyone so I could hear the rest of his statement.

"After much careful consideration, my cabinet members and I feel that it is best to let the dust settle as we continue to investigate the events of Christmas Eve. This is in assurance of everyone's safety so that no more precious lives will be lost. There will be no arrests or prosecution of the attackers at this time, however, we have not ruled out prosecution all together. Please note that we are still taking these attacks very seriously. In light of our concession, we have been assured that power will be restored to the Washington, DC area in the very near future. I thank my fellow Americans for their continued support and understanding during these difficult times and may peace soon be restored to our great nation once again. Thank you. No questions."

It was clear that Hood was attempting to appear in control despite the uncertain circumstances. But, it was easy to detect the agitation and uncertainty in his voice. I wanted to believe his words, but he was like a snake waiting in the hedges. I feared that if we made one wrong move, he'd strike. Hood stood there for a moment, his eyes blank, and then walked off, ignoring the sea of cameras and raised hands.

I gave Barry the signal to turn the power back on, then motioned to Apex, Ray, and Tyra to join me next to Barry. It was time to include them in my final plan to ensure our victory.

"I didn't want to tell anyone my plans in case any one of us was captured and tortured. I couldn't put that pressure on any of you. But here's the deal. Barry is now turning on power for every part of DC except for the Capitol power plant.

"This power plant only services about fifty thousand residents surrounding the areas closest to the White House — and it keeps us in the dark. This is our moment to throw another wrench into their plans. I believe Hood only placated us as a trap. I think he's still waiting for the moment that the power is turned on to trace our signal and come annihilate us."

As a look of concern fell on everyone's faces, Barry interjected, "Harrison, the power is coming up; however, once I get the green light that the power is up I'll be shutting the power back off in our surrounding area."

The Capitol power plant was one of the few coal-burning power plants left in the United States, and it was not an emphasized power generator. In my research on the power infrastructure in DC, it appeared to me that the government placed very little emphasis on this power facility. This was probably related to the government's current disrespect for the White House and what it stood for. The area had fallen to shambles and the Capitol building itself was, like the White House, a relic and no longer consistently used for official government business.

I had a few concerns about turning the power back off in this facility. There would be a relatively small number of residents affected in this area; about fifty thousand. But turning this plant off was an essential part of our plan. We knew that if this plant was turned off, any military infrastructure in the area would have to be fueled by generators. While this would not prevent the military from discovering us or affecting our operations, it would prevent them from being as efficient as they would like. We had already placed generators outside the White House, and we'd have ample power for a couple of weeks.

After another five minutes of simultaneously revving up the gas-fueled power plants in the DC area, we turned the Capitol power plant back off. I knew that the president and his administration were aware that we'd commandeered the Capitol power plant. I hoped they'd see it as a mistake on our part, but couldn't count on it. We braced ourselves, knowing that as soon as the president was informed that the power had been turned off in this small area, he may begin to suspect our whereabouts.

Still, I was hopeful that information would take time to solidify and would not be known until at least tomorrow morning. We needed the time to complete our infrastructure here at the White House. Most of our staff had already arrived and was getting to work. We had electricity, we had food, and we had a plan. And isn't that all you need? More significantly, we now had momentum with the American public. We were becoming a credible resistance. But only time would tell.

As the evening progressed, Tyra issued orders for about half of our team to take the first sleeping shift. And she insisted that I go to bed. I had chosen the Lincoln Bedroom for myself. Lincoln was the last president to fight for an end to slavery, so I felt it was only appropriate. I felt a strong need to stay up and support my team, but everyone insisted that I needed sleep.

Ray said calmly, "We are only as strong as our weakest link, and you look like a feather can knock you out. Go rest!"

I smiled and headed to bed without further objection. My first night in the White House was in one of the most hallowed beds in Union history. Maybe it was forbearance, but my mind would hardly let me sleep, no mattered how loudly my body protested.

I drifted in and out of sleep until the sun woke me up. I opened my eyes. I was indeed in the Lincoln bedroom. No, it hadn't been a dream. I had to laugh. I'd so many times read about the White House when I was still a slave in the Crops. I'd seen photos of the Lincoln bedroom and even daydreamed about it a few times. Now my dreams were finally becoming reality, but I still had a long way to go. Fancy bedroom and all, I was still not free. To the outside world, we were terrorists and had been given a temporary reprieve by the president. I knew that our time was short and we had limited leverage. We needed to capitalize on our fullest intelligence, ingenuity, and faith in this movement.

It was Sunday morning and the sun was rising into a beautiful day. In the Crops, we'd had an opportunity to go to church on Sunday mornings. Even though we were limited in the type of service we could attend, it was one of the few activities that allowed us some creativity. The church services allowed me to wonder about Jesus and God and issues that were greater than me. They allowed me to explore my own individual potential if only as it related to my religion. Sundays provided a brief window to freedom.

This could be the beginning of a new life for us all. Somehow this morning, I didn't feel the weight on my shoulders. I got up out of bed and took one small step and then another. Our actions over the next couple of days had the potential to affect millions of people, yet I felt no anxiety.

As I entered the main lobby, I was not surprised to see Barry already up and organizing. He had structured the large dining hall as an operations room with about fifteen laptops. In one large conference room, he and several workers had already begun the process of setting up additional computers and monitors. This would be our main command room.

All in all, we'd transferred about fifty of our workers into the White House and they were making good strides as the morning progressed. I was excited to see several workers setting up kitchen areas. There were no electric appliances in the main kitchen area, given the antiquity of the house. However, there was a smaller kitchen area that had been installed in recent years for the museum staff. While that kitchen didn't have a stove, it did have a refrigerator and a microwave. We could make it work.

As things began to run more smoothly, I thought about our people in the Crops. There were reports from NNC that the military was fully staffed at each of the attack locations. The reports indicated that the military was preparing to do final sweeps to "clear out" any final members of the resistance. It had been two days since we'd heard from any of our operatives in the field, and we began to question whether they were already lost.

The more critical question was whether the state would locate and advance against our operatives in the tunnels. We had been forced to leave behind several critical operatives who had full knowledge of our plans. If they were skillfully debriefed and tortured, they would likely disclose our plans and our location. I feared greatly for those we'd left behind, but the fact remained that we still had equipment and monitors that had to be managed and somebody had to do it. Barry monitored activities back at the tunnel while we continued to build our infrastructure at the White House.

There was one other glaring concern. We knew that if we did not continue to pressure the president and his staff, he might initiate an attack against us here at the White House. Despite Hood's assurance that there would be no imminent attacks, we were still seen as a threat to national security. It wasn't a matter of if he would retaliate; it was a matter of when.

CHAPTER 19
A NEW STATE

Iconvened a meeting during the late morning hours with Ray, Barry, and Apex. I was careful not to carry a demeanor that would cause Apex to feel I was trying to control the entire operation. It was important to me to illustrate that we were equals. The last thing we needed at this point were any personality conflicts or power struggles. Barry briefed us on the progress related to the growing digital infrastructure in the White House.

"A facility that has no modern amenities has certainly posed some difficulties, but we are working through them. Also, we have retained Charles and Lewis, the two security guards, in a position that's comfortable but stern. They are being held under close watch for the time being lest they go out and alarm the community concerning our presence. We want to delay our exposure for as long as possible," he stated.Picking up where Barry left off, I chimed in, "The president and his men should be able to locate our whereabouts any minute. We should brace ourselves for possible attack and be prepared to counter it by contacting the secretary of state as soon as possible. We need to convince him of our additional leverage."

Apex nodded. "Let's contact John in the early afternoon. That will give us an opportunity to finish some infrastructure building and cover our bases for this afternoon. In the meantime, let's look alive." He extended his hand and I shook it, happy to have finally established a productive partnership.

We dispersed and I stayed in the Oval Office, taking a seat in the president's old chair. I began to scribble some notes and organize my thoughts. My mind raced at the various possibilities and complications that lay ahead of us. An hour or so later, Barry came in and laughed.

"That seat looks good on you, sir."

I smiled. "Well, I mean, I thought I might just sit here and get a feel for it. Who would have believed that we'd ever find ourselves here?" I said with a sigh. "Man, we're in the White House! Even though we have a ways to go, at least we are in the game."

Barry looked down at the papers in his hand and then looked back up at me. Worry set deep in his face as he said, "Yep, we're here alright. But if I had to guess, I'd say we have less than a ten percent chance of success at this point. We are a small mouse going up against a huge lion. The president could swallow us whole at any time. We have to play our next card immediately. Let's head to the command center and call the secretary of state."

I shook off my awe and focused my mind on the next step of our plan. When we arrived at the command room, there were already four technicians working to make sure that the technical issues were met appropriately so that we could have continuous contact. Barry dialed the direct line of the secretary of state and Apex and Ray stood to either side of me. Tyra and the remainder of the council gathered around and we all took a collective deep breath. This would perhaps be our most trying conference of all. Barry sent out the signal and within seconds, the Secretary of state was on the line. The technician sent the feed to a large monitor at the front of the room, and once again we all got a glimpse of the Secretary's round face.

Without hesitation, he began, "Son, are you about ready to bring this situation to an end? The game is up. We will be sweeping the Crops today. Your forces will be taken down and we will be able to move forward with due diligence in locating you and the rest of your operatives. At some point, very soon, the president will take you all into custody and put an end to this entire crisis. The American people are devastated over the loss of life and President Hood has not taken that lightly. He will not rest until justice has been served. In truth, son, I'm praying for you. After we've got you in our hands, you'll need plenty of prayer."

I turned to Apex, giving him the opportunity to speak up if he wished. He didn't move, so I stepped up in front of the screen and replied confidently, "I think you've miscalculated in regards to the American people. The times are changing, John. Most Americans today believe in equal rights for all citizens. The flaw in the current system is that it doesn't utilize everyone to the effective benefit of the whole. That's why there will always be pressure to end slavery. We see this as a once in a lifetime opportunity to change the course. If we die for this cause, then at least we have taken the necessary steps to push our nation toward progress. It may not happen today. But we've already changed the course."

Moore's face one again grew red. "No! What you have done, son, is pushed us to the brink of death and heartache. So I am asking you one more time to give up and turn yourself in. It's time to relinquish the intellectual property and data you have stolen from the United States government, and restore the resources you've misappropriated, including all codes for power plants. That includes restoring power to the Capitol area." Apex and I exchanged a glance. "Did you honestly think we wouldn't notice? We need all citizens in DC to have their power back on, son."

The secretary dropped the last few sentences about the Capitol with a smile on his face, as if he expected me to be surprised that they'd noticed. Once again, the state had underestimated us.

I replied, "We will not restore the power to the Capitol power plant. The reason is that we now occupy the White House. It is important for you to know about the remainder of our operations. I'm certain that you're aware of a facility called Cove Point."

When I mentioned Cove Point, Moore backed up a little from the screen, panic beaming from his eyes. I could tell that he was in the "war room" in the executive mansion in Richmond.

His reply was short as he collected his thoughts, "Son, you need to hold on a second."

The screen went dead for a few seconds and I wringed my hands nervously. When the screen came back on, there were now two people sitting in chairs at the end of a conference table in another room. One was the secretary of state and the other was Vice President Benz.

Benz stared at the screen intensely. His tone was subzero. "What do you know about Cove Point?"

Before I'd retired the night prior, I'd briefed our council on the historical importance of Cove Point that I'd learned during my hours of fruitless research in the Crops. Cove Point was a coveted piece of prime real estate to the rest of the world.

I responded in a very calm and paced manner, "I know that Cove Point is one of the most critical places in the United States. When I was still a slave in the Crops, I did extensive research on Cove Point. Sir, as you may know, this nation's current economic success was built on energy, the energy that slaves injected into our economy and our industrial system.

"Over the past five years, natural gas has become more important than ever to the United States economy. We now produce more natural gas than any other nation. In fact, we now produce billions and billions of dekatherms of natural gas every day." Benz and Moore exchanged a look of bewilderment. Had a former slave really thrown the word "dekatherm" at them?

"As I'm sure you're aware," I continued, "our country has huge production facilities in both the Northeast and in the Midwest. Finds like the Bakkens and Marcellus have given us a huge advantage concerning natural gas production relative to the rest of the world. For many years, we were forced to use that natural gas domestically, because we didn't have the appropriate facilities to export natural gas to other countries."

I took a brief pause to wet my lips before pressing on. "But, you and I both know that three years ago the United States government gave full and final approval for the nation's largest natural gas facility to become operational. Cove Point. It's parent company, Dominion, receives billions of dekatherms of natural gas at its Cove Point facility each day. As a result, the United States now exports billions upon billions of dollars in natural gas to China and other nations each year. Those nations have become dependent upon our natural gas exports in the way that the United States was once dependent upon oil from the Middle East.

"Now, if any disruption, however minute, were to occur to that precious flow of natural gas from Cove Point, it would certainly spell disaster for our friends in China and other countries who rely on our exports. Even a small interruption in the activities at Cove Point would have global implications, affecting economies throughout Europe and Asia. You've got a great thing going with natural gas, don't you? I'm sure you wouldn't want any disruptions, would you?" With this last line, I glanced at Apex who shook his head, a wide grin spread across his face.

Benz pursed his lips and said smartly, "Well, I guess you know how to read don't you, boy? You have our attention and you're right. We can't afford any disruptions with Cove Point. Now tell me, why do you mention Cove Point?"

I couldn't help but laugh at his question. "Sir, you already know the answer to that question. When we advanced our teams to the power plant facilities in Washington, Baltimore, and New York, we hoped we'd be able to obtain codes for the targeted facilities and shut down power. Our efforts were only partially successful as we obtained codes for the Washington, DC area only. But that failure was not fatal, because it allowed us to get to this point. For us, the most important facility was the Capitol power plant. We needed a symbol, a place to operate, and the White House was a perfect location."

At this, Benz threw his hands in the air. To him, our prime real estate location was clearly new information.

"But the Capitol power plant wasn't our sole point of emphasis from a strategic perspective," I continued. "When we sent out those initial teams, we also sent out six teams of individuals to various natural gas compression facilities that service Cove Point. We knew that the government had inadequately failed to protect these facilities. After all, they are small compression facilities manned by only two to four individuals each. There is little to no security at these facilities, yet we all know that they're very important from a strategic standpoint."

A look of acknowledgement washed upon both of their faces as I pressed on saying, "Again, the disruption of the flow of natural gas into Cove Point would be devastating. The world has grown reliant upon our natural gas."

For a long moment, there was silence as Benz and Moore scrambled for an adequate response.

At last the vice president spoke up, "There have indeed been disruptions to several facilities feeding into Cove Point. Did you facilitate those attacks?"

I replied slowly and with iron in my voice, "Yes, we facilitated those attacks. We control the codes, sir. It's your move."

Benz tried to bluff. With a heavy sigh and glance toward John, he said, "That's fine. Even if you shut down those facilities, we can rebuild and restore operations to Cove Point."

"Oh sure, Mr. Benz. You could build alternate facilities somewhere along the pipeline, but that would take months. Years even. You don't have that kind of time. Russia has been making a push to regain its market share. They want to service our allies and current customers and we both know it's been a real issue for America to keep up with demands. Plus, Cove Point has provided Asia and Europe with a reliable source of natural gas. Now, if that source were to become less reliable, it would only take them a few weeks to start buying

Russian natural gas again. The net effect would be billions of lost dollars on our end. Overnight, we could become irrelevant."

Benz and Moore sat in silence — this was not a turn they were expecting. I turned toward Apex for assurance and he nodded. It was time to deliver the final blow.

With resolution I added, "Lastly, I would note that President Hood has used Cove Point for his own political gain on many instances over the past two years. I'm well aware of what a pet project this has been for him. Tell Mr. President that my team now controls his codes and unless he is prepared to cooperate, Cove Point will be shut down within seconds."

Moore exploded from the seat and shouted in a burst, "Oh no, you don't! If you turn those facilities off, we will hunt you down quicker than you can say help. I will order the attacks myself."

With a slow and steady breath, I maintained my composure and spoke without emotion, glad that the pair could not see my face.

"Fair enough, John. But keep in mind that if we come under attack, my great technicians have prepared a virus. If you so much as come near my men, we will release that virus into each of the computers at the compression facilities. It will destroy any digital infrastructure and I guarantee that it will take months, if not years to recover the data. So right now, with all due respect, I suggest you stand down, sir, and prepare to negotiate."

The gauntlet was thrown and I had to tell myself to take a deep breath. I knew it was a risk to speak with such aggression toward the heads of state, but I had no choice. This was the way it needed to be done.

Benz pulled Moore back to his seat and lowered his voice. "You really don't know who you're fucking with here, do you, boy? Don't make a move. We'll be in touch within fifteen minutes."

I don't know what drove me to say it, but I hissed, "Make it ten."

They terminated the connection and I wanted to collapse into my seat. But I had to stand strong — the team needed me.

I turned to Apex, Barry, and Ray, and said with urgency, "We need to finalize our plan of execution here. I don't know what their response will be. We need to be prepared if they attack. Talk to your men and tell them to be ready."

My head spinning, I turned and headed straight to the Lincoln bedroom. I closed the door behind me and with shaking legs, I fell to my knees and leaned my face into my hands.

It was Sunday, and the sun shone in thin beams through the old wooden shutters that I'd closed the night before. For a moment, with nobody to guide me, it felt as if I'd stepped off of a ledge and into the open air. Helpless, I prayed for the first time ever until I knew that God Himself understood my fears. I'd given my all — this was in His hands.

I'd only half finished my prayer when there was a knock at the door. I opened it and there stood Barry. He looked as if he'd seen a ghost.

"Harrison, you need to come see this."

Following Barry into the Oval Office, I heard a sound that shook me to my soul. Then, out the window I saw them: five or six tanks rolling in a convoy down Main Street. A number of military vehicles followed behind them and I could see a lot of movement and people. Within seconds, we'd be surrounded.

I looked over at Ray, "Man, they mean business, don't they?"

Apex said roughly, "Damn, heavy artillery!"

Ray chimed in, "We have to show them our resolve. It's now or never, Harrison."

Barry added, "It's time to show them and the rest of the world we aren't scared, ignorant slaves."

These three men, with resolve in their eyes, made me proud to be included in the fight to end injustice.

"You're right, Barry," I said. "It's time to show them how serious we are. Let's shut their shit down and show them we ain't afraid to fight!"

With that, Barry sprinted toward the command center to initiate shutdowns for Cove Point. As he ran he shouted, "Give me five minutes and we'll have them down!"

I stood at the window and watched as the president made his last attempt to make us cower. I gained confidence from the fact that as soon as the compressor facilities had been taken down, the state would be on the phone with more demands for our unconditional surrender.

In this moment I felt more powerful than ever before. Without a word, my people and I stood in solidarity, waiting for the call that would finally bring the president to the table to end this.

After an agonizing five minutes, the call finally came. We again convened in the command room and I took a moment to calm my nerves for the impending showdown. Then I nodded to Barry to connect the call.

Vice President Benz, appeared on the screen, standing in front of the camera with a self-satisfied grin on his face. The secretary of state sat behind him, lousy with the stress of it all. Benz spoke, "As you can see we have you all surrounded. We are just a hair away from taking the White House back and having you guys in custody."

Stepping toward the screen Apex responded harshly in his booming baritone, "You're going to have a lot of economic blood on your hands if you do that, man. As you know, we control the flow of natural gas into Cove Point and since you appear to be breaking your promise of immunity, we are honor bound to keep our threat. We are shutting down Cove Point. We hacked the servers at each of the compression facilities — easy doings for our operatives, as they were able to work directly at the servers. We have a virus prepped and ready to be placed into those servers. The second your men take action, that virus will be activated. So, I suggest that you stand down and let us take a more realistic approach to resolving the issues that started this whole mess."

The vice president spoke again, his voice almost as loud as a shout, "What do you guys want from us? What are your demands?"

I then spoke up, "Our demand is that all slaves in America immediately be granted freedom and complete citizenship. We also request that President Hood resign immediately and that a special election take place to elect a new president."

Benz let out a crazed laugh, "Well, I can guarantee you that neither one of those 'demands' will ever be met. I think for now we should just call it a day and let you guys marinate on the predicament you've found yourself in. People have died as a result of your actions. Then you hurt the residents of Washington, DC by turning off their power. Even now, there are people in the Washington, DC area who don't have power because you won't turn the Capitol power plant back on. And you expect us to just give you your way?"

Benz laughed once again, clearly relishing in his taunts. He continued, "Now you've threatened America's national economic interest by interrupting operations at our largest natural gas facility. Your acts are selfish and destructive. We would have happily initiated a dialogue without the chaos you've caused. I call on you again to immediately surrender. We are even willing to discuss amnesty."

It was my turn to laugh, "I think you're right, Mr. Benz. May I call you Frederick? Maybe we should both take the evening to consider what we do next. But no matter how much you threaten, we will not relent concerning our call for freedom. I would rather die here in the White House than exit a slave. You need to let the president know that we are here to fight 'til the end. If we need to take down every compression facility on the east coast to initiate a dialogue about freedom, then so be it." Benz rolled his eyes and in disdain responded, "I'll relay your message, boy."

He terminated the connection and we were left with a silence so thick you could touch it. For a moment, not a one of us could speak. Finally, I decided to take post in the command room and monitor the NNC for the rest of the evening to see what developed.

We were at a standoff. There were tanks outside, but for now they were standing their ground. We had our technology, our people, and food to last us for months. Inside these walls, we were still free.

Tomorrow was Monday — the first day of our proposed slave strike. Barry sent another email blast to the Crops communities requesting that no slaves attend work tomorrow. We knew that this was a shot in the dark. Many slaves from a mental and emotional standpoint were probably not ready to stay at home. However, in light of all our efforts, we hoped we'd affect some. But how many?

Our plans continued to advance, but we'd run out of bullets. We had no other major initiatives planned. We were stuck in a delicate balance that could tip against us without warning.

CHAPTER 20
INTO THE NIGHT

It was early evening and the compressor facilities had now been fully shut down. The flow of natural gas into Cove Point would be reduced to a trickle, and as of Tuesday, the gas that remained in the pipes would be exported. Without the necessary pressure in the pipe, transporting gas into Cove Point would be impossible. The facility was dead in the water. It was a bold move, but we had no choice but to play.

After a few hours' contemplation, I called Barry, Ray, and Apex to the Oval Office for a quick meeting.

"Alright guys," I said, "We need to set up two calls. The first is to Xi Jinping and the other is to the folks at NNC. We're going to schedule a press conference."

They all stared at me in a quizzical manner.

"Who the hell is Xi Jinping?" Apex asked with a raised eyebrow.

With a smile, I responded, "The president of China. Months ago, when you all thought I was just sitting around making puppy dog eyes with the women in the tunnels, I was doing research concerning world economics. Slavery isn't just a national issue; it's a global issue. We need to reach out to the world to help us bring the president to the table and discuss the end of slavery once and for all. We start immediately."

Again, the group just stared. It was a major leap, but one that we had to make. "Go, I'm serious!" I said to Barry. Bolting upright, he bounded to the nearest terminal to call the president of China. I'm sure he thought I was crazy.

Continuing I said, "Ray, I need you to contact the NNC and schedule a press conference for the earliest time we can get in the morning."

Ray left the office with a nod and headed to contact the NNC.

Barry then spoke up hesitantly with the receiver to his ear, "It may be a little tough to get the conference call with Xi... um... the president of China. We may run into issues from a credibility standpoint."

I accepted the uncertainty but pressed forward and replied, "Well it's a call that needs to be made, so keep trying. Start by advising them that we are the leaders of the insurrection here in the United States and we control Cove Point. Work your way up through the administration and get me to Xi Jinping!"

Barry shook his head a little bit but stayed on the phone waiting to speak to someone of authority in China. It was the first time he'd showed doubt, but to his credit he stayed the course.

I then turned to Apex and noticed the concern etched in frown lines down his hardened face. "Harrison," he said, "we need to make sure we stick to a solid plan. We can't get too creative here. We've come a long way and we must take very small, smart meticulous steps. You don't think you're getting a little too fancy here, do you?"

His doubts stung me, but I averted my eyes back down to my laptop and quietly said, "I know what I'm doing."

Apex shook his head and left the room quietly. I let out my frustrations in one long breath. As I stared out the window into the winter evening, I knew they were out there on the other side of the fence, looking at us. I didn't want to shut Apex out of my plans entirely, but I had to make choices for our survival. Now was not the time to question my resolve; I knew this was the right course of action.

Outside, the lights from the tanks shown across the lawn. They were situated side by side with their guns aimed at us. I knew that any stimulant would cause them to attack, and yet I was about to take our boldest step yet. It was time now for me to be more aggressive. We needed allies. This would be a once in a lifetime opportunity and the lives of millions of slaves were in the balance. The very institution of slavery was being challenged and with support, victory was in sight.

Now hustling to the command center, Barry worked feverishly with his technicians to get a message out to the political infrastructure in China. I knew that it would take him some time, but it was already approaching ten thirty here on the east coast, so I knew it was morning in China. I wondered whether the Chinese were already aware that the Cove was under our command. If so, its mention would grant us some access.

Just then, Tyra ran to me with a smile on her face and said, "You won't believe what the NNC is reporting right now!"

The lot of us ran to the TVs in the command center to hear the latest development.

As we entered the room, Tyra added excitedly, "Senator Bradley Crest is making a statement."

It was very unusual for a statement to be made this late in the evening, but apparently the issue was important enough for Crest to make one anyway. The caption on the NNC said, "Breaking News," and I knew this would gather some attention. Crest walked confidently to a podium inside the legislative building in Richmond.

He spoke slowly and solemnly, "My fellow Americans, we are in the midst of some challenging times. As you are aware, we recently experienced several attacks in various Crops locations throughout the east coast. The same group also attacked several power plant facilities, shutting down power to the Washington, DC area. It is now with grave concern that I must convey to the American people that our most treasured natural gas export facility, Cove Point, has also fallen under attack."

Cameras flashed and distant sirens could be heard as Crest continued, "Various compressor facilities that feed into Cove Point have been disrupted. It is our understanding that this disruption was caused by the same group of slaves. This is disturbing news. Cove Point is by far our largest export facility for natural gas. Billions of dollars of natural gas flows from that facility to China and Europe each day. Its disruption could affect our strategic interest in both Asia and Europe. Additionally, this shut down could allow the Russian government to step in and infiltrate our economic opportunities."

Crest's words momentarily calmed the flashing lights of the paparazzi. Looking sternly into the camera Crest continued, "This is serious news. At this point I must hold the Hood Administration responsible for their multiple failures related to these attacks. Not only was there failed security in several Crops locations, there was failed security at our power point facilities, in the White House, and concerning Cove Point, as well. These failures are indefensible and have placed the lives of millions of Americans at risk. They have threatened the very economic underpinnings and stability of our country. Because of his many failures to the American people, I am now calling for the president's resignation. I am also calling for the resignation of Vice President Frederick Benz. I am requesting that these resignations take place immediately. If these resignations do not occur, I am requesting that impeachment processes advance immediately."

We stood in the room in silence, too stunned to realize the gravity of Senator Crest's statements. His words were in direct support of our cause. His call for a resignation couldn't come at a better time.

I turned to Barry and said emphatically, "We need to get the president of China on the line right now! The timing here is critical!" Barry nodded enthusiastically and bolted to his computer to get to work. It was clear that Crest's support had renewed his confidence. I stayed to listen to the NNC's commentary. I was emboldened by Crest's challenge of Hood's leadership.

About twenty minutes later, Barry looked up from his desk. "I've got traction. We've got contact with one of the minister's offices in China. However, they are still skeptical and I think that you need to do the talking."

I nodded and picked up the call with an assistant in the minister's office. "Hello, sir," he said sternly. "Please tell me why I should bother our president with issues that are of no concern to the Chinese people?"

After mentioning Cove Point and Crest's pleas, the assistant immediately placed me on hold. A minute later, he responded, "We will call you back. The president is far too busy to take your call." Before I could object, he hung up.

The dial tone left me feeling defeated. We needed to speak with Xi Jinping if we were to have any real traction. This was perhaps the most critical moment we'd faced yet.

Miraculously, China returned our call within 30 minutes. However, the call was from one of their economic ministers, not the president. The elderly gentleman, Gao Hucheng, through the use of a translator, informed us that he was a minister of commerce for the Republic of China. He indicated that a conversation with the president would not be possible and that he wanted to understand why we were trying to contact him in the first place.

Speaking slowly so the translator didn't confuse my message I said, "These are concerns that directly affect your president and the people of China. Speaking with your assistant, I did detail why we were making the contact. I made it exceedingly clear that these were issues concerning Cove Point. My men currently control Cove Point, and we have shut down its operations."

I told him to turn on the NNC and pay special attention to their reports. Then, to show him I meant business, I terminated the call. I knew if I showed any flexibility in terms of getting in touch with the president, I would never get that chance. Again, it became a waiting game.

China called us back once again after twenty minutes. A harsh-sounding translator advised us that we had just fifteen minutes to state our case with the president and that was it. He then added that they would be transferring the call directly to Xi Jinping's office. Cove Point was a critical issue for the Chinese and with the recent announcement on NNC by Bradley Crest, I hoped their president would take me seriously. It was an ambitious reach, but not an unrealistic one. One final critical piece of leverage was coming to the table. Everything depended on this call.

Seconds later, I heard the voice of Xi Jinping himself, a tone of authority in his voice. His translator communicated, "Who are you and why are you bothering me?"

Slowly and calmly I replied, "Mr. President, my name is Phoenix, and I, along with my brothers and sisters, are the individuals responsible for the disruption in the power plants here in the United States. Surely you've heard about us on the news by now." I paused, expecting his acknowledgement. When it didn't come, I continued speaking, "Sir, we have closed off the compressor facilities to Cove Point and there will be no more gas flowing there by midnight on Tuesday."

After a brief pause, the president of China said in flawless English, "I had to be certain as to with whom I was speaking. Your facts are consistent with what my ministers and I have learned. What is it that you want from us, Mr. Phoenix?"

"Sir, you and I both know that this disruption will affect your nation's economy in a significant way. Although Russia can be used for a backup, by the time you adjust to obtain their natural gas at a higher price, the damage will already be done. We know you need Cove Point gas for both heating and generation. We are asking that you partner with us — with one concession."

"You have my attention, Mr. Phoenix," Jinping replied with concern in his voice.

With resolution, I continued, "We are willing to restore operations to Cove Point if you agree to pay an additional half-cent per dekatherm.

These funds will be used to offset the changes in infrastructure that would be necessary to free our slaves here in the United States."

Again, I was met with silence and I felt my stomach tighten to lead. I pressed on. "This is an opportunity for China to have a direct impact on the inner workings of our American infrastructure. If the Chinese government were to deal directly with us and were willing to pay an extra half-cent per dekatherm, we could facilitate the end of slavery in the United States. Sir, just think of the economic implications that an end to American slavery would have for countries such as your own. The US economic advantage concerning free labor would end immediately."

Everyone looked at me in awe. They didn't expect any of this. This new dynamic had potential to even the playing field concerning industrial production relative to Chinese exports. Our cheap labor had always been an issue; thanks to slavery, American goods were manufactured at almost no cost from a labor standpoint, thus America held great advantages in terms of exports to other countries. If slavery were to end, it would create a new balance in terms of competition with China.

I reiterated, "All I need is an extra half-cent per dekatherm, Sir, and your public announcement on the NNC that you are now fully supporting us."

I knew that the extra half-cent would translate into billions upon billions of dollars in additional revenue. But it was a small concession by the Chinese government from an incremental standpoint. I was certain the president would be intrigued at the opportunity.

After a brief pause, Jinping said, "This is a most intriguing proposition you've presented to us, Mr. Phoenix. I will call you back within the hour with our decision about your terms."

When the call ended, Barry looked at me like I was crazy.

"How in the hell are you coming up with all this?" he said, flabbergasted.

I responded, "Man, I have done a lot of research. Cove Point is critical. It's just by chance that the government left those facilities unprotected. Crazy isn't it? Taking down Cove Point is a critical issue and if we can get these concessions from the Chinese government, I'm going to definitely need that call into NNC. We need to show our country that we have support."

Apex shook his head in awe and said, "I'm so glad I let you lead this. If I had been stubborn, this revolution would've ended a long time ago. And it would not have been a good ending."

I smiled and patted him on the back. "Apex, if you hadn't started this revolution, everyone here would still be in the Crops as slaves without the audacity to even dream of being free." We shook hands and there were embraces all around as everyone celebrated this new turn of events with China.

The president of China kept his word and called back exactly an hour later. He spoke firmly, "We will agree to pay an additional half-cent per dekatherm for all natural gas moving out of Cove Point, if you will guarantee that there will be no more disruptions in the gas flow. I will also need some security that America is advancing toward the goal of eliminating slave labor as a source in its industrial base."

I responded immediately, "Thank you, sir! And yes, of course. Now we need you to announce this new dynamic to the American public. Will you do that for us?"

"Mr. Phoenix, on my honor I will make that announcement." I pounded the table in excitement. The deal was set — this was the leverage we needed and the ball was once again in our court.

Ray made contact with the NNC concerning the press conference to be held the following morning. This would be a dangerous move, since the conference would be me by myself, speaking during daytime hours in full view of the world on the White House lawn. The president's tanks were still waiting for any reason to blast us, and I felt certain that I'd have thousands of sniper rifles aimed at me the moment I walked to the podium.

We agreed that everyone else would stay in hiding in case the president gave orders to shoot me down. Ray had advised the NNC to allow no reporters inside the gate during the conference. The NNC's team would be allowed to enter, set up their podium, microphones, and cameras, and then exit and wait outside the gates as the statement proceeded.

The imagery would be stunning. One sole black man standing on the lawn of what used to be the most significant building in the United States; and outside the White House gates, tanks, soldiers, and the rest of America waiting to hear my statement. For the first time, I'd be directly in the line of fire. I had no idea if I'd come out of the conference alive, but it was a chance I needed to take.

CHAPTER 21
ALONE WITH THE WORLD

Now I had only to prepare and rehearse my statement. Of course, I'd never done any public speaking and I didn't consider myself to be an especially articulate person. But I'd spent night after night scouring the Internet, watching the news, and gaining an understanding of how our government works. I'd watched our nation's political figures give speeches to millions and I'd studied their diction and poise. Somehow I had absolutely no reluctance in terms of speaking. It wasn't that I was confident, it was that I had conviction.

After much debate and a few hours of restless sleep, it was finally time for me to face the music and deliver my speech. A half hour beforehand, a technician from the NNC had been allowed access to place the podium and microphone on the lawn per Ray's specifications.

The distance from the door of the White House to the podium seemed infinite and I didn't remember walking up to the podium. The blinding lights from the cameras and the blood pumping through my veins made every second excruciating. I almost didn't see the technician countdown with his fingers and then point to me to speak — it happened so fast.

"Good Morning, my name is Phoenix. I was a slave from the Crops in Baltimore for the first thirty-five years of my life. I don't know who my parents are. I don't know if I have any brothers or sisters. For years, I believed I was nothing more than just a pack mule to be used for the benefit of others."

Looking down at my speech for a moment and licking my lips nervously, I decided to abandon my script and speak from the heart.

"I've seen my fellow brothers and sisters beaten, raped, and then transferred when they were too old to be of any use. I have been used as a breeder when my master and the state wanted to create more slaves for their benefit. I was given no choice in any matter and I figured that would always be the case. Such is the life of a slave."

A gentle breeze washed over my face and gave me strength to continue, "I say 'No More' to that life. No more being used like animals. No more having our lives snuffed out when my fellow slaves or I question the status quo. The events of the last few days have been orchestrated and implemented by former slaves like myself. We have disrupted Cove Point and now control its access and flow. We have also partnered with the president of China, Xi Jinping, and he has given his word that China will enter into a new era of economic dealing with the United States. Jinping has agreed to pay an extra half-cent per dekatherm for all natural gas being exported out of Cove Point. This will result in billions of dollars in revenue for the United States. In light of this commitment from the Chinese government, I would like to extend a personal invitation to the president of the United States to come here, to the White House, so we can finally begin the conversation we've been asking for since day one." A gasp fell across the crowd.

Breathing in deeply and squaring my shoulders, I continued, "We will not be slaves anymore. We are African Americans and it's high time that America sees us as the citizens who built this country, and not the ignorant savages we were assumed to be."

With that, I stepped down from the podium and walked confidently back to the White House. A whirlwind of fear and vigor coursing through my blood.

The adrenaline was so intense I felt dizzy, so I headed straight to the Lincoln bedroom to sit down. As I walked through the halls and past the control room, all eyes were on me. A few shouts of "Bravo!" reached me but I wanted nothing more than to be alone to collect my thoughts. When I finally reached the bedroom, Ray, Apex, and Barry were there waiting.

Apex reached out to shake my hand, "Good speech, my friend." I looked at my feet, not knowing how to respond. In truth, I was just happy that I had not been shot.

Barry came over and patted me on the back, saying, "That was some great improvising."

Ray nodded and added, "We have started watching the reactions come in and they've all been favorable. I think the country — and the rest of the world — is stunned that a former slave could be so articulate."

I shook my head. "We still have a long way to go. The military is in full force and still surrounds us. Do you know what it's like to stare at a dozen tanks? I thought I was a goner," I said, staring out the window.

With the military watching our every move, we had no real means of ingress or egress. We were in need of a way to get things in and out of the complex.

Raising an eyebrow, I asked Ray, "How many days of supplies do we have left?"

Ray frowned, "We have a month or so worth of food if we tightly ration. Our supplies are diminishing fast."

Barry chimed in, "Another concern is that our generators are going to run low at some point. Additional supplies and new generators can be here as early as tomorrow, but without government cooperation, our guys will never get through."

I nodded. I was also waiting on news from President Xi Jinping to announce his support and partnership for Cove Point. So much lay in the balance. Despite our many victories, the end was nowhere in sight.

I sat on the bed and Apex turned to leave. Before he exited he said, "Great speech; great strategy. We might get there yet, Harrison."

Ray and Barry looked at me expectantly and with a sigh I said, "Guys, I need an hour. Back to work — I'll check in soon." They nodded and returned to their stations.

As I lay back on the bed, I could hear increased commotion outside. There were crowds gathering. The crowds were a mix of military, media, and citizens who were just plain curious. I was exhausted, but this was no time for shut eye. In an effort to collect my racing thoughts, I decided to take a walk around the White House, having never completed my tour.

I quietly walked out of the bedroom and up one of the stairways. On the walls hung dozens of painted portraits. I didn't recognize most of them, but I did see a painting of George Washington. When I got upstairs there wasn't much activity, just a few of our assistants walking around and inspecting to see what spaces could be used. In one room was an elegant dining area with a small table and ten ornate chairs around it. I disconnected the velvet stanchion that cordoned off the space and took a seat at the head of the table.

I imagined myself hosting dinner for eight dinner guests and a lovely wife; and for the first time in weeks, I thought of Meagan, praying that she'd survived this ordeal. I reclined back in the head chair and put my feet up on the table, lost for a moment in my dreams. When I began to feel drowsy, I shook it off and continued my impromptu tour of the remainder of the house. I walked around for another thirty minutes or so, examining every room. I knew from my research that this home was built by slaves, but it was never intended for us. No matter what happened next, we'd already changed the fabric of history. I came downstairs feeling renewed. When I reached the bottom floor, I noticed a huge group of our assistants gathered in front of the TVs in the command room.

The president was speaking and I knew it was his response to my statement. He had a somber tone in his voice and was disheveled — almost aged — in appearance.

Hood spoke calmly into the camera and said, "America, I'm in the midst of responding to domestic terrorist activity. As the duly elected president, I have a sworn duty to honor the wishes of the majority of the American public."

He lowered his head for a moment, and then with a fury in his eyes, he said, "To that end, I will preserve the institution of slavery to the benefit of all citizens. I will, however, issue a subcommittee to study how to make slavery more efficient and how to prevent these types of issues from ever happening again. Rest assured that power has been restored to Washington, DC and will remain active. The threats posed by the slave terrorists have been contained and negotiations are moving forward to bring this crisis to a full and complete resolution without any additional loss of life. Any questions?"

The media erupted into a swarm of raised hands and Hood anxiously called on a couple of reporters. Their questions evolved around Cove Point, the Chinese government's endorsement, and the continuation of slavery. Hood's answers were short and vague as he struggled to contain his frustrations. He had also omitted several key facts from his speech. It was clear that he was trying to save face and maintain the illusion of power.

Finally, he said, "Yes, the flow of gas into Cove Point has been disrupted. But our administration is still awaiting verification that the Chinese government has agreed to pay an additional half-cent per dekatherm for natural gas exports."

Barry said, "He didn't give you credit for that, Harrison."

Laughing, Apex added, "As if he would!"

Hood ended the conference by adding that he would adamantly oppose any initiative to disrupt the institution of slavery. Just as abruptly as he'd begun, he stormed away from the podium. The man was president of the United States, yet here he was so shaken and uncertain. Barry asked if I wanted to make an additional statement in light of the president's comments.

"No, man," I said. "The president has already done more damage than any rebuttal statement I could provide. He looked sick."

CHAPTER 22
A NEW TEAMMATE

My next point of concern was the work boycott. Slaves were still living in the Crops. Things had to change. Today was our chosen day. As coverage continued, the NNC confirmed that about ten percent of the slave workforce had not reported to work. This was more than enough to cripple the daily operations of every city across the United States, and it proved that there was some solidarity amongst slaves across the country. We had momentum.

Just then, Barry signaled to me from his station. He looked like he might explode with excitement. "What's up, man?" I asked.

"Harrison, I've got Senator Crest on the line."

My jaw dropped. This could mean only one thing. I put on Barry's headset and with excitement in my voice said, "Hello, sir."

Crest's words were abrupt and to the point, as he spoke with determination. "Phoenix, this is Brad Crest. That was a great speech this morning and I agree: it's time to put slavery to rest once and for all. I'd like to offer you my direct support." His words hit me like a wave and I had to sit down.

"Sir?" I said, dumbfounded.

"I would like to meet with you and your supporters tomorrow morning at the White House. I'll alert the president's team that I am coming so security shouldn't be an issue. Let's say nine AM."

I had to force the words from my mouth. "Yes, absolutely. Thank you, sir."

"Call me Brad," he added before disconnecting the call.

My expression had drawn a crowd in the command room and I blurted out, "Brad Crest is coming to the White House!" For the first time, I began to see the finish line. With that, everyone returned to work with a fresh energy and drive. I headed to the Oval Office and began jotting down notes for what was to be the most important meeting of my life.

Several hours later, Barry walked in. After watching me let out a giant yawn, he said, "You starting to look a little tired, my man. You've been working too hard."

I nodded and spoke through another yawn, "Yeah, we've all been working too hard. But there's still so much to be done — and let's hope we don't get attacked in the middle of the night by these crazies. This meeting with Crest is critical and I really need to get my thoughts together for that. This could determine our failure or success."

Barry nodded and said worriedly, "I understand, but I'm very concerned that you'll collapse from exhaustion if you don't rest soon. This is going to be a marathon, not a sprint. We need you to be alert whenever you interface with an official or the media. Get some rest and we'll hold down the fort for you. We really need you to be ready for tomorrow morning."

Before heading to my bedroom, I looked out the window and, as I expected, the tanks were still there. The media was still there, too. I decided to take a shower and put on fresh clothes to calm my nerves.

The shower relaxed me enough to allow me to think more pointedly about our current situation. *Everything is riding on tomorrow,* I thought. As I walked through the halls. I took a look at everyone still running around to complete their individual tasks. I felt an overwhelming sense of responsibility for everyone.

Arriving at the command center, I peeked out into the darkness to confirm they were still out there. After checking one last time with the council for an update, I finally headed to my room to get some rest. I trusted the council to run things in my absence.

As I lay in bed, my mind raced through all the possibilities that could go wrong. We needed supplies to replenish our stock, but with so many tanks and soldiers stationed outside the White House, it would be impossible to make this happen. We had no weapons and no security compared to the arsenal of weapons aimed at us from the outside. The glamour of moving into the White House was beginning to fade. Despite everyone's commitment to my plans, I knew I had to do something soon to boost morale. The major question on my mind as I tossed and turned was how I could make the end game happen to our advantage without engaging in bloodshed and persecution.

I greeted the new morning with a little bit of reservation. Senator Crest would be here soon. I needed to make sure I was comfortable, so I opted to wear my old clothes rather than the suit that Barry had provided for meetings with officials. I planned to meet with Crest in the Oval Office. It was about seven fifty AM. *It's now or never,* I said to myself as I headed to meet the council one last time before Senator Crest arrived.

In the command center I said to the group, "Thanks for letting me rest, everyone. I hope you will take an opportunity to do the same. But first, it's time to greet our guest. Remember: although he talked a good game on TV, we must advance our agenda. We don't have an ally just yet, nor do we have an enemy. Let's all pray that he's a friend and not a foe."

While preparing for my meeting with Senator Crest in the Oval Office, I took a moment to enjoy the view. The windows looked out to the garden and I opened them for some fresh air. I'd lived most of my life in the Crops where the only views were dilapidated buildings and broken spirits. Now, as I looked into the garden, I was impressed at how well maintained the area was despite the inactivity. Although no president had lived here for over one hundred and fifty years, it was still beautiful and luxurious.

Several minutes later, Barry and Ray greeted Senator Crest in the main entryway. I watched from the doorway as they turned the corner and walked the hall to the office. Crest walked with a bounce in his step and smiled when he saw me. As he got close enough, he extended his hand and said, "You must be Phoenix. It's great to finally meet you. You've done a tremendous amount of work here, but we have a lot to discuss."

Shaking his hand, I said, "Thank you, Senator Crest, and I wholeheartedly agree. If you would kindly follow us into the Oval Office… ."

The desk was set up for us with some water and juice. Considering how low our supplies were, I could only imagine the difficulty our staff had in making this look presentable. Sitting down behind the desk and placing both of my hands on top, I looked directly at Senator Crest to measure what kind of man I was dealing with.

He wore an expensive blue, pinstriped suit, custom-tailored to fit his athletic physique. I'd cleaned this type of suit for many years at the cleaners. His tie was a beautiful orange color with decorative gold designs. His shirt was a pristine white with medium starch. I'd never seen a man so finely dressed. Crest smiled assuredly and said, "Well, where do we go from here?"

I narrowed my eyes in response, reluctant to give him my complete trust just yet. "Well, our options are limited. We are in an all or nothing scenario. Here we are, former slaves occupying the White House. We only have two choices: freedom or death. At this point, we are willing to die for the cause in honor of our millions of brothers and sisters across the country who still find themselves imprisoned. It's time for slavery to end and we will do everything in our power to make it happen. Even if we fail, I am certain there will be those who come after us to take up the cause."

Senator Crest sat back in his chair, and folded his arms across his chest as he took in my comments. I continued speaking to ensure he understood the depth of my commitment to our cause.

"The slave boycott yesterday was an important beginning. We will be calling for additional boycotts to express to the American people our weariness with forced labor. It's time that we were recognized for our contributions to the American economy and society." I paused, making certain that I had his complete attention. "I am hoping that you can help us in advancing this cause."

Senator Crest nodded and said, "That's why I'm here, my friend. Today is an important day. You have my support, but I will need a couple of things from you. First, I will need a pledge that there will be no additional acts of violence. If you give me that pledge, I will relay that to the American people. Second, I will be again calling for President Hood's resignation. Based upon his response to your statement yesterday, he isn't going to change his mind about slavery. It's time for new leadership in America, and it's time for slavery to come to a quick and abrupt end. Now, in the event that Hood does resign, the question remains: will we be able to affect a slow and meticulous integration of former slaves into American society? The truth is that integration will be tough. There will be pockets of resistance regardless of what the government says; it's always difficult to take something away from people. White Americans have grown accustomed to using slave labor for many, many years."

Nodding my head in agreement I said, "I know the transition will be tough, but we are in a fortunate situation. Slaves are already participating in many vocations across the United States. The key issue is to provide them a foundation of freedom and the rights to be educated. We must have immediate freedom of movement. We are of course willing to look at a gradual transition from the Crops, but I would ask that the government implement programs aimed at properly affecting this assimilation. We can't just be thrown unprotected into a still oppressive society. However, I do expect that

African Americans would gradually move into all aspects of American society from an economic and geographic standpoint. Another clear necessity is our immediate ability to vote."

Crest said in earnest, "One of our first orders of business will be to attempt to implement the Universal Suffrage Act. This act will allow for all slaves in the United States to vote in elections. This would allow former slaves a sense of pride and belonging concerning the United States. Voting is a critical right. Without you having the right to vote, there will be no accountability in government."

The look of shock on my face made Crest smile. I shook my head in awe and said, "This is way more than I expected, sir. The social and symbolic significance of such an act would be a landmark, to say the least."

"Please, call me Brad. All of my friends do."

"Thank you, Brad," I said.

Smiling, Crest said, "I've been fighting this for a very long time. I refuse to have slaves of my own, I'd just want to set them free. But we know the law prohibits that. I've been working on a grassroots anti-slavery initiative for years. We needed a fresh fire to shake things up, and your revolt was just the thing to do it."

I nodded. "I understand, and I want to ensure that during this time of transition, all African Americans living in the Crops will be given fair wages with increased benefits and healthcare included. We also need autonomy in terms of how those wages are spent."

Crest seemed a little surprised at the depths of my plans for assimilation. He was pleased to learn that we were so in synch in our efforts. And I was relieved to know that he was a legitimate ally. He was not only an advocate for the end of slavery, but he was onboard for fair and beneficial programming to complete the ultimate assimilation.

"So, what's the next step, Senator?" I asked, and took a sip of water.

Crest said, "Our next step is to ensure that your deal with the president of China isn't sabotaged. Although you have control over the compressors for Cove Point, I can guarantee you that our president is working on a way to circumvent your access as we speak."

I remained calm while he discussed Cove Point. I didn't want to give him the impression that I hadn't thought of it.

He continued, "The moment I leave here, I'm going to hold a press conference out on the lawn to discuss with the American people what has transpired between us. I've also given word to my associates to supply you with whatever your team needs. I'm sure you'll be running low soon."

Relief washed over me knowing that my crew would be taken care of. Standing up and shaking his hand, I said, "Senator... I mean Brad, thank you for your help and your contribution to our cause. We couldn't take another step without your assistance."

"You're more than welcome and please don't hesitate to call me if you need anything else, Phoenix."

With renewed assurance I smiled and said, "Please, Brad. Call me Harrison."

Escorting him out the front door and to the podium, I felt better about our prospects. I stood by Crest's side as he gave his speech. True to his word, he publically denounced President Hood and once again demanded for his and the vice president's immediate resignation. He also mentioned his plans for communication with the president of China to ensure that we had his support. He then made it clear that we had the full support of the Democratic party to end slavery once and for all.

He finished his speech saying, "President Hood won't go quietly. He's a fighter and right now he is desperate. We need to be aware that this is going to be tough. But I have no doubts that we will persevere. Thank you." With that he stepped down and shook my hand once more, this time for all the world to see.

I stood there for a moment and looked him in the eyes. "Why are you doing this?"

As we walked back toward the White House, he said, "Because it's the right thing to do and because it's the right thing for America.

Sooner or later, we were going to face a situation where our moral inadequacies would affect our ability to remain at the very top of the world. Russia and China would eventually align and because we deal from the moral low ground, we'd be unable to mobilize the rest of the world. This is clearly the right thing to do for all Americans."

I needed and wanted to believe that this would eventually end without another life lost. But later that day, Brad's delivery of supplies was seized by the military. I knew it had seemed too easy, but I also knew that Brad wouldn't stop fighting for us. The real question was how soon and how hard would Hood fight back?

CHAPTER 23
HOOD WINKED

That Tuesday evening, Hood gave an address that was broadcast worldwide. "My fellow Americans, we are facing some very, very difficult times at this point. As you all know, the United States has come under attack via a group of slaves and various other parties who have fashioned a somewhat effective operation. It all started with attacks on various Crops, as well as attacks on several energy facilities in Washington, DC, and the ultimate occupation of the old White House."

"These are troubling developments. The stated goal of this resistance is to end slavery and it is now our understanding that the same slaves who initiated this operation also instigated the slave boycotts this week. Approximately ten percent of the slave work force did not show up for work today or yesterday, and this has affected the operations of many businesses across the United States. At this point, I am fearful that this group of indignant slaves will take more violent actions. I'm fearful that their calls for boycotts will become more affective. My gut reaction is to initiate military action against the operatives of this initiative, starting with those who have occupied the White House. My desire to do so is tempered by the fact that these same operatives still hold various codes that are essential to our energy infrastructure. So, at present, we are at a standstill. I continue to wait for the earliest appropriate time to advance military action. As soon as that opportunity presents itself, the military will bring its full force against these individuals."

"Cove Point has been compromised. Gas flow into Cove Point has been disrupted, which has caused severe problems with our continued exports, especially those exports to China. We are working to find a prompt solution to this issue, however as you are aware, today, one of the slaves, 'Phoenix,' announced to the media that he has been in direct contact with Xi Jinping. The slave indicated to the media that Jinping had indicated a willingness to pay an additional premium per dekatherm in return for an agreement that the gas flow would not be interrupted into Cove Point."

As we watched from the command room, Apex and I exchanged a glance. "Good development," Apex noted.

I shook my head in awe, "He may have spoken with Jinping directly. If Jinping confirmed his support of us directly to Hood, then the ball is in our court."

Hood continued, saying, "We are in negotiations with the perpetrators to ensure that our access to Cove Point is reinstated immediately. I am confident that within the week, we will have this matter resolved." Hood left the podium and the NNC commentators took over once more.

Jinping's support was a major body blow to Hood. The president of China had disrespected him in front of the entire world. Our agreement was a clear indication that the president was losing control. Not only was he facing a scenario where the vestiges of slavery were collapsing all around him, he was also facing an international situation where America's largest customer of commodities would now look at alternatives if he could not guarantee supply. The president was losing ground with the American people and the international stage. Polling showed minute by minute that those affected by the boycott or the energy scenarios were now vastly opposed to Hood, and, more importantly, to his position on slavery.

There was a growing general sense across the country that the foundation of slavery was about to implode. The NNC broadcasts showed interviews with white men and women inside their places of business or walking down the street. Many felt that slavery should end immediately. There was certainly very little sentiment in favor of a civil war that would involve mass bloodshed. The country had been there once before, and Americans had simply grown too comfortable to consider the prospect of a war in their own backyards.

It was late in the evening when Senator Crest called. Barry put the call through and Crest spoke briskly and to the point. "Harrison, it's Brad. It's time for me to respond to Hood — man to man. I'm going to keep you on the line, muted, so you can be aware of our conversation. Understood?"

I was baffled by the opportunity to finally hear the president's words uncensored. I stumbled to find my words. "Brad — yes. Thank you."

Within minutes, Brad had Hood on the line. I held my breath and put the call on speaker phone for the rest of my council to hear.

Crest spoke with fire in his voice, "Mr. President, you're at an impasse. There must be no intervention from a military standpoint. Any aggressive or violent action would wipe out those responsible for codes related to continued operations of the DC power plants and the compressor facilities at Cove Point. With all due respect, sir, I urge you not to do anything stupid."

"How dare you…" Hood began, but Crest cut him off.

"Also, if you turn on your television right now, sir, the president of China has officially confirmed his full support of the former slaves."

Hood was well aware that China had spoken with the resistance and made a deal concerning Cove Point. Apart from one long, deep sigh, he was silent as Crest continued.

"There's one critical concession that might help this process move along, Mr. President. The African Americans who are confined to the White House are growing short on supplies. My men are already there with the supplies they need, but have been barred from entry due to your standing orders. If you allow my men to pass, America and the rest of the world that's watching this unfold will see this as a positive step toward peaceful resolution."

Hood, grasping for even a single thread of power to adjust the equities of the conversation said, "I'm not willing to allow those insurgents to move in and out of the White House like they're free! They are terrorists who have threatened everything that we stand for! Besides, I'm not sure this Phoenix character is all he's cracked up to be. Captured slaves are talking. My sources at the FBI and CIA have informed me that the initial leader of this group was a slave by the name of Apex. If I'm to speak to anybody, that's who it's got to be. Not some kid." As he spoke, Hood's resolution diminished. These were empty words that held no validity — and he knew it.

Sounding deflated, he spoke more softly and said, "However, I'll allow a small concession of supplies to be entered into the White House, providing they do not try to escape their confinement or shut off any more power."

Crest, hearing the defeat in the president's voice responded respectfully, "Mr. President, thank you for allowing this. I'll be in touch as soon as matters develop."

After I heard the president hang up, I unmuted my phone. "Brad, thank you once again."

"Absolutely," he said. "How about you have one of your assistants talk to mine and give them the list of everything you need so we can make sure all of your needs are met?"

I gestured to Barry who had just returned from a much needed respite. He nodded and sat down to make a list.

Crest continued on, "I have to ask you a serious question. Are you the actual leader of this group, or is there someone else?"

Taken aback by the bluntness of his question, I said, "Hood was right. The original leader of this group was Apex. I'll let him know that the president wishes to speak to him directly." It was then I realized that Apex was nowhere in sight. I'd commandeered his leadership so successfully that he hadn't even thought to be present.

Crest said, "I'll talk to you later, Harrison, with any more details that may arise."

"Thank you, Brad. We'll be in touch about supplies," I replied and then disconnected the call.

Walking up to me with hope in his eyes, Ray said, "Man, this could end up working. We've got the president reacting to us. We have to keep the pressure up. We can't let this momentum die."

"You're right, my man," Barry added, and the two of them continued in conversation.

I heard them speaking, but my mind was on Apex and the reason why the president wanted to speak to him. There was no room for ego and I didn't want to feel slighted, but my pride stung a little. I walked to the TVs and watched as the NNC replayed Jinping's statement. I knew I should feel proud, yet something didn't feel right. Blaming my paranoia on lack of sleep, I tried to locate Apex so we could discuss his conversation with the president.

However, my body had other plans. As I searched for Apex, I paused for a moment and took a seat in a large, luxurious chair in the West Wing. Before I knew it, I had dozed off. The next thing I knew, Barry was shaking me awake and telling me to come downstairs. The supplies were arriving.

It must have been about two in the morning. Rushing downstairs, I could see a lot of activity outside the window. Cameras flashed as dozens of figures moved about in the darkness. Barry and I exited through a side door to greet Crest's associates in the driveway.

As I stepped outside, I presented a mask of confidence. These last few days had left me physically and mentally exhausted. But I was determined to move forward and face new challenges. Crest had sent about ten of his own people, and twenty or so of our crew had come outside to meet them. They had a ton of supplies with them: boxes of food, clothes, and toiletries, and new generators to boot.

As I hurried about shaking hands with Crest's men, Barry grabbed my arm and with a grin on his face, said, "Hey, Harrison. We felt like you needed an extra morale boost." He turned me to face down the dark driveway.

Just then, a slender figure stepped out of the shadows and I couldn't believe my eyes.

It was Meagan.

CHAPTER 24
INTO TO THE FUTURE

I almost had to pinch myself. For months I'd wondered if Meagan was even alive. Here she was, in the flesh, looking more beautiful than I could ever remember. With a smile, she ran into my arms and forgetting the cameras and the watching eyes, I hugged her back. It was a long, comforting, but uncertain embrace. I didn't know how to act or what to think. It was all so new — this freedom to touch and to speak freely.

"Meagan. God, it's so good to see you." She smiled bashfully and Barry patted me on the back, pleased to see how happy I was. "Barry, how did you know where she would be?" I asked, continuing to look into her eyes.

"Remember way back when you submitted that complaint regarding a slave being mistreated by her master? I intercepted it and I've kept tabs on her whereabouts ever since. When the Crops went under siege, Meagan fought. I thought we could extract her. We need all the fighters we can get don't we?"

With that, Barry left us to ourselves. We stared at each other in silence for a moment and tears began to flow from Meagan's eyes.

She spoke with emotion, barely pausing to catch her breath, "I really didn't know what happened to you, Harrison. I figured they'd taken you away and killed you. So, I gave up all hope of having anything more than just a slave's life in the Crops. I was practically suicidal. Just when I felt it couldn't get worse, one of the Monitors approached me in the courtyard — and they brought me to you. I can hardly believe it. We had been under substantial restrictions at the Crops following the attacks and there were soldiers lining the hallways. The soldiers had even threatened my life. To them I was just another number."

Brushing the hair from her eyes and gently wiping her tears, the only thing I really wanted to do was kiss her. I pulled her close as she continued with her story.

Instinctively lowering her head, Meagan continued, "The Monitors had restricted our movements — we were only allowed to leave our buildings to go to work. There were some slaves who were still not being cooperative. There were even slaves who had decided not to go to work because of some call to boycott. I saw the request for the boycott come over on my computer."

Laughing gently, I lifted her chin so her eyes once again met mine. I said soothingly, "Yes, that was part of our plan. How did you handle it?"

"I was terrified. During the last few days with this boycott, there were more soldiers and more shootings along with an increased presence of Admins in the building. This morning, a Monitor stopped me and said I was needed to help transport supplies to Washington — to someone named Phoenix. I don't know who Phoenix is, just that he is a symbol of hope for us out there. People have been saying that he's the one fighting for our freedom. It wasn't until I arrived and spoke to Barry that he told me you were here."

It was clear that not all of the news of our revolt had reached the slave population. I wanted to tell Meagan that I was Phoenix, but I was anxious to hear more about happenings in the Crops.

"The Monitor escorted me past the Admins and they didn't do a thing. They didn't even check my identification number. They put me in a car and brought me here. I was so scared — I assumed I'd been targeted for elimination, as well. They kept telling me on the way here that everything would be okay, but I figured that this would be the end. And now... well..."

Meagan, coming to the end of her story, rested her head on my chest. I squeezed her again. I knew that it had been a long, trying journey for her. She had gone through what all slaves go through. She had been degraded and humiliated, she had feared for her life, but she still carried herself with a sense of dignity. Her words gave me renewed energy to keep fighting.

As I held her, I thought about how our actions of the past week were about more than us. Our actions were about liberating human beings, giving them true hope, and providing them with the opportunity to live and love. It was time to live freely without anyone to call "master." We were on a long journey toward freedom, but this was my first taste of the implications of our actions.

I don't know if Barry knew the favor he had done for not just me, but for us all. I now had clarity about why we had to be successful. There was no alternative. Failure was not an option. We needed to make sure that every slave in the United States experienced what Meagan and I were experiencing.

Walking Meagan up out of the garage and into the basement of the White House, I held off giving her a tour of the place. It was late, so I took her straight to the Lincoln bedroom to rest. We took a seat on the bed and I could tell she was exhausted.

"I know you're exhausted. If you want to lie down here, you can. But of course, you're free to do whatever you want."

She smiled timidly and said, "Then I choose to lie down here and do nothing." Then she gently lay down, her small frame dwarfed by the luxurious bed.

I joined her and we stared up at the ceiling and the ornate chandelier. An old, gothic-style painting surrounded the chandelier, and beautiful moldings spread out in a circular design from the center of the room. After a few minutes, I finally had the courage to look over at Meagan. She was smiling and looked so peaceful. It was amazing to lie there, looking at such a wonder.

Turning her head toward me, Meagan said, "I always knew you were special. Even when we were stuck in those two apartments with virtually no hope — even then, I knew. When you left, it seemed like all the air went out of me. I don't know why we're here or what's really going on, but I can say I'm happy to be here with you."

Pulling her close to me and embracing the comfortable silence between us, I finally felt at peace. I didn't really know what the future held for us, whether it be friendship or love, but I did know that right then, for the first time, I was happy.

We lay there and talked for hours. Meagan and I had a natural ability to communicate with one another. It was something that I sensed was true even when we were in the Crops. We talked and talked until we were both exhausted and fell asleep.

When I woke up the next morning, we were both still on top of the covers, lying there with the sun shining through one of the windows. I got up and went to wash and get dressed. By the time I came back to the bed, Meagan was still asleep. I walked out into the hallway to look for Ray or Barry, but I found Apex instead.

Apex put his hands on my shoulders, "You know something? We have a chance now, but we must be precise about our next step. I think you need to renew the call for a boycott. We have to keep the pressure up. We can't allow the state an opportunity to develop a plan. We must keep the president in a situation where he is reacting, versus acting. Put some thought into it and find me this afternoon in the command center."

"Yes, sir. I will meet you there," I said. "Did Barry fill you in on your meeting with the president?"

"Yes, he did, thanks. Gotta run — I'll see you this afternoon." Apex turned to leave then paused and added, "There's one more thing that I need to tell you."

Raising an eyebrow I asked, "And what might that be?"

Smiling Apex said with a laugh, "I'm glad you have your own woman now."

I smiled and shook my head. "Thanks, man."

I headed downstairs and found Barry, as usual, already up and running. As soon as he saw me, Barry waved me over and had one of his assistants put a call through to Senator Crest. He then handed me a cup of coffee and a headset and I took my seat, waiting to be connected to the senator.

Sounding upbeat, Crest said, "Good day, my friend. I hope you all got your supplies last night."

"Yes, sir. We've received the supplies and we're very thankful for your assistance. Now tell me, when is the earliest you can come meet us so we can hammer out the final details before the president has his meeting with Apex?"

I could hear him shuffling papers and he said, "The earliest would be this evening around seven."

"That's perfect! I have to debrief my team and prepare Apex. Please reach out if anything changes. Thanks, Brad."

After the call, I felt I had some breathing room and time to unwind with Meagan. I knew we had to be on our toes and keep applying pressure to President Hood, but I also wanted to be sure Meagan was fully acclimated to her new surroundings.

After a quick check in with the council, I ran upstairs to the bedroom where I had left Meagan. It was reaching midday and I wanted to make sure she was okay. Before I could reach the bedroom, she rounded the corner, walking toward me with a smile on her face. It was good to see her smiling, and I knew the feeling. This was her first day of freedom, and even though we were locked in this oasis and surrounded by military presence, we were free to communicate and, perhaps even more importantly, touch.

I gave Meagan a quick hug and a kiss on the cheek. Laughing in her shy way, she asked, "Where do I go to get something to eat?"

"Downstairs in the kitchen next to the command center. Come, I'll show you."

Walking hand in hand, I finally began to tell her more about how we ended up here. The chef provided us with a great lunch and we found a secluded spot for us to eat as I continued to tell her the history of the revolution. I told her about the tunnels and Apex. I told her about Barry and Ray and the separate plan we had concocted. And I told her that I was in fact Phoenix.

"I knew it," she said with a smile. "I mean, I hoped. Somehow, I just had a feeling it was you all along."

Meagan was full of questions about the revolution, speaking with the heads of state, and what it was like to finally be free. During a pause in the conversation, she looked at me quizzically and said, "You're so not the man that left the Crops, nor the man I shared a dance with. You've changed, and I can tell you're coming into your own. Freedom looks nice on you."

Blushing slightly, I said, "If it weren't for Apex, then none of this would've been possible."

Meagan looked deeply into my eyes. "You hold Apex with high regard. After everything he accomplished, I can see why."

"The man created something out of nothing and then turned my simple act of individuality into a personal mantra for this movement. I respect Apex a lot, and for him to allow me to make his vision a reality says a lot about his character."

I didn't want to burden her with the details of the fighting that took place for Apex and I to get to where we were today. I explained to her that I was a little uncomfortable with being called Phoenix. The name, I thought, raised expectations of me to an unattainable level and glamorized my small act of resistance to legend. But I also acknowledge that the aura of being Phoenix was a great tool to motivate the others. She listened intently to everything I said, and her questions made it clear that she was fascinated by all that had happened.

I could have talked all day, but eventually an assistant came by and said it was time to prep for our meeting with Crest. Glancing at the clock, it was four thirty-five. Where had the time gone? I told Meagan that I'd have one of the staff members give her tour and that I needed to prepare for my meeting with Crest.

Standing up, Meagan embraced me and then, unexpectedly, gave me a soft, gentle kiss.

"Go be the best Phoenix you can and then come back to me alive, Mr. Harrison."

"You have my word, Ms. Meagan."

As I headed to the meeting with Ray, Barry, and Apex, I felt invincible and ready to tackle anything.

Apex, looking fully rested for a change said, "Harrison, have you thought of anything new to add to the boycott?"

"I have some ideas, but the main questions we need to ask before Senator Crest arrives are as follows: What's our end game? How can we attain this goal? And how can we ensure President Hood doesn't go back on his word?"

We tossed around several ideas before coming up with an outline that would be flexible enough to change if the need arose. Judging from the unfolding of events lately, we had to be both prepared *and* flexible.

We adjourned the meeting with nearly three hours to spare. Crest was running late and wouldn't be here until closer to eight. I took full advantage of this opportunity to spend some downtime with Meagan. I found her waiting in the Lincoln bedroom and we decided to watch some TV.

Barry and his team had worked their magic to ensure that the TVs could now receive all types of programming, including movies. This kind of TV was a luxury — in the Crops Meagan and I had both only had a handful of channels to watch. Flipping through channels, we came across a movie called *Toy Story.* Meagan and I watched in amazement. The animation was fantastic and it was a story of cooperation; a story of achievement. I liked the character Buzz Lightyear. He intrigued me, because his capabilities far exceeded those he possessed in reality. In the end, Buzz was still able to make a contribution, ignoring those same limitations. The movie was a great diversion, but immediately thereafter it was back to business. We turned to the NNC to catch up.

The NNC was once again conducting interviews with white Americans regarding the recent crisis in the Crops and our efforts toward ending slavery. Many interviewees indicated their amazement that a group of slaves could impact the American public so profoundly. There was also a consistent theme: Americans were starting to lose faith in President Hood. To many, the most compelling issue was that I was able to communicate with the president of China. They found it shocking that I had received Jinping's immediate concession. This really seemed to be a point of emphasis. These actions represented not only my group's strength, but Hood's weakness. He was failing, and the American people knew it.

Concerning the overall issue of slavery, most of those interviewed said they thought it was time for slavery to end. The sentiments were surprising to me; I had always believed that the overwhelming majority of Americans favored slavery. But when I thought back to my experiences, I began to realize that most of my interactions with white Americans were not oppressive. Many of the whites with whom I had contact simply acted as if I didn't exist. They expressed neither sympathy nor concern about me or my fellow slaves. We coexisted and we all had our roles, and that was it.

Most of the oppression I'd witnessed came from the Admins or those who had official positions, including masters and employers. Sure, there were some clear oppressors, like Meagan's masters who took advantage of the situation. But overall, people had seemed indifferent to slavery — it was just something that existed. Perhaps America was ready to abolish slavery and start a new path after all.

Interviews conducted overseas indicated that foreign opinions were much stronger. Many felt that Americans were hypocrites; after all, our government officials felt they had a moral mandate to take the lead concerning world affairs. And yet, America was the biggest oppressor of human rights in the world. Talk about morality. Those interviewed in Europe and other countries expressed that America needed to abolish slavery in order to truly become a leader concerning world affairs. Several people expressed disgust that America had become such an overwhelming economic power. Countries like Russia and China wanted to even the playing field by removing the cheap labor offered by slavery, and many there noted that a competitive balance was healthy for world affairs.

"It's amazing that you were the tipping point for this to happen," Meagan said after the broadcast had finished.

"Well, it was Apex who pulled me into his world. If it weren't for him, I would've been dead a long time ago."

It was true. I couldn't take the credit for what had transpired. Apex was the genius and the Founding Father of the resistance. I had simply been a cog that fit. But now I was dedicated to helping us reach the end game.

Meagan took my hand in hers and I was immediately flooded with warmth. She was the calming influence I needed. I knew that there would be difficult and complex times ahead, but, with her by my side, I felt complete and ready to take on the world.

CHAPTER 25
THE PRESIDENT

As it grew closer to our meeting time, I felt more comfortable. The supplies Brad had sent provided everyone with a new change of clothes. They were nothing fancy, just some jeans and t-shirts. But, they were fresh, clean clothes. I also had a new pair of underwear and those were, indeed, a welcomed sight. I ensured that Meagan received new clothes as well, and then prepared for the meeting with Brad. We'd decided that the meeting would take place upstairs in the Blue Room. It was a quiet location away from all the activity.

I arrived early to clear my mind and took a heavy gulp of cola. I hadn't had this beverage since my time as a breeder and it was uniquely refreshing. Soon enough, Senator Crest appeared, escorted by Apex.

Shaking his hand, I said, "Welcome, Brad! Apex, please have a seat and join us."

Apex shook his head. "I must respectfully decline. I have to prepare myself for the meeting with our president, but Phoenix, please fill me in later. Carry on men; I know I leave you both in good hands."

Apex closed the door behind him, and Crest and I sat down. Initially, I was prepared to discuss our overall plan. However, it still bothered me that Apex would meet with Hood. "Brad, what do you think about Apex meeting the president? Seems kinda odd, doesn't it?"

Crest leaned back in his chair and folded his hands in his lap, "It does. Honestly? Hood is a snake. Apex doesn't appear to be the type to be manipulated, but Hood is probably setting us up in some way. He could also be planning some divide and conquer tactic. Apex should coordinate with us extensively before making any statements or having any conversations."

Crest was right, and we agreed that the best course was for Apex to avoid meeting with the president at all. But this would be an almost impossible sell and it would likely be difficult to get Apex to listen. Apex had spent the past several years planning and training for this opportunity. For him, like me, meeting with the president would be a dream come true. Although he had given ultimate control over to me, this was still his baby — his design. And his demeanor revealed that he still presided over it all. Still, Crest and I agreed that I needed to convince Apex not to meet with the president, no matter how disappointing that would be.

My conversation with Crest complete, I shook his hand and then walked to Apex's room. He answered the door gruffly, clearly not wanting to be interrupted. His shirt was unbuttoned and there were clothes strewn across his bed. I said sternly, "We need to talk."

"Not right now man. I've got to get dressed. Big meeting for us today," he replied, turning his back to me.

I entered the room and closing the door behind me said, "We need to cancel this meeting with the president. I think he is using you."

Apex continued to go through his clothes as he shook his head. "Cancel? No, it's too late and too important. We've got to keep moving forward. This may be the most important meeting in African American history. Can you imagine? A former slave meeting directly with the president?"

I stepped between Apex and the bed, "This is not just a meeting between you and the president; this is a meeting between you and Hood. The guy is a weasel who will do anything to remedy the fact that he has been embarrassed and humiliated by slaves. Why else would he want to meet with just you instead of meeting with us both? Why is he making you come to him? How does this meeting advance the resistance? What are the specific goals for the meeting? C'mon Apex think… this is a set-up. Even Crest sees that we're being manipulated."

Apex pushed me to the side without looking up. "Ah, I see. You and Crest. You are now the face of the revolution and he is your master, huh? What's he got you doing next? Tap-dancing on the White House lawn? You can't stand that the president wants to meet with me and not you. Well, I started this, Harrison. And now I'm gonna finish it. This revolution is bigger than just us. It's not about who; it's about what. And that 'what' is freedom."

There was something close to malice in Apex's words, and for the first time, I sensed a pettiness in his actions. As noble as Apex had always been, he had also exhibited an impulsive side. But this? It felt like jealousy and desperation to remain relevant to the insurrection that he had started.

Just then, Tyra walked into the room and began helping Apex with his tie. I stood there silently, acutely aware that there was no way I was going to change this man's mind. "Apex, I really think you need to consider not going." Neither Apex nor Tyra acknowledged my comment as he continued dressing. I walked out without saying goodbye.

About two hours later I stood in the garage with Barry and Ray, waiting to see Apex off. As he entered the garage, Apex gave a quick nod and we approached him, doing our best to show some support.

Barry spoke, all business, "Ok, Apex. Your meeting will be at the old Capitol building. It is secure and they would only allow three people to attend with you. The press will be there and you and the president will each give a brief speech prior to your private meeting."

Interjecting, Ray said, "Be careful, Apex. It would take just one lunatic to take you out. Frankly, I wouldn't put it past Hood to coordinate something like that. Security is a major concern here, man."

Waving at him dismissively, Apex said, "Ray, stop being such a mother hen. The president would be an idiot to try something in front of the whole world. I'm good."

As Apex spoke, a car pulled up and out stepped Apex's assembled entourage. The men included two guards and Christian, Barry's younger assistant who I'd met during my first night in the tunnels. Christian had distinguished himself during the move to the White House and I'd taken a liking to him. He was a taller, darker kid who seemed to have an endless amount of energy. Lately, he tagged along behind Ray and he was always thoughtful and eager to help. I was happy we were sending a "team" with Apex, but my mind kept returning to Michael — the young operative we'd spoken to on the day of the attacks. We had never heard from him again. As the weeks dragged on, I assumed he'd been killed in the Crops. I was concerned that we were sending these guys into a similar situation, and I couldn't bear losing more lives.

Not only were Christian and the guards unprepared, they seemed terrified. I really wanted to pull rank and abort this whole mess, but I knew at this point, nothing I said would make a difference. Apex was determined to fulfill his destiny and I couldn't stop him.

Putting in his earpiece, Apex looked at Ray and said, "Like I said, we have this covered."

Ray's eyes still spoke of worry, but his voice didn't convey it. "I'll always have your back, Apex. Just need to keep you safe is all."

"I know. Thanks, brother," he said. Then turning toward me he added, "Harrison — you're in charge, my man." I smiled and shook Apex's hand, once again humbled by the faith he continued to carry for me but still apprehensive about his negative comments earlier.

Barry quietly said, "There goes Samson on his way to the lion's den."

Raising my eyebrows in question, I asked, "Don't you mean Daniel?"

"No, that's Samson. Apex will not be passive in the face of danger." I shook my head and thought to myself, *it's still a lion's den.*

CHAPTER 26
INSIDE MAN

It had become a frenzied circus around the White House, and we all watched intently as the news broadcast Apex's departure. As soon as Apex's car reached the White House gates, it was joined by a procession of police vehicles. The drive between the White House and the Capitol Building was less than two miles, but it was clear this trip would take a while. Outside the gates, the tanks still sat along with crowds of people, all waiting to see what happened next.

The newscast showed the entire procession. It took almost forty-five minutes as people flooded the streets, banging on the car windows and shouting words of encouragement or words of malice. People waved signs reading, "Go home, slaves," or "Freedom for all," or "Commit to Resist." It was an overwhelming sight to see. Amongst the sea of white bodies, a handful of black slaves could be spotted, some holding white children, and — astonishingly — a few holding hands with their white allies who had come out to support them.

Once the vehicles reached the Capitol, Apex's car was mobbed by reporters. He and his men were escorted out of the vehicle and onto the steps of the old Capitol where the president and a group of dignitaries were waiting. Apex's eyes were wide and sweat dripped from his brow as he began shaking hands with people. For me, it was odd to see him look entirely vulnerable. As he approached Hood,

Apex stood taller and set his shoulders back; he had quite a few inches on the president even when slouching. Hood managed an exaggerated smile and his eyes were almost wild as he shook Apex's hand. To Apex's credit, he didn't flinch but just stared back with a blank face that would impress the most seasoned poker pro.

I didn't like the subtitle the NNC put on the screen: "Slave to meet with president." How demeaning of them despite all our efforts. I looked over at Tyra. She was standing in a group, also watching the broadcast. She had her arms folded and fidgeted uncomfortably. I understood; none of us were used to seeing one of our own so exposed.

After several minutes of handshakes and schmoozing, Hood stepped up to the podium. "The past few days have been trying for our community and the country," he said. "Many have died. Others have had their lives changed. Despite it all, the institutions that form the fabric of our great country remain intact. Those great institutions will continue to be the pillars that hold up our country through all difficult times."

I listened closely to the president's speech. One of his so-called "pillars" was the institution of slavery and now he was planning to use Apex to his advantage. Unfortunately, Apex's ambition and arrogance had made him an easy target.

The president wrapped up his speech by noting that he and Apex, "the leader of the slave insurrection," would have lengthy talks about how to resolve the crisis and ensure that nothing like this ever happened again.

Apex then stepped to the podium. He looked around at the crowd and the cameras and looked for a moment like he may faint. It was apparent that Hood had played him for a fool. Hood was likely betting that Apex was inarticulate and that there would be a stark difference in his appearance. He hoped this would reinforce the difference between slaves and their more intelligent masters.

Apex spoke in a smooth, even tone, maintaining his composure the best he could. "Thank you for coming. This is a new beginning.

This is a day that African Americans have dreamed of for centuries. It is an opportunity for us to start over. Former slaves must have their rights. And the time is now for our country to respond." Apex then backed away from the mic as applause rang through the crowd. Several agents then came forward and quickly escorted Apex and the president away to begin their talks.

I turned around in the crowded control room and saw Meagan in the back. I motioned for her to come stand by me. I took her hand and we walked over to Tyra to lend some support. Meagan patted Tyra on the back and said, "He'll be just fine. Apex has it under control." But Tyra's eyes were wet with tears.

Over the next few hours, there were periodic breaking news reports of the interactions between the president and Apex. The first report showed video footage of Apex and the president meeting. They were in some huge conference room with about fifteen of the president's advisors seated around a large conference table. I couldn't help but think that this image was calculated to make Apex look small and insignificant versus the government officials. If that was the plan, it worked. Apex looked overwhelmed, his usual poise gone by the wayside.

Later, there was a live report showing Apex having dinner with the president. They were seated at a formal table with three other gentlemen. Apex still had on his same clothes but the president had changed into a more formal, dark suit with a shiny blue tie. In his worn, charcoal suit, Apex seemed unsophisticated and out of place.

The more I watched, the angrier I became. Meagan sensed my anxiety, noting, "Doesn't look good, does it? I mean he looks out of place."

"Yeah, I mean, I told him but he still fell right into their trap. Someone on the fence would buy into that crap that our race is naturally inferior. Apex is just helping the president's argument."

After the live coverage of the dinner ended, the reporters noted that Apex and the president would have one final meeting and then

Apex would be on his way back to the White House. The report complete, the broadcast switched to footage from a New Year's parade that had been held several days before. The New Year had come and gone without our knowledge as we all focused on the task at hand. I prayed this would be a year of positive change for us all. I walked to the window. Even though it was now early evening, there was still a massive crowd of reporters and on-lookers waiting for Apex's return.

The wait was agonizing. Three hours passed and there was no Apex. There were no new reports and no updates concerning his departure and my anxiety grew. My first assumption was that the president and Apex were engaged in additional talks. So I was not immediately alarmed. But after a fourth hour with no contact, I was really concerned. I located Barry and asked if he had any intel. But none of his calls to officials in Richmond were answered.

After several failed attempts, I was finally able to reach Crest. "This is bad, Crest. It has been hours with absolutely no contact. Have you heard anything?"

Crest was confused as well. "I haven't heard a thing concerning Apex's whereabouts. But it seems we were right — this whole thing was a set up to make the resistance and Apex look bad."

I begged Crest to look into it further and he promised to call me back within an hour. Then, just prior to midnight, before Crest could call me back, the activity level picked up outside the White House. A police escort slowly worked its way through the crowd. Behind the first three police cars was Apex's car. Meagan and I ran downstairs and onto the White House lawn. The police cars gave way and allowed Apex's car to enter through the gate. As we waited, we were joined by the rest of our team. Everyone was eager to greet him.

The car drove up and stopped in the driveway. There was a brief pause and then one of the car doors opened. It seemed like a thousand cameras were flashing outside of the White House fence. One by one, Apex's three men stepped out. Their heads were down in the old submissive stance we'd all grown accustomed to in the Crops. I immediately sensed that there was something wrong. I walked up to the car and looked in but Apex wasn't there. I turned to one of the men who travelled with Apex, "Where is he?"

Christian replied, a look of concern on his face, "They took him from us. Separated us. We haven't seen him since dinner."

Just then I felt a hand on my shoulder. It was Barry. "Harrison, you need to come inside and see this." We rushed inside and headed straight to the control room. There was breaking news. The reporter was explaining that the slave leader, Apex, had been taken to Georgetown University Hospital and was in the intensive care unit after a suspected allergic reaction. The reporter noted that security was tight at the hospital and that the president's spokesman was scheduled to speak in minutes.

I sent Meagan to console Tyra and called Crest again. There was no answer. Before I could make another call, the reporter was interviewing the president's surrogate. The spokesperson was somber, "The slave leader fell sick immediately following tonight's dinner. He developed convulsions and lost consciousness. He was immediately transported to the medical center and is receiving the best medical care. That is all the information we have at this time."

I pulled Barry and Ray aside. Ray, with his usual concern asked, "Should we try to get to the hospital? Somebody needs to check on him."

"No," I said, though it pained me. "This is Hood's doing, I just know it. It's too risky for any of us to leave right now."

Barry asked, "Are you sure? Apex started this all. He's the heart of the revolution. If something happens to him…"

I responded without hesitation, "This revolution is bigger than any one individual. We can't risk it. We really don't know where he is. What if he's not even at the hospital when we get there? We don't know what the real circumstances are. If we get out there and we're captured, it's over."

Ray blurted sharply, "This isn't about you being the leader of the resistance, is it? With Apex gone, it's all about you." Ray's voice clammed up with his last words, and I could tell he regretted the comment.

I took a step toward Ray, "I'm hurting too, man. Apex is my friend as well. But we must remain focused. Hood is a powerful man — and a dangerous one."

I walked up to my room. It was now past two in the morning. Meagan was waiting for me and we both lay awake for hours, trying to muster the strength to face tomorrow.

CHAPTER 27
IN THE MOURNING

The sunrise had little significance. I had only dozed off for moments during the night. I was up and calling Crest right after seven o'clock. When he answered, it was clear that he had also been up most of the night. He anticipated my questions and spoke with anger in his voice, "Apparently Apex is still at the hospital. Security is extremely tight, and I can't get through. I don't know what his condition is. But this stinks to high hell. Hood orchestrated this."

I felt trapped. There was nothing I could do. I asked Crest, "Do you think I should try to get to the hospital myself? It would bring more attention to the situation."

Crest's response was swift and precise, "No way. You are too important. Apex is either sick or captured. Either way, I'm sure Hood would love to get his hands on you. We need to let the facts develop and react in the best way we can."

Crest promised to get in touch as soon as he had additional details. I went back to the room to see about Meagan. She was still sleeping and I was glad of it. I would need her to be well rested as the day progressed. Most of our White House team was already up and working. I paused to observe the activity: former slaves all over the White House. It was an amazing sight. Everyone wanted to know whether I had additional information about Apex.

I sought out Barry and Ray, and found them in the kitchen. Ray was the first to speak, "Harrison, I'm sorry about what I said last night. I'm kinda stressed about Apex."

"I understand." I replied. "It's tough for us all. How is Tyra?"

Barry chimed in, "She's holding up well, but she wants Apex back here as soon as possible."

I started to reiterate the reasons why we simply couldn't pursue a more aggressive posture in pursuing Apex's return. Before I could get a full sentence out, someone yelled "No!" in the hallway. Then we heard a few screams and frenzied movement. We rushed out into the hallway. About fifty of us were gathered around one of the large monitors. One of the girls was turning away from the group with her hands over her face. I pushed through the group and up to the monitor. There on the screen in large letters was: "BREAKING NEWS... Slave Leader 'Apex' has died at Georgetown Hospital."

Everything went silent as I stood there frozen. All around me was chaos people crying and shouting — but I heard none of it. Ray took Tyra to Apex's room. I slowly made my way back to the Lincoln bedroom, waving away anybody who tried to stop me.

I opened the door and looked over at Meagan. She was still asleep. I parted the curtains and glanced out the window. The tanks were still there. The police cars were still there. Reporters were gathering. Apex was dead. Storm clouds had begun to gather in the sky and all at once, I felt like I was standing naked in the rain. Who was I and what was I doing here? I was wholly inadequate to handle Hood and lead this revolution.

Behind me, Meagan stirred and rolled toward me. She said sleepily, "Good morning."

I did not mince words, "Meagan, Apex is dead." In silence, she crossed to me and threw her arms around my waist. Her warmth and comfort meant everything to me in that moment.

For the next few hours, I isolated myself in the room with Meagan. I refused to answer the door. I knew everyone had questions, but I had no answers. For now, I needed to be alone with the one person who I felt would never judge me. By mid-afternoon, I had mustered enough inside to exit the room.

Crest had left me a message that he would immediately initiate a special investigation concerning Apex's death. I didn't call him immediately. Instead, I asked Barry to convene our leaders. Maybe — collectively — we could come up with some strategy. Tyra was understandably absent.

I started the meeting by pausing for a moment of silence in Apex's honor. I then clarified that I had no additional details about Apex's death. Barry summarized all that we knew about the events, and he noted importantly, "We decided not to venture out and try to rescue Apex. We would not have been successful and it would have been too dangerous..." Christian gave a summary of the events leading to their separation from Apex. He noted that, prior to the dinner, he and the guards were treated with respect and allowed to remain together. However, as the dinner approached, they were escorted back to their car and provided food and drink to eat on the way back. They repeatedly requested to see Apex, but were not allowed. Christian noted in a hoarse voice, "I knew something was wrong when they told us it was time to leave and Apex was nowhere to be found."

In truth, there were no solutions readily available. There was no quick fix. We debated the possibility of me making a statement, but we decided against it. What good could it do us at this point? Our main priority for the time being was to recover Apex's body so we could pay our proper respects.

After the meeting, I returned to my room. Strangely, I briefly yearned for the uncomplicated moments I had experienced in the Crops. Oppressive as it had been, at least there my big decisions had all been made for me. My decisions were simple: cook a little Salisbury steak? Watch a little television? I quickly dismissed the thought. No matter how tough the times, this was better than being a slave. I took a seat in my bedroom so I could think for a minute. That minute lasted all night.

Chapter 28
An Awakening

Around nine o'clock, a gentle knocking came on the door and upon opening it I saw Barry standing there with a tray of food and a meek smile. He spoke quietly, "You need to eat and get dressed. Everyone is calling to speak to you and I can't lie anymore."

Taking the food, I said flatly, "Why would anyone want to speak to me?"

"You're the leader of the revolution, aren't you?"

"No, Apex was. I just helped him live his dream."

"Harrison, Apex isn't with us anymore and the mantle of leadership now clearly falls on you." Barry said solemnly. "You can do this. And you're not alone," he added, placing a hand on my shoulder.

I gestured for Barry to follow me to an adjacent living room so Meagan could sleep. I was trying to chew over what Barry just said, but the taste was bitter in my mouth. This was a responsibility I'd never asked for — it had fallen in my lap and I wasn't sure I could carry it.

Placing my food tray on a table, I said, "Barry, listen, we don't know where we stand with the government at this point, much less anything else that really matters. Has anybody been in contact with Hood, Moore, or their men? I'm trying to get my head together here."

For the first time since we'd met, Barry raised his voice, his brow creased with anger, "You act like the rest of us aren't grieving! Right now Tyra is down there talking to the press and setting up interviews for you while Ray is talking to new contacts in Mexico. Heck, the whole staff is trying to keep this thing going despite our loss. Emotions have to be on hold right now. This is about abolishing slavery. It's about more than any one person."

Barry's words hit me hard. His once peaceful face was disfigured with rage and he shook his head, no longer able to look me in the eyes.

My voice broke a bit as I replied, "I'm so sorry, Barry. I didn't know everyone was doing this for me."

Pausing to swallow, Barry spoke more calmly, "Harrison, this isn't for you. It's for the rest of us who are counting on you to lead us toward freedom. This isn't just about you, and you need to get that through your head right now, man."

He left me there stunned and speechless. The entire team had rallied over Apex's death — unwilling to give up — and here was I, letting them all down. I didn't hear Meagan approach until I felt her delicate hand on my shoulder.

"Is everything okay?" she asked with a raised eyebrow. Her hair was tousled from sleep and she wore an old, worn shirt from one of my cleaner's uniforms that fell almost to her knees. She looked more lovely than ever.

"Yes, my love. I just found out that while I'm here wallowing in self-pity and licking my wounds, the rest of our team is down there pursuing our freedom. I'm an ass." I sank into a chair, resting my head in my hands.

Meagan stepped toward me, and cradling my head against her stomach, she said, "Harrison, we both needed a moment to be alone and breathe. But now it's time to get back out there and fight."

After kissing her hands, I left to take a quick shower and face the music that was playing at the dawn of a new America. Even if it killed me, I was determined to see us through to the future that Apex envisioned.

An hour later, Crest arrived to discuss plans going forward. Before entering the White House, he stopped briefly to speak to members of the press who continued to hover outside our gates. For now, his words would serve as a statement from the rest of us. We needed to lay low.

Our core team met in the entryway to greet Brad. He handed a bouquet of white roses to Tyra, who accepted them graciously while fighting back tears. I escorted Brad to the Oval Office and we took a seat, ready to get down to business.

Brad started, "My good friend, it appears that many of your activities are starting to take hold across America. Polls show that despite his careful staging and propaganda, the American people are soundly against the president. Certain individuals have started to form a coalition for the abolishment of slavery. This is all happening very rapidly and we must capitalize on it."

I smiled. This was the first good news in days. "First, thank you for taking that leap of faith before you even knew any of us. It took guts to step out and advocate for us, and I know you've put your career on the line. We appreciate you more than I can express, Brad."

"This is not about my career. This is about ending slavery. It's about what's right."

"This resistance — " I began and Brad cut me off with a wave of his hand.

"This is no longer a resistance, Harrison, this is now a *movement*. This is history and you must start recognizing the profound nature of what you are achieving. You may not take full stock of it, but you are sitting in the White House discussing the abolition of a centuries old institution in America. Your actions could profoundly affect the lives of millions upon millions today and forever."

Letting his words sink in, I replied after a moment, "Well, then let's make sure the history books get my name right." Crest laughed.

"What's your last name, Harrison? You know, for the books," Crest smiled warmly.

I paused — nobody had ever asked me that before. "Vance. Or at least that's what's on my papers. I, of course, never knew my family."

"Harrison Vance," Crest said smiling. "That has a nice ring to it. You should own it."

Own it. A year ago I'd never dreamed of owning a thing — let alone myself. Now I was a free man. I smiled and nodded my head. Crest was right — this was history in the making and if we held on, millions of people would be afforded the same opportunity.

I wanted to find out from Crest what the next move should be from his perspective. My thought was that we look at additional boycotts. Crest agreed but added that the boycotts must start immediately. The economic pressure placed on the American businessman would be compelling and it was a way to place indirect pressure on Hood's administration. If the boycotts picked up momentum and we could get at least half of the slave population to stay home, it would crush our economy and Hood would have no choice but to reconsider.

Crest noted, "The president will likely experience additional loss of support in light of Apex's death. A lot of good people are suspicious about how he died. Hood is vulnerable. It's time to propose a new option for president. We need a new president who can not only unite us, but show that the United States is serious about ending slavery and moving forward with the rest of the world. This new president must send a message to the world that we are a free state ready to deal with the world economy on equal and fair footing. This would open doors to more trade and more success for Americans abroad. Many international doors have been closed for years because of our reliance on slavery. We need to open up those markets immediately to ensure a better future for our children and grandchildren."

These were glorious words to me and I said, "Well, this will be an exciting time for all of us if we can achieve the end of slavery. As Speaker of the House, you're the next in line, Brad, and you'd make a fine president. With your leadership, we could build an infrastructure to eliminate hypocrisy in America." It was true. I could think of nobody more suited for the presidential seat than Bradley Crest.

Looking down and smiling, Crest said, "Oh, I would love to become president. It has been a dream of mine ever since I was a child. But I'm not the right person for the job."

Dumbfounded I responded, "Well, who then?"

"We need someone who's sympathetic to the cause and who's willing to sacrifice everything to initiate change. Even if given the opportunity, I'd turn it down because I'm not the best choice. That person is you, Harrison."

My heart stopped and for a moment I thought my eyes would fall out of my head. "America would never go for this, Brad! It has to be you!"

Crest spoke with firm authority, "This is all about putting the right person in place and sending a bold message to America and to the world. It's you, Harrison. I will fight for you to be our next president."

I sat in silence for a minute or two as the room spun around me. I was stunned by Crest's faith in me and shocked that I was even considering the possibility.

Finally, I said slowly, "There's no way this could ever happen, Brad. I'm just a former slave seeking freedom for my fellow man. America isn't ready to have a slave lead them in the highest office of the land."

Crest leaned forward and grabbed me by the shoulders, "Harrison, it will happen. It is already happening. I will be pushing for a special election to be held this November. That gives us eleven months to campaign and prepare. I will then push for Congress to do something unique. I will call for them to pass the Uniform Suffrage Act, which calls for an immediate end to slavery and the right for all slaves to vote."

I opened my mouth to speak but Crest cut me off, "I know it sounds far-fetched, but listen to me. This movement has already made a tremendous impact. People have had it with Hood, and America by and large favors abolishment. I have my men on this and it seems that many in the Senate are behind us. This *can* work."

Crest continued, stating that, under his proposal, blacks would be granted freedom to land, healthcare, and a host of other benefits. I could tell that he had been planning this for a long time. He patiently answered my every question and even presented the full details of the Act on his personal computer.

Wrapping up his pitch, Crest said, "The Uniform Suffrage Act will include a provision that states, in the event Hood and Benz are removed by impeachment or other means, Congress will have the right to initiate a special election to select a new president. This would clear the path for a special proceeding whereby a majority vote in Congress would select the new president.

"It is my hope that you will be able to gather enough votes to become the next president of the United States. I would expect the congressional vote to be impacted by the fact that African Americans will be able to vote in the next election. That is the path we are embarking on this evening. I really hope you'll stand with me on this, Harrison. We can't do it without you."

I really didn't know what to say. All of it was unimaginable. Less than a year ago, I was a slave in the Crops with no possibility of becoming anything more. Now Bradley Crest and I were sitting in the White House as he suggested that I become the next president of the United States. My first thought was to turn and run, but then I thought of Barry's words. Our whole team was determined to see this movement through to the end and they were counting on me to lead them to victory. Perhaps this was my destiny — and perhaps it could work. I needed to do this; for my team and for Apex.

With Apex's resolve as my strength, I said to Crest, "If that is the course as you see it, sir, then I am more than willing to fulfill my duty."

Crest grinned, "Great. You will not regret this decision. We should keep this to ourselves while the plans are unfolding. You need to call for a press conference tonight and immediately announce additional boycotts in response to Apex's death. America needs to be reminded that their quality of life is dependent on slaves whom their president doesn't even consider human. This will wake them up for sure."

Standing up to signal the end of our meeting, I said, "It certainly sounds like a plan that could work. I just hope that the country is ready to consider this."

I held my hand out for a handshake but Crest pulled me in for a hug. It occurred to me that I'd never hugged a white person before. It was hard to believe that we'd just had a conversation that could change the world. Crest left down the hall and I walked toward the window and inhaled deeply. As I watched the setting sun, I saw our future on the rise.

I called on Barry to set up a press conference as soon as possible. We scheduled it for eight o'clock the next evening. Since it would be an evening press conference, I decided to hold it inside the White House in one of our conference rooms.

We agreed to allow eight reporters in for an exclusive tour and photoshoot with our team prior to the press conference. Barry and Ray worked diligently to set up a security infrastructure to easily escort people through the gate and to their designated locations without fear that they'd wander off. During the previous days, Ray had worked tirelessly to put in place some infrastructure at the White House that would allow us to remain relatively secure. With everything in place, I sent our team to bed for some rest. Tomorrow we'd announce the boycotts and Crest's plans would be set in motion.

The next evening arrived in the blink of an eye. At eight o'clock I strode confidently to the podium. Barry's assistants had set us up with some microphones. The room was packed with camera crews. The eight selected reporters were seated; a mixture of men and women who were eager to hear what I had to say. I recognized a young female reporter from the NNC and knew that we'd have global coverage.

Meagan had pressed my suit and placed a white carnation in the lapel — "For Apex," she said. I touched the flower and lowered my head for a moment as I gathered the strength to speak. It occurred to me that not only was I doing this for Apex and our team, but for every person who had ever lived as a slave in the United States. It was time for me to prove myself as presidential material. The pressure was almost overwhelming.

I cleared my throat and spoke, "In light of the tragic death of our leader, Apex, today we mark the continuation of a series of actions aimed at creating equality across the United States. Our goal is to not only to create domestic equality, but to create global opportunity for the United States. For far too long, the United States has suffered from an inability to benefit from the exercise of its full potential internationally. We have been unable to affect affairs in the Middle East because we lack the ability to speak from a moral high ground. We have been unable to maximize our true economic potential with Asia, because we relish in an artificial economic advantage. We have been unable to fully benefit from our close relationship with our European allies, because we have engaged in hypocrisy. My desire is for *all* men and women — black, white, Hispanic, Asian — to benefit from the true potential that our country offers. As such, I present a continued call for the end of slavery here in the United States, and I urge President Hood to heed my word. It's time to bring this mutually beneficial goal to realization. Furthermore, I call on all of my slave brothers and sisters across the United States to boycott their work activity starting tomorrow and take a stand to end slavery once and for all."

Cameras flashed in my eyes, making it impossible for me to see my notes. I was thankful that Ray had made me memorize the speech just in case. He was a mother hen for sure, but with good intentions.

"Our call for a boycott is based on a desire to demonstrate not only our unity, but our importance to the American economy. We have lived as slaves for decades upon decades, unable to speak for ourselves or enact change. But we are no longer slaves; we are African Americans. We are part of the fabric of American society. We are all one team and we share one goal: to maximize our ultimate potential. We see this boycott as a means to an end. To my fellow slaves: I look forward to working with you to bring our situation to a glorious conclusion where *all* Americans, including *African* Americans may reap the benefits and rights that were first articulated in our own constitution. May the Blessings of Liberty be bestowed upon us all. Goodnight, and God bless you all."

With a firm nod, I stepped down from the podium and exited the room. I once again decided not to answer questions, it was simply too dangerous at this point. I returned to the command room to watch the reactions from the various news stations. The responses coming in were decidedly positive and I could have wept with relief. This moment was an affirmation of Crest's promise that this was an opportunity to change the world.

I watched the monitors for a while with Meagan cozied by my side. I hadn't yet told her about Crest's plans for me to become president, and I wondered how she'd react. For the first time it occurred to me that she could be my first lady. After all, I couldn't image doing any of this without her. After several hours, Meagan and I headed back to our room and went to bed. It would be a sound night with all the incredible possibilities that lay ahead tomorrow.

CHAPTER 29
CHANGE GON' COME

The next morning started with a flurry of activity. Waking up later than I intended at nine o'clock, I got ready to speak with Brad Crest, who was waiting for me on the phone.

"Well, your speech had a major impact on the workforce," he said. "Over thirty percent of the slave labor force in the United States decided to follow the boycott. Your speech last night hit home and now it's being repeated over and over for everyone to be reminded how important it is to end this."

"I can't take all the credit now, Brad. Barry edited the speech and sent it out all over the Internet." It was true. I'd be lost without my team.

"We need to show that we are in talks to end the boycott and then we can begin the other phases of the plan. Right now Congress is abuzz about your speech and the support from other African Americans. The idea of ending slavery has gained traction."

Apparently, the effectiveness of the boycott was a big blow to the president. Hood was fighting public relations issues from all fronts. And even his most loyal supporters continued to question Hood's role in Apex's death.

The Hood Administration was hoping that our actions would have a limited impact, however, the boycotts permeated every aspect of American life. Not only were small businesses disrupted, but larger businesses like the utilities and transportation industry were disrupted as well. Crest noted that he would speak to the press and would focus on a reconciliation concerning the overall situation as soon as possible.

"The pressure is on to resume normal activities in the United States," Crest added. "We need to meet publicly soon to show that you're sympathetic to ending this peacefully."

"I agree," I said. "But, first we need to bury my good friend Apex."

Crest responded, "True. But, we'll also be honoring Apex with our progress. We need to inform the public that you are ready for negotiations. I'll respond on behalf of the government."

This image was the antithesis of what many Americans expected. As a former slave, I was supposed to be impulsive or instinctive, incapable of complex strategy. The American people needed to understand that this was not about some unsophisticated plan to simply inflict damage. We had created pressure and now we needed the American public and Congress to be an ally.

I was surprised that Hood's people let us claim Apex's body. The casket was delivered in the middle of the night. I knew that this was a ploy by Hood to allow for minimum coverage related to Apex's death. I came downstairs as soon as the body arrived. I didn't want to see it, though. I needed to remember Apex with all of his vibrant power, not as a shell.

We decided to bury Apex in the White House gardens early the following morning. I took consolation in the fact that a black man would now be buried at the White House. Apex was now a martyr, to be remembered forever as the founder and inspiration of the revolt. The funeral was somber and sobering for everyone. Tyra wore a black dress that Meagan used from her former job, and walked behind the casket as several of our men carried Apex's body to its resting place.

A cool breeze blew across the lawn. We were in a part of the garden that was private to the outside world. Apex's casket reached its final resting place and we took turns offering our comments. It was odd; I had now spoken to the world several times about the end of slavery, but my words about Apex seemed entirely inadequate. I shed a few tears when Tyra spoke.

"Everyone was important to Apex," she said, adding that the thing he worried most about was loss of life. It was interesting to hear her say this because Apex always seemed to be an uncompromising warrior. She discussed his dreams for the African American and how much of a shame it was that he had only come so close to seeing that dream come true.

As we lowered Apex into the ground, it struck me as ironic that his death was necessary for the movement to transition. Apex had done his part to advance the revolution from a physical standpoint. It was clear now, however, that we needed more than manpower. We had to out think our adversaries; fortunately, they were vulnerable. They had underestimated us and I intended to capitalize on that.

As soon as the service ended, I turned my attention to the tasks ahead. I was not going to make the mistake of wallowing in self-pity a second time. I gathered my composure to speak to the reporters who were waiting for a statement. I straightened my tie and walked out to the front lawn of the White House where several news teams stood gathered.

I spoke solemnly but confidently. "Today we lay to rest the true leader of this revolution: Apex. His vision was that every African American live free. His intention was to impact not only the American public, but the world at large. On Apex's behalf I'm telling the world today that my fellow African Americans are tired of being seen and not heard. We strive to end this revolution on a positive note, with no more deaths and an end to the tensions and anxiety of the past several weeks. Therefore, I am calling on all Americans to reach out to your fellow man and begin to consider each other as equals. And, I am requesting that President Hood issue an executive order prohibiting any violent act or prosecution against any slave, including those here at the White House, until these matters are fully resolved."

It was a bold but calculated move. In this case I was asking for restraint and tolerance rather than freedom. These were baby steps, but they'd buy us time. Hood would seem irrational if he refused this one, reasonable request. I had done my part. It was up to Crest from this point forward.

It was about noon when Crest made his statement to the media. Gathering around a large screen, our team watched intently. It had been a long day and things were moving quickly. Apex's funeral felt like it was already days ago.

An interesting scene was developing outside the White House. Since Apex's death, the crowd on the street had steadily grown larger. People of every color chanted slogans that favored our resistance, and others held signs that said, "Freedom Now!" and "We are all human." It was great to witness so much positive energy. There was also an almost equal number of protestors with signs that spewed hate, including one that said, "Get those niggers out of the White House!" Although the naysayers were in a slight minority, it was clear that there was a visible segment of American society that didn't appreciate our efforts. There was still much work to be done.

Someone turned up the volume on the TV and Crest's comments echoed throughout the White House. "It's time for change here in America. President Hood had years to anticipate the overwhelming winds of change that now push us toward a more progressive and righteous society. This dynamic has been approaching for many years and it's something the president should have planned for. His lack of vision and foresight has caused death, destruction, and uncertainty. It is now time to address the core issues confronting American society. I believe that the time has come for slavery to end."

The broadcast cut to a wider angle of Crest, a crowd of supporters gathered behind him. The sense of support was almost overwhelming. "I believe that every American, regardless of race, should have the ability to live freely and to vote. I'm calling on Congress to immediately pass legislation that ends slavery in the United States. I am also calling on Congress to pass the Uniform Suffrage Act, or "USA." The Act will allow every American, including former slaves, to vote. Finally, in order for us to restore confidence in our nation's government, I am requesting that the legislature pass an amendment to the Constitution allowing for a special election. These are unprecedented circumstances, our nation is at a turning point, and we must elect a new president as soon as possible. Not only is this an issue that is central to our progress here in the United States, but it is also an issue of international importance. Our president has proven himself impotent — both here and abroad. His incompetence has caused immeasurable damage. We must act on these issues immediately and move forward. This is not a time for uncertainty. These actions must be undertaken with urgency, purpose, and focus. I'll also be speaking to Phoenix, the leader of the slave revolution, to solidify an end to any hostilities. It's time for all to act in the best interest of our country. Thank you. I'll take a few questions."

Crest beamed with confidence, emboldened by the circumstances and the support our revolution was receiving both across the country and abroad. He answered every question with articulation and strength, and it was obvious that he had been waiting on this moment for a long time. Our actions gave Crest the platform to seize the moment. It was a great speech and it set the tone for us to proceed with our plans.

In the early evening, Meagan and I walked back in our room hand in hand. We were both elated about the day's events.

She smiled up at me. "I didn't know how well you guys had everything coordinated. It's almost too good to be true. Are you and Senator Crest truly on the same side?"

I nodded my head. "Crest and I are completely in harmony. We're playing off of each other. I set him up with my speech and he rolled right off of it. We are hitting Hood from different directions. It's a great strategy, but it may or may not work. As well as today went, I don't want to get ahead of myself."

Meagan frowned at my uncertainty and I added, "It's a tough situation. Crest is our only way out right now and he's right. We must find a balance between aggression and earning respect as peace-seeking people who want nothing more than to live as everyone else. Although our actions were in some ways violent, our intentions were pure; our sole purpose was to abolish slavery."

Crest and I agreed that it was time for me to start becoming the voice of reason and compromise. The resistance had accomplished many of its original goals. We were situated in the White House. Other African Americans were emboldened to the point that they were boycotting their work. And the American people were beginning to see African Americans as both positive and influential.

Crest's plan was burning in my chest and I couldn't keep it a secret any longer. "Meagan, I have to tell you something. And it's big."

She raised an eyebrow in suspicion. "Okay... ."

"Crest wants me to become president. That's his intention with the special election. We discussed it just yesterday and, crazy as it sounds, the idea is growing on me."

Meagan's mouth fell open and her eyes bulged in disbelief. I couldn't help but laugh; her reaction was the same as mine when Crest had made his proposal.

"I really don't think that our country is ready for a black president!" she blurted. "I mean, sure, the public may want to help us abolish slavery, but that's probably where the good will stop. Don't you think you and Crest are pressing too hard?"

I sighed deeply. She wasn't wrong. "You're right on some counts. I have no credentials and no real education. It's hard to believe that any white person, other than Crest, would want to vote me into office. But how can we make progress if we never try?"

We stood in front of a large window in the Lincoln bedroom as the sun set outside, casting warm, orange light in beams across the room. Meagan took my hands in hers and spoke softly, "It's okay to dream big, honey. Sometimes you reach for the stars. Doesn't mean you'll get there. I dreamed for years that one day I would escape that hateful master of mine. But I also dreamed that my life would mean something. That it would affect others. You have given me and many others that chance. It's true that one person can make a difference. And sure, maybe that *could* be you. You could be the one to elevate all slaves. You could be the one to serve as America's first black president. You could be the one to set a shining example for African American kids for decades to come. I believe in you, Harrison. It's just a hard thing to understand and comprehend," she paused, pulled me in closer, and squeezed my hands tighter. "But... here we are in the White House. We made it. This is a unique moment in time. And you, my dear, are a unique person. If anybody can enact this change, it's you, baby. I say go for it."

Meagan looked up at me, her eyes dancing in the room's dim light. I leaned down and kissed her softly. Then she placed her head on my chest and for a moment we stood there and breathed in the evening.

"Thank you, Meagan," I said. Then with a slight laugh I added, "It's crazy to believe that I could be president and you my first lady." It was the first time I'd uttered my intentions aloud. Meagan said nothing, but smiled and bit her lip coquettishly. Just then, my stomach let out a loud growl.

"How about we feed you first before you die of starvation, Mr. President?" she said, tickling my belly.

We went downstairs and joined the rest of our team for dinner. Today had been victorious and soon enough, it would be time for me to meet with Brad and solidify our future.

CHAPTER 30
THE OVAL OFFICE

The time had come for my next address to the American people, and we all knew how important this evening would be for the rest of our lives. Brad even had his personal tailor measure me for a new suit, and I wore it with pride. I'd never worn something custom-tailored before, and it made me feel official. Our team had even begun to call me "sir," though I hadn't yet warmed up to the moniker. We had planned a speech for about eight-thirty in the evening. Slaves and other workers across the country would be comfortably situated at home; it would be the perfect time to catch as many people as possible. We were headline news now, and we knew that people would tune in.

I had growing concerns about us being sequestered at the White House. The crowds outside were becoming more aggressive and we couldn't just come and go as we pleased. While the majority appeared to favor what we were doing, there were others who were not quite so complimentary. The hateful signs kept appearing.

One sign read, "There's a reason it's called 'White House.'" Another said, "Niggers, go home!" I chuckled at the simplicity of this one and thought to myself, "I *am* home." Comments like those just made me want to stay in the White House.

On a more positive note, some of the tanks were gone, though I noticed that there were a lot more guards and police. Some of the guards had what appeared to be automatic rifles and I worried about some type of attack. For every positive move we made, our opposition had three negative ones in their back pocket. There was still a lot of work to be done.

Early in the evening before my speech, Ray echoed my concerns, stating, "The military has replaced their tanks with more men."

Barry, looking up from his laptop added, "Harrison, I'm worried that Hood's military could make a move at any moment and take us down."

Doing my best to hide my concern, I said, "Well, we still have the codes to Cove Point. I doubt that they would make a move and put Cove Point at risk once more. Plus, public perception is on our side after what happened to Apex. Let's stay the course."

I felt confident the military would not advance against us so long as their precious codes could still be compromised. On the other hand, I wasn't about to test their patience. We had to keep applying pressure while simultaneously defusing any threat of attack with our public statements.

With a quick glance at the clock I said, "Barry, it's around seven thirty. Did you contact all the networks to ensure that they'll be covering this?"

Barry shook his head. "I didn't have to call them because they called me. Trust me, this is big news and they want to be front and center to report it."

"Good. This time I'm giving the speech from the Oval Office. We need to make sure we're secure. Expect the unexpected."

Crest had recommended that the press conference be used to send the message that we were postponing any boycotts for the next few workdays. His goal was to appear as if we were compromising. This would show America not only our sophistication, but our willingness to work with the government toward a reasonable solution. It was all a balancing act.

Fifteen minutes before the start of the press conference, reporters were escorted to the Oval Office. The public must have been made aware that the press conference was forthcoming as the crowds outside the White House grew even larger. Our isolation made it impossible to know just what the sentiment was on the streets, but the crowds outside our windows told me that at least we were being heard. I was no longer afraid to speak to the American people. Instead, I felt ready and, more importantly, I felt powerful. Our recent experiences had prepared me for this moment and my successful prior interfaces with the media had given me a substantial amount of confidence.

Upon entering the room, I gave a little wave to the reporters, took my seat, and then gathered myself in front of the three cameras that had been positioned in front of me. Amazingly, I wasn't nervous. An NNC cameraman counted down and pointed his finger at me to let me know we were live and broadcasting.

"Tonight is a significant night in the history of our country. It is time to start the healing process. The past few weeks have been difficult and many lives have been lost since our efforts began. Those losses are not in vain, but rather were the wakeup call our country so desperately needed. Many of our partner countries around the world no longer respect the United States. Our global potential, both economically and politically, has diminished due to the moral challenges we have faced here at home. It's time for the United States to become the true global power that I know it can be. Our country can only reach its potential if it eliminates the primary obstacle to its greatness: slavery.

"All of our actions thus far have been geared toward creating a platform for discussion concerning how we, as a united people, can bring the cruel practice of slavery to an end. As a part of that process, we called for slave boycotts across the country. These boycotts were intended to illustrate the importance of the African American population to our economy and also served as an illustration of our resolve to end slavery. We are fully committed to our purpose. At this point, many of us believe that the only alternative to freedom is death. Despite that, we have no desire to undertake any action that serves to threaten the prosperity of our country. To that end, I am now calling for any and all boycotts by the slave population here in the United States to be suspended."

As I paused to collect my thoughts, several reporters nodded their heads in agreement. I cleared my throat and pressed on, "Our goal is continued prosperity, not disruption. I encourage every slave to report to work tomorrow. I am requesting that you proceed in a manner that is consistent with the best interest of the United States. Lives have already been lost and it is now time for our mutual healing. As a further offer of peace, we have flipped the switch such that all natural gas pipeline delivery through Cove Point will proceed without disruption. This will allow the American people to benefit from the higher prices that my team has negotiated with the Chinese government. Again, our goal is to create a better America, not to disrupt our society. As an American, I'm trusting in our legislative process to do right by us. We have conceded on several points and I hope you will meet us in our one request: equal rights for all Americans. Tonight signals a new beginning. It is my greatest hope that we can move toward a prompt end to the practice of slavery in the United States. Thank you and God bless."

I sat still at the desk in the Oval Office and marinated. I didn't want to get up. I felt powerful and liberated. We were playing a high stakes game, we were playing it competently, and we could not rest. We needed more. I had to tap into some additional reserves. The cameramen signaled that we were off the air. I slowly got up, shook a few hands, and walked out of the Oval Office.

Out in the hall, everyone was clapping and I high-fived several members of my team. We hugged and laughed. This was a winning moment for our side, no doubt. I thought about Apex. He would have been happy with our progress. This was his legacy and I knew I was doing him proud.

After making sure that I greeted everyone, Meagan and I headed back to our room for the night. We lay down in front of the television that Barry's crew had set up for us and watched the news reactions. Much of the commentary noted that this was a revolution of necessity — one that had been "a long time coming." There was also great emphasis placed on our country's reputation abroad.

I was so relieved. This was the message we wanted to spread: that the United States would be unable to reach its overall potential while still ensnared by slavery. To my delight, the NNC now called for immediate approval of the act proposed by Senator Crest and according to polls, many members of the public were expressing the same sentiment. Apex's death and the prospects of a stronger US economy had led many former supporters to distance themselves from President Hood and his Administration. Many also felt that Hood had left the US infrastructure vulnerable to our resistance. His popularity continued to plummet.

Senator Crest offered public comments concerning my speech, stating that he was in full support and would continue discussions with our team concerning the resistance. He reiterated that he wanted to expedite the Uniform Suffrage Act and noted that passing the act would have immediate ramifications for the United States, not only domestically but also abroad. Slavery would no longer be available as a platform for the world to criticize the United States. The goodwill created would allow us to repair our global relationships. Even though I was excited, I was exhausted. I was asleep before I knew it and would let Meagan fill me in on the rest of the highlights.

CHAPTER 31
CREST CHESS

The next morning, I called Crest first thing to follow up on the previous day's events. He expressed to me that he was anxious that we had no "official" momentum and felt we needed Richmond's political insiders to express their confidence in me as a potential presidential candidate. I agreed but couldn't help but feel self-conscious. I was nervous as it was about being a competent candidate.

In Richmond, the situation had become very difficult for the administration and the cabinet. The Secretary of State, John Moore, the Secretary of Commerce, Donald Leske, and the Secretary of Interior, Evan Thorpe had all publicly expressed their concern about the president's diminishing strength. Crest had heard reports that Moore, Leske, and Thorpe's meetings with Hood had left them unconvinced that the president had a clear strategy to manage the whirlwind of ongoing events; the president was stubbornly resistant. Still, the groundswell settling across the country was that Hood had mismanaged the slave issue. Something had to give.

After our conversation, Crest decided to travel to Richmond for a private meeting with Moore, Leske, and Thorpe. I was concerned about Crest tipping them off to any of our plans before we'd had an opportunity to develop them further. After all, our last communication with Moore had not been positive and Hood was a big threat. I was concerned that meeting with Moore could trigger action against us by the government. But Crest felt it was a risk worth taking and I was so busy working with Ray and Barry to increase my knowledge of international affairs that I put my trust in Crest to represent us.

I was no expert concerning international trade, though I was fast becoming functional. I felt lucky concerning the negotiations related to Cove Point, but now I wanted a good two weeks to study trade issues. Crest was eager to press forward, however, and I received a call around eleven at night, asking if he could come and meet with me immediately. I was tired but eager to hear what he had to say about his trip to Richmond.

Crest arrived around midnight and we sat in the Oval Office sipping on whiskey. I let him do most of the talking as he filled me in on the details of the day. Apparently the four had met in a luxurious steakhouse in Richmond where Crest felt they could all speak more openly. According to Crest, Moore had been somewhat aggressive during the meeting and had suggested they find an immediate resolution to the crisis. Moore's focus was on both the domestic and international implications related to an end to slavery.

Leske and Thorpe had been even more adversarial. "Harrison," Crest said, shaking his head, "Those two started the meeting by chastising me for aligning myself with your resistance. I spent the better part of thirty minutes trying to calm them down so we could discuss matters like gentlemen."

"Their reaction isn't surprising," I said, and took a big sip of whiskey. "We are, after all, asking them to make a big change."

Crest nodded. "Yes, but I told them it was critical they consider both sides of the equation. I explained that balance is the issue. Hood is starting to be seen as an extremist. His pro-slavery stance is a liability concerning trade and this is starting to hit people in their pocketbooks — and affect their sense of security. Especially in light of the resistance."

"Good," I said, pleased that Crest had been so firm.

Crest chuckled as he puffed out his chest, "I told them, 'You need to get your asses on national television and say that slavery is done for and that you fully support the Uniform Suffrage Act. Endorse it all with no question.'"

I was shocked by his candor. "What did they say?"

"They just stared at me," Crest laughed with exasperation. "So, I said, 'You still want to be around when the new president is elected, don't you? Save your asses now. Get on board.'"

"Damn!" I said, as I refilled both of our glasses.

"It was what they needed to hear, Harrison," Crest said with a smile. It was a bold move, but it seemed that Crest had finally gotten through to them.

Crest continued, saying that he'd focused on my negotiations with the President of China and the higher prices I'd been able to demand for gas at Cove Point. He'd described the move as brilliant and counter to the assumption that slaves are just ignorant animals. Apparently, Moore had chuckled when Crest suggested that I was clearly more savvy than Hood. But then again, he hadn't exactly disagreed.

"I ended my argument with an ultimatum," Crest added. "I looked them in their faces and said, 'The point is, gentlemen, a new day is coming and you need to decide right now if you want to be on the side that is remembered forever for ushering in a new America. Or will you occupy just a small paragraph in the history books, all because you opposed our movement? Choose wisely.'"

I leaned forward in my seat, equal parts excited and terrified by what Crest might say next.

"Moore was receptive — even to the prospect of you exploring a leadership position. I think we may win him over after all."

"Great! I think…" I started, but Crest held up his hand to interject before I could continue.

"Leske, on the other hand was less convinced. He even suggested that electing you for president would be the same as supporting a terrorist." I wrung my hands, not sure how to respond. It wasn't a surprising reaction, but it wasn't promising either.

"I didn't relent, however," Crest continued. "I emphasized the fact that you had already outmaneuvered them all. I told him, 'Hey, this resistance has been chaotic for everyone involved. But for the rest of the world it has been a long time coming. The whole world is looking to us to make the right move here.' I pointed out how every success only proves your effectiveness as a leader."

Leske and Thorpe had the most to lose here. Under their leadership, a slave had executed a revolt from inside the US. Then our resistance had outmaneuvered and outperformed their entire Cabinet concerning deals with other countries. Crest had provided them a way out. By joining our effort, they could take some credit for what we had achieved. If they refused to cooperate, the government would survive, but their political careers might not.

"I used the last bullet in the chamber by appealing to their moral instincts," Crest added. "What got them was when I said, 'Not that that matters to guys like you.' Their entire demeanor changed when I said that." It was a good move. He'd made them examine themselves and do a moral gut-check.

Before he left, Crest asked that each gentleman call their aides to set up a press conference in support of the Uniform Suffrage Act.

"As my car drove off, Thorpe and Leske just stood there watching me. I could tell — the looks on their faces or something — that they had already made up their minds. They're not going down with a sinking ship. They have careers, financial obligations, and families to protect."

I smiled and slapped Crest on the shoulder. "That's excellent news, Brad. Thank you. Thank you on behalf of our entire team."

"It means a lot to me, Harrison. But there is still work to be done. I also met with President Hood."

I nearly spat my whiskey. "Really? And?"

Crest shook his head. "He's still unwilling to compromise. Says that slaves are inferior — all that usual racist, preservationist crap. Apex's death only confirmed the depths of his hatred. I'm still convinced that he had a hand in it, though it would be hard to prove."

This information wasn't new; we'd already seen what Hood was capable of. His stubbornness, however, was even more infallible than his hatred and would be a tough wall to climb.

Crest continued, "Hood still views the resistance as a temporary setback. He believes that once we negotiate a resolution, things will be back to normal."

"He's infuriating," I said, my face growing hot with a combination of frustration and booze.

"Honestly, Harrison, I'm happy that he's held onto this posture. Hood thinks that Apex's death was the final straw and views it as an end to the resistance. He's underestimated you, your team, and his own administration. Public opinion is changing. The more he misinterprets this, the more vulnerable he'll remain."

I took a moment to digest Crest's words. "You may be right, my friend. Thank you again." With that, we wrapped up our conversation and called it a night.

I was pleased with the results of Crest's meetings, but there was still a ton of uncertainty. Despite Crest's best efforts, the United Suffrage Act had not yet been passed and I was still far from being a legitimate presidential candidate. There was work to be done and many questions to be answered, but I was prepared to fight like hell.

CHAPTER 32
PASSING THE USA

"Any more updates, Barry?" I asked with an exasperated sigh. It was late Saturday morning one week after my meeting with Crest, and I was struggling this weekend as activity had slowed. Congress was debating the Uniform Suffrage Act (or "USA," as Crest had dubbed it), and I had seen a report that some of the president's cabinet had publicly endorsed the act. This news was welcomed, though somewhat surprising. I had feared that the president's cabinet would continue to support the president's oppressive posture despite Crest's optimism.

Still, we needed to find more leverage, so I'd focused every second of my free time to informing myself about current affairs. I focused on the Trans Pacific Partnership and NAFTA and learned all that I could about both agreements. I sensed that there was a play there, especially in light of my prior success with China.

America was part of a global economy and we dominated various industries. We were dominant from a manufacturing standpoint and countries around the world imported American goods. Almost non-existent labor costs fueled low prices. About the only thing that restrained American prosperity was our reliance on foreign oil. But that dynamic was changing with various oil and natural gas finds in the United States. I had already exploited this dynamic with Cove Point, so I probed to see if I could learn more.

America had become a powerhouse because of slavery, yet our international relationships were fragile because we were not respected as a moral power. I understood acutely why Crest felt that American success abroad had been suppressed because of slavery. A combination of jealousy and disgust served as a barrier to good business between the US and the rest of the world. Many other countries had started to place limitations on their economic transactions with the United States as they felt the US was engaged in unfair trade practices.

The competition between the United States and Russia concerning the world's natural gas marketplace was also a critical issue. The trade agreements that were being formulated now concerning the energy industry would set the pace for the rest of the world for many years to come. The United States could either be a world leader concerning the energy trade, or lag sorely behind due to its lack of moral mandate. It was a two-horse race; and as distasteful a trade partner Russia was to many countries, the slavery issue made them a more attractive partner than the US to many suitors. This dynamic gave pause to many in Congress, and I knew it could be exploited.

In addition to taking the time to further educate myself concerning political and economic affairs, I also spent a great deal of time with Meagan. It was amazing how well we fit. Maybe it was the oppression that we experienced together in the Crops. Maybe it was the time we'd spent together recently, simply talking with one another. Whatever it was, my time with her felt very natural. I needed the comfort and calmness of our relationship during these stressful times.

I also worked to develop a stronger relationship with Tyra. She had understandably withdrawn since Apex had passed, but I was determined not to let her become isolated. She and Meagan were becoming closer and Meagan spent the majority of each day with Tyra. The impact was significant. Tyra was coming back to life and was newly focused on helping us complete our goals in the resistance.

That Saturday evening, Meagan and I took some quiet time on the balcony outside our bedroom. "Tell me more about Apex, if you don't mind. Was he that strong? Tyra is devastated," she said.

Sitting down next to her on the loveseat I said quietly, "He was an amazing person. Imagine coming up with a way to free the slaves and recruiting new supporters, all while growing the tunnels. He wasn't just some huge muscle man; he was a prodigy. And he could write code out of nothing. He was one of a kind. If I hadn't wasted so much time those first few months, we probably could have fully integrated our plans. He might even still be alive."

Resting her head against my chest, Meagan replied, "He sounds like a great man."

"The best that I've ever known," I said, running my fingers through her hair.

We sat in comfortable silence and looked out into the night. I remembered being on that bench in the Crops, staring across the bay toward DC. Now here I was. With Meagan. In the White House. It was unbelievable.

We rejoined the rest downstairs after a while to make sure everything was running smoothly. Barry approached with a smile on his face and said, "Harrison, apparently there is progress related to the Uniform Suffrage Act. Senator Crest is on his way over."

"Finally! Thank you," I said, giving him a slap on the back. I kissed Meagan on the cheek, and Barry and I walked to the Oval Office.

As we settled into chairs, Senator Crest came in with several of his associates. I searched his face for signs of anything positive, and from the gleam in his eyes I knew it had to be good news.

"We have made some progress in getting the act approved," he said. "Politicians love to hear themselves argue and the debate may take a while, but I'm hoping for a vote early in the week. I'm optimistic."

Outside, the crowd was growing rowdy. A chant of "Abolish! Abolish! Abolish!" could be heard and for a moment silenced our conversation. Just as soon as the chant picked up, it was drowned out by another group chanting, "Kill all slaves!" The powder keg was growing.

Turning my attention back to Crest I said loudly so all could hear, "Congress needs to make a move soon. We are at ground zero. This thing could explode."

CHAPTER 33
TRANSITIONS

The weekend passed by quietly and the crowds were beginning to thin out since no new developments had come up regarding the USA. Monday came with no final answer. The calm was beginning to concern me. We had tried to reach Crest with little success. The masses outside, although reduced, continued to be vocal. I continued to monitor the news awaiting any word from Congress. We needed to fuel the fire.

Our story had not subsided. Every so often, there would be a picture of me on the news and several speeches were cut and pasted to highlight my leadership. The media had tried in vain to garner more information about me and of course couldn't find any records of a man named "Phoenix." I knew I would eventually have to address this with the public.

Monday morning came and the news highlighted more supporters for the Uniform Suffrage Act who were becoming even more vocal, including several conservative Republicans. From my perspective, the pressure was enormous and I could only wonder what the deliberations were down in Richmond. I found it very difficult not to worry about my personal well-being and the well-being of those who had made this journey with me. I was desperate to speak to Crest.

Monday night I slept restlessly, even with Meagan by my side. I maybe slept for three or four hours and the remainder of the time I just lay there looking up at the ceiling, wondering when it would all collapse. Here we were sleeping in luxury, knowing it was all a facade. Everything was so impermanent and I couldn't shake the feeling that at any moment, my security could fall away. This was no time to get comfortable.

My nights were filled with thoughts about worst case scenarios: What if we did achieve our goal but those who worked with us were arrested or even executed? What if I myself were imprisoned? Or worse? We had seen what Hood was capable of. My whole future at this point was up in the air and the more time I had to think about it, the more my present circumstances bothered me.

I had even begun to think about running and taking Meagan with me. Hadn't we done enough already? The end of slavery was now in sight and my running for president still felt like such an impossibility anyway. No one could criticize me for leaving at this point. It wouldn't be selfish. After all, I had given up so much to get us here.

It was in these moments of fear I had to resign myself to the fact that I was the leader of this resistance and that quitting wasn't an option. Sure, in a few small ways I longed for the simplicity of being back in the Crops with no worries and no challenges. Though I'd lacked freedom, I had been secure and relatively comfortable. But no, I had to snap myself out of this funk. This was better, even with the uncertainties. And with that thought, I was finally able to rest.

Just as I'd finally eased into sleep, a pounding on the door startled both Meagan and me awake. Throwing on a robe, I went to the door. Barry stood there, his face fraught with worry, and said, "Harrison, you need to look outside. This is very bad news!"

Even though it was only about nine o'clock in the morning, the crowds in the street had grown immense and were becoming increasingly agitated. More concerning, however, was the group of soldiers that had gathered outside the gates, as well as the dozens of police and military vehicles with their lights blazing. The cacophony of voices was piercing but unintelligible, like an angry monster that roared for our attention.

I dressed in a hurry, gave Meagan a quick kiss goodbye, and met Barry and the other council members to learn more.

Barry said what we were all thinking. "They've come to arrest us and send us back to the Crops."

"Or it could be worse and we're all about to be 'transferred,'" added Ray. The council became a chorus of gasps, and my stomach turned over as my greatest fears were realized.

I raised a hand to silence the room and spoke honestly, unwilling or unable to sugarcoat the truth. "Well, this is it. This may be the end of our journey but we can take comfort in knowing we have made tremendous steps in advancing rights for our fellow African Americans. Regardless of today's outcome, hold your heads up and be proud of your part in creating history. Take a quick moment to look around you. We're in the White House. Just a month ago, we were all living in the tunnels — or in the Crops — just hoping this day would one day come. Now we've become the engine that pulled our people closer to freedom. So, no matter what happens today, we have achieved our goals. I pray that each of you holds your head up high, proud of what we were able to create."

The silence in the room was thick and we all gathered around different windows to watch the crowd as it undulated with cries of freedom and hatred. The police and military had aligned and would soon breach our gates. The only thing we could do was wait.

Ray asked calmly, "Harrison, should we arm ourselves?"

Part of me wanted to be like Apex, a warrior ready to fight to my last breath. However, I knew this wasn't the best course of action and said, "No, that would only agitate the situation. We need to remain positive and peaceful, especially if the media is covering this. We don't want to jeopardize any gains we've achieved."

The gates swung open and a hundred or so soldiers spread out across the lawn. In one swift movement, they all turned toward the crowd, weapons pointed at the sky. This was perplexing; for the time being they seemed more concerned with policing the crowd than arresting us.

Meagan found me at the window and joined in what was inevitably the end. Then, just as abruptly as they had entered, the soldiers parted, creating a pathway for several gentlemen to walk through. To my surprise, the man leading the pack was Crest.

I squeezed Meagan's hand and then ran to the door before Crest could reach it, exclaiming, "Brad what is going on? I thought for sure we were about to be arrested!"

Brad shook my hand and in a surprisingly nonchalant way, said, "Well, can I come in?"

I nodded, allowing Crest and his team to enter along with several members of the police and military, though the majority remained in their positions. Brad motioned for me, Barry, Ray and several key council members to follow him upstairs and we all headed toward the conference room on the second floor.

As we took our seats, Brad said with a grin, "Well, Harrison, the time has come. The Uniform Suffrage Act has officially been passed!"

For a moment, we sat there staring in amazement. Then Ray started a clap and the room erupted in cheer. There were hugs all around. Crest, raising his hand to calm us down said, "Just as importantly, Congress has initiated impeachment proceedings against Hood and Benz."

This sobered us up a bit. The impeachment process would be problematic. Would the House actually vote to impeach Hood? What would happen if Hood survived the process? He would be empowered and rejuvenated.

Crest continued, "The Uniform Suffrage Act mandates that all individuals who have suffered under slavery will immediately become United States citizens. I have included a number of provisions that may be controversial. One of the provisions states that all former slaves immediately be given the right to vote. Each slave's former identification number will be used to complete the registration process. We will get the names situation straight later."

"That's not too controversial. Long overdue, more like," Ray said.

Crest replied, "True, but the second controversial provision I have attached mandates that if the president or vice-president resigns or is impeached, the presidency shall not move in order of succession to the secretary of state, but instead, there shall be a vote by a majority in Congress to determine who will become president. That election must take place within thirty days after the resignation or impeachment to ensure continuity of government. We need Hood and Benz to be impeached and removed from office."

Barry was seated at a computer sifting through the flood of Internet articles that were popping up concerning the act. "Crest, it says here that anyone who is thirty-five or older can run for president if the impeachment process is completed. Hell, I might run!" he said with a chuckle.

Crest, nodding his head in agreement said, "You would be a great candidate, Barry. But it would be kind of awkward for you to run against Harrison."

A hush fell over the room and all eyes were on me. Ray and Barry both looked as if they may faint. I knew this moment was coming but it still felt overwhelming to hear Crest speak the words out loud.

Ray shouted, "America will never vote for a black man! Especially after the stink that we've caused!" Barry added, "Not to mention the death threats, hate mail, and Lord knows what else some closed-minded racist could cook up!"

Others began speaking up, voicing their concerns, and a few seemed almost angry with the decision. I let everyone get their fears out into the open, "Ray and Barry, your concerns are the same ones I voiced to Crest when he first approached me with the idea. But, just imagine, a former slave as president!"

"Yeah, that's the same type of thinking that got Apex dead," Barry huffed.

Patiently, Crest and I went through the details of our prior conversation with the crowd. It was critical that our decision be unanimous, as our future success would rely on the strength and unity of our organization. So we all sat and talked strategy for hours. It was after midnight when we adjourned.

By the end of the night, we were energized. It was as if the resistance was starting up again. We decided to meet up in the morning to determine when and how to release the statement for my bid to run for president. We ended the night with a champagne toast; this was solid progress.

As we parted ways, I walked toward the second floor banister and Meagan was there speaking with Ray. She waved at me, smiling.

"So tell me, what did Senator Crest have to say?"

I responded in a somewhat nonchalant tone, "He still wants me to become president." Despite trying to play it cool, I couldn't help but smile.

She smirked and said quickly, "President of what?"

"Oh, really? How about you give the future president of the United States a kiss?" She leaned in and kissed me softly with a sweet laugh. I would marry that girl someday.

I put my arm around her and we leaned over the rail, watching the activity below. Maybe this was the ultimate new beginning. I was ready to make the push with Crest, but I also wanted to make sure African Americans were properly integrated into American society. The bid for president almost seemed selfish, however, I knew it would benefit African Americans for an eternity. I needed to anchor myself in the goals of our community. Crest could never understand how we felt, what we were going through. I resolved to be guarded concerning his goals. I needed to make sure we stayed focus on the best interest of all former slaves across the country. To do this, I had to maintain independent thinking. It would be tough. Crest had done a lot for us all, but at the end of the day, this was still our ball game.

CHAPTER 34
RISING ABOVE

Every news station was talking about the Uniform Suffrage Act, and it had become a certainty that President Richard Hood would be impeached. Still, there was a little confusion amongst the public about whether slavery had already come to an end. The Act stated that involuntary servitude would also be prohibited, however, it was becoming clear that the most appropriate course would be to enact an amendment to the Constitution. Crest and his team had already proposed language for an amendment:

"Neither slavery nor involuntary servitude, unless as a punishment for crime whereof the party has been tried and convicted, shall exist within the United States or any place subject to our jurisdiction."

I thought the language was beautiful. The bar was high, but Crest felt that the dye had been set. We were still riding on momentum and he felt the votes were there to pass the Amendment and achieve ratification.

Hood had been alarmingly quiet during these developments, though unbeknownst to us, he was about to raise his ugly head. Many of us had mistaken his silence for conceding and that was clearly not the case. Hood had issued a statement to the press acknowledging the passage of the USA, but he'd argued that the act itself could not free slaves. That, he claimed, would be an unlawful taking of property from both the state and those citizens who held licenses. A constitutional amendment would be necessary to overcome this issue. Thank goodness that Crest had seen this coming and the effort to mobilize necessary votes in both the House and Senate was underway. The president was merely reacting at this point rather than controlling.

The dynamic at the White House was starting to change. With the enactment of the USA, we were finally free. We all walked around with a different type of demeanor. My steps were no longer as calculated. We went outside more, though we continued to be cautious about leaving the premises. There were still people gathered outside, and I knew that there were bound to be some crazies mingling around.

Even more amazing was the fact that Crest was now sending staff to work with us inside the White House. Many of those staffers were white, and technically, they worked under me. I struggled to get used to giving my new team orders, but I needed their information and we needed to run our operation efficiently. Plus, I would be running for president. I couldn't be shy about giving orders to anyone. Even Crest.

Crest had been busy mobilizing public opinion. He was all over TV and I paused to listen to one of his statements on the NNC.

"Of course, the overwhelming majority of slaves in the United States were born right here. So, in truth, they are already natural-born United States citizens. We don't need a constitutional amendment to establish that fact. However, we do want to ensure that all future generations have certainty concerning their freedom and rights as citizens of this nation. We can leave no doubt that, as of this time, all slaves are free."

Crest seemed to be everywhere in Washington and Richmond all at once. I knew that he was wheeling and dealing. My role would become more active later. For now, I was more than willing for Crest to set it all up; after all, he had connections that I didn't. I wondered to whom he had told our plans for my candidacy.

This was the calm before the storm, so on a sunny afternoon in mid-February, I decided to talk a walk with Meagan in the gardens. It was cool outside and Meagan was radiant and more relaxed than I'd seen her. I intentionally avoided Apex's burial site. We had to complete this deal before I could face him.

"If we're free, why do I still feel so strange walking around outside?" she asked.

I felt the same way. "I know what you mean. It's just too early. For a lot of us, it will take years before we are comfortable. Still, it's a whole lot better than being at a social and knowing I won't be able to talk to you again for months. Crest is right. Ending slavery sends one message. But a black president will send a deeper, more long-lasting message."

We sat down on one of the old concrete benches in the garden where we were secluded. I needed Meagan's opinion. "Do you really think I should trust Crest concerning this presidency thing? Or are we trying to move too fast?"

Meagan hesitated briefly and then said, "There will be many people who will fight true integration. But with you as president, that integration process would take years instead of decades. You will prove to people once and for all that African Americans are equals in this nation."

I smiled, knowing I'd fallen in love with a woman who was smarter than me.

CHAPTER 35
COOKING SOMETHING UP

The mood inside the White House was light-hearted. I looked outside at the thinning crowds. We were no longer the epicenter of change, as that distinction now belonged to the Congress in Richmond. Next up was the vote on the constitutional amendment and the impeachment of Hood.

I knew I had to keep the ball going, so I found Barry and said, "I have a very important task for you, my friend. Tomorrow morning, I need you to call Joachim Joc, the president of Germany. This is critical; I need to talk to him by tomorrow morning."

Barry smiled at me and said, "You have another surprise planned, don't you? Whatever you need, just consider it done. I'll reach President Joc as soon as possible."

I needed to continue this progress independent of Crest. While I was grateful for all that he'd done to help our movement, I had to remind myself that I had only known him for a short period and our progress with the resistance had not been premised on Crest's assistance. I had to avoid becoming complacent and dependent on his efforts. As a leader, I needed to stand on my own two feet.

Midweek, I learned that Crest had arranged for the White House to receive complete and unlimited access to the Internet and other vital information that would assist my preparation for the presidential run. In addition, Barry received access to a more complete database that would allow communication with former slaves across the United States. Crest argued that, as the leader of the resistance, I could help manage the morale amongst former slaves and help avoid any civil unrest.

My first mass communication was directed at creating a bridge between the former slave population and myself. I asked all former slaves to report to work in a timely manner until the details concerning our full transition to freedom could be worked out. This move created some much needed equity as businesses across the country that relied on slave labor could continue their operations without interruption.

My decision was well received. When I scanned the Richmond and Washington newspapers, the prevailing headlines were that slaves were now, in effect, free and that we had the right to vote. But there was still concern in some circles that the transition would become violent if I continued to lead the former slave population. As such, I felt compelled to arrange to speak to the public because of the goodwill that was being generated. I convened our inner circle, including Barry, Ray, Tyra, Christian, Meagan, and a few of the new staffers, making sure to include several white staffers.

I noted we were gaining national goodwill by the moment, but that the real question was how we should leverage it. We needed to determine our next steps from a public relations standpoint. Barry and Ray suggested an aggressive approach, including immediate press conferences. Meagan advocated a subtle wait and see approach including a week-long moratorium on communications with the press. "The more information we have, the better prepared we will be to communicate," she added.

Tyra suggested we take a combined approach, noting that we needed to start growing infrastructure to communicate with all African Americans. She clarified by saying, "We have an agenda today, but we will need organization and an agenda for many years into the future. Apex was always into planning ahead. Let's not lose his essence. Think outside of the moment. As former slaves, we will face challenges beyond the simple freedom to choose our daily course. How are we planning to address these challenges? If we don't, we could find that the freedom we've fought so hard for is not as sweet as what we desired."

Tyra's words stung me. I'd made it more about the presidential campaign than executing a proper plan for freedom.

I nodded toward Tyra, "Thank you. I definitely needed that honesty. You serve Apex's legacy well." Then turning toward to the group, I added, "Change in plans. Tyra has set us on the right course. Let's meet again tomorrow."

As we adjourned, I pulled Barry and Christian aside. "I need you two. Let's find a quiet place and a computer."

Settling into the control room, I asked Barry to pull up a map of the United States. I had an interesting observation, "Hard to believe we're now free to travel anywhere on this map."

Barry quipped, "Really? Then, let's go! I'm tired of being stuck here at the White House!" We all laughed.

"Listen, guys. We need to select seven cities across the country — and they need to be spread out geographically," I said. "Now, this is not going to be science. So, don't ask me for some master plan. We just need to pick the spots where we'll begin to build our national community."

On the west coast, I picked Sacramento, the capital of California. I also picked Houston, Atlanta, New York, Chicago, and a city in North Carolina called Fayetteville because it was near the country's largest military base. I still needed a city in the middle of the country. I settled on Lincolnton, Nebraska, a city named after the president who had unsuccessfully sought to abolish slavery. Seemed like a great pick to me.

I disclosed to Barry and Christian that we need to develop small teams in each of these cities to assist with the regional advancement of integration, just as Tyra had suggested. Regardless of what happened concerning my run for president, we needed a strong plan concerning integration. I would press Crest to develop an interface with the central government to make sure there was pace concerning the integration process and that the concerns of African Americans were addressed systematically.

Finally, I added, "Christian, I want you to lead this process. Stay organized. This may be the most important job of all."

The young fella didn't look up but simply said, "Yessir!" and maintained his focus on the map. There was no doubt in my mind I had selected the right guy for the job.

CHAPTER 36
GETTING OFFICIAL

Another week passed and at this point, the police presence outside was more to protect us than to agitate us. There were still a few protestors with signs outside, as well as a consistent flow of reporters. But much of the pressure was gone and we were no longer under constant scrutiny. It was a welcomed feeling.

Crest arrived midday with a young, light-skinned black aide in tow. The aide was carrying an armful of clothes and boxes.

We shook hands and Crest said, "Harrison, this is Anthony. He's got some clothes for you, and it's important you dress the part."

Anthony nodded to me and handed me the stack of clothes. "It's a pleasure to meet you, sir," he said with a smile.

Crest continued, "We have some very important meetings today. This continues to be a very fluid situation and we must move quickly." I'd learned I didn't have to question what Crest was doing and was willing to follow his plans for the most part. He'd informed me that we'd be meeting with officials in Richmond — including several members of Hood's cabinet.

The new clothes were of a much higher quality than I was used to. I quickly dressed in a new suit with some fancy leather shoes. Crest said, "Alright, you need to leave here and make your way into the public so they can see you face to face."

Instinctively, my eyes lowered to the ground. I was afraid to leave the relative safety of the White House. "I'm concerned about safety, Brad. There are still some hard feelings out there, and I'm sure there are folks who would love to knock me off for participating in the resistance."

Without hesitation, Crest responded, "Security is top notch. You're going to have to get used to being surrounded by a security detail. Even if you don't win the election, you will have to get use to that. You're already famous, Harrison." My gut wretched at his words. I was simultaneously excited and terrified.

There was a long black car waiting outside for us. Crest called it a limousine. Crest, Anthony, and I climbed inside. The car had polished leather seats and contained a stocked bar with bottles of water, spirits, and champagne. There was even a small television tuned to the NNC.

I startled a bit as the limousine began to move. Crest asked, "This is your first time in a limo?"

"Yes, and it feels kind of weird." We both laughed.

There were three additional black sedans with us. Two police cars took their places in the front and back of us. We were so well protected that I began to ease up.

Crest, handing me a folder, said, "This next meeting is probably the most important one you will have. We will be meeting with several members of the president's cabinet and I anticipate that there will some who are not happy with the events that have transpired. Be on your toes. If they smell weakness or a lack of preparation, they will come for you hard. Relax, be yourself, but be confident."

I looked over the documents. They included bios of the various cabinet members, including their positions on abolition. "So, is this the kick off for my presidential bid or is the focus still slavery?"

Crest opened a bottle of water and said, "It's time for us to start building the foundation for the presidential campaign. It's important that you establish as much credibility as possible as a presidential candidate. There will be individuals across the country who will question your experience. It's a natural response. They know that, just a short while ago, you were just another slave in the Crops. They will underestimate you. But we can use that to our advantage."

The limo ride was smooth and I almost fell asleep. Incredibly, I had no anxiety related to the upcoming meetings. I had been through so much that I no longer feared meetings.

It took us about two hours to get to Richmond. Crest filled me in on the topics that might be discussed at the meeting and I felt particularly well-prepared concerning foreign affairs. I had been relentless in studying our economic relationships with other countries and how those relationships affected foreign political policy. I hadn't been sure, however, which foreign affairs issues would be a priority during the meeting. Crest did his best to bring me up to speed.

We finally arrived at our destination: a restaurant in downtown Richmond. Anthony stayed behind as Crest and I exited the limo. It was a classy place with polished wood floors, warm bread, and butter molded into the shape of coins. There were only a few patrons present, giving the place a feeling of intimacy.

Our security team walked in ahead of us and were met by another security detail at the back of the room. We were then walked through two doors and into a private section of the restaurant. A round, ruddy-faced gentleman stood in the shadows with a glass in his hand. I recognized him immediately as John Moore. Donald Leske, Collins Wright, and Evan Thorpe were seated at a table. At each place setting was a perfectly arranged salad and a short glass of some type of reddish brown liquor. "Single malt scotch," Crest would tell me later.

Seeing these key players in person hit home for me. I felt my old nerves come creeping back, knowing that I needed to convince this room full of former preservationists to back me, an African American, to run for the most powerful position in the country.

Moore stepped toward me and I extended my hand to shake his. Instead, he gestured toward an empty chair with a terse smile. "Have a seat, Phoenix. Maybe this time we will have a more civil conversation." Crest and I found our places at the table as the others nodded and waved their silent hellos. Moore continued. "These have been unique times. An impeached president. The end of slavery. Hell, even I'm wondering what's next. What's on your mind, boys?"

Crest spoke up before I could answer, "Gentlemen, whether you like it or not, Hood is done. Benz is going down with him. It's time for America to start the process of rebuilding the executive branch and we need strong leadership. But we also need to send a message to the world. We must cultivate a high moral authority if we're to become the true global force that we know the United States is capable of."

Leske chimed in, "Agreed on all points."

"This new administration must be put together in a very calculated manner from the top down and it is critical that we select the right person for the job. I think that that person is our Phoenix. Meet Harrison Vance. My strong recommendation is that we collectively support Harrison in a bid for the presidency."

Crest's comments were met with blank stares and silence. Moore, who had been gnawing on a crust of bread, coughed and reached for his scotch.

"Hello, gentlemen," I managed, my voice shaking slightly.

Crest smiled confidently and continued, "America needs a new image abroad, but it also needs effective leadership. There's no doubt in my mind that Harrison is the right person for the job. Of equal importance, we must surround Harrison with the expertise and leadership that will assist him in being an effective leader both domestically and abroad. Harrison and I want to preserve a sense of continuity concerning the US government, but there is only one way to advance the prompt integration of former slaves while preserving and advancing our interest abroad. Harrison is the key. He is the positive message we need to send to our country and the rest of the world. We need your support and, if we succeed, we would like for each one of you to remain in the Cabinet." The silence in the room was almost suffocating.

Crest continued, "We recognize this will be a difficult transition. This is the beginning of a new era. But what is most exciting is that it's not just about ending slavery, it's about taking advantage of America's potential. With the end of slavery will come an opportunity for *all* Americans to earn a living and fluid wage. This will create some additional costs, but those costs will be more than offset by the new international dynamic created by our ability to execute trades internationally. All of the existing trade sanctions are likely to be removed once we eliminate the argument that America is an immoral country. This will allow America's manufacturing base to grow and will greatly enhance our exports. I also anticipate an increase in domestic productivity as our newly freed brothers and sisters receive fair wages for their hard work. Now these individuals will be working to retain their jobs, working to advance their careers."

To Crest's surprise, I interjected, "Yes, these will be exciting times indeed. As a former slave myself, I can attest that my productivity was depressed when I had a ceiling on my potential. Once you free an individual to benefit from his hard work and his successes, you will immediately have a more productive worker. When we begin to — "

Before I could say anything further, Moore interrupted, "Okay, okay. Before we get too far, I want to apologize for our prior interactions and I need to apologize for the institution of slavery itself. The institution has placed a terrible blight on America and I for one am excited to be a part of this movement." Crest and I exchanged a glance; this seemed an abrupt change of heart for a man who had previously been so unrelenting.

"However," Moore continued, "I must be honest and let you know up front that I believe President Hood to be a man of great integrity. He is also a man of great abilities. His administration has done a tremendous job in advancing our country economically. Therefore, I have some deep reservations about supporting someone who has very little political, governmental, and international experience."

"Yes!" chimed Thorpe.

"Well said, John," added Wright.

Moore nodded and continued, "These are very delicate times both domestically and abroad, and a president who has no experience with the system — not to mention zero formal education — could serve as a huge detriment to our country."

I opened my mouth to speak but felt my throat knot up. Moore's concern was legitimate. Crest, however, spoke in his usual cool, collected tone.

"I understand your concerns, John. But Harrison has already exhibited the qualities of a successful president many times over. I mean, it's clear he's a survivor. He survived the degradation and pain of slavery before leading one of the most unusual and complex movements in American history. He did so with limited access to external resources. His interpersonal skills are genuine, and he is a quicker study than any man I've met. Sure, he may lack formal experience and education, but that is where we come in. With our support, there's no doubt Harrison possesses the characteristics necessary to be a successful leader on a national scale."

Finding my words, I added, "Thank you, Brad. Gentlemen, I too understand and appreciate your concerns regarding my credentials. However, I think what I bring to the table most is an acute understanding of people and how to motivate them to achieve their potential. I'll rely on you on for a more formal understanding of how to navigate our nation's government and for a strong understanding as to how I should manage international issues."

Once again, my declaration was met with nothing but silence. Crest cleared his throat and offered, "Look, this is it. We have a path to choose. Here today, we have the opportunity to determine the direction of our country for decades to come. My belief is that, without Harrison, it will take years to integrate African Americans into our society. With his help, it may take a year. Once our black brothers and sisters are successfully integrated, we can begin to take advantage of our continued manufacturing strengths and leverage our new moral standing internationally. The decision we make this afternoon is critical to the future of our nation."

I took a cue from Crest's statement. "I've already gone to work internationally. It's clear the world favors a United States that is inclusive. I know this because I've just brokered another deal." With these words, Crest eyes opened wide, almost in concern. I hadn't yet shared my latest progress with him. "I have had extensive talks with Joachim Joc, the President of Germany. Joc has agreed to pay us the same price in gas that China is paying for natural gas out of Cove Point. The more countries we negotiate with, the fewer there are that will be purchasing from Russia. Hood may be a decent president from a fiscal standpoint, but he is largely considered a hypocrite internationally. I realize I'm the underdog here. But I may be the voice we need. After all, several leaders have already been willing to work with me."

My words were answered with smiles all around. Even Crest appeared surprised, but impressed.

Thorpe let out a deep laugh and said, "Well, this is impressive, Harrison. But, tell me this: How the hell did you learn to speak like this? I mean, you've lived in the Crops forever, right?"

"Yes, Evan," I said. "But I spent every night on the computer studying. As a slave you spend most of your time in isolation just thinking. In the evenings I had nothing to do but read articles and gather information from the Internet. Thanks to the Crops, I was well prepared for the resistance." There was a pause, and then Moore and Crest laughed.

Moore smiled, "Dug our own grave, did we?"

I couldn't help but laugh. "You've got that right, John."

This broke the ice. Our discussion became a meeting. Crest was artful and the group allowed him to describe what my administration might look like with only minimal hesitation. As we spoke, one prevailing issue arose: we needed to get rid of Benz. That would clear the path for the selection of an alternate administration.

Wright spoke up, "Don't you guys worry about Benz." He turned to Leske, "Isn't that right?"

Leske responded without looking up, "Benz has a problem with pictures. The kind you send to friends when you forget there's a mirror in the background. And an underage girl in your bedroom."

Crest and I exchanged a glance — Benz was toast. With both Hood and Benz out of the picture, we could move forward. It was sinking in; this could really happen. By the time we finished our conversation several hours later, I felt as if I were gaining a critical level of respect from those who would potentially form my cabinet. We all shook hands, and then Crest and I returned to our limousine as the sun was setting.

During our drive back to the White House, Crest said, "You know, you surprised the shit outta me mentioning that deal with Germany."

I chuckled. "I know. Sorry. I wanted to keep it on the down low in case they showed some resistance. Moore started in with me having the no education or political credentials. I knew I had to wake them up and show them I meant business."

Smiling he said, "Harrison, it was a great move. But we still can't trust those guys. We have to keep the pressure up."

I looked through the limo's skylight and could see the stars clearly. They were the same stars that shone over the Crops when I was a slave, but somehow they now held many more possibilities. I said a silent prayer for Apex. He'd made all of this possible.

As our caravan winded its way through DC, Crest spoke up again, "Harrison, you should know that I'm also going to be making a request of the legislature to consider moving the national seat back to Washington, DC. It's the birthplace of our country, and Washington is now the largest city in the world by population. It's time we brought the government back home."

"You want to bring the White House back to its formal glory?"

"If we can force this election and succeed, DC would be a better option for our capital. Richmond brings back too many images of slavery — not only for us, but for the rest of the world. We need to start anew."

"I agree with you," I said, looking at the Washington Monument in a new light.

By the time we pulled into the White House, it was late in the evening and I expected that everyone would have retired for the evening. I was wrong. Ray, Meagan, Tyra, Christian, Barry and about twenty others were up waiting to hear what happened and greeted us in the foyer.

With Crest by my side, I said, "I guess you all have been wondering where Mr. Crest and I have been today. These are very exciting times for our people and there may be even bigger changes ahead. As you all know, the Uniform Suffrage Act is now law. Included in that act are certain key provisions, including a confirmation that slavery is unconstitutional. Another provision mandates that in the event a president and vice president resign from office, there shall be a new national election held within thirty days. This election will be conducted via votes placed by Congress. The final mandate under the Uniform Suffrage Act grants every slave born in the United States both citizenship and the right to vote. Bearing all of this in mind, I would like to officially announce my candidacy for president of the United States. It is my hope that my presidency will mark a new era for our nation where African Americans are considered equal citizens, thereby strengthening our unity and relationships both domestically and abroad."

My speech elicited gasps from those who didn't serve on our council. After a moment, the room broke into applause. Seeing Meagan's smile and the look of joy on her face gave me the strength to continue with confidence.

"Thank you. As a result of my presidency, African Americans would gain not only freedom, but respect as well. No longer will we be considered a people outside the true fabric or our nation;

instead we will be an integral part of the United States' government."
I paused as my friends once again offered their applause. A sense of
gratification washed over me.

"These are exciting times indeed," I continued. "But we are not
there yet. It could all fall through and I may not even be elected. We
must be diligent over the next few weeks as we work to impeach
President Richard Hood and Vice President Frederick Benz.
Hopefully, we can force a special election. Now, I must thank Senator
Bradley Crest for his tremendous efforts. Brad is a true friend and a
remarkable strategist. If, in fact, I become president of the United
States, I would like Brad to serve as my vice president." I glanced at
Brad who put a hand to his heart and mouthed, "Thank you." For
a man of many words, I'd managed to render him speechless twice
that day.

I concluded my speech, saying, "We are well on our way here.
There is no doubt that we are close. I also recognize that there
are contingencies that could derail all of our carefully laid plans.
However, if it all falls into place, I may very well be your president
within a matter of months. Thank you."

Adrenaline pumping through my veins, I wasn't ready to turn
in. Instead, Meagan and I held hands while I answered everyone's
questions. It was a good moment to pause. We had accomplished so
much and this was our biggest victory to date.

It was four in the morning or so before Meagan and I headed to
bed. That night we made love for hours. If this was as good as it got,
I was beyond satisfied. Early in the morning as I lay in bed waiting to
drift off to sleep, I remembered Apex and the promises I'd made to
him. My responsibility was to see this through to the benefit of all. I
could rest later.

CHAPTER 37
DAYBREAK

As the weeks faded away, change came very rapidly. Crest had arranged for an emergency hearing in Congress in regards to the special election. The election would be held solely through votes placed by senators and members of the House. However, with slaves now having the right to vote, there was accountability by members in Congress to this new constituency. There was a massive number of African Americans in the United States and the new wave of abolitionism was spreading. Because of evolving sentiments and the changed electorate, Crest knew that both the representatives and senators would be forced to vote in a way that was consistent with their potential re-election. It would be in their best interest to support me.

Crest had already assigned a team of seven assistants to help me elevate my understanding of all the various issues that would come up during the course of the presidential election. I met with them diligently, determined to be as well prepared as possible.

Crest's team presented many issues both foreign and domestic for discussion and seemed surprised by the knowledge I'd already gathered. I already had a comprehensive understanding of the workings of our government and had continued to bone up on domestic issues since moving into the White House. I now had a decent understanding of how our economy worked, but there were some issues like stocks, and issues related to foreign trade, trade imbalance, and the national deficit about which I was still weak.

I was also in dire need of additional information about foreign affairs. There had been periodic wars in Israel and there was a consistently unsettled situation with both Russia and the Ukraine. The Middle East always seemed to be in conflict, as well. We talked a lot about terrorism and how the United States had failed as a leader in the fight on terrorism due to its compromised moral standing in light of slavery.

I told the team that it would be best to assume that those moral issues were off the table. We needed to assume a new world order in terms of foreign politics and that the US could effectively interface with any country in the world as it was no longer handicapped by hypocrisy.

To me, some of the preparations arranged by Crest were premature. Neither Hood nor Benz had resigned and my intuition was that Hood would continue to ride this out. I wondered what direction I would need to take if the presidential bid never happened. Meagan and I had long discussions about what we'd do if I didn't get the chance to run. We decided that we'd try to find jobs and save up enough money to build a house. I imagined a home just like those that I saw on the side of the highway when I was being transported to the breeding complex. There, I could have a free life with no monitors, no Admins; just the chance to sit in my own backyard would be intoxicating.

But those plans would have to wait. Finally, on March 28, 2019, it happened. Frederick Benz announced that he was resigning his position as vice president of the United States. In addition, Benz expressed a vote of no confidence concerning the president. On the day of his resignation, we all gathered in a conference room to watch Benz give his statement on the NNC. He stated that his resignation was in the best interest of the United States and that the end of slavery should be complimented by a new administration with a new, inclusive vision for the country. One of his statements struck me: "We should move with diligence to erase all doubt domestically and internationally that we are a changed country. Never again will we look back on times when African Americans were not treated as equals."

The line seemed aggressive to me; it suggested drastic measures and it had Crest's fingerprints all over it. Remembering our conversation with Leske and Wright and their concerns with Benz's illicit affair, it was clear they were helping to pull the strings here.

Hood was now the only barrier to the special election and Crest wanted to meet to discuss next steps. I had become accustomed to Crest handling all of the political maneuvering in advance of the election and I was ready to meet, but felt that I had little to offer in terms of strategy.

Crest arranged for us to meet at an office building in DC. Instead of coming to the White House, he had his security detail pick me up, as he wanted me to be more comfortable venturing out alone. And it did indeed feel strange to leave the safety of the White House without him; I hadn't realized how much I'd relied on Crest as a security blanket of sorts. Instead, I brought Christian along with me.

As our limo winded through the streets, Christian marveled at the many high-rise buildings. Washington was an amazing city and I wondered how all of the thousands of buildings could be occupied. It seemed impossible that there could be so many people in one city.

After twenty minutes or so, our police escort turned into a parking deck where we rode down a ramp and stopped in front of a gold-framed doorway. There were security personnel everywhere as we entered the elevator and rode up the 32nd floor.

Crest was waiting for us as we stepped off the elevator and was smiling ear to ear. "Harrison, Christian, good to see you. Time to get this done." He patted me on the back and we walked into a large conference room. I took a seat at the end of a long table with Crest and Christian to either side of me.

I raised an eyebrow at Crest. "This table is for fifteen people. Didn't you have anything more intimate?"

Crest laughed. "You better get used to being at the head of the table. Listen, we have a significant challenge ahead. Benz is gone, the tide is turning, and the pressure is building for Hood to resign. Many of his Cabinet members have pushed him to do so and I've also had a discussion with Hood. But he has made a request: he wants a private meeting with you."

I exchanged a look with Christian and then shook my head firmly. "A meeting with me? What, so he can poison me the way he did Apex? Hell, Brad, let's go ahead and schedule my funeral now! Christian, how much room is there beside Apex's plot at the White House?"

Crest responded, "Well, we would have a ton of security for the meeting. And, of course, you don't have to eat anything."

I blasted back, "Crest, no amount of security would be enough. The guy is a snake. He killed Apex. You should be ashamed for even asking me to do this!"

Crest bought me right back down to earth. "It's not about you, Harrison! It's about African Americans, the future of this country. If we get Hood to resign... ."

I didn't let him finish, "Fine. But Meagan's going to be pissed. We can't tell her. Just set it up."

CHAPTER 38
OUT OF THE SHADOWS

The upcoming meeting with Hood was making me queasy. Leske, Wright, and the other members of the cabinet had been informed about the meeting, but I hadn't told Barry and Ray. Of course Christian knew, but I had instructed him to keep quiet. I was most concerned about Meagan finding out. She would immediately equate the meeting with Apex's death and she didn't trust Hood — or even Crest for that matter. I remembered how her master abused her night after night in the Crops. She had every right to distrust white men.

I scheduled a briefing with Crest. We needed to define exactly how the meeting with Hood would take place and to clarify our goals. This meeting could define how our country looked over the next decade.

Crest came into the meeting as relaxed as could be. I, however, was in a very serious mood knowing that so much — possibly my own life — could be at stake.

Crest said, "You know that Hood has some hidden agenda. This will be a complex meeting and we need to be careful in case he's recording your conversation."

"A valid concern. But for starters, where will I be meeting him? Surely not the Capitol," I said, thinking of Apex's final moments.

"I've given it some thought," Crest said, scratching his head.

"I think it would make a powerful statement if you made a sitting president come to you and met at the White House."

"It might make a statement, but it's not the best choice. I have a particular place in mind. I'd rather meet Hood in Richmond."

Crest was taken aback. "Richmond? Are you kidding? If you thought the Capitol was a bad spot... ."

I interrupted, "The address is 818 East Marshall Street. Set it up."

Crest did not seem happy at all with my choice of location. Hood controlled Richmond and a thousand things could go wrong. Plus, Crest was unfamiliar with the address I'd given him. Even so, I insisted.

We moved on to discussing how the meeting would progress. Crest wanted to go in with a formal agenda. The first key would be to establish my credentials and begin to convince Hood of my ability to manage the government as president. We would focus on the "Commit to Resist" movement, how I helped build the infrastructure in the tunnels, and how my team had successfully executed the resistance.

Crest felt that Hood was already at a breaking point. His vice president had abandoned him, his cabinet was no longer supporting him, he was being impeached, and he'd allowed a group of former slaves to out-maneuver him. He could save face by allowing a peaceful transition. If he bowed out now and let me move forward with my candidacy, he could preserve his legacy. It was certainly more advantageous for him to resign rather than being impeached.

It all sounded sweet, but I knew Hood. Apex had lost his life dealing with that snake. I doubted that there was anything I could say that would move Hood one way or another.

After meeting with Crest, I decided it was time to tell Meagan. For her, I knew this news couldn't come at a worse time. Things had begun to settle at the White House and we'd finally established a relative sense of normalcy. Crest had arranged for some of our team to be moved into apartments in the area. I'd visited the new living quarters and approved the move. I wanted my friends to start their new lives; being stuck at the White House had sometimes felt like we were imprisoned. We replaced those individuals with new staffers who were there to make the environment more comfortable. There was now an even greater mix of whites and blacks, professionals and former slaves all working together. And the new staffers worked for us. For a former slave, these were good times.

Meagan and I were at a place where we had a choice to make. We had done our job. Freedom had been achieved. Who would blame us for asking Crest to find us some anonymous, non-descript apartment or home somewhere so that we could begin a new life?

Meagan and I walked into the Oval Office, and I gestured toward the large, antique desk. "Look at this, sweetheart. This is where presidents once made major decisions, and soon it may officially be mine. Can you believe it?"

She smiled. "It's amazing. You and Apex got us here. Things were so hopeless in the Crops. Sometimes I feel like I'm dreaming."

I reached for Meagan's hand. "I feel the same way, too. But here we are. My only concern is our next step."

Meagan held my hand tighter, "What next step?"

I turned away and walked toward a window. "We have a responsibility to the American people to finish this. We have secured our freedom but we now need to secure our future. Crest is right. The one way to accelerate a positive future for all African Americans is for me to become president. Unfortunately for us to achieve that, I have to meet with one person: Richard Hood."

Meagan's demeanor changed. "Meet with who? President Hood? No. No! Harrison, he killed Apex. I won't let you do this. You're too important."

I knew she meant "too important" to her. But this was no longer about me and Meagan and our future. It was about our race, our people, Apex's legacy. My perspective had solidified.

"Please don't go," Meagan begged.

"I have no choice. I won't be able to live with myself if I don't do everything I can for our people," I said. I reached out to grab her hand, but she turned and stormed out of the Oval Office, crying. I knew inside that nothing would placate her until I returned safely from my meeting with Hood. Though I was uncertain as to whether I would actually return.

Crest scheduled the meeting for the following week. This gave Barry and I plenty of time to prepare for the meeting. Hood agreed to the location and I suggested that the meeting be held at four o'clock. But I planned for Crest and I to arrive at the house on Marshall Street at least two hours early. I had Christian accompany us.

The limousine ride didn't seem quite as long this time. I had gotten comfortable with limousines. I sipped from a bottle of water and reclined, my back facing the limo driver. "Christian, what do you think? Hood killed Apex. Am I doing the right thing here? We could be driving right into a trap."

Christian looked out of his window, "I think you're a brave man. Hood is a nightmare, but I understand why you're doing this."

"Why *am* I doing this?" I laughed.

"So all of us can live better lives than we ever imagined. I want to be more than just some freed slave begging for respect and opportunity. I want to live like they do. Freedom is not enough. I want to be equal. Somehow, I think I'd have a better chance if you were president."

I looked down to review some of the notes that Barry had given me, "Well said, Christian. Well said."

Despite the fact we were two hours early, the president's secret service staff was already in place when we arrived at the John Marshall House. Marshall was a scenic two-story brick home that had become a historic landmark. Christian was held back in a waiting room by the secret service staff, and Crest and I were escorted through a set of double doors. The secret service staff then began to frisk Crest and me. Crest's face turned bright red and then purple as they patted down our arms, back, legs, and even our crotches.

Crest yelled, "I'm a United States senator! And you guys are frisking me? This is a joke!"

My mind flashed back to the examination I'd undergone prior to breeding; I had been through worse. I let them frisk me without uttering a word.

We were taken in through the double doors to what appeared to be another waiting area where Crest and I sat for nearly two hours. There were two guards stationed at the door. Finally, one of the guards approached me and said, "The president will see you now." Crest attempted to rise from his seat. But the other guard placed a large, firm hand on Crest's shoulder and held him down. "Only Mr. Vance, sir."

Crest grimaced and spoke in a loud whisper, "There is no way in hell I'm letting Harrison go in there by himself."

I put my hand on Crest's other shoulder. "It's got to be done. I'm ready."

Crest was still shaking his head as the guards led me through the door and into a dimly lit room with polished, hardwood floors and beautiful, flowing curtains. At its center was a dining room table upon which sat a large bowl of fruit. I sat down at the table. As tempting as they appeared, I decided against eating any of the fruit.

After a moment, a corner door opened. In walked a guard followed by Richard Hood, the president of the United States. Hood stopped at a side table and without acknowledging my presence, poured himself a drink of some type of brown liquor. He then walked toward me and I stood to show my respect. Staring into my eyes with stern, cold calculation, Hood offered me a slow, firm handshake. He was taller than I expected, around six foot three or so, and I was eager to sit down and even the playing field. He directed me to sit at the head of the table, then sat his glass down and took a seat, reclined in a casual fashion. He put both hands on his glass and stared at me. Finally, after a painful thirty seconds or so, he spoke.

"Interesting decision to meet here. I applaud you, Phoenix."

I wanted to make sure Hood understood I was not intimidated. "It's Harrison," I corrected him. "And thank you, sir. John Marshall was all about a straightforward interpretation of the Constitution. He believed in key principles like 'we the people,' 'justice,' 'general welfare,' and the 'blessings of liberty.' Those principles are inconsistent with slavery, don't you think?"

Hood raised an eyebrow and smirked, "You are a smart guy, Phoenix. But maybe not smart enough. Go back and look at Article IV, son. You'll see how much of an abolitionist Marshall was. He favored states' rights, including the right to elect to maintain slavery. You can't just read a few books or articles and hope to have a meaningful conversation with the president of the United States," he smiled and took a deep swig of his drink. Something, maybe the color in his cheeks or the tone of his voice, told me this wasn't his first drink.

I was not persuaded. "Marshall owned slaves but he was an abolitionist. Perhaps you were briefed improperly."

Hood sat back in his chair, "You're a smart guy, Harrison. Smart enough to understand that you guys messed it all up. This was about order. You're *so* smart. Have you read the Constitution? That's one of the first words in the preamble: Order. The order was whites, then slaves. Order is what has brought our great nation this far. Our industrial advantage worldwide was a direct result of our observation of the natural order of things. Now, because of your so-called insurrection, things are turned upside down. They are uncertain. The United States had it all and now people wonder what the next day will bring. You guys did this. Now it's time for you to correct it."

I leaned forward, "Correct it how?"

Hood got up and filled his short glass with more brown liquor. "Harrison, I have a deal for you. You have distinguished yourself, and I need someone in my administration who will help me calm things down and move our country forward. Whether I like it or not, you helped end slavery, son. Now, help me move our country and your people forward. I am creating a new position in my cabinet. I need you to serve as my secretary of African American affairs."

I slowly got up, walked over to the side table, and grabbed a glass. I grabbed the bottle from which Hood had been pouring. The label read "Jack Daniels Old No. 7." I poured a little into the glass, raised it to my lips, and took a sip. It tasted like bitter, hot medicine, but I kept my composure. I sat back down and moved my chair closer to Hood.

"Richard, I must respectfully decline your offer. This is not just about order. It's also about justice and equality. It will take years, if not decades, for African Americans to enjoy the same rights as white Americans unless something drastic happens. That something drastic ought to be an African American president."

Hood's demeanor immediately grew darker, "Are you out of your fuckin' mind? I just offered you a position in the cabinet of the president. Just a few months ago, you were a slave in the Crops. Come on, Harrison. You're smarter than this."

I remained calm, "I am smart enough to recognize that this is about our country. Working in your administration won't achieve anything but add a title to my name, and this is not about me or my journey. What about 'We the People?' It's not about me. It's about everyone having a better life."

Hood raised his voice to a near shout, "Son, it's never been about everyone having a good life! You think that's how we got here? You think that's how we became the greatest country on earth? No, son, this is about the elite! Those who are in power."

Hood took another sip of his drink, and lowered his voice once more. "The Hood family has stood up for our country since before the Civil War. Through perseverance, we gained political and economic power. With that power, we helped shape this country. It was people like us who led the way. This ain't about some lower middle class farmer from Nebraska or some newly freed slave from New York. You think I give a fuck about people like that? This is about the overwhelming might that is our country. That might comes through the strength of leaders like me and leaders like you, Harrison. Those of us who worked our asses off to get where we are."

I leaned back and began to clap my hands. "Great speech, Richard. I don't know whether I should be honored or insulted. But there is no way that I can accept your offer."

Hood's eyes narrowed with rage. He walked over to the counter and screwed the bottle top tightly on the bottle of Jack Daniels and carried it back to the table with him. "You know, I've never had a drink with a nigger. I always avoided it. Didn't want to get my glasses dirty. Same reason I never slept with a nigger woman. But I sure would have loved to get me a taste of that... what was her name, Meagan? Damn, it would have been nice to get a hold of her license. Be sure to send her my regards." Hood took another drag of his Jack Daniels, waiting for my reaction. But, I simply sat there unwilling to let him get under my skin.

Without taking his eyes off of me, Hood hissed to his guard, "Get this nigger out of here."

As the guard approached, I stood up. Despite my willingness, he grabbed my right arm and roughly pushed me out into the waiting room. Crest was standing there, waiting for me. Placing a hand on my back, Crest pulled me out through the next set of doors and past Christian who jumped up to follow us. Our security was waiting and we climbed into the limousine.

As soon as we were safely seated inside, Crest spoke, "Well, that didn't go to well. I could hear that asshole through the wall. I guess we'll have to go it alone. He'll never resign now."

Traffic was thick and it was a long, uncomfortable ride back to the White House. By the time we returned, it was almost ten o'clock. Only a few staffers were still mulling around. Crest hastily said goodnight as he promised to develop a new strategy by daybreak.

Christian and I walked into our main meeting room where Ray and Berry were waiting. I walked over to Barry and slowly took off my jacket. I then opened my belt, saying, "You were right, Ray — too much respect! They only patted down my arms, legs, chest, and crotch." I reached behind my belt buckle and pulled out the thin recorder that Barry had taped inside.

I tossed the recorder over to Barry. "Get this to the NNC as soon as possible." With a wink at Christian, I added, "I guess a resignation is in order after all."

The following morning, the NNC aired soundbites from my conversation with Hood. The entire nation heard his slurs and his disdain for the working man. Minutes later, I received a call from Crest.

"What the hell is this, Harrison? You recorded a conversation with the president of the United States? If you'd been caught, all bets would have been off."

I was quick to respond, "Well, I wasn't caught, was I? Let's just see how it plays out." I was gaining my footing with Crest, but I wanted him to understand that I had independent thoughts and plans. Our success was not entirely contingent on him and I needed his trust.

I spent the afternoon watching news reports in what one of the old guards called the "Blue Room." I was starting to become very comfortable there. I had also started spending time in the Solarium at the top of the White House. It was beautiful and quiet and afforded me time to collect my thoughts.

The reporters voiced their amazement that, once again, we had outsmarted the president. I thought the entire story would revolve around Hood's disrespect for the American people and his obvious elitism, but it also focused on my patriotism and my selection of Marshall House for the meeting. Apparently it "suggested a real depth of thought." One reporter even mentioned that this was the type of thoughtfulness that you would expect from a president of the United States. These were the types of endorsements I needed.

Hood really had nowhere to go at this point. His choices were clear: either limp through the impeachment process and become the first president removed from office, or resign while citing that he was doing what was best for the country. I really had no need to contact or meet with him again. I had inflicted a fatal political wound and there was no way out and no way to recover.

Another key benefit was showing Hood's Cabinet that I could stand face to face with Hood, or any other leader for that matter. I was certain our conversation had gained me some further measure of respect. I knew I had momentum, so I decided to call John Moore directly.

When I finally reached him, Moore seemed surprised I was calling without Crest. His first comment was: "Is Brad coming on?"

"No. I haven't spoken to him, but I needed to speak to you about where we are."

Moore sounded confused, "Where we are?"

I went straight to the point, "I'm going to need all the support I can get during the election. Some in Congress will never vote for a former slave. Others will vote in the country's best interest. All they need is a nudge and I'll need someone to legitimize me. Crest will not be enough, but with you and the cabinet . . ."

Moore cut me off, "I've already confirmed with Crest that we will support you. There has to be a plan, however, and you need to stick to it. And we need to remain an active cabinet. You have a lot to learn, Harrison. If you win, you will need guys with experience around you. We're taking one hell of a risk here, but country first."

I replied that I understood and agreed. I then noted. "I'm gonna need another favor from you. The Logan Act... you know that I will need immunity for all that I've done." Moore promised to assist with the grant of immunity as the Act prohibited a private citizen from negotiating with foreign governments.

I promised to advise Moore concerning every step we took. Our conversation was liberating. I was branching out and speaking directly with officials on my own. It was a critical step, but Hood still needed to resign.

It didn't take long. Two days later we were met with breaking news that the president would be making a speech. Crest came over and we headed to a reception area in the West Wing to watch the broadcast.

Hood was seated at his desk in the presidential mansion in Richmond. The camera zoomed in on a clean-shaven and composed president. This was a sharp contrast to how he appeared when we met at Marshall House.

Clearing his throat, Hood began, "Good morning. First and foremost, I'd like to thank everyone who has supported me throughout my presidency. Without each one of you, I would have not been able to accomplish so much." He then proceeded to rattle off a short list of prime right-wing accomplishments including economic developments and international negotiations.

"As you all may know, my administration has always been deeply committed to our country and its institutions; institutions that have enriched the very fabric of our nation since its beginnings. Unfortunately, it seems the tides have turned and many in this country have lost faith in the very institutions upon which we have relied for so long. It has long been my guiding principal to do 'what is best for our country,' and today is no different." Crest and I exchanged a glance and he placed a hand on my shoulder.

The president continued, "In light of my love for our country, I recognize there are times when we all must make individual sacrifices. And while it is my strong desire to continue serving the country I love, circumstances demand a transition. The world must know we are a stable democracy, united in our desire to lead the world in a positive direction despite any internal debate. To that end, I am resigning from the presidency of the United States effective tomorrow at noon. Thank you, and may God bless America."

I was almost moved by Hood's speech, though he had not mentioned the end of slavery, nor had he made mention of equality or justice. And he had certainly not referenced Apex or me. As surprisingly humble as his speech was, I quickly moved on. Hood was now a non-factor. Crest and I had a campaign to run and Congress was waiting.

Crest and I decided I should announce my bid for president on the steps of the Capitol in memory of Apex. This way, we figured, we'd show the world that Apex's death had not prevented our progress. I began my speech by requesting a moment of silence for all who were lost during the crisis. I then spoke about the strength of unity, emphasizing how the diversity of our talents would do more than just balance the loss of free labor. During my speech, I also mentioned my deal with the President of Germany, Joachim Joc, who gave his own speech in support of my bid for president.

I discussed how the United States was becoming a player on the world stage, which presented a challenging thought for the members of our team. For years, the United States had simply practiced isolation in terms of world affairs. We moved unilaterally on many issues, not wanting to give up the benefits of slavery in return for a more effective international presence.

I looked up on several occasions and noted the stunned faces of those in the crowd. They simply weren't used to an African American being articulate and comprehensive in his thinking.

I ended my speech by talking about the "staggering brightness" of our new era. We had ended slavery. Now, together, we could erase many of the remnants of the oppressive past and move forward with a clear conscience and a clean slate. If I were elected president, it would send a signal to the entire world that the United States was committed to justice and equality.

For the first five minutes of our ride back to the White House, Crest was completely silent. Finally, I spoke up. "You okay?"

Crest looked up at me, bewildered. "Man, where did that come from? That was an incredible speech. I'm amazed. Didn't you feel any pressure at all?"

I smiled. "Just a few months ago I was a slave, Brad. I could have been arrested, beaten, or even killed at a moment's notice. So, sure, I was a little nervous before my speech. But it's just a speech. How bad could it be?"

According to the NNC, the speech was a great success. The world now saw me as a credible candidate, and in truth, that was the best we could have hoped for. The stage was set and we now had a strong platform concerning our campaign.

Meanwhile, my staff at the White House had become larger. I found myself presiding over meetings of twenty or more people. I knew I was equipped to handle our meetings, but I still had much to learn. Fortunately, my new associates were eager to teach. After each session, I would spend hours drowning myself in the knowledge we had covered.

At the end of each day, I would head to the TVs to watch the status of the election and debates that were set to come up. The abolishment of slavery was still headline news across the country, the news arriving later for those further inland. In some areas, slaves didn't have easy access to the Internet and their former masters were reluctant to share the information. But the word was quickly spreading that freedom was the new law of the land.

One evening, I found Tyra alone in the command center, holding a framed picture of Apex that we kept at the front of the room. A glass of wine sat on a table next to her, dripping with condensation.

Sitting down in a chair opposite her, I said, "Hello, Tyra. How are you feeling?"

Not looking at me she replied, "You know, I should be out there celebrating with everyone and rejoicing that we've accomplished so much. But honestly? I'm split in two right now, wondering why I had to fall in love with a man who had to be braver than he needed to be."

Handing her one of my handkerchiefs, I said, "I want you to know something; I too have those same fears and reservations. Apex left some mighty big shoes to fill and I'm afraid I'm not ever going to live up to his expectations."

Tyra looked up at me with her eyebrows furrowed in confusion. "What are you talking about? Harrison, you've done more than Apex dared to dream of. If it wasn't for you being involved, none of this would be happening."

"That's the issue," I sighed. "This is a whole lot bigger than anything I ever imagined while I was in the Crops. The truth is, it's all been luck. I wrote on my shoe, for crying out loud. Just a simple act. I wasn't aware of any resistance, and I didn't have any plan beyond that. I only did it to satisfy my personal desire for retaliation and my motivations were entirely selfish. I never knew my little act of rebellion would make such a big difference."

Wiping her eyes, Tyra said, "I guess it's about time I told you more about the argument Apex had that night in the tunnels when you found out about the two of us." Clearing her throat and taking a sip of wine, Tyra continued, "After you pointed out the holes in his plan, something everyone saw but dared not question him on, Apex knew you would be the one to lead us further than he could. He wanted to free everyone by any means necessary; he hated feeling helpless. Apex watched his mother being raped by her master when he was just seven years old. Ironically, that same master was the very person who taught him all he knew about technology. This created a bitter dilemma for Apex: hating the very person who helped him achieve his potential. Apex grew into an idealist militant. He firmly believed all of us were ready to kick ass in the name of freedom," she smiled and gestured "cheers" before taking another sip of wine.

"He called you 'Phoenix' due to your perseverance. He had written a program that gauged a slave's activities on the Internet. If you met a certain criterion, including engaging in particular searches on the Internet that suggested a desire to rebel, we would begin surveillance. Apex became enamored with you because you always went to work with a smile on your face. Even with your head down, you always smiled. Even after all the hell you'd been through, you never lost your smile. After Apex met you, he quickly realized you believed something bigger than the misery you were experiencing. That's why he expected much more from you when you came down to the tunnels, Harrison. But he forgot one key thing: You're only human. You wanted to be lazy for a change and enjoy the freedom of doing whatever you wanted. We told him it was unfair to place so much responsibility on your shoulders. After all, it was such new information to you and you had no way of knowing what to do."

I nodded, uncertain of how to respond. After a moment, Tyra continued, "I want to thank you for supporting him despite everything. And for being brave enough to face Hood after all that…" Her voice trailed off as she took a ragged breath.

"Tyra, I'm — " I began, but she held up a finger to stop me.

"Please let me finish, Harrison. If it had been me, President Hood would be six feet under in a million pieces and that would've set us back decades, if not eons." Her eyes were fiery pinpoints of rage as she took a deep sip from her glass.

"Hell hath no fury like a woman scorned," I said.

Tyra let out a loud scoff. "That's why you're the best choice for all this, Harrison. I still want to slip into Hood's office and slit his throat, but I know Apex wouldn't want me to endanger this revolution. We worked so hard to get here and my personal vendetta cannot take precedence."

Tyra stood up, and placing a hand on my shoulder, said warmly, "Make sure you love Meagan with the same intensity that she loves you. We black women have to be strong for our black men. With that kind of dedication comes something one hundred times more deadly than any object, animal, or man if anything comes between us and our men. Remember that when you get up there and speak for us, Harrison. Remind our women that we are all warriors underneath the pretty words and genteel smiles. Remind our women that we are royalty and we are ready to die for what we believe in."

With that, Tyra left me alone to ponder all she'd said. She'd revealed a fierceness that had always been just below the surface, something I'd sensed the first time I met her and looked into her uniquely piercing eyes.

As I stepped outside the conference room, I spotted Meagan standing alone. I slid up behind her and embraced her, taking a deep breath of her rose-scented perfume. Everyone else was off in their own groups, celebrating the power of being free and living their lives as they saw fit. Every night since the USA had passed, there had been a reason to celebrate. With the added excitement of my candidacy, everybody wanted to spend this night with someone special.

I stole Meagan away into the Blue Room for some much needed privacy, thankful there was no one there to bother us. Meagan sat down on blue, velvet couch and I lay down next to her, my head resting in her lap. Tyra's words still echoed in my mind. *Love her with the same intensity that she loves you.*

"Meagan," I said softly, "I love you. With all my heart, I do. I know this first year of transition will be hard for all of us — African Americans and white citizens alike. But no matter what, I know we have a future together. If I'm not elected, I'll get a job. Maybe go back to the cleaners…"

Meagan laughed. "I love you, too. But you and I both know that after everything you've accomplished, the only thing you'll be cleaning is America's assumption that African Americans are just some poor, silent stereotype. This is what you were made for, baby."

I smiled. She was right, as usual.

As for the rest of our team, they would all have to stay in their same jobs, at least for now. It would be a long and difficult integration process, and there would be a great deal of uncertainty and friction from people who were less than enamored with the idea of a black man being their equal. Nonetheless, we were on our way.

As Meagan and I sat in silence, I wondered about Crest's plans. How did he see his role going forward? Although I trusted him, I needed to make sure I controlled my destiny and the destiny of my people. No one, not even Crest, could take that control away from us. Crest was becoming a trusted and loved friend, but this was bigger than either of us and I needed to know his true intentions. This was my last thought as I drifted off to sleep.

When I awoke the next morning, Meagan had left and I had a blanket covering me. I was awakened by Reggie, one of our staff members. He said, "Mr. Vance, you need to come downstairs immediately. Your staff meeting started 30 minutes ago."

Many of our staffers had taken to calling me "Mr. Vance" already. It was strange to hear that. As I walked downstairs with the blanket around my shoulders, I was shocked that the clock read nine thirty. There was already a flurry of activity as I rubbed the sleep from my eyes.

Reggie walked me over to the conference room where the team was already assembled. Tyra, Barry, and Ray were seated along with three members of my new preparation team.

One of the members of the preparation team spoke up, "Thank you for joining us, sir. A number of congressmen have announced this morning that they will be supporting your candidacy for president."

Everything in me woke up. I became instantly focused and said, "Well, I guess you guys know what this means; we're in campaign mode. These are delicate times and any mistake I make with the media could be devastating. This is not about convincing people I'm some type of super candidate. This is about convincing Congress that I'm competent and serious about this run. Crest and I believe Congress has a desire, because of our situation internationally, to elect someone who will have an immediate impact on our domestic and foreign interests. So, we have an advantage, but that advantage will be our weakness if I appear to be inexperienced or uninformed. It will be your job to make sure I'm fully prepared and I want you all to be tough on me."

Tyra gave a firm nod that encouraged me to keep speaking from my heart. "This is the chance of a lifetime and although we're no longer slaves, the perception of the African American is critical. We must set a platform for success and freedom; we must set a shining example of what the African American can be." Ray handed out folders, and I knew it was time to get down to business.

CHAPTER 39
WINDING PATH

rest arrived at about two o'clock that same afternoon with more staff and more supplies. Despite Crest's considerable efforts, my fellow former slaves and I had found ourselves in a confusing situation. We were now technically free, but we didn't know what to do with that freedom. I felt constrained. From a legal standpoint I could walk out the White House gates and onto the street. But, I didn't feel comfortable doing so. And, I wasn't the only one. Attitudes were shifting, but it would still be some time before African Americans could feel comfortable walking down the street, let alone shopping for groceries. Furthermore, until a new payment system was established and African Americans began earning fair wages, we had little money to pay for supplies anyway.

The crowd outside the White House had evaporated to just a few individuals on the streets with signs. The armed guards were now *inside* the White House gates, there to protect us. Every time I looked out the window I'd see a few curious onlookers checking out the situation, but for the most part we felt secure. The imminent crisis was over.

As we settled into the Oval Office, Crest loosened his tie, rolled up his sleeves, and took a few drags on a cigar — a nasty habit I was glad I'd never been exposed to. He spoke with confidence, "Well, Harrison, the stage has been set. You're now in a situation where those additional provisions under the Uniform Suffrage Act will be triggered. There will be an election of the president via Congress within thirty days and there's very little time to campaign. There will be time for just one debate. Do you think you'll be prepared for a debate against a seasoned opponent?"

"Well, I guess it depends on who that opponent is. Who do you think would face us?" I asked.

"Well, it's tough to determine right now; I'd expect most Republicans to stay away from the opportunity, honestly. The heavy abolitionist spirit in the United States means it would be very difficult for a Republican — or at least a preservationist Republican — to win this election. However, there are a couple of candidates who could give us problems. Thomas Raines could be a problem if the ultra-conservative element gains momentum. Ashton Bragg is also an issue. He's a young buck of a politician with military ties. Dale Broyles from my home state could also be a problem; he's viewed as moderate and appeals to both Democrats and Republicans. So sure, we may face some stiff challenges. Especially if you're talking about someone who's held leadership in their party for many years and has a good understanding of both domestic and foreign affairs."

I said confidently, "Well, I guess it doesn't really matter who our opponent is. The reality is we're running against history and losing is not an option. We're running for all Americans — no matter their race or creed. This is about the future of the United States, so we have to do everything we can to be prepared regardless of our opponent."

Crest agreed and we discussed plans for me to formally introduce myself to members of Congress who would have a vote in the election. I needed to learn the personalities of each congressman and begin to sway them to our side. The moment I felt a lull in the discussion, I raised a question that had been on my mind.

"Brad, these are unusual times for you as well. I've got to ask you something."

Crest's eyes narrowed somewhat. "What's on your mind, Harrison?" Lowering my voice to a confidential tone, I said, "Despite all your accolades, you've never taken that next step to run for president. Why settle for vice president now? It seems like a step below your true ambition. Why not run for president yourself? You're white and would have an easier time achieving the same goals. Plus, you'd likely win this election hands down, no questions asked. Will this be enough for you? Where do you see yourself down the line?" Despite my overwhelming gratitude for all he had done, I needed to know where Crest's heart was. Was he truly in support of my candidacy and all it could provide for our country, or was I just a foot in the door for his own agenda? I sincerely hoped the latter wasn't the case, but I couldn't shake the feeling. I needed to know how much I could trust him going forward.

Crest stood up and turned toward the window as he contemplated my words. "Well, that's a very interesting question. Yes, I've always wanted to look at obtaining a higher office, but the timing was never right. Plus, I've always had my family to think about."

I walked over to Crest, and looking him directly in the eyes, I said, "Be honest with me, Brad. Is that really the case? Or did you never run because you knew you couldn't win? Maybe you knew it would never work. An abolitionist candidate in a country that was totally dependent on slavery? For you to win, it would take something drastic. Perhaps even a revolution of sorts. And you'd need to enable a new electorate so that you achieve your goal. And lo and behold, the tides have changed and now you're just one step away. Isn't that convenient? If I become president you're my vice president, that would mean you're only a 'me' away from where you need to be, right? And if something were to happen to me, you'd be the next president all by circumstance, isn't that right?"

Crest's face reddened and he opened his mouth, dumbfounded. I knew I'd caught him off guard, but this was something that had been on my mind for quite some time. I knew Crest was a good man with a benevolent spirit, but he was also a politician. He had to have his own agenda and I needed to know his heart.

"Harrison, I don't — " he began, but I cut him off.

Turning my back to Crest, I said forcefully, "Brad, I need one thing from you before we move forward. I need a signed agreement that you will not seek the office of president should I die in office."

My words were met with silence and when I turned to face him, his brows were furrowed in disbelief. He looked heartbroken.

"Harrison, what are you suggesting?" Crest asked quietly.

I softened my tone, "I'm not suggesting anything, Brad. I just need to know, for my peace of mind and for the peace of mind of my people, that you have no agenda other than creating a new and brighter America. You said it yourself, this is not about us — this is about the future. I need to know this isn't some rouse where I die unexpectedly and you wind up in the position you've always dreamed of. So let's take that situation off the table right now."

For the first time since I'd met him, Crest looked tired. His silence frightened me.

Finally, he spoke up, "Look, of course I would never want anything to happen to you. This has always been about the betterment of our country and the African American people. But if it helps you sleep at night, sure, I'll sign your agreement. Before I sign, however, there's something you should know about my family. You were bound to hear about it sooner or later, and I'd prefer to tell you the truth before the rumor mill reaches you."

My heart sank at the mention of family. I'd always dreamed of having a family of my own, and the thought of hurting a friend or compromising his family's happiness put me back in reality.

"Brad, what is it?" I asked.

Speaking in a soft tone, Crest began, "During my youth I was full of bright ideas about abolishing slavery. My family didn't want to support me; they owned several stocks in Crops across the country. When I was nineteen, I went with my father to visit the Crops in

Boston. It was there I fell in love with a beautiful black woman named Lucy. She was charming and intelligent and she could sing like an angel.

"Lucy belonged to someone else, a rival family, the Richards, who gave her to their oldest daughter as a wet nurse. You have to understand that, as a white man, you do not touch another man's slave for any reason whatsoever. But Lucy and I were in love. I violated that law and would do so again without question. Lucy and I married in secret and I helped her escape to Canada where she could live freely. I promised to move there with her as soon as I could secure a job abroad. But we both knew it would be months before we'd see each other again."

I was shocked. Crest's actions were without question illegal, but they also confirmed his dedication to our cause without a doubt.

He continued, "When Mr. Joseph B. Richards finally learned what I'd done, he declared war on my family and threatened to sue us for all we had. He sent bounty hunters to find Lucy and bring her back to him. My family left me alone to fend for myself. I knew I needed to protect Lucy and I flew to Canada as fast as I could. But I was too late. Lucy had taken her own life. She had given up. I was riddled with guilt. She would still be alive if she'd never met me. I was... I was cold inside for a long time after that." Crest cleared his throat and brushed away tears that had begun rolling down his cheeks.

"Brad, I'm so sorry. I didn't know."

He shook his head and continued, "What I didn't know at the time was that during our separation, Lucy had given birth to a little boy who she'd sent to live with another family for fear of his safety. One month after Lucy died, a frail old black woman came to my home in Richmond and told me the news. She reunited me with my son and I brought him back home with me. Since he was born in Canada, he was free. But, he could not enjoy the freedoms of being an American citizen."

I now understood Crest's passion as an abolitionist. "This is why you became such a strong advocate for ending slavery. He's the aide,

Anthony, who came with us to Richmond a few weeks ago, isn't he?"

Crest nodded. "Yes. I want my son to be free to be anything he wants here in the states. He shouldn't be hindered because he was brought into a world that considered him property and not a human being."

"I understand and I'm sorry," I said, placing a hand on Crest's shoulder. We wrapped up our conversation and I saw him out.

I understood Crest's desire to ensure that his son was able to enjoy the rights white Americans had. But was he just using this story to gain my sympathy? My gut told me he was a good and honest man, but this was a game of chess and I couldn't take any chances.

I not only had to think of young men like Anthony, but also of everyone else who wanted to live freely without fear of their loved ones swinging from trees. I couldn't allow myself to be a pawn and I prayed Crest wouldn't make me out to be one.

CHAPTER 40
SUNDAY'S BEST

I dedicated my Saturday to preparing for the only debate that would be held during this special election. I spent almost the entire day sitting with the team and gathering information related to the upcoming campaign. Decision day was approaching and there was simply no time for me to take a break.

Crest and I had spoken numerous times by phone. The day after our confrontation he'd sent a written statement that he'd signed and had notarized stating that he wouldn't seek the office of president upon my untimely death. This alone restored my faith in him, and I would no longer question his loyalty.

My advisors and I were sequestered for the entire day and as the evening wore on, I resolved that Sunday would not be like this. Yes, we had work to do, but for my own sanity, I needed to take a break and I wanted to spend time with Meagan.

Before retiring that night, I advised Barry to send an email reminder to the former slave community that Monday morning they should all return to work. We needed to show we could be productive and earn the fair wages that were finally due to us. My team feared there were some out there itching to take up guns to avenge Apex. I was more concerned about showing our competence as a workforce.

I had requested that Crest have a limousine available for me during the mid-morning hours on Sunday. As my role and stature in American politics grew, it was critical I receive necessary protection. He provided me with a car and twenty-four-hour security detail.

Sunday morning around ten o'clock, Meagan met me in the foyer wearing a beautiful blue silk dress and matching heels. I'd worked into the wee hours of the night and now we both wanted to spend some alone time together. Unfortunately, we'd have to get used to being "alone" with our armed security.

Meagan climbed into the back of the limousine and looked around nervously. "I always ordered these things for people at the hotel, but I never imagined I'd ride around in one, touring the very city that made me a slave since birth."

I was elated that Meagan was here with me and there was only one place I wanted to go. As our car drove through DC and headed toward the bay, we looked out the windows, seeing the city in a new light.

DC on a weekend morning wasn't quite as frantic as a normal business day. People sat outside at cafes, walked in and out of shops and churches, and appeared relaxed and serene as they enjoyed their Sunday.

Our driver broke the silence asking, "Mr. Vance would you like to go to Baltimore?"

Meagan and I looked at each other. We both knew it was too soon to go back there.

"No, sir. Baltimore is in the past and we are living in the present. Take us to the docks that face the Chesapeake Bay, please."

A few minutes later we pulled into an open dock area. Our security vehicles surrounded us and made sure all was safe before they let us out of the car. Meagan and I got out and walked toward a small pier with a few boats anchored to it. The boats were small and modest. I assumed this was a docking area for local fishermen.

This dock was isolated and I took a deep breath of fresh Chesapeake Bay air. This waterway had defined my life until now. As a slave, I'd often looked over the water and envisioned it as a gateway to the life I desired. Not in my wildest imagination could I have dreamed of being in this position. As I stood there now, my arm around Meagan, I laughed out loud thinking about how just months ago, we'd both been slaves. Now we stood here with full security detail watching our every move simply because I wanted to take my girlfriend out for a "private" moment. As I leaned down to kiss her, I realized I'd never been happier.

When we returned to the White House that afternoon, Crest had left a message reminding me for the thousandth time that we had the key advantage of preparing for a debate even before our opponent had been designated. I bid farewell to Meagan and set to business.

I couldn't rely on charisma alone; I had to prove to the world I was the best man for the job. My story and tenacity combined was the one thing no one could take from me and I wouldn't let anyone else define me with their words.

I worked well into the late evening with my prep team, which included Ray, Barry, Tyra, Christian, and several of our new advisors. One by one they all came for my jugular with no mercy. They hit me with questions aimed to get me angry and throw me off my main objectives. A few folks even threw out the "n" word and I found myself apologizing to one white advisor for cussing her out after she called me that name. Ray, in usual peacemaker fashion, reminded me that this word only had power if I gave it power.

After a short break for dinner, my prep team came at me even harder than before. Each round, they exposed more and more flaws I'd have to keep under control. I don't remember what time I fell asleep, but upon waking up around seven thirty Monday morning, I was more determined than ever to be on my A game. Everything relied on my proving the world wrong about their negative assumption of slaves, and I couldn't give them an inch less than everything I had in me.

Crest arrived at the White House shortly after breakfast. His son, Anthony, was with him and offered me a couple of new suits with an option of two ties: a beautiful pink and lime green tie or a royal blue one.

Picking up the blue tie and feeling the silk between my fingers I said, "This is the one."

"Good choice, sir. Blue is a powerful statement; it represents hope," Anthony said.

"Thank you, Anthony," I said. "You're a wise man like your father." He smiled and left to take the items to be pressed.

"Okay, all the small things are done now," I said to Crest. "I want to talk opening statements. What can I say from the start to calmly address people's concerns from the very start?"

Crest sighed, "Pettiness can destroy even the greatest of aspirations. This is not about you or me as individuals. You and I both know you'll be judged harshly from the get go. I would talk about your reasons for the revolution and the actions that lead you to speak to China and Germany to get them to agree with your deal. Once they hear this and know you're sincere, even the harshest critic will be silent and listen."

I reached out my hand to shake his. "I apologize for what I said earlier about any assassination scenarios. I was just scared, and to be honest, you're the first white person who's treated me like an equal. I thank you for signing the letter and having it notarized. I know for sure you're a man of your word."

He smiled and shook his head. "Harrison, I know actions speak louder than words and once you have your first child, you'll understand how much I want to make sure Anthony has every opportunity possible."

We then talked strategy and focused on my opening statement, ensuring it was a strong platform for any question the moderator threw at me. We'd gotten way ahead of the game and I would be fully prepared for the debate regardless of the opponent.

"So then what do we do now?" I asked.

Crest smirked and said, "Pack your bags and get ready to fly, Harrison. Our plane leaves in the morning. It's time to play the campaign trail game."

CHAPTER 41
THE CAMPAIGN TAKES FLIGHT

rest and I knew we only had a short period to begin the process of campaigning. Fortunately, the Uniform Suffrage Act was a well-designed piece of legislation. It gave someone like me the opportunity to campaign for the presidency in a very short time, while focusing on a relatively small number of targets. Unfortunately, those targets didn't live in Washington, DC.

Crest had arranged a private plane to fly us from DC to Richmond that Tuesday morning. Meagan squeezed my hand upon hearing we'd be flying instead of driving. I returned her squeeze, knowing this would be a new experience for us both.

Although I knew it would be important for us to meet the senators and representatives who would be voting, our plan of attack had been to meet them after the debate. Switching gears like this added some urgency to our efforts. The winner of the election would need to gather the majority in both the Senate and the House to be elected. If neither candidate obtained the majority in both the House or Senate, a national general election would be scheduled. This put a lot of pressure on any prospective Republican candidate, given the changing demographic of the American voters. If no candidate won the election during the initial process, it was likely that some thirty-eight million new African-American voters could swing the election in favor of the abolitionist Democrats.

Crest had done a good job of putting pressure on the Republicans. Their nominee would run hard in the early period, and they would likely try to discredit me early in the game given my lack of formal education and my lack of experience in United States government.

As we approached the airport, Crest continued to relay new instructions and he seemed to be more excited than usual. It was obvious he was concerned about my upcoming performance in these meetings. While some congressmen were sympathetic to our cause, there was a minority who wanted nothing to do with the ending of slavery. They were staunch believers that slavery should continue to the benefit of license holders. Many were becoming increasingly vocal about the fact that as soon as living wage for former slaves was mandated, businessmen in the United States would be paying a lot more money for labor. The result would be a possible slowdown in the economy.

As we zipped down the highway, Barry said, "Before we board, you need to speak to the prime minister of Canada and the president of France. These are calls you've been waiting on for a couple of days. I know you've already spoken to Joachim Joc in Germany, and we need to get these two out of the way quickly."

Taking the phone from Barry, I only spoke for about ten minutes each; brokering two more deals for not only our gas, but opening trade talks, solidifying another bulletpoint for my debate. At that point I was ready to hop out of the limo and head straight to the plane.

When we arrived at the airport, we were moved toward an isolated area. I watched several planes with their jet engines screaming at takeoff and landing. I had always wondered what it would be like to fly on an airplane. I'd glamorous and spacious interiors in every plane, especially private jets.

After we checked in, we were escorted to a small plane that was sitting off by itself. As we boarded, I let out a whistle. It was remarkably lavish. The cabin housed a plush couch, tables, a small refrigerator, and other supplies with room for about ten people, not including the flight attendant and pilot. Crest and I sat across from each other at the front, while everyone else took seats behind us.

Noting the fear in my eyes, Crest said, "You've never been on a plane, have you? Don't worry; you'll get used to it. You're going to be doing a lot of flying over the next three weeks."

No amount of words would comfort me at that moment. I didn't know what claustrophobia felt like until the flight attendant closed the door and informed us to buckle up. I felt a tightening in my chest as the plane started moving toward the runway and I leaned back in my chair as we began to pick up speed. Finally, I heard a thump as the wheels tucked in and with that, we were airborne.

I took a deep breath and as I looked out the window. I couldn't believe what I was seeing. We were moving up into the clouds. I looked back over DC and saw office towers everywhere. This was the epicenter of the financial world and it was incredible to see the overwhelming breadth of the city. I looked back at Meagan, Barry, and Ray; it was their first flight too and they all stared in amazement.

The flight took about an hour. By then, Crest had already called ahead for a reinforced security detail, stating, "The security team from DC will be flying out to clear our next destination."

As we climbed into one of three black limos, Crest mentioned we'd be spending three nights in Richmond. First we'd go by the hotel to freshen up before we initiated any of our meetings. He then began to talk through the agenda for the day. We'd be meeting with elected officials on a group basis for about five or six hours. I was nervous, but excited for the opportunity.

We eventually arrived at the state government facilities in Richmond where our meetings were to be held. The first group of senators entered with swagger in their steps, looking like a bunch of roosters in suits. I walked over and shook each of their hands. Two of the senators were about sixty or older, and the other two were young.

They were white, and one of them had a southern drawl that kind of unnerved me. They took their seats and we began our meeting.

I began with an explanation of my background and how we got where we were. I acknowledged my weaknesses and my need to understand issues and verticals that could affect the United States government. But I also I noted that despite those potential inadequacies, I had equipped myself with knowledge concerning the inner workings of Congress as well as domestic and international affairs.

A question came up about foreign affairs. I was asked if I supported the state of Israel and their efforts to rid Hamas of its base of weapons. I responded that we would always be allies with Israel, but that it would be difficult to send any American, black or white, into a battle from which many wouldn't return. My concern relative to any foreign contact was that we fully understand the conflict and how our intervention may impact its resolution.

Clearing my throat, I said, "Gentlemen, I would think long and hard about sending our soldiers into harm's way. There can be no consoling a family or friend who has lost a soldier in war. So while I would endeavor to take any and all steps necessary to protect our borders and our interest abroad, I readily acknowledge that the United States would be reluctant to inject themselves into conflict internationally."

The senators looked at one another and nodded. They seemed relatively surprised at the complexity of my comments. I had done a lot of studying and although I didn't have a thorough understanding of government operations, I had enough knowledge to articulate issues related to our domestic and foreign well-being.

The rest of the afternoon and evening went well. To our surprise, there were only a few meetings where the overtly racist nature of a senator or representative became apparent. The anomaly was Representative Thomas Raines from Mississippi. He had long been in favor of slavery and felt somewhat angry that he wasn't able to preserve it. When he first met with us, he seemed like a nice enough person. However, his demeanor changed when we began to talk about politics. He let it all out.

"Boys," he said, "I have a genuine concern about whether Mr. Vance has the mental capabilities to serve as president. It would take a lot to convince me. I just don't think you people have the brainpower, and a president is going to face a complex set of crises at least once a month. If you don't have the intellectual engine to absorb and manage this new information, it will be a disaster if you become president."

I looked at Mr. Raines and felt pity for him. He was unable to open his eyes to things going on around him, and that failure to adjust would be damaging to him and his interests.

It was a complex journey to meet with those who would have votes in the upcoming election. Crest's access and power were critical assets. Those assets allowed us to quietly campaign without an opponent being named. This put us in an excellent posture. We controlled the dialogue up to this point and I could meet with as many congressmen as necessary to pile on our agenda.

That evening we settled into our hotel. It was exceedingly luxurious and I was intrigued by the concept of room service. It reminded me of when Thomas brought us special deliveries into the Crops. Just for the heck of it, I called room service and asked if they had Salisbury steak. They didn't have Salisbury steak but they did have a cut called a ribeye. I decided to try it, and I had to admit it was one of the best pieces of meat I'd ever experienced. I put a little bit of sweet sauce called "Heinz 57" on it. It was juicy and delicious. It was at that moment, I fell out of love with Salisbury steak and in love with the ribeye.

The following morning, we were awakened with news that the Republican Party had honed in on their likely nominee for the presidential election: Ashton Bragg. Bragg was a Virginia native whose family had a long military history. Bragg's ancestors had fought and led during the Civil War. One key concern was that Bragg was a lawyer. He was sharp, uncompromising, and very calculating. He had a stoic but clean image, and being in his late forties, he could appeal to a broad age demographic. He was as tall as I was, and from a visual standpoint, his presentation was very much like ours. If Bragg were indeed the Republican candidate, he would be a challenge.

Throughout the second day in Richmond, Crest and I continued our meetings. The majority went well, though I think many of the attendees had low expectations of me. Even though they were intrigued by the uniqueness of my story, they were blinded somewhat by their experiences with slaves. To me, it was a great advantage. I enjoyed being able to use shock value. Once the platform was even and they realized I was both articulate and confident, it would always take them some time to recover. It was during that uncertainty that I was able to seize the moment and pile it on. I wanted these voters to understand I was a serious and aggressive candidate. This wasn't about charity; it was about opportunity.

And the future.

One of our final meetings was with a representative from the state of North Carolina, Thomas Lind. From a social standpoint, Mr. Lind was about as conservative as you could get. He, like Raines, had been a super strong advocate for slavery and had been aggressive toward abolitionists in the past. Ironically, Lind was a Democrat, though he took a conservative approach on many issues. He would not be very happy at all to support an African American for president.

When Lind came into the meeting room along with a few other representatives, he walked over to Crest and hardily shook his hand. This was a true example of the impact Bradley Crest had. His presence and strength of personality could influence both sides of the aisle. In this case, he was trying to influence someone who had every inclination to vote Republican, but the mutual respect between the two was obvious.

After greeting Crest and before I'd had a chance to say a word, Lind turned to me and said, "What makes you think you should be president of this great country? That would be like turning over the wheels of a fancy car to a baby. I can't imagine you'd be able to handle a crisis. Managing such situations requires extreme intelligence, integrity, fortitude, and an understanding of the international matrix. It's obvious to me that you would be unable to obtain those characteristics within the next couple of weeks."

Lind then took a seat and I stood there with a calm demeanor, knowing he expected some type of emotional response from me. Instead, I looked down, clasped my hands, and said, "I agree. Those are very important characteristics you mentioned. But life experience is critical to the development of character. My life experience has been tough, sir. I'm a former slave. I have lived every nightmare a slave could live. But I'm also an intellectual. I have an in-depth understanding of our government and the economic keys necessary for it to advance. I've not only learned a great deal about our foreign policies and affairs, I have already affected them." Lind raised his eyebrows and smirked, clearly still doubtful.

I continued, "There was a reason I chose Cove Point as a target for our resistance. Cove Point was a critical point for us internationally. I had an acute awareness of the relationship between China and Russia, and I understood that strategically, China's economic alliance to Russia was dangerous to the interest of the United States. That's why I brokered an agreement with China to continue the flow of natural gas from Cove Point on a consistent basis. I also negotiated a price concession related to the sale of that natural gas to the great economic benefit to the Unites States. So as I said; I've not only learned about foreign affairs, I've improved them." Lind raised his eyebrows once more, but this time he nodded slowly.

"Sir," I said, "I have already proven I can talk with heads of state, and I have proven I can accomplish things. But more important is what I stand for. My presidency will inspire newly freed slaves across the country to excel. From the beginning they will have an example of how to achieve success.

"What's more — my presidency will allow our country to move past the criticism we've faced abroad due to our reliance on slave labor. It is critical that America make a change. We've abolished slavery, perhaps the most substantial impediment to America in regards to business abroad, and now we'll be respected as an international power.

"Whoever the new president is, they must also understand the importance of the freed slave as a resource to our country. There are so many things this manpower can generate for our country, but it must be marshaled and directed. All in all, I have a good understanding of what this country needs to be. And I have a good understanding of how to move this country forward to achieve those goals. But the greatest benefit of my presidency will not be my actions; it will be who I am and where I came from. I anticipate I will be a true inspiration for all of America, black and white.

"In short: I appreciate your reluctance and suspect there's not much I can do to lessen it. All I ask is that when you do vote, you vote in favor of a candidate who can do the most for America from every perspective."

Lind looked over at Crest and smiled, then turned back toward me. "Well, well, well. You have a lot more substance than what I expected. I suspect I will be advancing my support for you after all. I look forward to our next meeting." With that, he got up and shook our hands, leaving the remainder of the representatives to finish our conversation.

We were changing minds. It was not a minute too soon. The nomination process would take place in the next few days. At that point we would find out for certain if Crest and I would be the Democratic nominees for president and vice president. Crest was confident. I understood why. He had a ton of contacts. He had a subtle, but commanding demeanor. Flat out… people liked him. Still, Crest had expressed his concern about Bragg being our opponent.

It was rumored Bragg would select a gentleman from Florida to be his vice president. That representative also brought significant appeal and was also in his mid-forties. Interestingly, Bragg was trying to balance off his ticket by selecting someone who was less conservative. It was clear he was working to advance a diverse campaign to match ours.

If it came down to me versus Bragg, we had about two weeks to duke it out. There would be one debate and one debate only. Although I eagerly waited for the nomination to be finalized, I also anticipated a whirlwind of activity and travel as we tried to convince the most critical individuals that I was the perfect candidate for the job.

I was starting to enjoy this. I liked talking to white men on a level plane. My articulation was growing by the moment and so was my confidence. If we didn't win, it certainly wouldn't be my fault. I was winning over congressmen and I had absolutely no reason to look back.

CHAPTER 42
WHOSE HOUSE IS THIS?

C rest and I returned to DC feeling optimistic. The meetings with the congressmen had gone well. I hadn't made any missteps and we both believed I'd gained a bit of respect from all those I'd met. With that said, we were a little reluctant, not about the nomination process but about the election. Crest had a limousine drop our team off at the White House.

As soon as we walked in the front door, I called a meeting with members of our council. I highlighted a few of the key successes of our trip and then opened the room to questions. Ray continued to have reservations about Crest and believed he may have motivations that didn't coincide with our goals and aspirations.

"This is all about politics for him," Ray said. "He doesn't care about the fact that we're free now. He only cares about being a heartbeat away from the presidency! We gotta watch that guy. He's trying to use us and disregard us."

I assured Ray of my great appreciation for Crest and all he'd done to help our cause. I mentioned how he'd agreed in writing not to seek the presidency if something unexpected happened to me, and how he and I were gathering genuine understanding of each other.

Having addressed their concerns, I told the team we had two big events coming. One, I was scheduling a meeting between them and Crest over the next few days to make sure we were all on the same page. And two, I had requested that many of our assistants be moved out of the White House and into an alternate house around the corner. This would give us some needed space to operate fully outside of a survival context. It would also give my fellow former slaves the opportunity to see more than just the inside of what had come to feel like an informal prison. Crest had agreed to facilitate the request and the move would begin immediately.

Crest had also suggested we move in several capable and qualified staffers to assist with the campaign process. Over the next few days, a team would move more technology and equipment into the White House to make it a functional location for the campaign. Barry questioned this move as I had not yet been officially designated the Democratic nominee. "A valid point," I said. "However, the Democrats in Congress will be voting for their nominee this week. The reality is that I am the only active candidate. Crest made sure of that. We'll have their decision, soon and I feel confident it will be in our favor."

"Are you sure we're not counting our chickens too early?" Tyra added.

I shook my head firmly. "Crest is a very powerful politician. If he'd run by himself we wouldn't be having this conversation because we all know he'd win, right? I know it's risky, guys, but with Crest's strength in the party combined with the emotional energy I bring to the table, I feel strongly that we'll carry this through and win the nomination. I need you all to put your trust in me and in Crest. We can win this election, but we need your help. Okay?"

"Got it," said Ray. The others nodded their heads and as we adjourned, I felt more confident than before.

The nominations process played out just as Crest had suggested. He was clearly the most powerful Democratic politician in the United States. We also had the momentum that resulted from my inspirational story of being a former slave. Support was pouring in from all over the world. People as far away as Europe and Asia were commenting that the election formed a turning point for the United States from a moral standpoint..

As the excitement around our campaign grew, the crowds outside the White House returned in full force. Hundreds of people would gather at all times of the day and night to shout their support. Unsurprisingly, there was also a small spattering of naysayers who held up signs; some of them even called me "monkey." But the overwhelming sentiment was positive.

Amazingly, we were virtually uncontested concerning the nomination process. We watched as the votes were counted and the decision was announced on NNC. I had become the Democratic nominee. It was an exciting time, however, the response from our staffers was unlike what we experienced when slavery ended. We were all excited, but we recognized the steep road ahead and set to work immediate. First on the agenda: the meeting with Crest and our team.

Crest was met with new energy upon arrival at the White House. We were now the official Democratic nominees for president and the vice president. We had cleared the White House of many of the participants of the rebellion, and replaced them with staffers who were solely devoted to the campaign process.

Our meeting began with a round of applause as the team congratulated Crest and me. We each gave a brief speech and then settled down to business. Crest updated the team on our latest progress and our top priorities. We now had a little bit over two weeks to prepare for the upcoming debate. Those two and a half weeks would also be filled with more meetings with representatives and senators as we pressed to gather their votes.

"Our highest hurdle will be gaining the majority in the House," Crest explained. "There are more Republican representatives than Democrats, and if the vote goes along with party lines, we'll lose the House. We have a greater opportunity in the Senate, however, we can't take it for granted. As we all know, many just aren't interested in voting for a former slave. Now, it'll be up to us."

Before Crest could finish his sentence, an assistant poked her head in and asked Barry to step out.

A moment later, Barry returned and said, "Harrison I've got France on the phone and Italy is in ten minutes.

I asked the group if they could excuse me for about thirty minutes; these were important calls related to trade issues. Crest looked at me, baffled. *What the hell,* his eyes seemed to suggest.

"I've got this," I said quietly.

Crest nodded and I ducked out as he continued his conversation with the group, explaining pertinent steps leading up to the debate.

When I returned thirty minutes later, I voiced my concern that we reach all of America and put pressure on Congress from the outside in. Although this wasn't a general election, we could use each senator's or representative's constituency as a foundation for leverage. This would be complemented by my consistent dialogue with those who would be voting.

"We need to lay out a strategy related to both domestic and foreign issues and get in touch with the media. Barry, you're our man to interface with the NNC," I said.

Before I could continue, one of Crest's new staffers chimed in. He was a younger white man, early thirties, and spoke with an air of authority. "With all due respect to both you and — Barry, was it? Sir, I ask that you let me handle communication with the NNC. I have worked with the media for over ten years now and I have been effective in formulating strategies aimed at maximizing our effectiveness. We need to begin with a grassroots media relations campaign and then escalate that up to the NNC."

Barry jumped on his comment. "That would be a mistake, Mr. —" Barry paused, searching for a name.

"Stephen," he said.

"That would be a mistake, Steve," he continued. "We already have a ton of equity with the NNC and national stations. We don't have time to go local with this. We have to start big and end big. We need to use the influence we've already built and reach as many people as quickly as possible. I also anticipate the need to use daily email blasts across the country to continue to press our message. There's no time to be reluctant and there certainly isn't time to grow some complex media relations strategy. We have to hit them hard and hit them hard now."

Stephen shook his head and flashed a confident smirk. "Well, if that's what you guys want... . But I must note that you guys are still inexperienced. It's not your fault. It's just that my team has been at this for long time. And successfully."

"We're following Barry's plan," I said sternly. "And that's final."

Stephen sighed and let out an exasperated laugh. "Okay, but it's your funeral."

"And you're fired," I added.

"Fired?" he asked, looking over at Crest and back at me. "Mr. Crest does the hiring and firing here."

I replied, raising my voice and looking him in the eye, "No, he doesn't. I'm the presidential candidate here and we need uniformity on the team. If you aren't capable of that, then I need you to leave now."

This was the first time I'd put a white man in his place and I almost shook with a combination of exhilaration and fear. Stephen stood up, stared at me, licked his lips, and tried to decide what to do next.

I continued, "Son, your best bet is to sit your ass down and do what we tell you to do. This is not about you or me. There are huge issues at stake here. But one thing is for certain: Anyone who works on this campaign or ultimately my administration will follow my directive. You are no exception."

Stephen looked at Crest one last time and sat down. I glanced around the table.

"Any questions from anyone?" A few people shook their heads while others looked as if they may laugh. "Well, with that, I believe this meeting is closed!"

As our staffers new and old shuffled out of the room, I looked over at Barry and Ray. Ray's jaw had dropped and Barry was looking down at his note pad, chuckling to himself. They each patted me on the back as they left, and Crest and I were left alone standing by the door.

"Fair enough?" I asked him. Crest shook his head, grabbed his pen and pad, and laughed.

"Fair enough for me, boss." He chuckled again and I put my arm around his shoulder as we walked out.

CHAPTER 43
THE UNION

The next two weeks were a blur. They became an endless series of meetings with advisors, senators, representatives, and the media. I was now very well versed on just about any conceivable issue that could come up concerning foreign or domestic policy. Our advisors had done well and I was an eager student.

Oddly, Austin Bragg and his running mate were not aggressively asserting that I was a former slave. Instead, they focused on my inexperience in politics and governance, hammering on about it in their interviews with the national media while touting their superior knowledge of politics. In several interviews, Bragg expressed concern about America's well-being should I be elected. He argued that the world was a dangerous place and that my inexperience could cause crises in both the Middle East and Israel. He also warned that the domestic instability of our economy required someone who was familiar with our systems, claiming my inexperience would be a dangerous dynamic relative to the reorganization of the American economy.

Bragg voiced his concerns with a sense of authority, always appearing calm and articulate. I'm sure many of his concerns resonated with the American public, and truthfully, we had no rebuttal. The fact was that I did suffer from a lack of experience. And it was true I wasn't an experienced participant in the inner workings of Congress. I was truly an outsider to the political system.

We responded with a series of interviews and advertisements aimed at voicing my views on domestic and foreign issues. We touted my achievements relative to Cove Point and the fact I had already generated billions of dollars for the American economy. We also noted that a newcomer was needed to marshal this "brave new world," and how African Americans would be a key asset to our labor force moving forward.

We had a tougher argument relative to my foreign policy experience. I understood the various crises abroad, but I could only comment via the recent knowledge I had gained. I had never been a direct participant in any foreign affairs and Bragg was right to focus on that as a weakness.

I was certainly concerned about the state of our union both domestically and abroad, but there was another union I was even more concerned about. I had decided to marry Meagan. Our common experience and our newfound love had bound us together, and I knew she was the right person for me. I'd known it from the first moment our eyes met in the Crops. As a secondary benefit, I knew the marriage of two former slaves would create a lasting image that African Americans were a true part of the American experience.

We decided to hold a simple ceremony on the south lawn of the White House knowing the gardens would be in full bloom on that May afternoon. What we didn't anticipate was the media stampeding our gates, nor the massive crowds that gathered to catch a glimpse of the affair. "Simple" and "quiet" had clearly become things of the past. The majority of those in the crowd were African American, a stark testament to what we had accomplished. All of them were former slaves who now had the opportunity to attend the wedding of a presidential candidate — and a black one, at that.

Crest and Meagan made sure we had the best wedding attire, "just in case anybody takes pictures." I thought it appropriate for a presidential candidate to wear a gray tuxedo and Meagan, of course, looked like an angel in her traditional white gown. The wedding party was very small. I chose Ray to be my best man. He was my quiet companion, and I thought he would be the most appropriate pick. Crest and Barry were groomsmen. Tyra and Barry's assistant, Nora, were Meagan's bridesmaids. I had the chaplain from our Crops in Baltimore preside over our wedding. It was fantastic to see him in a different light.

Of course, there was no time for rest following our wedding and we had no plans to travel anywhere. We did, however, plan a quick private reception at the White House to celebrate. When we returned inside, we were shocked to note there was already international coverage of the proceedings. Fortunately, the coverage was all positive. The NNC featured comments from citizens across the country, both black and white, stating how beautiful it was to witness the marriage of two former slaves. And I had to admit myself that we made a good-looking couple on camera.

Crest approached me during the reception. "I have to tell you Harrison: that was an absolutely beautiful wedding."

"Thank you, Brad," I beamed. "I have to tell you how much I appreciate you being here — not only for Meagan and me, but for our people."

"I wouldn't miss it. And I've got to say, you couldn't have picked a better time to get married! Polls are already coming in that your marriage has elevated Americans' perception of you as a candidate. I've even heard comments about how well you articulated your vows. The public likes family men, Harrison!"

I chuckled, with a glance toward my bride. "Well, that clearly wasn't my primary intent, but I'm glad to hear it."

"Of course not," Crest laughed. "But hey, this is critical stuff. This is bigger than just our potential victory. It's about generations to come."

Meagan crossed toward us and I put my arm around her. "I'm just happy to be married to the love of my life."

We partied through the evening knowing that tomorrow, it was back to business. I thought back to the socials in the Crops. What a long way I had come.

CHAPTER 44
THE DEBATE

The night before the debate was intolerable. Everybody was nervous, including Crest. He didn't have to in the debate. All pressure was on me. Incredibly, however, I was calm and felt no pressure at all. As a slave I'd faced much more grave challenges than standing at a podium, debating political issues with an opponent. Besides, I was well prepared. I had an arsenal of information concerning foreign and domestic affairs. It now flowed out of me naturally.

Despite the fact that it would be Congress placing the votes, we needed to present a positive image to the American people to influence how those congressmen voted. If we didn't stay on our A game, Congress might go with the safer bet: a man who was far more experienced in politics.

In a way, I considered Bragg's experience to be a negative. Political insiders had placed the United States in its current crises. It had become obvious that the American economy was fragile. Our image had been tainted by the hypocrisy of slavery. Something had to give, something radical, and we'd be at a great disadvantage competitively if we stuck with the status quo.

Crest called one last meeting the evening prior to the election, and I insisted my original core team be present along with just one of Crest's new staffers. Crest began by discussing the historic significance of not only the next couple of days but of the last few months.

"You all have a lot of courage and I am so proud to be part of a team that has accomplished so much," he offered. "Even if we lose, we have accomplished more than any of us could ever have imagined."

As Crest continued with his speech, I could feel the excitement pulsing throughout the room. This was the end of the road — one way or the other. With the election on the way and the debate tomorrow, our world was about to change yet again. A new era had begun, but we could make it even better. Much better.

That night I lay in bed next to my Meagan. She was now my wife and our union was sealed. "Here we are, man and wife," I smiled as I brushed the hair away from her face.

"Soon we may be president and first lady," she added, planting a soft kiss on my lips.

President and first lady. It sounded incredible, but I didn't really know what it meant. I had read a lot about the duties of president and the presidencies of all those who had come before me and I knew it would be a tremendous responsibility. Still, I felt like I had been challenged more in my previous life than I ever could be as president of the United States. And with Meagan by my side, I was certain I could get through anything. I was ready.

The next morning was all about prepping my image. I needed to have the right suit, the right tie, and of course, the phoenix tie clip from Meagan. I chose a dark suit and made sure I was clean-shaven. I even received a fresh haircut from Crest's personal barber.

I met one last time with my advisors. We all felt I was prepared for any scenario. I had my doubts about whether a good debate performance alone would be enough to win over the American people and Congress, but it was just a piece in the greater puzzle. Therefore,

I would take a passive, calculated tone during the debate to avoid any perceptions of being an aggressive person.

Our private jet arrived in Richmond at one o'clock in the afternoon. Meagan had joined us for the trip, but Barry, Ray, and the rest of our team stayed behind to hold down the fort at the White House. I squeezed Meagan's hand one last time and then headed with Crest to the preparations headquarters at our hotel.

About mid-afternoon we got dressed and began the drive over to Capitol Hill with a substantial police escort and several secret service agents. As we traveled across Richmond, I looked out the window and noted the mass of people who had lined the streets to watch our motorcade pass. When we arrived, we were ambushed by media and spectators alike. I climbed out of the limo and could hear thousands of people cheering. I turned and waved and the cheering got even louder.

Crest placed a hand on my back and said, "This is it."

We walked into Capitol Hill and made our way to the back area to await further instructions. The debates would be broadcast nationally on the NNC and there would be only one moderator. The Hall would be filled with citizens, but there would be no questions from the audience. And there would be several points during the debate where we would have the opportunity to interact one on one as candidates.

I was certain Bragg would use those one on ones as an attempt to bait me into becoming an "aggressive black man," but I was well prepared for that.

Around five thirty we began final preparations. An assistant put some makeup on my face. I wondered whether the powder made someone really look better. Then Crest and I were led into what they called a "green room." We sat down together and I crossed my legs.

I leaned back in my chair and said, "Nervous?"

Crest chuckled. "I can't believe you're this calm. This is probably the biggest moment of our lives and you're sitting there with your legs crossed as if this were any other interview."

"Would be better if I uncrossed my legs?" I smiled. "You know this is about being myself. I'm not going to put on any act. I know what I know at this point, and the truth is all I need to do is give my best and then let the American people decide."

Crest nodded, "Well, there's really not much I can say at this point. Good luck, my friend. You know I will be out there in that audience rooting for you."

I stood up and we embraced, then Crest headed out into the audience. It was good to have a few moments alone with my thoughts. I needed to think about how important this night was not only for me, but for so many others across the United States. I needed to be at my best, and I truly believed my best would be more than enough. In my mind, Bragg had become irrelevant. This debate was me against me. If I performed up to my expectations, I would be successful.

There was a knock on the door. It was time for the debate of a lifetime.

Bragg and I met at the middle of the stage and shook hands. I was surprised to note I was just a little bit taller than he was, and I hoped the image would resonate well with the American people. We then took our places at our respective podiums and awaited the first question.

I had some notes set up at my podium, but I'd resigned myself to avoid using them. The first question was about domestic affairs. The moderator asked us both how we thought the end of slavery would affect the American economy. Bragg responded first. He talked about how slavery was a huge engine for the American economy. It kept the prices of our exports low and it allowed business owners to keep their labor costs low. The end of slavery, Bragg noted, would cause a lot of unrest related to the American economy. He felt the end of slavery was a "disaster" for the American economy.

"Unless certain safeguards are put into place, this disaster will not be reversed," he drawled. "In the future, with the cost of American labor going up substantially, the few exports that America has at present will eventually dry up. Furthermore, the small businessman in the United States will collapse. The ultimate result is that we are going to see the disappearance of the middle class. The middle class can't afford a living wage for former slaves. This will be a deathblow for small businesses. We must put in safeguards now. We simply can't afford to pay former slaves a living wage." Bragg's comments were met with nods of agreement from many in the audience, but I still felt confident.

I countered with the exact opposite perspective. I noted how there were substantial limitations on trade abroad due to the negative image slavery projected onto America.

"As a result of slavery," I argued, "There has been a decreased demand for American products. We've very limited internationally concerning trade markets. However, with the end of slavery those markets are now open and set to thrive. We have an opportunity to sell far more commodities abroad than ever before. I am confident we will see our exports rise, creating increased revenue for American businesses that can be used to support a living wage for former slaves across the United States. I believe we'll witness more fluidity in the American economy as slaves earn a living wage, and more money will be put back into American society. Take your average dry cleaner, for example," I added with a smile. "African Americans will need their clothes cleaned too, right? As a result of new opportunities and increased clientele, we should see a boom in American business and a new injection of capital back into domestic markets."

The discussion concerning domestic affairs was a stalemate. We were simply coming from two different perspectives; one Democratic and one Republican, but it was becoming clear there was no difference in capability. And that was all that I had wanted to prove.

The next section of the debate revolved around foreign affairs. Bragg, as usual, was quick to point out my lack of experience for the position.

He stated bluntly, "The American people are thinking about electing a person who has no international experience whatsoever to lead this country through a myriad of potential international problems and difficulties."

Perhaps the loudest response from the crowd came when I responded, "And sir, how long have you been president?"

The debate went on and on. Bragg mentioned how America had long been reluctant to enter the fray concerning issues related to Syria, Russia, Iraq, and Israel. He felt we'd delayed too long in Iraq, allowing militants to create a "terrorist state" that would be able to attack us "here on American soil."

I rebutted, arguing that America was not now and would never be imperialist. We were not about using our resources to stake out a permanent position in other countries.

"We will continue to serve as military advisors in Iraq," I argued, "and we will continue to address terrorism by supplying Iraqi citizens with weaponry and technical support. Furthermore, we will always be allies to our close friends in Israel and we will reject any growth in imperialism by countries like Russia. My primary goal is to protect American interest abroad and limit the growth of terrorism internationally, but I must insist that we avoid the loss of American lives at all costs. Every person's life is precious, including our soldiers."

Bragg was quick to agree with my statement about American lives. "However," he added, "being proactive is far safer than being reactive." The crowd murmured in approval.

And so it seemed the debate on foreign affairs was also at a stalemate. And a stalemate simply wasn't good enough.

As we moved into latter parts of the debate, it became exceedingly clear that we were equals in terms of intellect and awareness. However, Bragg was white and I was a recently freed slave. My concern was that Bragg would be seen as the safer bet in light of his experience.

We were both given an opportunity to make closing statements. Bragg went first and offered an eloquent and articulate closing, focusing on his long history as a servant to the American people in Congress. He mentioned his family's long history of service and reiterated how he was the best candidate to move our interest forward both domestically and concerning foreign affairs.

"Ladies and gentlemen," he crooned, "while Mr. Vance's rise to prominence makes for a beautiful and charming story, we mustn't get caught up in some fairytale to the detriment of our country. We must choose substance over glamour. This *isn't* a fairytale. Real problems deserve real solutions and I'm the only one on this stage equipped to deliver and restore confidence in the American people moving forward."

Bragg's was a very strong closing and I knew I had to do something to sway the American people. I looked around the room and noted it was almost completely white. White reporters, white spectators. There were a few blacks in the room, though they were almost certainly there as workers. In one corner near the stage, sat Meagan and next to her stood Bradley Crest. I knew he was nervous. This was the end of the debate and at best it felt like a tie.

With a nod to Crest, I began my comments. "Tonight is about you, the American people, making a determination about who is best to lead our nation forward. Mr. Bragg is obviously well equipped to lead this country. His experience as a politician would bode well and he is a very dedicated public servant. My story is somewhat different. Less than a year ago, I was a slave in the Crops in Baltimore. I could never have envisioned being a freed man today, let alone standing on a stage, vying for the office of president of the United States. Mr. Bragg is correct: it is a truly unbelievable story, but it's much more than just some fairytale. My story has become an inspiration, not only to people in the United States, but to those around the world. My story is an example of America's willingness to achieve its true potential.

"America for many years has failed to meet its potential because we have been hypocrites. We have claimed to serve as moral leaders to the world while at the same time promoting the institution of slavery and the oppression of our own people. We ignored the contributions of African American slaves to our economy, to our growth, and to our strength. Now for the first time we have begun to recognize the true potential and contributions of all people. I embody that new

America. But this is a presidential campaign; it's not about potential, it's about performance. And to that extent I have performed." I paused for a moment to take a sip of water and was in awe of the silence in the room. My crowd was riveted, and I felt a power I'd never experienced before.

I continued, "I was fortunate to broker a deal between the United States and China concerning Cove Point, and I have been in touch with allies across the world who have also agreed to favorable prices for our natural gas. But I have even bigger news tonight. I have received reassurances that America has officially been accepted into the G8 economic organization. And because we have divested ourselves from the institution of slavery, we will be provided full rights as a G8 member." Gasps echoed across the hall.

"I have confirmed our status with the leaders of several G8 countries including Italy, Canada, the UK, Germany, and others. It has taken the past month and a ton of advocacy to close this deal. However, this development is substantial to our country. The G8 will provide America a new and historic marketplace concerning international trade."

"My fellow Americans, I have performed. I have leveraged my status as a former slave to advance the cause of all Americans and if elected, I will continue to do so. I may not have the years of experience. But I have the capability and willingness to lead America into a new era of prosperity, both domestically and abroad. Congratulations to all who are watching tonight. As a part of the G8, we are now prepared for a prosperous future. If elected, I will do everything in my power to ensure a bright future not only for ourselves, but for our children and our children's children. Thank you. Goodnight. And God bless America."

It was a devastating development; I had pulled the ultimate trump card. Barry and I had been planning this in secret for months, though it seemed like every time I had a conference call with a G8 leader, Crest would show up. We had purposely left Crest out of discussions for fear he'd find our plans too extravagant. I knew he'd be stunned.

As soon as I left the stage, I found Crest. He shook my hand saying, "Man, you really did it. I can't believe what you've done. What a night!"

Meagan was speechless as she threw her arms around my neck. Our G8 negotiations had been a secret even to her and I could only imagine the environment back at the White House. Barry of course knew the deal, but the rest of our team had been in the dark.

Now the world knew I'd accomplished the first major benchmark for our country following the end of slavery. Our affiliation with the G8 would be key to our economic future both domestically and abroad. We were building bridges with other countries that had never existed. President or not, I'd played a major role in that process.

Crest, Meagan, and I prepared to fly back to Washington, DC during the wee hours of the morning. I was eager to get home to our team with the election approaching. I had done all that I could do to be a strong candidate. All we could do now was contact several congressmen who may still be undecided. But the truth was: we'd already reached millions of people. It was reported the debate had the largest audience in televised history.

Over the next few days, I took time to relax between phone calls. Even though the election was approaching, I reduced my schedule. I still managed to conduct several televised interviews from the White House, and I ensured that Barry's team continued our efforts via email blasts.

I noticed a difference in tone when I spoke to congressmen. They were no longer sounding arrogant. In fact, many of them spoke as if I were already the president. It was a surprising dynamic. And with the election approaching, poles showed that the American people favored me by a sixty-one to thirty-nine percent margin. Congress now faced a constituency that weighed heavily in our favor.

On the day of the election, I invited everyone back from the original team that had escaped the tunnels. A few of our partners who had been injured in the initial raids on the Crops were in attendance; I'd promised them that if I were elected president, they would all receive executive pardons.

Crest stood by my side as we all gathered across several rooms to watch the results. Anticipation was something we'd become accustomed to. Though a Senate victory seemed likely, it wouldn't guarantee us a victory overall. The votes started coming in toward the latter part of the evening and all cameras were pointed toward Richmond.

The Senate results came in first; Crest and I had won by a landslide. The vote was seventy-five to twenty-five, a convincing result. Incredibly, I'd received a healthy number of Republican votes. Crest and I exchanged a nervous glance as the minutes ticked by. Finally, the results from the House came in about thirty minutes later. I had won the House as well: three hundred to one hundred and thirty-four.

When the results were announced, it was absolute bedlam across the White House. Meagan jumped into my arms and after a moment, Crest hugged me as well. I looked up into Crest's face, and his eyes were full of tears. We'd allowed several camera crews into the White House and the scene was broadcast to the world.

I had to make a speech, but I elected to keep it short.

With a slight tremor in my voice I spoke, "Wow. Ladies and gentlemen, thank you. It has been a long journey for me. I was born a slave and lived the majority of my life in the Crops. Thanks to my brother, Apex, I was brought to tunnels that paved the way for our resistance. My team and I came into the White House under the cover of darkness, and today we find ourselves bathed in a new light as I begin my new journey as president.

"My journey is not unlike that of America. America began with the early years of our forefathers and the age of discovery. We were led into the Civil War and found ourselves in the vestiges of slavery. At last, we are all free.

"I couldn't be more thrilled, and I assure you I will do everything in my power to serve all Americans to the best of my ability. I must thank Bradley Crest for his advocacy and support. You, sir, will go down in history as one of the greatest and fairest men of all time. And thank you to Ashton Bragg for your class and dignity throughout the campaigning process.

"As your newly elected president, I will petition to change the seat of government from Richmond back to Washington, DC. DC was our nation's original capital and it is the financial capital of the world. It feels only appropriate that I preside from the White House. Richmond will always hold a treasured place in American hearts and mind. It has served as the capital of our country for many years, and we will always remember the contributions of not only our elected officials in Richmond, but of American citizens throughout the south. This is a great nation and all geographic regions have contributed to our ultimate success.

"We've come a long way in a short time and now it's time to start building. The road ahead will be tough, but not nearly as tough as what we've already been through. Let's build this country together. Thank you."

CHAPTER 45
A BRIGHT FUTURE

My inauguration was a wonderful experience. It was held on the Capitol steps in Washington, DC, and the NNC reported that there were over a hundred thousand people in attendance. There were people as far as I could see. Following the inauguration, Meagan, Crest and I traveled back to the White House. The streets were lined with well-wishers of every color and ethnicity cheering and throwing confetti. It was an exciting time for our country. This diversity was what the new America was all about. I had a ton of responsibilities facing me, but, amazingly, I felt no weight.

When we returned to the White House, I walked in knowing that, for the first time, it was officially *my* house. This was my home and Meagan's as long as I remained president of the United States. Meagan was overjoyed, stating she was glad we were finally no longer "squatters."

One of our staffers asked if I had any belongings I needed gathered and brought to the White House. I responded that I never had any real belongings of my own. But I did ask him to arrange a trip back to the Crops. I wanted to visit Baltimore and take a good look at my old home. I wanted to speak to the former slaves who still lived there and assure them they'd have ample opportunity for success in our country. Besides, I knew the best motivation for success would be to always keep in the forefront of my mind where I had come from.

I settled in at my desk in the Oval Office and opened my laptop. Just as I began reading an article, Crest walked in.

"I've got something for you," he said as he slid a manila envelope across the desk. On the front of the envelope was a large red "C." Underneath was the word "Classified."

Crest's tone was serious, "You need to read this."

I opened the envelope and pulled out a set of documents. The cover sheet read, "Internal investigation re: death of Aaron Washington." Confused, I flipped over the first page. The second page was a death certificate with the heading, "Aaron 'Apex' Washington." I scanned down the death certificate to the section headed "Cause of Death." The cause of death was listed as "congestive heart failure" with a secondary cause of "pulmonary edema." I scanned the report and found no indication of trauma. And the toxicology report showed no signs of poisoning.

Crest pointed at the papers. "There are two different autopsies in there. I'm familiar with one of the medical examiners. Both confirm natural causes."

I was stunned. "I wonder why Hood didn't just release these."

Crest shook his head and replied, "He was so caught up in that 'slaves are weak and fragile' bullshit. This would have erased a lot of suspicion."

After all this time, it was clear. Apex had given his all to the cause and had no more left. I thought back on how much weight he seemed to lose during our final days in the tunnels. I felt a strong sense of relief as I'd always I struggled to imagine anyone killing Apex. He was too strong, too determined. He'd run the race until he couldn't run anymore.

I looked up at Crest. "Thank you for this, Brad. By the way, I have an envelope for you too." Crest looked at me, perplexed, as I handed him a smaller envelope. "Open it."

Crest carefully opened the envelope, reached in, and pulled out pieces of a torn document. "What's this?"

I sat back in my chair. "It's the agreement you signed saying you wouldn't become president if something happened to me. I don't need it anymore."

Crest smiled and put the torn pieces back into the envelope. As he walked out of the office, he glanced over his shoulder and said, "'Bout time you trusted me, Phoenix." I couldn't help but laugh.

I stood up and turned toward the window, looking out over Pennsylvania Avenue. There were no more tanks, only guards. There were no more angry crowds, only tourists. And remarkably, I was the president of the United States of America. Arguably, I had become the most powerful man on the planet.

I walked to the door and informed one of the staff members that I wanted Salisbury steak and rice for dinner. Then I sat down and began writing a memo to Barry. We had lots of work to do.

www.ingramcontent.com/pod-product-compliance
Lightning Source LLC
Chambersburg PA
CBHW031218010425
24427CB00037B/360